The Village of Pointless Conversation

Kersi Khambatta was a sailor for twenty-three years, until the itch to write became too urgent to ignore. He wrote the screenplays for *Being Cyrus* (2006) and *Finding Fanny* (2014), and is currently developing a third script, to go on the floors soon. He continues to pursue his big love: travel writing. He lives in Mumbai, and this is his first novel.

The Village of Pointless Conversation

KERSI KHAMBATTA

HarperCollins *Publishers* India

First published in India in 2015 by
HarperCollins *Publishers* India

Building 10, Tower A, 4th Floor, DLF Cyber City, Phase II,
Gurugram Haryana – 122002, India
www.harpercollins.co.in

P-ISBN: 978-93-5177-240-8
E-ISBN: 978-93-5177-241-5

2 4 6 8 10 9 7 5 3 1

Typeset in 11/13.7 Perpetua Regular at
Manipal Digital Systems, Manipal

Printed and bound at
MicroPrints India, New Delhi

To Homi, for all the voyages into the absurd, seeking that edge just to fall off it.

To Divia, for all the patience and grace that I will never have. For being the mystery and reality, all at once.

I am sick to death of cleverness. Everybody is clever nowadays. You can't go anywhere without meeting clever people. The thing has become an absolute public nuisance. I wish to goodness we had a few fools left.

—Oscar Wilde, *The Importance of Being Earnest*

Prologue

The boy and girl, they walk in at ten to seven that evening, just as the sun is going down behind the churchyard, taking Pocolim from golden-ochre to blue-black in one hour and twelve minutes of gorgeous twilight. There is nobody else in the tavern at that hour. The boy and girl, they have that beaten-yet-contented look of tourists who have been at it all day, that fire of new discovery in their eyes still flickering after a day of dusty roads, spicy foods, thumbing guidebooks and speaking broken English in kindly tones.

'It doesn't matter where you go,' I tell them. 'Travelling just means getting out of where you were.'

Which is my half-assed way of saying, if they have stumbled through my doorway, they are lost as hell. Off the guidebook grid. Bumfuck nowhere, in other words. So if they like, they can drop that stoic Columbus-must've-felt-this-way look. Unburden their load. Sink their buttocks in my creaky chairs.

'We're just passing through,' says the boy, clutching a knapsack that looks heavy enough to sink teeth into his sciatic nerve. 'Thought we'd stop for a bit. Take a breather.'

'Long day?' I ask.

'Very,' sighs the girl, scratching one blue-jeaned asscheek. She stares dazedly at my wall, the paintings and photographs. 'Nice place you have here. Are you Braz?'

'Braz's my father's name. Dead. I'm Bob. Call me Bob.'

'Oh, the name outside said—'

'Everyone tells me, why don't you change the name? I say, why fix something that is not broken?'

When you ignore the bigger picture of your own dreams and aspirations, I tell them, and focus on the minutiae of others' lives, running a bar is better than television.

Which is my way of explaining why I came back after my dad kicked it. To run this taverna. In a village represented by a black dot on a map, a dot so small, the dot on the 'i' in Pocolim might be larger.

'I got six types of feni that will get you frisky as a rabbit,' I tell them. 'No hangover.'

My father's specials, on the other hand, still brewed in the backyard, those will give you delusions of a marauding African lion. Yes, and maybe a hangover.

The boy sits alpha-male style, a cocky tilt to his torso, butt sliding down to the edge of the chair, legs splayed out. The girl keeps pushing her glasses up her nose and staring at the portraits and photographs on my wall.

'We'll start with something light. Two beers?' says the boy.

I let him have it: not much of a traveller, I say with my eyes.

'Lovely little village this is,' he says, his finger cutting an aimless swathe through the condensation on the bottle.

'Quaint, quiet, sleepy,' says the girl.

'Does anything ever happen here?'

It doesn't matter where you are. Travelling simply means you're not where you always are. Anywhere you're not nodding howdy to your neighbour day after day, or not scooping up your dog's poop, or not watering your plants.

Czechoslovakia, Mongolia, Lapland, as long as you're not couch-surfing internet porn or changing light bulbs, arranging flowers on your dinner table or taking your car in.

'Nothing,' I say.

The only thing that makes your patch of land different from another is, take this test: is your life chasing its own tail right now, round and round, like a demented dog? If it's not, you're travelling.

'Nothing ever happens here. Nothing, except for the greatest love story you've ever heard.'

'The grea—? Oh, really, now.'

Well, maybe not the greatest. Daftest, perhaps.

'This village, there is plenty of love, but never a story. Look outside.'

Through the doorway, we see a fat, elderly couple walking arm in arm, and because of our oblique angle to the door, they stay in view for a while.

'See that? Tomaso D'Souza and his wife.'

Or it could be Tomasz, or Taimur, or Tuomas, as long as you're not calling the repairman to fix your coffee machine.

'Every day he drops her to the bus stop at seven in the morning. She's the head matron at a hospital. Every evening comes to pick her up and they hug like they've not seen each other for twenty years. Then they walk back home. Look, even their bums move together: up down, up down.'

The boy takes a swig, mooching his lips around the mouth like he is sucking on a lemon popsicle. Marking territory with saliva. Either not a sharer, or too much of one.

'Sweet,' he says.

'And look, there's Joel, our pharmacist, his wife Serafina. Every evening, they close their shop for an hour to go for a sunset walk, he holding her hand like she is a child crossing a road.'

Love seems to be filling up my doorway, moving right to left.

'Plenty of love, but no story,' I sigh.

The boy and girl, they exchange a glance. A moment of shared condescension.

'If you have the time, I'll tell you the great love story,' I say. 'If not, no problem.'

The boy belches, the girl smiles. Their guidebook says, always humour the locals. Blend. Belong.

You would never do it back home, never take the time to listen to a stranger. That's travel, says their guidebook on How to Travel.

'Oh, I don't know. It's been a rough day…'

'Oh gosh yes. And hot.'

'Took us forever to find an ATM.'

'One that worked.'

'Yeah, this one ATM, it said, open from 8 a.m. to 3 p.m. I mean, what the heck?'

Habits die hard. Conditioning is fast, slippery and armour-plated; like a cockroach, it will survive long nuclear winters. Strangers with stories are just lonely bores who think you've got nothing better to do.

'Is it long?'

'Damn, this beer does taste good.'

'My feet could do with a little rest.'

'Go on, tell us then.'

'The short version.'

'I'll bring a glass,' I say. 'And one of my daddy's specials.'

Ferdinand D'Cruz has a dream. Not your average dream, a jumble of disjointed images we sift for allegory the next morning, never believing for a second that perhaps our subconscious might just be yanking our chain every once in a while.

What is also so unusual about this dream is that Ferdie is an insomniac, and as such, cannot remember having dreamt at all these past thirty years.

No arcane symbolism. This dream comes with signposts, translated into languages he knows.

BOOK ONE

THE FOOLS RUSH IN

1

FERDINAND

If he jack-knifed up any faster, he would've left his head behind on the pillow.

The first thing he hears is his heart, a distant African drum. Every fifth or seventh beat a healthy thump; in between a haphazard patter of a drunk stumbling over a wooden floor.

The sensation is that of being washed up on a beach, some tropical island where the water is warm. Realization dawns like a weak sun through thick fog: he has pissed his bed. Again.

Attenshin-seeking, dat's wat it is, which bleddy fifteen-year-old does dis? His father roaring through twisted lips, tyrant's eyes dancing around in his alcohol-sodden head. But that was then and they are all long dead, his mother with the perpetual tiredness, his father whose liver and brain were racing each other to oblivion; whose attention is he seeking now?

Fingers go out to investigate; they grope and feel, and come back telling him his bladder is sealed shut and throbbing safely with pressure. He yanks out the flaccid hot-water bottle from under him and holds it up in the dark, seeing nothing, smelling the odours wafting off its scaly skin and its withered insides: old rubber, a reliable archive of fragrances that squirrel into its pelt and never leave. The bag has survived two generations of deep sleepers, his granddaddy and his daddy, and it is simply not equal to the task of outliving a third who thrashes his body sleeplessly into it night after night.

He touches the soaked sheets. *Maybe I di'nt tighten the cap good. Maybe the lining tore. Maybe*... The moist warmth dreamily distracts Ferdie from any more maybes, which is just as well, for maybes are the bane of his life.

It is still dark out. A cat mewls in the distance. Hideous creatures! Rubbing their horrible fur against this or that like perverts in a crowded bus ... The mewling is very close now, getting closer and closer, until he realizes it is coming from his own mouth.

Ferdie was crying in his dream.

He rubs sleep out of his eyes. His heart still doing its arrhythmic routine; as the day wears on, it will feel more and more like an ox grunting and labouring to pull a cart that has sunk in mud up to its rims, his body.

How vivid that dream was, the force of his emotion carrying on into his waking world.

He reaches out and flicks on the bed-lamp. Joseph, Mary and Jesus, surrounded by feral sheep that seemed to be eyeing the infant with carnivorous lust, come to life on a bed of cheap plastic hay. He remembers the happy dreams of Millie *way* back then, when he would get out of bed with a badly erected tent in his trousers. These days not even a bursting bladder can get his penis perky.

Minutes pass; he does not know how many – the wall clock is deep in the penumbra of the bed-lamp glow, each tick more a tut tut of disapproval, the second hand stuck in place, tripping over itself for eternity until the battery juices out.

He turns to the window which is ajar just enough to let a little air in. The colours of the night are running, the velvety violet already bleeding into a brooding teal, the 5 a.m. March sky peeking in, and the shadows disappearing like wood-smoke. A new day is here and there is no stopping it now.

The fear in his heart lies down and takes a nap, though it will always be a light sleeper.

In his little toilet, he goads and pushes as if it were not urine but adhesive paste he is squeezing out of his urethra, his flanks shivering and shaking with exhaustion. Then he walks around his little room, turning on the stove and putting a kettle on. He does not steal glances at the empty bed with its soaked sheets speaking of the years no one has ever shared it with him. He wonders if he will get his two hours of restful day-nap before heading off to church. Two hours in which Millie will not drop in again with her real-world vividness and frighten him.

It's no fun waking up with so much sadness, so much dread.

He makes minor adjustments to photo frames hanging on the wall, photos from sepia to black-and-white and then to faded colour, photos of his life-journey through the Pocolim choir, from an angelic trilly soprano to a dodgy warbly tenor, from when his balls were strung up tight as two lynch victims, to when they sagged and fell one day while belting out the final bars of a crystal-shattering '*O Lord I Am Not Worthy*'. The look of bliss on the parishioners' faces, followed by the gasp of horror as their favourite soprano's testicles descended just five notes before the final bar, that day always feels hot on his cheek as the memory of a branding iron might.

Add that to the existing sadness and dread. Add self-pity too.

On cue, the tears well up, an unstoppable force, except he is in the act of stuffing a half-eaten chicken patty from the oven into his mouth; all that comes out is muffled, stoppered sobs that send fine bursts of chicken mince all over his stove and floor.

The kettle whistles. The sun is turning up the wattage. Soon Angie will be here and the day will unfurl with its horrors and delights. The monkeys of Dread and Hope have their daily morning slugfest in his head; they will stop only when it becomes clear neither can win. Around mid-morning. Or late afternoon. Sometimes never, carrying forward to the next day.

He scratches his itchy bum and pours himself a cup of boiling hot water in which he mixes a teaspoon of salt, testing it with his tongue, correcting it for perfection under the tap. He gargles throatily, spits, takes a deep breath and lets out a long unwavering hum like a jet engine revving up. A dog barks, a vicious cur that goes for his ankles every time he cycles past. He grits his teeth and hums again.

Another volley of barks, which sound like uncivilized eruptions of disgust. The canine has sharp teeth, but there is no way he will be cowed by the coarse criticism of a vulgar animal. Emboldened by this lofty thought, he bursts into a high-pitched, ululating warble that rises majestically in pitch and frequency. For one brief, eye-watering moment, Ferdie almost makes it back to his most-golden soprano moment, but like an exhausted mountaineer he misses the final finger-hold and crashes back to the plebeian earth.

The effect outside is devastating. The four-legged opera critic is dashing around in circles, howling in a blood-thirsty manner: any minute now it will come flying through the window and rip out the throat of this atonal charlatan.

He hears an angry human voice over the din: *Shut up, you son of a tone-deaf dog!*

He hears that one and nods in satisfaction. Yes, that tone-deaf dog deserves it.

2
POCOLIM

Outside the window through which the comforting light of a new day gives Ferdinand the courage to face it, the village emerges from its own slumber. Unlike Ferdinand's fitful variety, this slumber is usually a deep, dreamless one; it awakes every morning not unlike a fat, overweight giant coming out of an alcohol-induced coma.

A thin ground-fog dusts the earth, top-lit by underpowered halogen street lamps, every third one lit, creating spooky spotlights of shifting shapes and shadows. Nothing seems to move at all. And then, through the changing light, as black gets its first tinge of blue, the sickly halogens go off.

The village twitches then, the overweight giant's comatose neurons sparking to life. Ghostly shapes emerge from the giant's pores, and they shuffle with sleepy, sullen gaits to my little watering-hole, Braz's Taverna it is called, sandwiched between Alfonso's Photo Shop and Oscar's Laundry.

The 5.30 a.m. patrons rarely make conversation; an eavesdropper would hear incoherent murmurs as I lay out a row of glasses filled with coconut feni.

Feni: where would Goa be without it? Where would I be without it? They come in every day, the toddy tappers in their threadbare coats, with their cocks and balls and scrawny butts all sacked up in brightly printed lungis, their skinny thighs shivering against the feel of the cold sickle blade. They knock back two each and then go and climb their trees, the ubiquitous *Cocos nucifera* with its rustling palm fronds, supplying 40 million coconuts per year all over Goa, one per family per day. They're all Hindus, they're my brothers, and every morning I wonder which of them might never come back.

Forty feet above ground is no place to have a bad day at the office.

5.30 a.m. is also the time lights appear in Joao's bakery; it is the time to bung soggy dough in the oven so that it will be ready to mop up xacuti and sorpotel at lunch, except he hardly ever gets his eight hours. Too often, in those magic moments when sleep has burrowed in deepest, he is yanked awake by plaintive sounds, some of pleasure, mostly of anguish, which continue all the way to his alarm clock going off. Joao typically starts his mornings with a black murder-mood, resulting in a complaint or two about the gummy texture of the bread that has a deceptively fresh crust on the outside. 'Bad sleep,' he says sourly, shooting the complainants a sideways look that suggests they should understand, no?

That particular morning, after yet another night of truncated slumber, he has given up, lying in bed staring at the ceiling, eyelids flapping like storm-shutters in a hurricane. He surrenders to the familiar, horrible sound of, first, a cow trying in vain to shed its bowels, followed by an eerie pant-shitting mating-call of some neurotic prehistoric bird. Which prompts his first words of the day – Shut up, you son of a tone-deaf dog! – which he screams in a throat-tearing, eye-popping, hoarse rage.

The next couple of hours, as the sun asserts its gimlet-eyed authority, see the emergence of bright colour-print dresses being strutted by ladies of advancing years, with prim, knock-kneed gaits and gossip-gleams in their eyes. They walk past shops whose doors are banging open with desultory squeaks and thwacks to embrace another day of sleepy commerce, past crumbling houses with jungles of wildflower and weed in the front-yards. Their tight hair-buns and thin lips are accessorized with shopping baskets and frilly umbrellas and bright handbags; they convene outside the courtyard of the Church of Our Lady of Perpetual Succour. Banter, bitchy and censorial, floats in a sing-song manner on the light morning breeze, the first conversations of the day.

Vendors unfurl their dun carpets outside the church walls, offering the early goers colourful votive candles crudely shaped to look like body parts that the sufferers light reverentially once inside, symbolically burning away the sicknesses trapped in their flesh or ravaging their organs.

Father Francis, sunglasses firmly in place and hoping his chain-smoking will smother the brandy fumes during any accidental conversation that might ensue, doffs an imaginary hat to these lovely ladies as he throws open the church doors in the grand style of God opening up the kingdom of heaven. He is already composing the late-morning sermon in his head, a little rant on Loose Morals and Responsibility to Elders. Soon his flock will come in, by which time he will be three more brandy goblets down and his bloodshot eyes mistaken for righteous fervour.

He leans on the doorway. I have always known Father Francis to lean on something or the other like a toddler unsure of his first steps, like his adult muscles never adapted to hold him up on their own. If there is nothing to lean on, I have seen him steer people away mid-conversation to the side of a road so he can lean on a tree. He smiles at the ladies, catching sing-song snippets of the subject under discussion. He knows they secretly talk about him all the time, a man of God, a man of mystery. They wave to him and giggle; he gives a shudder of dread before disappearing like a territorial animal into the draughty protection of the church.

Bit by bit, the village of Pocolim rises for another round of calendar-day, another shot at life, one more haphazard cluster of Hours, Minutes and Seconds filled with torpor, sloth, drunkenness, broken dreams, ennui and contentment.

3

SAVIO

Three doors down from Ferdinand, a young man rocks his chair on the *balcão* of a big rambling house that stands around him. Every time the chair digs into the rotting wooden floor, the house buckles and groans in pain. He rocks back and forth, staring with hooded eyes at the dusty road beyond the walls of the property.

More and more, the house resembles an old tramp, struts and supports buckling like wounded knees, the roof a raggedy hat gone floppy in places. The wall around it is only three feet tall, weathered and broken. Age and erosion have kicked the shit out of it, much like the house it pretends to guard.

The look that lances out from the man's hooded eyes – there is the brick and mortar that really guards the house; iron spikes can be added, if an unwelcome visitor proves to be of the obtuse variety.

A bottle of feni stands by the foot of his chair, next to an empty glass. It is only noon, and he isn't too proud of the fact that there are only two inches left in a bottle that had been full only three hours before. He isn't proud, no, but he concedes that it improves his mood a little. He directs a baleful stare at the red soil, at the jackfruit tree across the road, at the shifting light as the sun ambulates across a bland sky, the only evidence that time is moving at all. He looks at the rusting Dodge sitting on flat tyres in the sparse scrub just inside the wall, frozen in time and place since he had been eighteen; it may as well be a faded snapshot discovered at the bottom of a forgotten drawer.

The sun, the passage of day, it seems superfluous. Time is a tool to measure, but if there is nothing to measure, what's the use of the tool?

A fisherman, enshrouded by a net he is carrying on his back, shuffles past. He turns to look at the house and smiles. 'Good morning, Savio. Sitting?'

The face is familiar, his own age or perhaps younger, but no name comes to mind. Perhaps it is just a generic fisherman's face, chiselled by sun and seawater by day, smoothened by booze and dull-witted conversation by night. Perhaps they had played as kids, smoked cigarettes behind the church wall. After *her*, none of the boys had mattered a damn. And then Bombay had pulled him away, or had he been pushed?

'Sitting,' he concurs with a growl.

This is no condition to be found in, sullen, sprawled, semi-coherent, looking and feeling like a steaming pile of dog-shit.

The fisherman smiles, satisfied with the information. The air flops down heavy, fat and bloated with silence.

Three hours earlier would have been good, his trick-bag full: motor-skills, speech, maybe even a shy blush of joy … it's all dead stuff now, everything drowned in a toxic pool of cashew feni.

A little firecracker of dread sparks to life deep within his bowels, the fuse fizzing and crackling. He struggles to form an image, based on how he had seen her last, the morning she had not come to bid him goodbye at the train station because she was getting married. The image settles into something twisted and bleary; the projector's inner works are floating in fermented cashew.

Sounds cut in from the left, human sounds. Humans in motion, feet shuffling red mud, the crackle of starched clothing, the rustle of polyester and silk. And voices: sing-song gossipy voices, authoritative men voices, whispers, whinges, opinions, cackles, bleats, baritones. Savio closes his eyes. Church has let out, three doors down. Some of the voices will recede, the others will come his way.

He sifts for a familiar lilt, that cadence, pitch, but they are bunched too close together. The fuse flares and charges. He experiences a tortoise-urge to duck back into the house, but nine inches of feni have skewered him to the spot.

The voices come, women voices, two of them.

'Hot, no?'

'Very. Oof, eef in March like this den what in May?'

'Eh Saiba. One time you wear and you have to wash every'teeng.'

They cackle, while his pickled stomach roasts on a slow flame. The one farthest from him pokes her head around. 'Kai re, Savio?'

He waits, knowingly, and then it comes.

'Sitting?'

'When you come back?'

'Did not come for Mass today?'

'Very hot, no? Better just sitting, doing nuttin'.'

They chortle and roll on past, bullets of perspiration running down their perfectly round faces.

Pocolim, the Village of Pointless Fucking Conversation. He reaches for the bottle, needing those two remaining inches inside of him immediately. Oblivion is the way forward. Gravity sucks him down further with thick, slurping lips.

He also needs a cigarette. He can twist the tobacconist's arm for a little credit. A muscle in his jaw starts up, the only muscle still capable of any work, as he wonders how he can get the cigarettes to come to him.

A little boy in school uniform, no more than seven or eight, comes into view from left to right. He is carrying a schoolbag big enough for him to crawl into; his little brown face is looking for stones to kick.

'Oi,' he hollers, his voice cracked and parched. 'Oi, chhotu!'

The reaction is slow, measured, almost adult in its resentment at being called a kid. He slows as he looks up, but does not stop.

'Oi, wait. What's your name?'

The boy stops and obeys some ingrained instinct to respond when an adult asks him a question.

'Jamie Silveira.'

'Can you do me a favour, kid?'

Blank stare.

'You know Peter's shop?'

Blank stare.

'Down the road, re, backside of Bob's Taverna. Tell him Savio wants three cigarettes. He'll give you.'

And then, suddenly, a reaction. A scowl, one foot tracing aimless patterns in the mud. 'That is not on my way home.'

'So what is your hurry to get home? School is finished, no?'

The boy slowly scratches the back of his pants. 'Why you don't go yourself?'

Some kids manage to look like shrunken adults, full-grown with age and wisdom poured into tiny, cherubic, unlined faces, eyes that flash in disgust easily and mouths that pinch up like a cat's anus. Where's the fucking innocence gone?

He tries to grin and the muscles resist; after much push and pull, he wins. 'I am expecting a phone call. Get a bar of chocolate for yourself. Tell Peter to put it on my tab. Three cigarettes, Gold Flake regular.'

Jamie Silveira scratches some more, bent over with his backpack, an eight-year-old torn between rebellion at adult authority and the knee-jerk helplessness to obey it. His eyes gleam. 'One bar of *foreign* chocolate, okay?'

There is a whirring sound from the direction of the church, a sound of something cutting up air. There is cloth flapping, and a low unsteady whine, fluctuating in pitch and timbre. It all grows louder, sounds tumbling over each other in great haste, and an unmistakeable human sob cuts through the wavering whine. A bicycle comes hurtling around the corner, its rider pedalling furiously, a great mass of tawny, white hair sticking up from the top of his head which is being bent backward by the wind. Tears flow out of the man's eyes, streaking in his wake like jet entrails. He is wearing some long white coat that billows up and around him like a faulty parachute. He steers recklessly past little Jamie Silveira, narrowly missing him. The boy sends out a hoot of cruel laughter after him, which no doubt he hears, for there is another sob, louder than the first, which hangs in the air long after he turns the corner and disappears.

'Who was that? Was that . . . ?'

Jamie Silveira still hoots and brays in that unfeeling way only children of his age can, chortling and jumping around like a little leprechaun.

'*Who* was that?'

'It's that Ferdinand, re,' Jamie snorts scornfully, waving a tiny finger around his ear. 'Completely off his head, that mad fellow.'

He waits for a little more information, but the kid has business on his mind.

'Foreign chocolate.'

'Take two Five Star, re. What you want with foreign chocolate?'

'I don't like Five Star. Stick in my teeth.'

A vein begins to pulse in the middle of his forehead. He has caught a movement out of the corner of his left eye. This is not good. Oh, God, not good at all. The fuse hits home, the fire-cracker explodes. 'Go now,' he hisses, 'take what you want. Bring back what I told you.'

'Gold Flake?' Jamie wants to get all the facts straight in a loud piercing falsetto.

His bowels burn. *Yes, you little rat, let the whole world know*. 'Go!' he snarls viciously.

Jamie Silveira legs it. Just in time, as the fat bitch Rosalina Eucharistica heaves into view like some behemoth oil-tanker gracefully sailing upriver. His breath snags. She is with her, right behind her.

The firecracker becomes a mushroom cloud. He digs and digs, willing the floor-boards to part, the ground to pull him and his chair down to the centre of the earth.

Rosalina is a majestic woman, big at the shoulders, even bigger at the waist. Her ballast shifts all about her under the shiny black dress, providing her stability and a rippling, liquid grace. Shadows swirl as sunlight dodges past her girth.

That shadow … that shadow had for a moment looked like her. But no, it's just this enormous water-bed that has decided to go for a little walkabout. She shoots Jamie Silveira a suspicious look as he beetles past her.

'When you come back?' her voice is part mouse-squeak, part fog-horn, the kind that jangles feni-soaked nerves. The question is directed at him, loaded with censure and derision, void of civility.

Well, fuck you too, fat lady. He closes his eyes, digs his chair in, and prepares to sit out Hurricane Eucharistica.

'Gone deaf?' she squeaks hoarsely, her big eyes blazing like prison spotlights nailing an escaping convict.

He hears faint rumbles of flesh under slithery silk as she scuffles past on fat ankles. He feels the heat of her vision sizzle his flesh.

'Sitting?'

Inertia and momentum are great enemies of statuesque people. People of girth and stature find it hard to stop once moving, and start moving once stopped. Her voice is to his right now, receding.

'No. Fucking,' he mumbles.

He hears a heartbeat of doubt in her walk, a nanosecond double-take, and then the flesh rolls on, whispering seductively against the sighing silk.

4

DON PEDRO

In mathematical terms, human interaction is really just a bunch of vectors converging, diverging, colliding.

Don Pedro Cleto Colaco is in the act of pissing over a wild triffid-like plant he doesn't have a name for when Rosalina Eucharistica enters his life.

He has been sitting there all morning, his lofty perch higher than the tree-line except for some freakishly tall palms that sway in the slightest breeze, lost in a state of no-thought, sipping his sixth cup of black coffee, enjoying the hand-jitters and the heart-palpitations. Unkemptness and dishevelment are creeping up on him like winter on autumn; washing and shaving feels outdated and overrated. How long has it been?

All over the planet, really, we're just arrows with magnitude and direction, flying around, criss-crossing, merging. There is the occasional fender bender.

His bladder has begun to agitate, which is when he decides to water his garden, the trees, plants and shrubs that dot and line his expansive courtyard. They look blow-torched by the sun, parched and weak. Not even noon and he thinks he can feel melanoma spots mushrooming all over his shiny pate.

Really, God is just a fucking Air Traffic Controller.

He walks around to each plant, tree and shrub, spraying first the leaves, then soaking the soil. It is three small plants for every cup of java. The bamboos and the frangipani that have pots the size of mini-bathtubs, well, they will need two cups *each*. The coffee is brewing non-stop. He supposes that a phase of drinking gallons of the stuff can't exactly kill you, but it will be okay even if it did.

The triffid-like monster, it has always been his favourite. It does not grow so much as erupt out of the pot, shoot up vertically and cascade splendorously down the sides, displaying a lust for life that he envies. He has a full, steaming cup of coffee in his right hand; his left is directing his flaccid hosepipe over the bombastic plant.

The church bell tolls, a sound that would have been more pleasant had the toller a better sense of rhythm or the bell better quality. The harmonics clash and collide with each other, fat sound waves stampeding through the air like a herd of brass hippos, causing extreme pain in Don Pedro's left temple.

He visualizes a monkey thumping a large kitchen utensil with a rolling pin, and then pictures beating that monkey to death with the same rolling pin.

Human voices rise and spread like a mushroom cloud through the dying metallic vibrations of the air. He goes up on his toes and looks over the wall.

And then: amongst the bent-over, shuffling, wobbling, boringly constructed hoi-polloi, this enormous dugong-like creature emerges from the church doors, solitary and singular, no one else even daring to share door space with her. It is love at first sight at 250 metres.

Don Pedro, Vector DPG462, meet Rosalina Eucharistica, Vector RAF847. You are cleared to collide.

All his involuntary muscles go into a spasm; his breathing seizes up and his bladder expels the last stream of piss over the wet foliage. He hurriedly reaches down to zip his pants.

Birds burst out of trees with a mad flapping of wings. Church-goers think they might have heard a buffalo that accidentally sat down upon a sharp sugarcane root, but they pay it no mind.

He staggers, stumbles, gallops across his courtyard, scratching himself violently on a badly placed rose bush, dropping the cup somewhere along the way. Once in the house, he spends what feels like an hour hurling to the floor anything that isn't nailed down. He must find his binoculars. Still streaming tears of pain, he gallops back to the place at the wall, briefly wondering if he should get some Burnol for his penis and balls and deciding against it, too much time wasted already.

A frantic scan confirms that the rolling, heaving, avoirdupois has not fled the scene. It had only been thirty seconds, and the road out of the church is straight as an arrow, visible for almost half a mile. Short of being air-lifted with the heavy-duty harness normally reserved for transporting elephants cross-country, there is no way she could have disappeared.

He demonically fiddles with the focus knob. Love flares. The vector arrow adjusts its trim and rudder; there is no stopping it now.

The binoculars, despite their age, deliver a clear picture. Her curves: sensuous parabolas of geometric perfection. As she rolls forward, her dress dimples and creases like dough being kneaded with ghost fingers. He is thunderstruck with incredulity.

He moves from the bottom up, slowly, careful not to jerk. Calves that look like luscious legs of pork that used to be strung up in the steaming, aromatic stalls in the Mercado de Carne on a Sunday morning on the day of the Festa de Infanta. A nostalgic tear breaks loose as memories of that smell, the springy texture, come flooding back. The hem of her dress interrupts the upward flow of flesh, but imagination replaces empirical data. Saliva laced with phantom filet mignon juice floods his mouth.

The scope goes up, up, over what looks like an acre of silk sheathing her hips.

When Galileo turned his telescope to Jupiter in 1610, his initial reaction was not recorded. In the 400 years since, no one has ever mentioned whether he moaned, shrieked, or danced around the room. Maybe all three. Maybe he spilled hot coffee on his balls too, who knows.

Here in Rosalina's hips is her mother-lode, her essence, her equator; here the movement is the most prodigious, most frighteningly tectonic.

Ahead, the road turns. He will lose sight of her in the next few minutes, seconds even. Who is she? Does she have family?

Sisters?

He has seen large women. Epicureans with oesophagi the diameter of storm drains. Dumpster-truck stomachs. Disastrous thyroids. But never one sculpted like this, a symphony of flesh. An ocean in motion, the symmetry of crests and troughs.

His lungs feel like hot-air balloons, scorched with hot gas.

He lowers the binoculars, eyes brimming with tears of joy, body shaking as if in the grip of a malaria attack. He turns away from the wall slowly and totters back to the house. Once there, he throws the binoculars on a bunch of newspapers he had earlier strewn to the floor, and like a man in the throes of a wet-dream, reaches for the telephone.

5
ANGIE

In the house that is reeling Rosalina in like a baleen whale at the end of a line, Angeline Fernandez looks up at the hexagonal skylight of the main hall of her adopted home and sighs. Her sigh makes the dust particles in the air flutter.

Dust is her friend. It is all around her, everywhere, like a devoted dog at the ankles of its mistress. She sees dust differently: in a cloud, she sees individual particles, each one unique, each one telepathically tied in to its neighbour, the tiniest movement cleverly choreographed.

A cloud of dust is just a million chorus girls kicking up their heels at the same time.

Her skin is flushed with sweat, it is the colour of milk sweetened by a sprinkle of chocolate, it is the texture of an unripe peach. Her posture is good but her shoulders have rounded in surrender.

The skylight is massive, and the afternoon sun pours in like hot liquid gold, giving all the hodge-podge of antique furniture directly below it the look of an over-exposed photograph. All the old teak, rosewood and mahogany that is drenched by this ultra-violet shower is completely bleached; no varnish can survive the relentless onslaught. Perhaps the Portuguese architect of Casa Fernandez had wished to create a sun room where natural light and heat prevailed.

Perhaps he forgot that the tropics were different; this was more suited to the gentle climes of Europe, where the sun's rays hit Earth at an oblique angle, like the passing caress of an outstretched hand, entering homes with subtlety and good manners. Here in Goa, several latitudes down, that same sun pounds a meaty fist downward, like a bar-brawler finishing off a sprawled drunk.

She looks up at the skylight, loving its design, hating its impracticality, looks at her trillion friends bouncing buoyantly in the white-hot light.

She had read about it in an old science magazine that never gets thrown out of Dr Britto's clinic where Rosalina goes every two weeks to get her gout checked. Dust from space, a hundred tons of it falling every *day* on earth, swept out of a hundred distant aliens' homes or from the streets of alien cities, the garbage of alien planets.

Or, as Rosalina had squeaked huffily when Angie had read the article to her, God also has to sweep out heaven once in a while, no? Heaven being after all merely a change of residence for ordinary dirty humans who continue their unwashed ways up there?

She looks up at the cobwebs at the edges of the skylight. They look like trapeze gear swaying gently long after the aerialists have gone. Through the skylight she can see the tall palm trees nodding and kowtowing like lanky sycophants.

The particular cant of the sun's light tells Angie that the mistress of the house will be clumping her way home and the cleaning is not yet finished.

She fetches a long broom and hoists it up, the handle longer than a vaulter's pole, the bristles bobbing hungrily like blind sci-fi monsters towards the cobwebs to devour them.

Five feet from where she is standing is Rosalina's favourite chair. Ten minutes from now, she will leave a trail of red mud as she cruises magnificently into the house, slick as a giant ball-bearing, balletic as an effete hippopotamus. Navigating at a safe speed, she will manoeuvre her bulk expertly past ancient footstools, sagging ottoman couches, crumbling chairs, floor lamps in the shape of harps and enormous wooden statues of medieval courtesans disrobing, some of them unfortunate amputees as a result of collisions with the mistress of the house.

When she lowers herself into her favourite chair, she will not specifically look up to see if the day's cleaning has been adequate.

The wicker cane will groan as it stretches to accommodate every inch, kilogram and litre of Rosalina Eucharistica as she sinks towards the centre of the earth. The bottom of the chair will bulge; it will typically stop two inches short of the recently swabbed floor.

She will not specifically look up because she cannot. She does not possess the neck for upward rotation.

Angie will drop the broom, rush over and say something like, sometimes you walk in so softly, even eggshells would not break under your feet.

But once she leans back in her chair, every untended cobweb will be visible to her eye.

If you want to get your mind off the dreary daily chores of cooking and cleaning, think of things worse than that.

The shoes, for example. The shoes that are bearing Rosalina along right now, scuffling the road so that from far she looks like she is floating on a little red cloud. Shoes that are biting into her feet, her pain threshold crumbling with every step, her lips and teeth clamped in a martyr's clench.

Even as she examines the ceiling, there is the Church Conversation. Followed by the Father Francis rant. Followed by the Thanklessness of Matchmaking. Topped, as always, by That Wretched Ferdinand.

When Angie pries the shoes off, little puffs of odours will escape, soft and smelly as puppy farts.

Sometimes she will lead with That Wretched Ferdinand.

When the shoes come off, the other bouquets on offer are: rancid talcum powder, Roquefort cheese on mouldy bread and old tea bags pickled in vinegar.

Father Francis, he always talks too fast. Eats up his words. He thinks God has the time to play fill-in-the-blanks.

Young boys and girls, you'd think they would have enough sense after all that scriptural teaching, to not be led into temptation based on breasts, or lean bodies in tight shirts. Or looks. Or shapely Sunday skirts. Or bare legs and bare arms.

If Jesus cannot understand what Father Francis is saying, how will her gout ever improve?

You'd think young boys and girls, they would follow the example of their parents and choose wisely.

Sometimes, it's just Ferdinand through and through.

Young boys and girls, their hormones make them stupid.

Ferdinand and his choir singing. Trying to jump in on little Maria's soprano part. And then pretend, oops, mistake. And then sulking for the rest of the hymns, missing his cues deliberately.

Really, if you find daily chores hard on the body, just think of the daily conversations that murder your soul.

On the dresser in the living room, on which the inevitable sprinkling of space dust reappears an hour after Angie has gone over it, amongst the photo frames of family snapshots and one ivory crucifix of a negroid Christ which Rosie's husband had found in a flea market in Ghana on his travels, are several plaques in various shapes: circular plates, irregular rectangles, faux hewn-wood shingles, bearing nuggets of wisdom stamped in old-worldly fonts, quotes that are timeless in their banality: 'Life is not a matter of counting the years, but making the years count.'

'Dance like nobody is watching, Sing like nobody is listening, Live like there is no tomorrow': this one strikes Angie as horribly out of place in a home where nobody has ever sung or danced.

The one that is the most accusatory says, 'Great minds discuss ideas, Average minds discuss events, Small minds discuss people.' That fat, mute lump of cheap plastic dressed up to look like weathered wood, presiding gloatingly over every trite and predictable sentence strung together on the walls of Casa Fernandez ever since Albert had put it up there.

Today, Angie resolves as the broom pokes air, missing one rat-tailed cobweb by three inches, today she is going to bring up the issue of Nereus once and for all.

Maybe it's not Rosie's fault after all. There was that programme on TV the other day, about zebra finches, tiny birds with exceptional singing abilities that learn to copy their father's song in the first four to twelve weeks of their infant lives. Before that it's just tuneless babble. If daddy's away in that crucial learning period, they will babble tunelessly all their lives. No mini-aria will ever burst forth from treetops if daddy is killed or captured in those four to twelve weeks.

Perhaps in Rosalina's growing years, she had never heard an idea being chewed and crunched upon, discussed and dissected. All she has ever heard was babble, never learning to shape that into song.

Still, today she will learn about narcolepsy. Today she will learn that cats can have it too. That is today's agenda, come what may.

Cats typically sleep thirteen to eighteen hours a day. So does Nereus. But cats never doze off mid-stride, walking along happily one moment, crumpling into sleep the next. That is just strange.

What is strange time for a cat? she will ask. Dey are animals, dey sleep when dey feel sleepy.

Cats never doze off in the middle of drinking milk. Cats are never found with their head half in, half out of the milk bowl. Milk sloshing up one pink nostril. Sleeping in a pool of milk like a murder victim.

You leave Nereus alone. He knows much better dan you how to behave like a cat. Next t'ing you will be telling me how much I should sleep.

On another day, Angie is going to bring up the photos. Some of them too small for their frames, because the person on the far right or far left has been deliberately snipped out. Those early days of colour photography, the hues shy and self-effacing, like the black-and-white erupted into colour on its own. The two remaining people in the photo are recognizable: a younger Rosalina on far left, the potential for roundness lurking even then, and her husband Albert, his arm around her shoulder. Albert is smiling widely, Rosie's smile is on a timer switch, programmed to go off after the shutter clicks. Around Albert's shoulder, a skinny arm snakes in and Angie recognizes it by the veins on the back of the hand that droops like a wilted flower over Albert's shoulder, recognizes the shape and length of the fingers.

But first, today, that cat.

If gardening breaks your back, broom handles blister your hands, rough floors scab your knees, scouring powder wrinkles your fingers, kitchen knives nick and cut, you're fine. If you want to rip your ears off so you never have to hear another word again, or claw your brain out so it won't devour you alive out of boredom, you're in real trouble.

6
SAVIO

He comes to with a start, still in his chair, head lolled over, causing waves of pain to shoot into the back of his skull.

His mouth is a land of drought and famine, and the nicotine craving that had temporarily gone to sleep along with its host, suddenly comes alive, like a feral animal gnawing at his vitals. He feels like shit.

That little kid, what was his name, did not come back with the cigarettes. Or did he, and walked on, with the fucking foreign chocolates in his pockets, without waking him?

He staggers out of his chair, noticing the empty bottle of feni. The road outside is deserted, and the air oven-hot. The fat, swollen jackfruit across the road stirs gently in the breeze like a prizefighter's punching bag. His legs do not feel game enough to hold him up. There is an uncontrollable tremor in his hands. I am twenty-four years old, he tells himself, and I feel like I'm ninety.

A yawn comes upon him out of nowhere and the whole body convulses. The brain deprived of oxygen, that's what causes a yawn, but a jaw-unhinging one like that? What is he doing to his brain?

She did not come to church today. He is thankful for that. His bowels feel blitzed and charred, like a forest fire had passed through them, but there is a sense of relief, the relief of a bullet dodged.

He totters from the bright balcony into the gloomy house, which smells of ancient dust, mould, dried feni and rotting cigarette tobacco. And snuff, his father's snuff, over and under everything else, deeply burrowed into every single grain of wood, every swatch of fabric. His overheated nostrils welcome the cool of the indoors. With blurred vision, he smells his way to a nearby ashtray that has a bulging meniscus of cigarette butts. He finds one that is almost half unsmoked, and with grateful, shaking fingers puts it to his lips. When he inhales – the sensation of something with sharp teeth and raking claws scurrying through his bloodstream like a frantic ferret subsides.

Slowly the room swims into focus, blurred edges crystallize, his legs feel a little more reliable and the shake in his hands slowly judders to a halt. It's the heat, he says, swaying on his feet, taking long deep drags. What's one bloody bottle of feni, I can knock back five of those on a good day.

Nothing a few jaw-dropping yawns won't fix.

He looks around the hall; the light is adequate without having to flick on a switch. Sepulchral, but adequate.

The room has that undecided quality about it: does it belong to an inhabited house? Are its occupants on their way out, or on their way in? It just hangs there in limbo, turgid with ghosts of the past, showing no inclination or gumption to have a future.

Our houses reflect our personalities, our outlook on life, our state of mind.

There is a dining table, a sideboard, a showcase that has some old porcelain and wooden figurines. The figurines are looking out in horror as they slowly disappear from view behind the crud growing on the glass, incrementally and relentlessly.

Just add a little light, he thinks, wipe away the grime, throw in a little laughter, gaiety, conversation and he can fleetingly bring that room back to how he remembers it. But fuck it, that's not going to happen, he muses, as he blows out smoke.

There are some old, dusty, framed photographs on top of the showcase. He doesn't need those; he remembers exactly what everyone looked like, his mother, his father, three brothers, four sisters, and an assortment of gruesome, inconsequential, irrelevant relatives that might've pinched his cheeks or tousled his hair. Always the baby, even when he had been old enough to not be treated like one.

Generation gaps among siblings are treacherous things. You are fondled like a soft toy the first three years, treated like a moron the next five and completely ignored after that.

Robert, the eldest, was twenty when he was born, and Filomena, the closest sibling to him in age had been twelve, eight kids in all, a conveyor belt running through Jacinta D'Gama's womb, carrying in a seed and carrying out a squalling tiny person, all of them psuedo facsimilies of each other, like the settings on a photocopy machine gone a little awry.

Today Robert is some fat cat marine insurance surveyor in Auckland with a plump wife and three sun-browned kids of his own, given to wearing polo-necked golf shirts and grinning shit-eating grins in every goddamn photograph that he regularly e-mails the entire family, holding up a hapless glassy-eyed fish freshly caught or flipping burgers on his outdoor barbecue, wearing an apron that says 'Step Back! Dad's Grilling' in some faux-flaming font, which is probably a birthday gift from his wife whose name Savio does not know but who always looks as happy as a pig in a shithouse, living in a land of sunshine and fair-skinned people.

After Robert, there was Janet, Walter, Theophile, Sandra, Maria and Filomena. Or was Sandra before Theo? He could never remember.

There is a map of the world in the living room on which Loyola has proudly stuck little colourful drawing pins representing the location of every one of his seven seeds, seven colours of the spectrum dotting the surface of the earth. NZ – 1. Aus – 1. Some North European country, Belgium or Holland or Germany – 1. And four dots in North America, two on either coast, two in Hicksville Bible-Belt.

No pin for Savio (no eighth colour, there *is* no eighth colour), because this little fellow who had come along twelve years after Jacinta had closed her legs for what she thought had been the last time, this little fellow has never really amounted to much.

Poor mum, he thinks, all that recurring distension, the back pains, the mood lows, the weight swings, those horrible hormonal wars. All so you could have a world map with colourful pins stuck up on your wall.

On a sofa with the stuffing knocked out of it are his father's belongings. Personal effects are transitory things; they have no place in the house after the person is gone. You can hold on to them as anchor-points for nostalgia to latch on to, but that is like grabbing air. He looks at the stack of clothes, shirts, trousers, neatly pressed. There is no memory of ever having seen his father in any of them. He looks at the shoes, all lined up under the sofa: ditto. A big chest, full of junk, lies next to the sofa. Cartons, packed and labelled, litter the floor.

All this detritus around me, Savio thinks, the old man's flotsam and jetsam somehow gives him more personality than his living self ever did.

That, and the smell of snuff. And engine oil.

So how the fuck do you grieve for someone when all the memory you really have is his *smell*?

He picks out another twisted butt from the table that has two centimetres of death still left in it and sparks it, mentally making a note to track down Jamie Silveira and smack his head.

The gloomy house is beginning to depress him. His shirt is sticking to his back, and sweat is running down the crack of his butt. He walks out again, into light, into fresh air, into the heat.

He stares at the Dodge parked in the front yard, hefty, masculine, resisting decay and rot, keeping its chin up like an old wrestler, but going down all the same. He squints into the white-hot light that sears the scene. He wonders what time it is; mid-afternoon probably, that spooky time of simultaneous siestas.

The Dodge was where he fell in love the first time. There is still a spectral imprint of his love right there on the front seat. The smell, the taste, the head-reeling vertigo, the soft white light of bliss, it is all there.

Her eyes, it was eventually her eyes. The playful touches, the mock hugs, all the buddy-slaps before, those were nothing. When she had turned to him, laughing at something he had said, nothing funny but something just *right*, he had stared into her eyes. And seen them for the first time. That brown. That gold and green. That supernova explosion, five seconds after the Big Bang. Not just a snapshot of her soul, but of the entire fucking universe, in those button-sized portals.

And did Gabo know, sitting in the backseat?

Savio squints unblinkingly until his eyes water, willing the ghost to bugger off, but the ghost stays.

An idea possesses him.

7

DON PEDRO

The phone rings, distant and muffled, startling Don Pedro out of a reverie of dispassionate evaluation. About his life up to this moment.

The afternoon is passing in a sweltering daze; he knows he has been mumbling to himself. Mumbling hateful stuff about himself, most likely. Like some medieval penitent, he has been lashing himself with words he cannot remember, no doubt. His ear is cocked for only one sound: the church bell tolling again.

The skin on his penis and scrotum still glows and smarts. The throb inside his genitals, that hurts more, he can feel that over the blisters. He welcomes its low motor-hum, like he's just received mail from an old, old friend. Who was by his side all those creative years, twenty or more, and then one day mysteriously went AWOL. All those years of filling canvasses and filling women, and then waking up one day to find him gone, his buddy, his wingman.

There used to be a billion trillion tons of water where the Sahara is now. What are a few litres of creative juices in a human compared to that?

If planet earth could not halt its fertile loins from becoming three million square miles of dry dust, what chance does a human have?

The abominations of that drying-up period still hang on his walls, in various stages of unfinished ghastliness. Ideas that went nowhere, or turned mutant, brush strokes that lost the will to continue, muses that disappeared with a blink, the language of picture that forgot its vocabulary mid-sentence – all the evidence of failure is still strung up, in the hope that one day the tide will turn and reclaim the parched earth.

While he was lashing himself with hateful words, Pedro had images of lighter fluid and flames. Of standing beside a roaring fire of his past work and hurling cathartic abuses of joy at himself. There was no lighter fluid in the house, not even petrol or kerosene.

Instead, he had drunk more coffee and pissed on every one of them.

The phone rings and rings. He follows his ears and finds it under a hill of dirty clothes, jangling stridently like a petulant baby demanding to be picked up. His initial thought is that it is the priest calling him back with news, but it is a single ring, indicating an overseas call. He unhooks the receiver and growls pleasantly into it, 'Yes.'

Paula, his agent, never loses time getting to the heart of the matter. 'Don Pedro, good morning, although I imagine it must be afternoon over there. How are you doing these days? I figured I'd give it one more shot before I asked the neighbours if there was a peculiar smell under your door.'

'Hmm,' Pedro rumbles noncommittally.

'Are you alright?'

'I'm on the line, talking to you,' he says, reasonably.

'Aah, splendid then. Might I ask how you are getting along?'

'Of course you may ask. No crime in asking.'

There is a silence on the line while Don Pedro fondles his genitals. Like you might do a loved relative who has just awoken from a long, deep coma. He can see Paula in her business suit and stockinged legs, tapping a pencil on her desk, counting to ten, her thin mouth getting even thinner.

'Well?' she finally says. 'I think this is your cue to speak.'

He looks around the big rambling hall, where everything looks like it has been picked up by a capricious wind and hurled around randomly. And those ghastly paintings look on in self-righteous disapproval.

In hindsight, as his eyes water, he concedes that lighter fluid would've been better.

'Well,' he deliberates, 'all I can say is I'm done scratching my balls with boxing gloves on.' He digs his fingernails into his scrotum, stopping just short of popping his testicles like quail eggs. Aah, the delicious pain.

'What on earth is that supposed to mean?'

'I have seen the light, Paula, and I am walking towards it.'

He marvels at how perspective can change in a second. One moment you are a lizard, the next an eagle.

'Well, Pedro, if you are about to put a gun to your head and blow your brains out, can you wait until I connect you to Mary, the curator, so she can hear the shot first-hand and save me the tedious explanations?'

One moment, you are ground level, scrabbling over stone and dirt, unable to see around the next corner.

'There is no gun, Paula. Keep your knickers on, as you English are so fond of saying.'

The next, you are soaring so high, you can see the earth curve all around you. Past, present and future in one glorious wide-angle snapshot.

'Tell that Mary, tell whoever you want, that it's going to be delayed. Until when, I cannot tell you, but when it shows, it's going to blow your little mind to a place it's never been blown before.'

The immaculate purity of objectivity. The only god-moment a human will ever have.

'Pedro,' a strangled sigh, 'I've heard that before, you know.' Instead of tapping the pencil, she is now probably twirling it.

'This time it's for real. As real as that pencil you are holding in your hand, as real as the shitty, grey sky you are seeing though your window right now.'

Beyond the vision of Paula's muscular calves emerging out of her tight black Debenhams skirt, beyond the window facing her desk through which bare twigs and branches of a sycamore sway in the foreground of Edwardian chimneys poking the belly of a fish-scaled sky, he sees his new canvasses clearly, lined up on some generic wall of some generic gallery, a hint of the Baroque in its vaulted arches, hushed footfalls and murmurs in foreign tongues humming through the halls like power lines, ingenious lighting that throws a calculated amount of shadow around the viewer, enfolding them, making them one with each canvas.

Oh, the clarity of eagle vision! That annhilation of doubt!

'Very vivid, Pedro. I wish I could say I see you too. Know that you really are on to something, instead of listening to that prevaricative, buying-time bullshit that I've heard before and—'

There is a tinkle of laughter, Paula playing both good cop and bad cop. Paula being friendly, wanting to find out more so she can sleep better, assured of her twenty per cent. Paula not letting on that she is actually wound tighter than a clockspring, ready to shit kittens if someone sneezes next to her. Paula reading from The Agent's Handbook of Mentally Disturbed and Volatile Whack-Jobs That Call Themselves Artists.

'You can't see anything, Paula. Not from your perspective, not from where you are.'

The perspective of a lizard, that is.

'You did not see me as I was coming down. I was the plane crash that you could have avoided. All you saw was the percentage and as long as that was coming in fine and dandy, it didn't really matter which way my nose was pointing, am I right?'

Is he blaming her for his dwindling inspiration, the encroaching impotence, not being his eyes and ears? The audacity of it. He holds back a chuckle.

'Well, I'm coming up again, Paula, up and up is where I am going, so relax and sleep easy, it's all going to be business as usual.'

A horn toots in Pedro's courtyard, an annoying toot specially designed to make you pay attention. Pedro picks up the telephone instrument and carries it as far as he can towards the open door. Joao the baker is standing in the middle of the piss-soaked courtyard; if he registers any peculiar smell, it does not show upon his deadpan face. Pedro waves the receiver at him and puts it back to his ear, to hear Paula talking in wary and carefully measured tones.

Rule No. 16 in the Handbook of Demented Artists: Never be baited by ridiculous uncalled-for remarks.

'Okay, that is very interesting news,' Paula says. 'Isso soa muito interessante. Eu adoraria kno mais sobre ele, Pedro.'

The artist smiles generously. It is the sort of smile Paula is lucky not to see. Portuguese, a language that could make a laundry list sound sexy. Speaking it in an English accent is vandalism. Like hurling faecal matter at a sixteenth-century Tsuzure-nishiki.

Joao toots his horn again, a double toot this time, grinning sourly from ear to ear. Pedro smiles at him, pleasantly aware that Joao's appearance does not annoy him today, despite the fact that he looks as loathsome as ever. Boot-polish black hair piled in an Elvis coif, that horrible little moustache, also painted black, crawling over his upper lip like a tapeworm. And that repugnant Hawaiian print shirt that stretches out over his gut, bits of hairy belly showing through the gaps between buttons. He stabs a finger at the receiver and motions him to wait.

'Pedro?' Paula is saying. 'Você ainda está aí?'

'All in good time, my dear. One cannot rush these things. Just focus on the fact that you, and the whole art world, might be very pleasantly surprised before long.'

'De quanto tempo estamos falando?'

He pictures yanking out her tongue with a rusty meat-hook. It is like listening to Bob Dylan sing Pagliacci.

'When I know, you will know. Be patient.'

Joao the baker, apparently, is anything but. He leans on his tooter like a geriatric leaning on his walker.

'OI!' Pedro roars, a lion that had just had a safari jeep go over its tail. 'Are you blind? Can you see I'm on the phone?'

'So you want bread or no?' Joao yells back, grinning. 'I haven't got all day to waste on you!'

'Bugger off!' Pedro screams. 'Do I look like I need your poxy bread?'

'Pedro? Hello? É este um momento ruim? Eu posso chamar de volta mais tarde.'

'No, it is not a bad time!' Pedro roars into the phone. 'And stop talking Portuguese. You sound like an ugly tourist trying to get laid in a bar!'

That nails her to her chair. When she speaks again, it is in a voice choked with rage and dripping with frost. 'I am connecting us to Mary. You tell her what you just told me, about the delay. I am done covering for you—'

'I make you rich, you hear?' screams Pedro. 'And I'll make you even richer, so don't you dare talk to me like that!'

The church bell goes off just then, announcing evening mass. Pedro looks around wildly for his binoculars. There they are. He puts down the bulky instrument at his feet and runs to pick them up, still holding the receiver. He is about to dart out to the courtyard, then remembers the phone cord will not make it that far.

'Paula? Paula? Can you quickly connect us to that silly cow, so we can get this over with? I have things—'

'Pedro,' hisses Paula through clenched teeth, 'Mary is on the line. Really, you are the rudest—'

The church bell tolls a second time. A shiver breaks out in his groin. 'Good. You talk to her. I have to go. Remember what I said. Rich, rich, rich.'

He throws away the receiver and gallops out to the wall.

8
SAVIO

He managed the 'L'. As he started on the 'E', the pen ran dry.

If the ghost won't budge, the Dodge will have to go, taking everything with it.

He scratches furiously, willing the last half-drop of ink out; nothing more comes.

The heat hits him like a physical force as he steps over the shade-line, the shade of the awning of his balcony, the tramp's hat that has gone wobbly in parts.

He holds up the pen to the sun; if it can fry his brains, surely it can melt trace remnants of dried ink.

His ears catch a sound of feet scuffling mud, the tread lazy and tired. His brain instantly goes into flight mode. Which *other* moron is out at a time like this?

A tall figure appears from around the corner, wheeling a bicycle, all stooped over with exhaustion. The chain has slipped off the back wheel, the pedals swinging gently, uselessly. The front of his shirt and trousers are smeared with grease, speaking of an unsuccessful tussle with the errant chain. A white robe hangs off his scrawny shoulders, flared open in front. The cuffs of his trousers are shredded and ripped. A shock of white hair lies in a tangled heap around the man's skull. Tufts of black hair clump out of his ears like little hardy scrubs growing off a rock-face. The face is dirty; sweat and road-mud form a pancake through which something wet has made furrows.

Savio racks his memory for a name.

The man stops, leans a scrawny neck in his direction like a curious tortoise, and then, as though a dimmer switch has been turned up, a light of recognition glows brighter and brighter.

'Savio DaGama? Loyola's littlest fellow, Savio?'

'Ferdinand. Ferdie the postmaster. I remember you now.'

The face lights up with a smile that is so radiant and genuine, Savio is a little embarrassed.

'Good memory you have. When you came back?'

'Last week.' A little alarm goes off in Savio's head. Sweet smile or not, endearing or not, this is nosy Pocolim .

'You were not dere for your daddy's funeral, no?'

'No, I was in Bombay. Heard about it too late. I had to wrap things up and—'

'Nobody came, not Walter, not Teo. I tot at least Robert would come…'

'They're all far away, everyone's far away.'

That is exactly what Robert had said in the e-mail, the fat-cat eldest taking it upon himself to speak for the family, '*…it will be virtually impossible for any of us to attend the funeral at such short notice…*' Like if you know these things are going to happen, you can hire baby-sitters and push your fucking barbie to another weekend. '*…dad's needs were fairly simple in these last days, and Walter, Theo and I have been sending him a cheque for a decent amount every month. There should be more than enough for the funeral arrangements, though not for much more than that…*' Except Savio had checked his mail four days too late because of that disastrous alcohol jag in Bombay that had left him legless, shit-faced and with a burning itch in his crotch that he was sure had been a gift from Saviya, that gaunt little nub-breasted hound whom he had banged non-stop over that weekend – probably just about the time his father was taking his final breaths, all alone with no one by his side in this rambling old house, six hundred miles to the south. '*…so we are relying on you to carry out the last rites on our behalf as you are the closest, geographically speaking.*'

Savio and Saviya, they had teased him, the boys at the garage on Charni Road, what a couple they would make. The boss's daughter, and therefore potentially a catch. As if that was good reason to overlook the fact that she had a face that would make an onion cry. And shoulder blades more pointy than her breasts.

But then there is the miracle of rum, lots of it, and the double vision had made Saviya's flinty face an alluring moving target, and he had conceded that he was no fucking oil painting himself, was he?

'Sad it was, very sad. All our time will come,' Ferdie intones morosely.

Savio peers keenly, then scowls. 'You been crying or what?'

Ferdie blushes. 'Eh, crying? Me? No. I jes' get dirt in my eye on de cycle, maybe.'

Savio points to the gown. 'What is that?'

Ferdie attempts a sheepish grin. 'It's de opa-mus, re. I sing wit de choir in church.'

'Uh-huh.'

This man reminds him of the father on whose gravestone he had placed flowers five days too late. The alarm had been raised by the kid who delivered the coconut water the next morning, possibly around the same time he, Savio, might have been waking up in Bombay, seeing what was lying next to him and needing more rum.

'What happened to your pants?'

'Dogs.'

Okay, he wants the old man gone now, this daddy-doppelganger. But the old man keeps talking.

'Joao says put fish oil on de pant. Den dogs won't come close. Dey don't like smell,' he says. 'I bin in the church choir since ten years old. When you come to church, you will see me.'

Savio shakes the pen, hoping the heat has done its work.

'See what I got dis morning?' From a plastic bag strapped to his handle, Ferdie removes candles and puts them on the low wall separating them. Mostly ears, crudely constructed question-marks with no features and tiny wicks sticking out of the top. There is one nose. The others, they could be anything.

Savio points to one. 'This is a pear. Why have they given you a pear?'

'It is a gall bladder,' Ferdie says, poking himself somewhere between his third and fourth rib.

Maybe it's the grease on his shirt, reminding him of the other grease monkey, his father, the one in the ground.

'And is there something wrong with your gall bladder?'

'Maybe. What if dere is?'

He pokes something else that looks like a miniature rugby ball that has lost air.

'What is this? Is this actually in your body?'

'It is my stomach. Everyone has stomach problems.'

Maybe it's the abject stupidity. All social retards inevitably resemble each other.

'So many ears? You have a hearing problem as well?'

'I am growing old, son. I have to plan for de future.' He fidgets with one pendulous lobe. 'Plus, dey was giving a very good discount.'

Savio wants to tell him, don't call me son. Instead, he glares at the pen and readies himself for a final assault. Ferdie follows his movements with big, curious eyes, a child following a magician's hands. 'Selling car?'

'You want to buy?'

Ferdie gives out a high-pitched school-girl giggle, and Savio checks an involuntary reflex to stab him in the eye. Instead, he merely uncorks the pen with his teeth, puts the nib to the cardboard and scratches hurriedly. The ink paints the backbone of the 'E', a vertical line, and then the pen dies for good.

'Shit! Fucking shit!' he yells, flinging it clear across the road.

Ferdinand, he looks thankful for the one-foot-thick wall that separates them. 'Ooof. Hot no?' he says, unnecessarily.

Savio turns on him speculatively, a predator wondering if the meal is worth the effort. 'You think so? I'm feeling cold.'

'Oh. It must be a case of fever, den. See doctor?'

'No, it's a case of sarcasm, actually.' He walks over to the wall. 'You knew my father well?'

Ferdie shrinks back. 'E-e-everybody knew him,' he says, deflecting the blame on all of Pocolim, just in case.

'The funeral went well?'

'Everybody was dere. I t'ink de whole village except Mrs Ferrao, she got all dat art'ritis no?'

'Good, he deserved that. He was a good father.'

By extension, giving the impression that he, Savio, was a good son too.

'You will see at the Mont's Mind. Everyone will be dere, you will see.'

'There is no Month's Mind.'

'In one week will be one mont', no?'

'Yes, but we have not asked for it.'

'Oh, I heard…' And Ferdie's eyes shift. The Adam's apple bobs like a yo-yo.

'Heard what?'

'Heard … umm, nuttin.'

Maybe it's the total lack of personality. People afflicted with that resemble each other.

'Heard *what?*'

'Nuttin, nuttin.'

Like two boiled cabbages would resemble each other.

'You!' he bellows, causing Ferdie to jump.

A little boy has appeared out of nowhere, standing next to Ferdinand, scratching the back of his pants, looking at Savio insouciantly.

'Where you went, re, you little *fucker*?' The last word is hissed through clenched teeth, not in deference to the little boy's innocent ears, but to Ferdinand's big ones.

'I came! You were sleeping. I d'int want to wake you.'

'When? How far is Bob's Taverna from here? Took your own bloody sweet time!'

'Dat Peter, he doesn't know you. Ten times he is aksing me, who is Savio, who is Savio? He tot I was taking cigarettes for myself! Den I told him where you live and he give.'

'So where are they?' Savio growls, observing Ferdinand from the corner of his eye, wheeling the bicycle in a wide circle around the boy.

Jamie Silveira turns his bright, dancing eyes on the postmaster. 'You fell? Hehehehehehehe.'

Ferdie is almost running, pushing the useless bicycle as fast as his weakened state will allow.

'Hehehehehehehe,' chortles Jamie Silveira. 'Fall again no, I want to see!'

'Oi!' Savio shouts angrily. 'Show some respect! This is how you talk to your elders or what? One I'll give you on your ear now!'

One can't have little brats making fun of father-lookalikes.

As Jamie turns full circle to jeer at Ferdie, Savio notices a huge brown stain on the seat of his pants.

The circle complete, the boy turns back to Savio, eyes now wary and watchful. He pulls out three crumpled cigarettes from his back pocket. Savio grabs the tiny wrist and whirls him around. 'Two pockets on your shirt, two pockets in front of your pants, and you had to put the cigarettes *back there*!' he bellows in rage.

Jamie squirms like an earthworm. 'If I put dem in front then somebody see dem in my pocket.'

'Shitting your pants like that! What, you can't run to the toilet or what. How old are you?'

'It's not shit. It is mud, you idiot!' Savio lets go, and Jamie Silveira sprawls to the ground.

'Dere were no foreign chocolates,' he yells, scrambling to his feet, his pride hurt. 'Gimme one cigarette as payment!'

'What? *What* did you say?'

'Gimme one cigarette as payment!' bellows the kid at a volume that might have been heard in the neighbouring state.

Savio walks along the wall towards the gate. 'I'll give you one on your ear, that's what I will give you.'

Jamie Silveira knows it is time to live to fight another day. He scampers away; before reaching the turn in the road, he gives Savio the finger.

Fucking modern-day kids, no respect for elders. Savio stands there in the broiling heat, clenching and unclenching his fists, then turns and stalks back into the gloom of his father's house.

9

ANGIE

And of course, when the time comes, her nerve fails.

In that magic time between three and five p.m., Pocolim lapses into a long continuous stream of silence, almost as silent as night, except for the occasional complaining bird-squawk occasioned by the heat.

He is back, goes the village buzz.

Between three and five p.m., Pocolim is a canvas of stillness and peace on which disembodied sounds splash: a cough like a firecracker going off, a stifled sneeze, a song on a tinny radio that may be playing in a faraway village.

She knows that house better than her own. From certain angles, you can't even see it through the thick foliage of the oak tree that abuts it.

It was Ferdie who mentioned it. 'Guess who I met today. Young Savio, Loyola's littlest fellow, you remember him?'

Between three and five p.m., you will hear the random squeak of bedsprings, the clink of glass on glass of another drink being poured, a creaky door-hinge, the shiver of leaves; it is the designated time for the tiny sounds to emerge and play.

'I almost d'int recognise him, so grown up he has become. He is a full man now. You met him?'

Around four, the muffled rumbles of earth-moving machinery can usually be heard rolling through the hot streets of Pocolim. If one follows the sound to its source, one ends up staring at the upstairs window of Casa Fernandez. It is Rosalina's nap time, and even in sleep, the lady demands attention.

'No,' she said, 'I seem to be the only one who has not even seen him, let alone met him.'

'You must have just missed him. Five minutes before you came, I was talking to him outside his house. He was doing sometin' on his car.'

That sounds like all the other sightings she has heard, he was just here, you just missed him, as if he possesses some magic genie powers with which he disappears in a puff of smoke every time she appears.

Around 4 p.m. or so, Joao too lies in bed next door, miserably concurring with that old chestnut spouted by real-estate agents – location, location, location. He seriously considers, not for the first time, rushing over next door and sitting on a pillow over Rosie's face. In the morning, it is that tall, droopy idiot with his singing and in the afternoon that fat pig next door with her vibrating uvula and three chins and her window wide open.

Ferdie had been weird today. Even by Ferdie's standards, he had been off the charts.

It had taken her a while to realize that the redness might not be all mud; there was a hint of overheatedness in his face, his brains perhaps a little scrambled by the sun, his bluish-brown lips speaking of possible dehydration.

And he was rambling about a dream.

After she fetched him water, there were the candles. The votive candles he was pawing through like a homeless vagrant scouring a garbage heap looking for food, eyes all dull and vacant and body bent over more than usual. Even as his shaking hands neared it, his fingers seeking like blind worms, she saw what it was, recognized it by its popular shape.

'Are you getting chest pains again? Did you go to Siolim to get your ECG done?' she asked him, even as his fingers curled around that candle.

She could see its round pinkness peeking out like some trapped exotic bird as he brought it up to his lips and kissed it reverentially with a slurping sound. Reluctantly prying away his lips, as if it were a delicious ice cream and not wax loaded with colour that was probably toxic.

He went to the bus stop the other day, he said. They cancelled the bus last minute.

So, she asked. There are ten buses to Siolim every day.

Not at three o'clock when he went. There was only one. The hand holding the candle came down, and the other went up to extract flecks of pink wax from his lips.

Any shooting pains down the left arm? The jaw? Any sense of impending doom?

No, no and no.

Was he regularly taking his medicine, his Nitrostat?

Yes.

Then why that candle? Why that particular candle?

What candle, he asked, one hand going behind his back and slipping it into his pocket.

She told him how exasperating he could be.

He rambled some more about some dream. How Angie reminded him so much of...

When the standing got too much for him, he slumped down heavily on the chair.

And then let out a yell of mortal anguish and jumped back on to his feet. Hand shaking as if in the grip of palsy, holding something round and flattened that looked like a pink pancake. Even after Angie fixed it, pieced it back, he kept caressing it, looking like a demented old man fondling his only possession in the world.

Then: a morose rant on Loyola. Died all alone.

Then: his closing lines. How is Rosalina?

She is fine. Come visit sometime.

Ferdie shook his head. That was then … when Albert was still living there. When both of them were merchant-ship men.

And then, finally: Guess who I met today.

'D'int recognize him, all growed up, he is a full man now.'

What did that mean? Fat, jowly and prosperous like his brothers? Or like Loyola, shrivelled and shrunken and defeated?

But Ferdinand was staring at the damaged candle as if it were sending messages to him in a language only he could understand.

That was when she vowed to stop off on her way home, march into that house if the door was open, or knock if it wasn't.

Of course, when the time comes, her nerve fails her completely.

Standing outside the rusted wrought-iron gate that she knows squeaks precisely halfway through its arc unless you push upward, she just stands there, the heat of the day gradually diminishing all around her. The front door is open, just a black rectangle. The balcony is accessed by stone steps that are overgrown with moss. Fourteen steps precisely; the stupid things you remember because you climbed those steps almost every single day of your life from when you were sixteen till you turned twenty-five, growing from a gawky, coltish teenager to a woman in her prime right on those very steps.

She hears music playing in the black interior, the sound tinny and lacking in body, a song she cannot recognize but judging by the wail of a guitar and the crash of what sounds like a wind-up monkey banging a toy drum, she guesses it is rock music, a departure from the country and western he used to like back in the day, influenced by the musical tastes of older siblings. The music sounds angry and edgy, a grown-up throwing a tantrum, as opposed to the softer child-like innocence of twanging box-guitars and sweetly plaintive fiddles. Perhaps it is a reflection of the change in his personality, a little of Bombay that he has brought back with him.

She does not go in to find out.

Everything seems to be decaying around her: Ferdie's mind, this once-bright, people-filled house.

She turns away from the gate and looks homeward, staring down at the well-travelled path that sometimes has the appearance of a muddy leash tugging at her.

She reluctantly succumbs to that force, ashamed at her weak resolve.

10
SAVIO

Inside, he is brooding over a monthly bank statement in the diffused glow of the evening sun that is battling its way past the grime on his living-room window.

A couple of electric lights would increase the illumination, but he isn't in the mood for cheap faux gaiety. He likes the earthy realness of sunlight and glass battling it out, the tyrannical star with its bullying force getting trounced by commonplace, lowly dirt. Loyola House has always needed a little extra help from electricity, something to do with it being hemmed in by extensive tree cover that Loyola would not dream of pruning. So he does not feel the least guilty about not keeping the windows clean.

He does not need extra light to read the numbers running down the page in clean laser printer ink that poke at his eyes.

If he rubs his fingers over those numbers, like a blind man reading Braille, he fears his fingers might get sliced open. *Goddamn*, is the word being pounded wordlessly somewhere in the region of the back of his mouth, the area where it hurts every time he swallows, as if his saliva is peppered with sharp pebbles.

Father Francis had called around 4 p.m. Probably wanted to get it out of the way, before he started on his evening brandy, before he slurred too much.

He was slurring even at 4, but later, he would be incoherent.

He had slurred that they needed to meet. He and Madame Rosalina, they needed to meet with him. Was he aware that a month was almost up?

Something about a Month's Mind.

No problem that he had not asked for it. He nor his siblings.

Loyola had asked for it. Before he died. Paid up in full, too.

Goddamn, goddamn, goddamn, the words thunder on ceaselessly, powered by some hidden battery source independent of his brain, an a capella soundtrack to the e-mail lines running in Arial font across the screen of his mind, the font as boring as old fat, bald, methodical Bob banging it out on his MacBook Pro down in Auckland, *Dad's needs are fairly simple these days*, isn't that what the pompous fuck had written? *There should be enough for the funeral, though not much left over after that*.

Well, let's see. Opening balance on the first of February, 1,40,000 rupees, Loyola of the simple needs, stacking up his nuts like a good little squirrel. A couple of modest withdrawals further down the page, money for cigarettes, for food, the odd bottle, all neatly plucked out from the nut-pile, nothing egregious or flamboyant.

At the end of the month, Savio's own transactions, using the power-of-attorney Robert had couriered over to him, to pay off the undertaker who had graciously interred Loyola without any cash up front while Savio had been porking the boss's daughter back in Bombay. Any surprise that he might have felt at the cost of the ceremony, questions like why walnut instead of pinewood for the coffin, were instantly squashed by his guilt at arriving late, and gratitude towards old Mr D'Sa who had sniffed and made it very clear that he normally did not encourage debt, and family should fork out the minute a member kicks it, in order to mitigate unpleasantness and resentment. After all, he is also a tradesperson, and it is not like there are people dying in Pocolim every week to ensure a comfortable livelihood, no?

Still, Savio's pen-hand had shaken a little as he had scribbled 'Rs 30,000 only' across the face of the cheque which Mr D'Sa had folded up and slipped into his pocket with a grave nod of thanks, don't be late again.

But somewhere in the middle of February, around the time when people in love all over the world start getting it on, buying flowers and candy and cards and condoms in honour of St. Valentine, around the time Savio was ignoring the glad-eye from Saviya and taunts from co-workers, the old squirrel seemed to have eaten a large chunk of his nuts all at once, enough to jam his digestion from end to end: a withdrawal of 70,000 rupees, which cause Savio's eyes to water and to ask himself, where the fuck is this money?

The only cash in the house he knows of is the 20,000 he has helped himself to by closing the account – not a lot considering the old man has left him nothing else, and you are supposed to leave a little behind for your kids, no?

Yes, he can spend the next two days looking for loose floorboards to peek under, or run a knife through every single mattress and cushion in the house the way those desperate people in the movies do, but he guesses that it would be a waste of time. So if it isn't in the house, what had he spent it on?

A big, grand going-away party with liquor and hookers? An Armani suit to be buried in? No, there is only one answer, and it is causing the two syllables to stomp the back of his head in jackboots.

His hands shaking, he puts the bank statement aside and walks through the still hot air of the living room towards the telephone just as Steven Tyler is exhorting in his standard throat-tearing snarl '*Don't get mad, get even*' from out of the Akai CD-radio boombox he had purchased in Bombay and carried back with him. Timing, he marvels, grinding his jaw; Spot-on Steve talking to him from a scratched CD of *Pump* that has recently begun to skip on the last track.

He dials Father Francis's number.

11

FERDIE

He paces the room in his pyjamas, moving in tight circles within the ghostly light thrown by the Holy Family lamp.

The low-wattage bulb reaches out with sickly yellow fingers but does not get too far. The dust accumulated on the plastic shell causes the First Family and their sheep to look like they have rolled around in the backyard minutes before posing for this most famous of tableaus.

By day, Ferdie can be reckless with his forays into the world. As long as the sun is out, his roaming radius can be substantial. By nightfall, as the shadows blur and thicken, his world shrinks and shrinks until it eventually becomes this little pool of light, the last haven of security and benevolence.

As always, he is delaying the final act of clicking off the lamp with fear of darkness thudding in his heart. Tonight, add to that the fear of dreaming.

The day has been exceptionally trying. He should not have butted into Maria's solo, but every time that upstart sprite puffs out her chest in preparation for her part, he experiences a vision of her precocious little mouth opening, and a sudden look of fright in her eyes as only a hoarse rattle tumbles out. He never can finish the vision – of her being booted out forthwith, flying out of the church door like some rag doll, serves her right – because always, *always*, instead of a dry, death-rattle, the most mind-numbingly soul-enriching golden voice fills up the highest nook and nave in church, a voice distilled from honey and nectar and the larynxes of a hundred nightingales.

The parishioners tremble and tear-soak the pages of their hymn books, and the Son of God looks like he would applaud if he could free his hands for a brief moment.

Ferdie always chokes back a howl of rage.

Today, he had almost succeeded; even as scrawny Maria was inflating her diaphragm with that cocky, spiritual look on her pimpled face, the trill had burst forth from his mouth, taking off and rising, rising, rising, wobbling like a dodgy bi-plane in a strong cross-wind, until that nasty fiend of a choir boy Joachim had kicked him painfully in the ankle, causing that flight to abort and crash-land in a howl of pain.

Then, that mad, reckless dash out of the church and through the streets of Pocolim on his bicycle, humiliation and disgrace snapping at his rear-wheel. Oh Saiba, and the dogs ... how they had fallen upon him, one cur in particular jumping high enough to brush his thigh with its slavering teeth, causing him to scream in terror and lose his balance, crashing to earth, twisting his wrist painfully. The crash had made the bicycle chain come off, which he had no strength to put back, and so he walked back in the putrid heat. What a day.

Tonight he wants to sleep. Not a sleep in which his dreams write their own weirdly real stories, frightening him, bringing back memories that make his heart ache. Not a wishy-washy thrashing-about sleep where his bed looks like a fight zone the next morning.

Tonight he wants to be in a coma, right up until the first rays of dawn enter the cracked-open window. And Joel, the clerk at the pharmacist, had taken one look at his red eyes and slipped him two tiny pills torn off the main strip, advising him to take just one and maybe another tomorrow as well if he feels like it.

He swallows one now with a tiny gulp of water; he has to be careful with the water intake if he is going to be out like a light. Tonight Millie will let him be. His heart feels like it is floating in a bottle of vinegar, pickled in pain. May as well take a Nitrostat too, right now, let it wallow and melt in his mouth before his head hits the pillow. Two pills, going their separate ways in his bloodstream to their respective destinations, working their magic; he feels safe tonight.

Picking up the misshapen lump of wax that Angie had put together that afternoon, he puts it down firmly on the night-table. Joseph, Mary and the dirty-woolled sheep eye it noncommittally.

When he lights the wick, the flame flickers hungrily, sending out longer fingers of light into the gloom of his room, reaching out even beyond the halo of the Holy Family. You are supposed to light it in church, in the presence of the son of God, but this is an emergency, and the Heir to the Kingdom is right there anyway on his bedside table – thirty-three years younger, still a babe in his mother's arms, carrying that benevolence in his innocent, blue eyes.

He does a recce, makes sure the pillow is in the exact centre of the bed, makes sure the plastic water-jar has the handle turned out at precisely the right angle and the glass of water is by his bed on the floor. All is right with the world, he tells himself with a twinge of apprehension.

The flame licks the air like a dog's tongue, hungrily feeding off the oils in the wax, shooting up tall and straight into the shadows that hang like a rain-cloud over the bed. He can see the basin, the kitchenette, the door to the bathroom, the dining table and chairs. He can even make out the other body parts arranged neatly on the table surface, clustered around their own kind, segregated from the others. His eyes move counter-clockwise groggily, sweeping past his front door, noting that it is triple-locked, and moves onto the bookshelf next to it. The book spines are blurs, propped up primly and colour-coded, a clump of whites, followed by oranges, then reds, a couple of greens and then the solo stragglers, kinless in colour. All my fadder's books, maybe one day I'll read them, he muses pleasantly and sleepily, a little happy that the pill is not losing any time at all.

All of a sudden, his attention snaps back to the right. Dread monkeys up his spine like a coconut-picker shinning up a palm tree. Something long and white is coming in from under the triple-locked front door. Ferdie hears short slithery sounds as it appears larger and larger; then, with one final sssshhhhh, it glides all the way in and stops. Even as his heart does hand-springs, he realizes it is only an envelope. But at this hour?

He chews his lower lip. His eyelids feel heavy and his spine yearns for the embrace of the mattress, but now fear has pressed the pause button on his stupor. His brain goes through the usual computations of whether or not this can be life-threatening, as it does with all events in his life, but even at his paranoid worst, he cannot see anything sinister about an envelope.

But at this hour?

Emboldened by the candle flame, he staggers a zigzag path to the front door, fumbles with the tumblers and yanks it open. He pokes his head out into the black night of Pocolim. Nothing moves; some street lights burn with feeble glows, others stutter, crickets confer busily, rodents squeak and cower as a hunter owl shrieks out a warning, but there is nothing out there that could have pushed that envelope under the door. He pulls his head back in, shuts the door and waits. He counts to ten, eyes gleaming with excitement, swaying under the unsteady effect of the Restil, then pulls the door open and thrusts his head out again. He squints, cranes his neck, not quite willing to actually step out into the black night.

He almost nods off in that position, leaning like a drunk against the doorframe; he retracts his head like a startled tortoise, slamming the door shut and triple-locking it. He quickly snatches up the envelope from the floor, and scurries over to his bed, into the safety corona of the Holy Light.

For the next ten whole minutes, serenity seems to settle over the village, the soft sounds of families tucking themselves into bed, of lights being switched off with muffled clicks, of restful sighs and duvets being pulled up and heads sinking into pillows, of murmured conversations as bodies snuggle up against each other.

And then it comes: the wail that slices through the air in all directions like a cluster-bomb explosion. This, people will reflect much later, is the record-breaker; it raises the bar for all time, on human expression of grief and distress. They just lie pinned down in their beds, stunned.

The wail goes on and on; it arcs through the Pocolim sky, going in and out through open windows or any crack in the masonry that it can find, chilling bloods and firing imaginations. Joao's wife, Jacinta, huddles closer to him, her face white as a sheet, and wonders aloud, 'E Saiba, *how* long is his breath?'

The arc of sound seems to hit a peak of sorts, and then begins to subside. The villagers wait, lightheaded from holding their breath. Down, down the sound goes, and then, as if effecting a bumpy landing, breaks up into a series of coughs and gurgles. Then there is a long silence.

'He stopped?' whispers Jacinta.

Joao, who knows better, buries himself under his duvet a little more and ticks off the seconds.

'Joao,' she hisses, 'maybe he died?'

And then it bursts forth again. This one is tinged with a rasp of helpless rage in its top notes, and that really makes hairs stand.

One by one, lights came on; some of the braver village folk, the ones farthest away, actually dare to look out of the window. In the distance, they see a ghost running towards Ferdinand's house, flitting into and out of the pale yellow streetlights. Some hear another voice, a fog-horn shriek of indignation and resentment whose lower frequencies somehow duck and dodge their way through. 'Yes, go ahead, never mind my leg massage, leave me! Go to dat fool, whose mudder should have slapped him more of-tin! Sissy boy!'

The stray dogs have started howling now, and bats are wheeling around the sky, frightened out of the trees.

The ghost reaches Ferdie's door, but instead of passing right through, seems to be rattling some metal outside it. Ferdie has landed again, coughing and gagging. In the silence, the villagers hear the ghostly rattle stop, they hear tumblers flipping thrice, and light streams out as the door is pushed open.

Ferdie is on his hands and knees, his pyjama bottom barely hanging onto the curve of his scrawny behind. His stomach and chest distend fully, and then the first string of notes canter out, primed to burst into full gallop.

The ghost slams the door shut just as Ferdinand strenuously attempts to outdo his previous eruptions.

'Sissy boy!' comes a scream from two houses away.

Joao puts a pillow over his head, and sobs freely and unabashedly into it.

The ghost runs to the little kitchenette next to his bed, returns with a soda bottle and a couple of towels. It kneels, gives the soda a vigorous shake, and sprays it ice cold into his face. The way one would turn a fire-hose upon a beloved pit-bull that has locked its jaw in one's thigh. Not a time for soothing words and pats on the back.

Mid-wail, he gags and sputters and flails his arms helplessly. He rolls over onto his back, launching into a series of apoplectic coughs. The ghost deftly throws one of the towels around Ferdinand's head, puts an arm around him and pulls him close.

Now there is just a strangled whimper; a sudden and violent storm has come and gone, the surface turbulence has ceased, but the ocean of grief still remains.

'Shhh,' she says, as she rocks him, aware of a painful ringing still in her ears. 'Shhh. You keep this up again and again, people will think you are possessed, Ferdie Padraon.' She frowns and looks down at his muffled head. 'Are you?' Without thinking, she clutches the crucifix around her neck. 'Sometimes I never know. It truly sounds like you are trying to expel the devil from your soul.'

Ferdie is beginning to twitch now; his whimper has segued to muffled sobs.

She looks around her as she rocks that feeble life-form, now fully spent and collapsed in surrender. Everything looks as it always is, nothing out of place. In the flickering glow of the lumpy candle, she sees the torn envelope lying on the floor.

The way it is cast on the floor, giving the impression of having slipped from fingers that suddenly went limp after near mauling it to death first, makes her ask, '*This? This* is the cause of all this?'

12
ANGIE

She cannot asleep. The last dregs of adrenaline the recent activity has cooked up, they're still good for a twitch or two.

There are little pools of moisture in her eyes, hot, stagnant, but not spilling over.

Regret, longing, loneliness: like common colds they come and go. They come, you whack them with a sledgehammer, they go. They come back again, when you're weak. Vulnerable.

Her ears are still ringing with Ferdie's naked expression of grief; all of Pocolim will sleep a little jittery tonight. It was like watching an open wound scream and run around in pain.

The letter is lying on her bedside table. She had taken it with her. The pools in her eyes shimmer. She blinks, and a hot trickle runs down one temple, quickly cooling as it goes.

What a beautiful letter, bumbling, earnest, so full of love. Who would not smile at the meandering train of thought, the compound sentences thrown together like snapped twigs, a language that could never be spoken, only written?

She shuts her eyes and touches herself, starting from her breasts, skimming the belly and coming to rest over her mound that has never been touched by another hand. Healthy, in the prime of its life, but never been touched by love.

Her fingers tinkle a silent intro over her vagina, feeling its sinking swampy softness through her underwear, wondering if she should reach past the waistband and bang out the entire sonata whose music will still all other thoughts. And then her hand is already there, teleported through cheap cotton, feeling its way through the first notes, tinkering with the thematic material of what's to come.

She thinks of Gabo, who had perished on their wedding day two hours before she would've been deflowered. Unvirgined. She feels no lust for him. He is there, on her bedside table, in their wedding photograph, drunk and grinning into the camera, his arm around her waist gripping a little too tightly. She remembers the feel of that arm because it was the only real contact they ever had.

One hour later he was dead.

Ridiculous, how quickly she went from almost-fucked back to never-been-fucked.

The photo, she just puts it up there as a perverse symbol of Almost. Almost married, almost had kids, family vacations, big Sunday spreads. A rotting daisy-chain of Almosts.

Her fingertips move on, cooking her loins slowly.

Rosalina suddenly snores in the next room, and her fingers lose their place. She tries to shut out the sound, but its bullying familiarity throws her off her stride.

When exactly did her life became assimilated with Rosie's, when exactly did the *I* and *you* blur into a *we*, when did the conquest happen?

Just as suddenly, the snores stop, and Angie regroups, bringing back the melody, picking up from where her fingers had paused. Now her thoughts are roaming, charting a zigzag course into the past like a bird in a cross-wind, back to the memory of another body cleaving itself to hers on her wedding day so many dirty moons ago, alien lips pressing into the bare skin of her neck. Abruptly, it's the present, and her mind is racing down a red road, running up fourteen steps; her fingers are skirting the fleshy rim now, one finger feather-stroking a swollen clitoris, two more standing-by for some spelunking, the *codetta* leading to the final bars...

A short scream rips the night, an atonal axe that slices her symphony dead.

Not again, Ferdie, not again.

Except, this one is really close, like just outside her window.

She jumps out of bed, and even from that distance, she can see he is quaking and trying to chew through all eight fingers at once.

He sees her and screams, 'Aaaaa-ghhh. A c-c-c-a' ... it was a c-c-c-a'. Aaaaaa-gh. It brush my leg. Aaaaa-gh. I tot it was a shnake ... a big hay-ee shnake.'

'Ferdie. Shhhh! What are you doing *here*?'

'Fi' oil. I use fi' oil. Kee-kee-keep de daw's away. But the ca', aaaaaaagh, the ca',' the words fractured and broken as they elbow past eight bunched fingers.

'Fish oil?'

'Dey are all aroun' me. Make 'em go away.'

'Oh sweet Christ, Ferdie, hasn't this been enough for one night?'

'Who is it?' Rosie bellows from the next room.

'Nothing, mama. Just a frightened cat outside.' She frantically waves her fingers, still a little moist at the tips, still fragrant with her essence. 'Go away.'

But he is rooted to the spot. When his hands drop limply to his side, she can see angry teeth-crescents on his fingers.

'I came to tell you,' he squeaks, 'I came to tell you I-I am going to find Millie.'

'Nereus!' Rosie screams from next door. 'Come down from de window sill! It's jus' anudder cat!'

'What?' Angie shouts.

Ferdie points up at the wall. 'Dere's one looking down at me. Dat one's wagging his tail. Is dat a good sign?'

'What did you just say?'

'I tot about what you said,' Ferdie shouts back, squaring his shoulders, keeping his eyes on the feline on the wall that is looking at him with unbridled lust. 'I am going to find Millie.'

The window next to hers suddenly bangs open. 'Ai Christo, *what* is that smell?'

Angie sees a big head jut out, like a gargoyle has suddenly grown out of the wall.

'Who is it you are talking to? Is it dat ee-diot again? And why is he smelling like de ocean jus' washed him up?'

'It's fish oil, mama. That Joao keeps giving him stupid advice.'

'Why is he covered in fish oil? Po' Nereus was jus' falling asleep!'

Like Nereus ever has difficulty doing that.

'Not covered,' Ferdie replies, a little indignantly. 'Just de pant. It keeps the dogs away.'

'And if Nereus does not sleep, I cannot sleep. Go home, you fool! Once an eee-diot, always an eee-diot!'

He looks up at Angie pleadingly. 'Can I come in? Can we keep them out?' he pleads. 'Is dat one dangerous?' He points up.

'You are calling me dangerous?' Rosie shrieks. 'And how dare you point at me like dat!'

A dark object whizzes through the night from a diagonal direction and crashes into the red mud a few feet away, scattering a freshly potted bonsai cactus. The cats yowl and disperse.

'I'll bleddy strangle you to det' now if you don't go home!'

'Shut up, you bleddy baker. Tell this impertinent rascal. Calling me dangerous. Pointing to a lady like dat!'

'He meant Nereus, mama. Please shut the window and go to bed. I'll deal with him.' She turns to Ferdie. 'I'm coming down. Don't move.'

'Don't let him into the house! Dat smell will strip all my good paint. Oh dear, my eyes are wat'ring now. How will I sleep? You eee-diot!'

'And you shut up too!' comes the near-hysterical scream from next door.

'Shut the window, mama.'

'What's the use? It is all in my nose now! It will stay dere forever! Oh, where is my potpourri? Go home and take a bath!'

Angie opens the front door and holds up her hand. 'Stay there. God, what a smell! Every cat in Goa is on his way here to lick your leg. Fine job, waking up mother like that.'

'Do you t'ink she is angry?'

'No, of course not. You think?'

'I'm going. I'm leaving. To find Millie.'

'What, *now*?'

'Not now, but – but soon. As soon as—'

'But … you don't even know where she is.'

'She was from Secaulim village, two–t'ree hours from here. She will be dere. Talk to her face-to-face. Aks her why she did not reply to my proposal.'

A couple of cats, wary of flowerpots, have returned to check him out again, but he isn't frightened now.

'You know, all dese years, I taught myself to forget,' he says. 'You cannot jus' forget, you have to *teach* yourself to forget. You know how difficult is dat?'

It's not difficult. It's impossible, she thinks.

'You know how long it's been?' he asks. 'You know how long t'irty-seven years is, to wait for a reply?'

After the first ten years, does it get worse? Or better, she wonders.

'Every day telling myself, every *moment* of the day, pretend like she was dead or sometin',' he says.

Regret, loneliness and longing. Turning up like bad pennies.

'Your heart telling one t'ing, your head somet'ing else.'

A bad penny is a swindler's penny, one with two heads, or one that is deliberately unbalanced. From Dr Britto's clinic, another magazine that will never be thrown away.

'Don't worry,' he assures her. 'I'm crying because udderwise my eyes will close and I will fall asleep.'

So that when you flip it, the coin will never turn down. A bad penny will always turn up.

'Last night ... I get dis dream, in which I see Millie. Everyt'ing I tot myself was forgotten in an instant.'

You take a sledgehammer to it, it goes, regret, longing, loneliness. And then it comes back.

'I had fooled my heart all dese years, but my heart never forgot. And den ... and den, dis ... dis letter. Tell me it is not a sign. Tell me I am a foolish ol' man. Tell me.'

When she eventually speaks, it is barely a whisper, 'How are you going? Is there a bus to Secaulim?'

That is the first time a car is mentioned.

'*What* car?'

'After all dese years, I don' want to go by bus.'

'Does she have cats? She will love you instantly if you go wearing those pants.'

'We never discussed pets. She tol' me once she was allergic to horses.'

'And I am allergic to you!' shouts Rosie. 'Go home and talk to yourself in the mirror! Is dis any time to visit somebody? Pervert!'

'Go away, now,' Angie whispers. 'We'll discuss this tomorrow. She will hear every word otherwise.'

'I'm doing de right t'ing, no?'

He just stands there, spindly legs anchored in the soft mud, upper body swaying. Then he smiles shyly and his feet begin shuffling backwards, keeping her in sight. She watches him recede into the gloom, their eyes still locked. When he is just a blur of pyjama top and postman trousers, she hisses in a loud whisper after him: 'Padraon, promise to throw away those pants – not wash, throw away – and I will come with you to find Millie.'

Whether or not he hears she cannot be sure, but she thinks she sees a smile just before he wheels around and disappears into the black, the stench of fish oil tailing him through the night like a smelly detective.

Following Angie's orders in a happy daze, the first thing Ferdie does when he goes home is strip off the postman pants and wear his pyjamas instead. It takes a while and he has to sit down to do it, because by now everything in his vision is trebled. And blurred. He picks up the trousers, and holding them at arm's length he stumbles back out into the black night, operating more on instinct than sight.

He returns minutes later with a happy smile in his tired eyes, collapses onto his bed and sleeps dreamlessly for twelve hours straight.

13

POCOLIM

The next day, Pocolim carries on as usual, although on the stretch of road that leads to church there are a few remarks by the early-bird coconut pickers about an awful smell. Several opinions are offered at the Taverna over shots of arrack, some a little closer to the truth than others, but all of them conceding that some living organism (perhaps many) has perished and is decaying somewhere in the vicinity of Joao's bakery.

An ocean full of fish, perhaps, have committed mass suicide, which although closest to the truth, is pooh-pooed because the ocean is five kilometres away.

A colony of rats, maybe, or a couple of buffaloes, these are some of the other astute observations, but nobody wants to get out there in the spooky gloom of the flickering halogens that blend into the pre-dawn night to find out.

Joao almost gags and pukes and runs back inside when he first emerges at six to do his rounds. That morning will go down in history as the day that Joao was in the blackest mood ever because all night, well after that idiot had almost given him a heart attack with his screams and yells and even later, after the shouting match with that bloated beast next door which had cost him one of his wife's carefully nurtured bonsai, cats had yowled non-stop outside his house, each yowl louder and angrier than the last.

But as he staggers and pushes his bicycle out past the stench in the gathering light of day, trying to keep last night's dinner in, he grudgingly admits to himself that the smell is familiar and associates a certain memory to it.

It is only when he returns from his rounds that, in the broad light of day, he sees the trousers draped over his garden wall, clawed to shreds by frustrated cats. He stares at the pants speechlessly, for long enough that the sun appears from over the roof of his house and blazes down on his dyed hair, making him sweat, making the dye run down his collar. His expressions reflect the several undercurrents of thought that flow through his head, but in the end he just walks up limply to the wall, bundles up the trousers and throws them in the garbage bin at the rear of his house.

14

SAVIO

That morning did not pan out as Savio's best either, not in a long time.

All through his feni bottle, the number 70,000 had kept flashing jerkily before his eyes, like a projector going on and off, and anger had grown in his gut like some mutant embryo and spread to the rest of his body until he was vibrating all over.

Just try sleeping angry, with one litre of 40% proof alcohol bashing through your bloodstream.

The next morning, waking an hour before his scheduled meeting, his breath smells like a dead dog decomposing in its own faeces, and his tongue feels like a dwarf has been stomping over it all night in muddy boots.

Five per cent of alcohol you lose through pissing and sweating.

Five per cent you exhale.

The remaining 90 per cent is pure hangover.

Even after he has shaved and showered and staggered to the back of the churchyard and into Father Francis's office, he is in no shape to deal with that first sight of Nosy Rosie sprawled into one of the priest's sturdier chairs, her back to him. It is the body language: a lioness that has devoured a few goats already, but would easily swat down one more just for the heck of it.

'Good morning,' he says, pulling up a chair next to her. She swivels her head, a challenging feat without a neck, and fixes upon him a practised look of scorn and disdain. 'You're late.'

'No, I'm not. You're early.'

He becomes aware of a little nimbus of aroma that he seems to have walked into, encircling him, making him its own.

'Punctuality is a virtue,' she says. 'And it's better to be five minutes early dan even *one* minute late.'

It is an aroma of stale perspiration mingled with a perfume distilled from dead, rotting flowers.

'Yes, I read that issue of *Reader's Digest*, too. Pardon me, is the window open? It's a bit stuffy in here.'

He walks to the window and throws the curtains aside. It is open, and it provides a view of the side of the church. Father Francis is leaning against a wall with his spine all askew, talking animatedly to a burly brute of a man. The brute is unkempt and unshaven, but impeccably attired in a fancy linen shirt and trousers, far fancier than anything Savio has seen in Pocolim. The priest seems to be calming the big man down.

Savio walks over to the opposite window and throws it open as well. On his way back, he turns up the fan a couple of notches. Rosalina is watching all his movements with her big toad eyes. The constant swivelling of her head does not improve her humour.

'Feeling very hot, I see.'

Savio sniffs the air. Still toxic, but better, much better.

'You must be hot as well, no?' He smiles thinly. 'Ooof, if in March like this, den what in May?'

'Well, dis is Goa. If you want cold, go live in Denmark or sometin'.'

'No, I like it here.'

'You young chil'rin, always complaining.'

'So is Father Francis joining us?'

'He went out for sum'tin', I don' know wat. He will be back soon.' Her bosom heaves, suggesting that he'd better come back soon. 'Den we will start. I don' want to repeat myself again and again. My time is preshis.'

He remembers her from ten years ago and not much has changed. There is no grey in her hair, no lines on her face, dye has taken care of the former, and gluttony the latter.

'So what are you going to do here, now dat you are back?'

'What is there to do here?'

'Lots of t'ings. For people who want to work and not lie around all day.'

Her viciousness and self-importance are now almost a fine art; ten years of practice have made them perfect.

'Uh-huh. Like what?'

'Your fadder never had to aks dat. He did so many jobs, and he did dem all very well.'

He remembers his father: good to start, hopeless to finish. Ten on ten for effort, zero for results.

'Better dan sitting on de balcony, drinking in the morning. Wasting all God-given yout'.'

'I am on holiday. I am taking a break.'

'What work you did in Bombay?'

Despite the fan and the slight breeze blowing through the windows, he sees tiny beads of perspiration on her upper lip. There is a baby-snake trickle of sweat coming down from behind her right ear, cutting a little furrow through the talcum powder and dirt that has caked up in the folds of flesh on her neck.

'God will be your judge, dat you did honest work. We may not be watching, but God is watching, remember dat.'

She is wearing heavy clothes, black as ash, of material normally used for circus tents, or hot-air balloons. Her breathing looks laboured.

Maybe she will have a heart attack right now, he hopes.

He cringes as a playful breeze sends a bright, sour odour his way, making his eyes water. Jesus.

Father Francis bounds in, a little hot and breathless, sunglasses stuck in place. A wide grin bares his tobacco-stained teeth, as he places both hands on their shoulders.

'So! Getting along like a house on fire? Do I even need to be here?' He laughs at his own joke, rubs his hands and walks around the desk. 'Now where were we?'

'Where were *we*? Where were *you*?' Rosalina demands, her face pink with fury.

'Er, yes. There is this fine gentleman, Don Pedro Cleto Colaco. He is an artist and he insists on meeting you, madam.'

'What does he want wit' my time?'

'It would be an honour, he said. When he knew you were here, he came down and *insisted* on meeting you *now*. Travelled the world, very successful. But I told him, today – now – was not possible.' He vaguely indicates Savio. 'We have this other business to finish today, yes?'

'Tell him he can come tomorrow afternoon to my house. For tea. Six o'clock.'

'Tomorrow, six o'clock. Very good, madame.'

Sounds like a butler, Savio thinks. A bloody priest, should be putting her in her place, sounds like her butler instead.

Father Francis suddenly bounds out of his chair and runs to the window behind Savio. He pulls the curtains together, bounces back to his chair and resumes his wide smile.

'I opened the curtains for a reason,' Savio snarls at him. 'To let some air in.'

'The window is still open. Perhaps I can make the fan faster?'

'De boy here is feeling hot. I am fine.'

'So,' says the padre, throwing a tentative ball up in the air, hoping someone will catch it.

'Why you keep your glasses on?' demands Rosalina.

'It's – er – maybe conjunctivitis. My eyes felt scratchy this morning.' He tries again, 'So.'

'So, I believe my father may have left a little money behind with the church, for things like memorials and … other stuff?'

'And?' Rosie asks.

'And? I want to know what it's being spent on. And why.'

'Why? *Why*? Because he aksed for it, dat's why.'

'How much money did he leave behind?'

'Dat is none of your business. We're jus' here to tell you w'at is planned wit' de money. As per your fadder's wishes.'

'Okay, so what is the money being spent on?'

'Deat' announcement. Funeral announcement. De usual.'

It is starting, he tells himself, his jaw twitching. This is the beginning, the tip of the iceberg that will be 70,000 feet deep and God knows how wide.

Savio clenches his fists. 'What else?'

'Den for de Mont's Mind I had to—'

'We did not ask for a Month's Mind.'

She actually bares her little teeth at him in a ghastly grin. 'You did not die. Your fadder did, and he aksed for it.'

Even though he is hearing it for the second time, he cannot believe it. 'My father asked for a Month's Mind before he died,' he repeats to himself.

'And de announcements in de papers for dat. If you read de *Herald* two days from now, you will see. And den the hall and refreshmints for everyone.'

He grinds his teeth. 'Another announcement. Great.'

'Prepared by your fadder himself, wit' dates lef' blank to be inserted later.'

'My father, the bard, composing odes to himself.'

'Yes. He didn't trust you and your siblings to do anyt'ing. You should hang yourself in shame. Your names should be *struck off* the announcements, useless chil'rin dat you all are. Never even aksed how he was.'

'I'll make it a point to stay in touch now. I wouldn't want to miss your funeral, for sure.'

Score one for the goat.

'Loyola was a fine, outstanding man of dis community. You – you are not worthy of de mud scraped from his shoe.'

A dangerous look springs into Savio's eyes, and the priest jumps in hastily like a good referee. 'Er, madame, young man, let's keep the – er – personal references aside. We are here to discuss and respect a deceased man's wishes. Now, about the first anniversary mass—'

'All de preparations are done,' says Rosalina.

'What, what, *what*?' He is sinking down past the wall of the iceberg, down, down, down indefinitely into the black. In terms of misappropriation, this is not just an iceberg; this is a whole fucking continental shelf. '*First anniversary mass?*'

The priest wishes, not for the first time, that his parish were only made up of little children and senile old citizens. The belligerent, argumentative middle lot can prove a little heavy on the soul.

Father Francis had taken up boxing briefly in seminary school, and dropped it when he broke his wrist on another student's jaw.

Priesthood is meant to be non-competitive.

He wishes these two would disappear so he can have his mid-morning snack with a little glass of something.

'People could not remember my father *five minutes* after they had met him, so – *forceful* – was his personality! One year after he is dead, you expect people to even remember he ever *existed*? Last wishes of a dying man? At what point does it become a *complete and useless waste of money*?'

He has blown his cover. He knows this by the sly, triumphant way in which Rosie defies neck-mechanics to look at him. By the bluish-brown tongue that snakes out and licks that hideous smile.

'Why? Did daddy not leave any money behind for de apple-of-his-eye son?'

Did the son expect to be taken care of? ask the moving lips. So he could lie in a booze-haze all day and never do an honest day's work ever again? While the rest of the world toiled and scraped, the son could bask like a lizard till the end of his days, speed-dialling in food and drink with daddy's money?

'What is next?' he hisses. 'A five-year anniversary? Then ten years? For a guy who had the personality of *boiled water*? Who the hell comes for these masses, I want to know?'

'People who rispeck the dead!'

'Yes? How many people came for the wake?'

Both answers come at the same time.

'About ten,' says the priest.

'At least fifty!' snaps Rosie, shooting daggers at Father Francis.

'These people come for *everybody's* wakes! They don't know if it's Loyola or Jacinta or Albert or Frederick. They just come because they have nothing better to do!'

Around the edges of her righteous, fake-sympathy look, triumph lurks like a chortling imp. 'Dere is a special place in hell for you. Though I wonder if hell will also take you.'

It's out in the open now, and the air is thick with eventual and preordained defeat, thick enough to bite into and spit out. 'Where is the proof of all this?' he snarls. 'Of these ridiculous requests? Of the bloody money spent?'

'You jus' wan' the money, don't you?'

'No! Yes! It's the principle of the whole thing! It's wrong!'

'Loyola trusted me. It doesn't matter dat you don't. Where were you when he died? Who did de running around?'

'You? *You* ran around?' Savio curls his mouth. 'Was that the small earthquake I read about in Goa?'

Goats have tempers. They can get in a gore or two.

She struggles for five agonizing seconds to get off the chair, but she is wedged in. Smacking his head will have to wait.

'There is an orphanage just outside Pocolim,' he is roaring now. 'Donate the money to them, so that way people who never knew he lived will thank God he died.'

Father Francis is moving around in his chair like a skinny white bear scratching his bum on a fallen tree trunk. He is wondering if he will be blamed if they start stabbing each other with sharpened pencils.

'Give them ceiling fans! They are boiling in that orphanage! Give them a bloody washing machine, for God's sake, walking around with dirty clothes like little urchins!'

'If he wanted somet'ing for the orphanage, he'd have mentioned it,' says Rosie icily.

'Give it to the SPCA! The bloody animals will be happy. My father liked animals.'

'He d'int say donation. He d'int say washing machine. And he d'int say dogs an' cats!' Rosie is screeching now.

He gets to his feet and stares down at her. He feels the spirit rise in him for one last gore. 'How much are you taking out of this?'

'Now, now,' says the padre nervously, 'there is no need for allegations.'

'No, no, let him speak. Let's hear wat de rascal has to say.'

'I saw that withdrawal from my father's account, which no doubt you held his hand and convinced him to do. Buy yourself a good perfume from that. And some soap. You stink. You stink like a pig that cannot stop eating.'

Her face turns pink, then red and then a dangerous shade of purple, suggesting an imminent life-threatening thrombosis.

'Please,' Father Francis whimpers, 'no personal remarks.'

'Look at you,' Savio continues savagely, 'if there is a drought or famine in Pocolim tomorrow, the entire village can feed off you for a week.'

Face twisted in rage, she grabs both armrests with plump hands and pushes strenuously with plump feet. The entire chair, with Rosalina wedged firmly in, rises off the floor a clear six inches, then thuds back down with sickening force, causing one of the rear legs to snap like a dry twig. The chair totters, the remaining three legs groan, she screams.

The goat ducks its head and delivers its final cut. 'I can't wait for the day I'll see your announcement in the papers.' He stalks out of the office.

As he leaves, he hears, 'Why can't you have wider chairs in your bloomin' office?'

As he storms out into the courtyard, he sees the burly brute who had been talking to Father Francis earlier, crouching below the window of the room he has just exited, reaching up a surreptitious hand to part the curtains.

'Mad,' he says. 'This whole fucking village is *mad*.'

15
ANGIE

In her head Angie flips a coin: friend or stranger?

She stands behind the large banyan tree across the road and watches him at work on the car. In her hand she has a thermos filled with ice-cold lime juice.

Every time the coin lands *stranger*, she makes it bounce again while she thinks some more. What had he been when he left, ten years ago? Without that reference point, she cannot project ten years into the now.

Her bright summery dress gives out the right measure of non-invasiveness and friendliness, she hopes. Harking back to a time before widow-black housecoats became the norm. Before her stash of lively colours got buried under predictable greys and blacks. Predating her personality sinking out of sight under the toxic smog of servitude.

The coin flips and bounces and flips.

The dress had felt strange, stretching reluctantly to accommodate a thicker, fuller body, chafing at her skin as if, in exile, it had developed a scratchy, neglected mood. When she smoothened out the kinks around the hips and her breasts, she had to admit she looked quite fetching in it, every curve cleaved by cloth. Her face is scrubbed clean and her hair tied back in a non-threatening school-girl fashion.

Her eyes feel tired in their sockets. After Ferdinand had slunk away, her fingers had gone back to finish what they had started. Excitement had galloped through her head like a herd of elephants, and when the first crack of light appeared between the curtains, she could still feel the weight of the stampede.

He has the hood of the huge car up, and he is poking his head around the machinery, skinny arms on a skinny body in a dirty singlet. There had had been a little more flesh on him, a little roundness and softness in the face back then. Now, from cheekbone to jaw, his skin looks stretched like cling-wrap, and some ham-handed sculptor has taken a chisel to his face. His hair is slicked back with cream, and the dark circles around his eyes suggest she isn't the only one who's had a bad night. There had been a little brightness in those eyes then. Now, it looks like a couple of bulbs have blown, leaving behind gloomy shadows.

This is not the boy she thought of last night as her fingers played their song.

She adjusts the straps on her dress and walks across the road, the coin still flipping away relentlessly in silver, glinting arcs.

He has set up a table next to the car for his tools and some dirty bits and bobs from the engine. She had not expected him to come running and give her a hug, but … not this either. She lets the coin plop in the soft mud, not taking off again.

His first words are, without looking at her: 'At least you don't ask silly questions like everyone else around here.'

His face is sunburned red, his eyes sullen and furtive and shoulders hunched over as if he expects a sharp blow from behind. His voice has a gravelly edge to it that speaks of an unending train of cigarettes trundling through his airways, a train ten years long and still running.

'What silly questions?'

'Kai re, Savio, you back? Hot, no?' He throws the spanner down, and picks up another smaller one. 'And everyone's favourite: didn't come for daddy's funeral?'

'Why are those questions silly?'

He looks at her for the first time, the first time since he has returned. After ten years, he has not dropped in to say hello, nor bumped into her on the road, in the market, at church, all those places where their paths used to cross, just flitted around like a ghost, leaving traces of himself: an outline in a chair on the porch, an imprint of fingers around the neck of a bottle.

He looks at her for the first time and she sees a spark of *something* jump into his eyes, she is sure of that.

'People talk to you because they are glad to see you,' she says. 'And it is hot. We had three sun-strokes last week.'

'They should stay at home then, listen to their fados and mandos. There'll be less pointless conversation all around. What's this?' He indicates the thermos.

Through tiny aural windows she hears snatches of his old voice, devoid of the shards of glass it seemed to have dipped itself in, like an old accent surfacing through the patina of a recently learned one.

'It's for you. Nimboo-pani. Perfect for this weather.'

'You made it?'

'Not exactly a secret recipe. But yes, I made it.'

'That's not what I meant. In that big house I thought you'd have servants to do everything for you.'

'*I* do everything.'

He grins and cleans a spark plug. 'No servants? What is she saving up for? A cruise on the QE2? You won't be going on the cruise, you know. You'll be here, cleaning out the cobwebs and scraping off the bird-shit, keeping the grand *palacio* spotless for the lady when she returns.' He jerks his thumb. 'I know it's a stupid question, but is there any feni in this?'

She looks at him with genuine curiosity. 'So this how Bombay people speak?'

He snorts. 'What Bombay people? And what way is that?'

'I don't know. You sound bitter. Or you're just being funny, I cannot tell. No, there is no feni in it.'

'Care a damn is more what I am. Fucked and resigned. That's what I am.' He looks the other way and spits gently.

'I never understand people when they come back after a long time. It's like watching those English movies where they mumble their lines. I always wish for subtitles.'

He looks at her again, startled again at what he sees. 'How perfect you are for her,' he says as he bends over and sticks his head under the hood.

He keeps steering the conversation into dead ends. The coin lies mute, stranger side up.

'So,' she asks. 'Will it ever run again?'

He grunts as he works the spanner in a difficult-to-reach place, then straightens up. 'She is in the ICU right now. If she were human, she'd be dead long back.' He wipes his soaked brow. 'But since she's a pile of American nuts and bolts,' he explains, 'made in a time when they gave a shit about quality, there is hope.'

'Your father used to be so proud of it, remember, in the early days? It was the *only* car in the village.' She pauses. 'Still is.'

The early days are what she wants to bring to the conversation.

This little boy seems to have grown up at thrice the human rate; taken a running jump from eighteen and landed somewhere in his forties, making even her thirty-five years seem gauche and silly.

She wants to bring in memories of the car, of the three of them, Savio barely fifteen and at the wheel, her and Gabo taking turns in the front, exploring the outer reaches of Pocolim.

'Ten years nobody knows anything about you. Are you alive? Dead?' She pauses. 'Married? Successful? Do you know Gabo died that same day? The train must have *just* been leaving the station when it happened. No sign of you at the funeral, no—'

'What would I have come back and done? Brought him back to life?' That flatness in his tone, it's like a fly-swatter smacking down on a bug.

'No phone call, not even a letter?'

'To what end? I heard about it the next evening. By then he was in the ground. I was committed to my new life. Nothing, *nothing* about this goddamn village made me want to come back.'

Not even you, Angie: the words he does not say.

Not even me? The words she does not dare ask.

'Who were you then, Angie? Did you have any personality left? What would I have come back to? A widow in black dedicating the rest of her life to pressing her mother-in-law's feet?'

He fetches a quarter-full bottle of feni that is lying on the porch and pours it into the thermos.

'It's not your fault,' he says. 'Fate dealt you shitty cards. Plucked you out of an orphanage and plonked you into a family with a mother, a potential husband, happiness. And then everything went tits up, and it all became a cage, too late, the key had been thrown away.'

He swirls the liquid in the thermos around, shooting fleeting looks in her direction. He had forgotten how … how *wholesome* she is. That is the word that comes to his mind. He has not seen wholesome in a while now.

Plenty of skanky, none of wholesome.

'Who are you now, Angie?' he asks. 'That's a, umm, beautiful dress you have on, but has anything really changed?'

Working like a servant all day long, slogging over broom and mop is good for the body, obviously. Eating scraps from a table can have its advantages.

When you tear your eyes off her breasts and move up, that is where it hits you, he thinks. Lines around the mouth, strands of grey at the temples. Bags under the eyes, the milky tiredness in them.

But still, at the core, that supernova explosion still blazes, the Big Bang only seconds old, and his mouth goes dry.

He turns around to look at the house behind him, the crumbling wreck that was once a thriving home. He looks at the car, at the 'FOR SALI' sign on it. He takes a long swig from the thermos and butts away the silence.

'Forget about all that,' he says. 'It's all in the past, whether I came back or not, did I call or not. How are you? How have you been?'

'People have grown older,' she shrugs, feeling a little nicked and cut by his words. '*You* have grown older.'

'Who's growing younger? Anyone?'

She expected a few jabs to be exchanged. Friendly pokes after ten years are normal. Except, she feels like she has brought boxing gloves to a knife-fight.

She runs her fingers along the side of the car contemplatively, chewing her lower lip. 'Are you really going to sell this?'

'Why, you want to buy?'

'I can't, it seems. It's for somebody called Sali.'

Savio looks startled. 'Funny. Very funny. So what, Auntie Rosie is tired of coolies carrying her around? A car all of a sudden?'

'Why are you going on and on about my mother-in-law today?'

'Yes, I wish I could get her out of my mind. But I just met her, what a horrible way to spend a morning. Now she's stuck there, like a ... like a ... bloody hippopotamus in mud.'

Then: 'So how is life with her, after, erm, you know...'

He is having a hard time saying it. Death has many connotations to different people.

'Nothing has changed. Do you remember how it was when we were growing up? Well, add a few years, plus or minus a person or two, and it's all the same.' Mostly minus, she thinks, the book of life running away into minuses, no plusses. 'How was Bombay for you? You look...' *Prosperous* is what she would have liked to say. That is what you told everyone who came back from the city, but her intuition is running the other way. 'You look like you've been working hard.'

He does not nod nor shake his head, nor does he offer an answer or comment to her observation, nor does any emotion flicker in his eyes. Another dead-end wall at the foot of which her words lie, crushed and useless.

'I came here to ask you for a favour, for help. But it's like asking a stranger; an unreliable, unpredictable stranger.'

'A favour. For you? Or...' He cocks his head.

'For me.'

'It doesn't involve that fat cow?'

Spots flare on her cheeks like sun-storms. 'You used to come over and play in that house!'

'So? She was a fat cow even then. Only gone fatter. Answer the question.'

'No it doesn't,' she says softly. 'But it involves your car.'

'What car? *This*? This baby has not had her engine turned for God knows how many years. Pistons have seized, the starter is fucked, the—'

'But? You are a mechanic, right?'

'I'll have more luck walking on water or healing lepers.' Or changing water into feni, that would be cool. 'Besides, it's not my car anymore. Sold. By my father. Before he popped it.'

'But then – why do you have a sign For Sale?'

He looks at her shiftily and shrugs. 'In case I get a better offer. Then I'll return that bugger's advance.'

'Whose advance?'

'That mad artist, lives on top of that hill, behind the church.'

'That ... what's his name? Don Pedro?'

'Last deal my father made. Took an advance on it.'

Loyola informed Auckland Bob, who informed him in Arial font. Advance amount not mentioned, but the balance after it is fixed and delivered to him.

'Deliver? This piece of shit?' He spits into the earth at his feet.

The advance amount that did not make its way into the bank account. Cash, obviously. Which is not under floorboards or sewn into a mattress, like in the movies.

She feels a lead-ball of disappointment go thunk in the pit of her stomach.

'What do *you* need the car for? Finally running away from that slave-camp or what?'

The sun-spots morph into a deep-red blush. 'Ferdinand and I – you know the postmaster? – we have to, er, make a short trip.'

He coughs out a cloud of smoke. 'You're running away with *him*?'

'Don't be absurd! You have a dirty mind.'

'Not at all. You've never had a father figure in your life. Stuff like this happens.'

'He received a letter in the dead of night. Last night.'

From a girl he knew thirty-seven years ago.

A return-to-sender letter. Except there was no return-to-sender stamp on it. The letter, unopened, unread, for thirty-seven years, just like that, reappearing in the dead of night.

Except, why is she telling him all this? Does he care? Does he give a shit? He is not even looking at her now.

She pushes herself away wearily from the car. 'I'll be back to pick up the thermos. And don't bother to wash it. I'll do it; I have a lot of experience washing and cleaning up.' She looks down and walks away.

'Listen,' he shouts after her.

She stops briefly and half-turns.

'I'll do you a favour any time, you know that.' He seems to find the words awkward, extracting them slowly and painfully, putting them one after the other in careful order. Avoiding her eyes. 'I just honestly don't think this heap of bolts will ever run again.'

She waits for him to say more, not turning around fully.

'And besides, will he let you use it, that artist fellow? Who knows?'

No more words come. His mind is full of a hundred thoughts suddenly, but his voice-box stays silent.

She walks away, holding her head high, feeling more tired than ever before in her life.

16

DON PEDRO

Don Pedro watches the tall lanky figure grow incrementally larger as it shambles towards him. There is an air of purpose about this man even as there is defeat writ in every step he takes. The defeat, Don Pedro deduces keenly, is in the man's nature, the sense of purpose merely an anomaly, an aberration.

There are still many yards to go, uphill ones, before the man will make it to the artist's lofty sanctum.

Six months ago, Don Pedro had taken one look at the estate and had put money down without a moment's hesitation, precisely because of its singular insularity: surrounded by a stream of flowing water on three sides, and a vertical hundred-foot drop into the churchyard on its fourth. There is a bridge over the gurgling brook, the only means of entry into the estate, unless you were a bird, a monkey, rock-climber or a burglar.

The bridge is guarded by an imposing gate, which Don Pedro has put an enormous padlock on earlier that morning. Today he needs quiet time that is not disturbed by bread-men, laundry-men, fisherwomen and other sundry humans who have no business entwining their lives with his. Today is by invitation only, and Don Pedro stares long and hard at this sundry human in a khaki postmaster's uniform who seems determined to break that rule.

Today, his favourite spot, the courtyard, is temporarily out of bounds. They say your own smells are rarely offensive to your own nose, they enjoy a forgiveness based on proprietorship. But there is nothing deserving of any clemency whatsoever in the stench of stale urine, his own, that hangs over the courtyard like a bad mood. Even the paintings that had earlier been in the house are now ranged outside, the colours bleeding and melting. He has, by his own admission, outdefecated himself magnificently.

The smell has a critical-mass quality about it; even one more drop could now lead to a cataclysmic event: low-flying birds might drop dead, or trees in a one-mile radius could wither and die.

Today, he merely awaits a meeting with Madame Rosalina Eucharistica at six.

Except now there is some lanky, droopy, defeated yet annoyingly determined, insignificant and ineffectual member of the human race slowly but surely attempting to invade his private space.

Earlier, the man had eyed the gurgling brook with a quaking fascination. Then he had sat down and removed his shoes with a snail-like slowness, as if haste would tear his feet off at the ankles. Then he had tied the shoes together by their laces in a neat, fastidious knot. Then he had proceeded to fold his pants over his knees, inch by inch, making sure each fold was neatly smoothed out.

Today is not a good day for imbeciles and retards.

Holding on to his shoes, the man had stepped into the gurgling brook. After two hesitant steps, he had slipped and fallen, all of him almost going under. Somehow, he had managed to dunk almost all of his six feet in two feet of water, almost as if he wanted to lie down on the stream bed. But then, with Herculean effort and all the attendant drama of Greek theatre, the man had righted himself inch by inch, until he was in a sitting position, the water running just below his breastbone. Five minutes later, he was standing again, his water-filled shoes dangling uselessly at his side, held in one weak fist.

This is not a time to be surrounded by the weak and the helpless.

The man takes a break every ten steps as he trudges uphill. Breath rasping loudly and body bent over like a sickle, he finally crests the rim and stands there, in total wonder and disbelief. Slowly he straightens up, like a wilting flower unbending towards a healing sun. He is wheezing as he breathes, as if a blunt knife is scraping the inner wall of his chest cavity.

A flock of birds suddenly break cover and fly overhead. Sunlight dapples the earth through the acacia trees, and a cooling late-afternoon breeze is picking up.

The man smiles, and squelches towards the courtyard filled with wild flora and the twenty-odd canvases arranged haphazardly. He stops and sniffs the air, his expression suggesting that this is an odour that is familiar, yet exotic.

17

FERDIE

He stares at the canvases. Even to his unpractised eye, they look unfinished, works in progress. He experiences nervousness, a voyeur's guilt. Should he be seeing these?

'Eh!'

A voice growls over his left shoulder, causing him to jump and void his bladder. He closes his eyes, expecting horrendous pain any second.

A muffled but menacing bone-rattling baritone says: 'It is my policy to normally shoot trespassers unless they can prove they have something useful for me.'

When he slowly opens his eyes, there is a big, burly brute with mad, yellow eyes burning brightly from over a colourful handkerchief tied over nose and mouth, wearing a stained singlet and shorts that hang well below his belly.

He cannot see the man's mouth, but he imagines this is someone possessing very large teeth, like those African gorillas he had seen on TV once.

The big ape slouches forward. 'So what is it? A letter? A parcel? Or a waste of my time?'

Fear paralyses his mind. 'W'at were de first two?'

The simian head suddenly fills up his vision, forcing him to take two steps back. A barrel chest touches his own humble one, and the handkerchief tickles his chin.

'Can you smell something?' the lips ask from behind the colourful fabric.

He isn't sure, but he thinks this big ape is grinning at him now. He wishes he would faint, but no fainting spell comes.

'Can you smell it?' the big lips move again.

Is he referring to my recent bladder-accident, he wonders fearfully.

The big head swivels from side to side, taking in the entire courtyard with those big yellowish eyes. Then they came back and settle on him. 'No? Can you smell *anything* over your own stench of uselessness and failure? Pah!' He steps back and rips off the handkerchief. 'So. No letters, no parcel. What good are you being a postman?'

'Er – I'm a postmaster.'

'Man or master, you're still useless. And you are a master of nothing, my friend, believe me.'

He stands there stupidly, wondering why a man like this is not locked up somewhere. He does not look safe at all. Unhinged. Mentally unstable.

'Does a closed gate with a padlock mean anything to you?' the man asks. Then, 'Do you have children?'

Very carefully Ferdie considers an answer to the second question, keeping in mind he is talking to somebody who might be homicidal. 'No I don't,' he finally says, considering truth to be the safest option. 'But Millie and I would have—'

'Shut up. Good thing you don't. Otherwise I would have suggested you go back and strangle them, so that your line ends once and for all.'

You and yours should be eliminated from the gene pool, the beast is telling him. 'But now that you're here, perhaps I can conduct a little experiment with you, so I may understand the rest of the retarded world.' He sweeps a hand over his piss-drenched paintings. 'What do you think of these?'

Nobody has ever asked for his opinion on art before. It makes him feel strangely special.

'You can take your retarded time. I have a meeting with a beautiful lady at six. Until then I will listen to your plebeian babbling.'

He looks carefully at each painting, walking from one to the other, keeping the bloodthirsty gorilla in his peripheral vision at all times. The paintings strike no aesthetic chord within him at all, but he stares at them the way he imagines art patrons do: hands clasped behind his back and squinting at them with a practised eye, except his earnest fake-squint make him look like he is half-blind and cross-eyed.

'Yes ... mmmm ... yes, er, It's ummm ... I think dey are very good.'

'Don't try and be clever,' warns Don Pedro. 'You are a simpleton, think like a simpleton. Tell me what you think in your own moronic language.'

For the life of him, he cannot think of a more moronic way to put it, so he nods myopically and repeats feebly, 'Dey are very good. *Really* very good.'

'Yes? How can you tell?'

He looks at Don Pedro helplessly.

'How can you tell if they're good?' the artist repeats.

He racks his brain for words. 'G-g-g-good colours,' his mouth blurts out, with no help from his useless brain.

The artist looms close. He cringes.

'Look carefully. Concentrate,' the baritone rumbles out on a bed of hot, fetid breath that tickles his right ear. 'It is a moment frozen in the blink of an eye. Frozen; but if you look close enough, it moves ... it's alive!'

He can only concentrate on the fact that his exposed neck is three inches away from the maniac's teeth. He stares sightlessly at one of the paintings and his mind wanders, for some strange reason, onto a vision of little Maria who would be in the middle of one of her solos right now, stoking the parishioners into a state of ecclesiastical frenzy. 'I don't see it move,' he mumbles.

Don Pedro smacks him lightly on the head.

He cowers down, covers his head and gibbers, the words coming out in a rush, 'Angie knows where I am if I don't come back she will wonder and I have a choir seshin and Fadder Francis will wonder please let me go please let me go I should not have come sorry about not seeing de lock and I tot it was important—' He runs out of breath and begins to sob, his heart beating like a bass-drum in eight-time.

Pedro steps back. 'You ridiculous human being,' he gasps. 'Sorry, you poor *excuse* of a ridiculous human being, are you suggesting that I am going to *kill* you?' And then he laughs.

To Ferdie's waterlogged ears, it sounds like the bloodthirsty braying of a hundred hyenas. He shuts his eyes.

Don Pedro laughs on. The sound is like apocalyptic thunder, the evil jollity of a demon prophet booming down from the sky, barrelling through every street of every town on planet Earth, filling hearts and minds with fear and dread.

Then abruptly the laughter ceases. 'Stand up,' a calm baritone voice commands. 'Stand straight. What is your name?'

He opens his eyes and sees a hairy belly protruding from below a soiled singlet. He focuses on the pattern of the hairs running down the curvature of brown skin and disappearing into the waistband of the shorts.

'Up, up, *up*! Stand up straight!' the voice bellows from high above. 'What is your name, postmaster of Pocolim?'

He is startled by how low he has crouched; there seems to be a long way to go, he is still somewhere in the region of the beast's upper belly. He pulls himself erect hastily, reeling from a head-rush.

'Name!'

'Ferdinand. Antonio. Lazar. D'Cruz,' he mutters, trying to still the quaver in his voice. 'At your service,' he adds, trying to sound important but sounding obsequious instead.

'Weak name. Perfectly fitting someone with no spine. With an opinion that is as useless as water to a drowning man.'

He shudders at the cruel choice of words.

'So,' the artist plumps both hands on his hips and sneers, 'Simpleton with useless opinions, Ferdinand whatever whatever D'Cruz, you like my work, is it?'

He nods solemnly, pretending to be a man of conviction, steadfast in his judgement.

'Well, that is a very good sign that other idiots like you also will. *But I don't paint for idiots!*' he suddenly roars, blowing the hair on his head back. '*Bloody mediocre obvious shit!*'

A flock of parrots squawk and fly away.

'Sit!' Don Pedro thunders. 'Your spine looks like it needs some rest.' He nudges the postmaster, gentle pokes to the chest with one big banana-like finger, making him totter backward until he collapses on the sitting-ledge connected to the wall.

'Would you like some water? In case you haven't drunk enough in the stream below?'

'Yes, er no, I would like some water, please, t'ank you.'

'Well, too bad. I'm not going back inside. Say your piece and get the hell out of here. It's getting late.'

He licks his parched lips longingly. His uniform is drying against his skin and it is making him itch madly.

'I – I need a car,' he says, morosely, scratching himself simultaneously on his navel and his left thigh.

Don Pedro looks down at him and blinks. 'Okay, one more time. Let's do this again. What do you want?'

'A car. I need a car.'

'Yes, and do I have Hertz Rental written on my forehead?'

He peers at the madman's forehead, transferring one hand to his left butt-cheek now. 'I – I cannot see...'

Don Pedro begins to count to ten, flexing his fingers like fat, writhing baby snakes.

'...but Loyola da Gama has a car,' he finishes brightly.

The artist thinks for a bit, then frowns. 'Wrong. He *had* a car.'

'Yes.' He nods vigorously, relieved that they finally seem to be on the same page. 'God rest his soul.'

'God can do whatever he wants with his soul. The car is mine, provisionally, and it is not for sale or hire.'

'It's for a very good cause. It will bring—'

'And *especially* not to morons.'

'It will bring two people togeder. Widout a car, dere will be...' He pauses dramatically. '...loneliness. Eternal loneliness.'

'Why? Are you planning on mucking around with someone in the back seat? At your age?'

'When I find her, she will ride in front wit' me.'

'Find? So somebody ran *away* from you, then? Good for her.'

'But I cannot drive, so I suppose we'll sit in de back.'

Don Pedro becomes aware that he might not be part of the conversation that they are having. 'That car,' he says harshly, 'is probably never going to run. That old fool who sold it to me promised to give it to me in working condition, and then died. Took the easy way out of the deal.'

'His son is a mechanic also. He is here now.'

'Another moron. I am surrounded by morons. Maybe I'll just take back my advance.'

'No, no, he is good. He worked in Bombay.'

'*You* are giving testimony for somebody? *You*? The most useless being on the planet?'

'I am only telling what I heard.' He suddenly sneezes violently. 'Oh no I'm gedding a cold.'

'Leave. Now. Before you infect me with your disease.'

He gets to his feet, tears of failure welling up in his eyes. This is a lost mission. And he is probably going to die of pneumonia, if a heart attack doesn't get there first. He is tired, and he just wants to sleep. 'Can you open de gate, please?'

'Of course not. Go back the way you came.'

'But I have a cold!'

'Keep away from me.' Don Pedro takes two steps back. 'If *I* get your cold, I will come and hunt you down.'

'I will wait here till you leave, and den leave wit' you.'

Don Pedro begins walking towards the house. He looks over his shoulder. 'I will give you five minutes. If you are still here, I will bring out my air gun and start doing target practice.'

'Ad leas' give me a glass of wadder! My t'roat is hurting.'

'Drink some more on your way across!'

'I will drown!' he screams. 'I cannot cross dat t'ing again!'

'Natural selection!' roars Den Pedro. 'Should have happened long ago!'

He disappears into the house.

18
DON PEDRO

Don Pedro wears a watch for the occasion, some old timepiece that he had discarded six months earlier. He finds it exactly where he had left it, in one corner of the living room, on an old, battered copy of *Thus Spake Zarathustra: A Book for All and None*. When he picks it up, it leaves behind a watch-shaped impression in the thick dust on the cover. He gives the book a baleful stare as he straps the watch to his wrist.

Pedro has groomed himself with meticulous care: he has washed copiously, splashing around in a jasmine-scented bathtub like a happy water buffalo, scouring every inch of his skin with a bristly dishcloth gourd, emerging red and raw and rejuvenated half an hour later. Thereafter, nose-hairs were snipped, talon-like toenails were clipped, fingernails emery-boarded, and a new razor-blade had done two passes on the stubble.

It had not come at an opportune time in Don Pedro's life, that book. All that rambling, allegorical hoopla about rising up to be a superman, a *ubermensch*, when in reality he felt himself slipping a rung or two on the evolutionary ladder, moving backward. The *ubermensch* laughs at man from his lofty plane, just as man sniggers at the ape for falling behind. If ordinary men had begun to snigger at him, that brought him down to the level of an ape, said the nutty

German. An ape with opposable thumbs, who could hold a brush, but could not produce anything of beauty with it.

A steaming hot towel had then caressed the baby-smooth face, followed by an assault with ice-cubes, relaxing the pores and then squeezing them shut. Hair is combed back and waxed, ear-lobes are tweezed and armpits fumigated. A freshly laundered white linen shirt is matched with well-creased cream trousers and crocodile-skin loafers. Finally, just as he is leaving, an original, classic Panama hat that he had brought back with him from Ecuador fifteen years ago.

He had discarded the book in one corner of the living room. The blinding headaches he would get trying to wade through phrases like 'What would be thy happiness if thou hadst not those for whom thou shinest!' Or words like forsooth and keepeth and promiseth, which when he read aloud, made him sound like a ponce with a lisp. The watch had joined it a little later, for more or less the same reason, when time for him had begun its backward tick.

But today, as he has gone from a urine-stained, crud-encrusted, tatty lout to a suave, slick, bon vivant aristocrat oozing sex, supremacy and savoir-faire, today he looks at the book with renewed interest. There might be a nugget or three in that tangled mess of obfuscating verbosity that might be of value to him in his new avatar.

On his way over the bridge, he scans the water for a drowned human being, even a stray shoe or two washed up. He sees none and is vaguely disappointed, a flaw in that bugger Darwin's theory. He righteously hopes it will be corrected soon.

By the time he reaches Rosalina Eucharistica's door, two large and sticky patches have grown out of his armpits, the humidity has made the magnificent Monte Cristi Classic sag a little, and red dust has caked his pant cuffs and filled up his shoes.

A handsome-looking lady opens the door. Don Pedro smiles charmingly as he sizes her up. Good genetics, lyrical lines of worry and tiredness on her face. Good working stock. He likes the honesty of working women, the poetic resignation in their eyes, the raw hands, the firm thighs. He doffs his hat and bows.

'And a very good evening to you, ma'am. I have come to meet the lady Rosalina Eucharistica.'

'Please come in. I am Angelina. Mai is expecting you.' She steps aside to let him in and shuts the door. 'This way, please.'

Pedro gestures with his hatted hand and bows again. 'After you, my dear lady.'

She smiles that simple half-witted smile of pleasure as when a master throws a slave a compliment, he thinks.

'I am Don Pedro Cleto Colaco,' he offers.

She lowers her eyes. 'I know who you are. Would you like a glass of water? Your throat must be parched with the walk.'

'Very gracious of you. Yes, it is a little hot, isn't it?'

'Oh, now it is much better. It was hotter at four o' clock. Were you outside at four o' clock?'

'I don't remember. Yes, probably.'

She smiles sweetly. 'You would remember if you were, Don Pedro. I think you were.' He blinks in surprise; is that a knowing wink she just flashed at him?

'I will get the water. In the meantime, please follow me.'

Poor peasant nutrition, he thinks; makes the brain a little soft, leads to incoherent rambling.

His eyes are drawn to her full, round bottom as she leads him to the living room. He admires the view, but this is nothing compared to what it is leading to, just beyond that door.

This is just the teaser; yonder lies the grand extravaganza.

This stuff is for amateurs, for gauche schoolboys fumbling with buttons and bra-hooks. Pah!

That is for the seasoned lover, the true connoisseur of the carnal, the gastronome whose mind rises above mere meat to the juices that oil it, to the musk that lies hidden in the folds. And to capture *that essence*...

He is ushered into the living room, and the peasant girl gives him a funny look as she leaves. He dismisses her from his mind as he looks around.

The jumble of furniture smites his eyeballs. It is like some passing tornado has swept through a hundred houses, picked up one item from each and dumped them all here. His mind struggles for a description. Louis the XV? Victorian? Baroque? Georgian? Indian Mughal? Art Deco?

And the layer of dust on everything. He cannot afford to be judgemental, he corrects himself sternly. His own house currently smells like a hooch-bar urinal.

'So. We finally meet de artist on de hill,' says a mouse with a cold from somewhere behind his back.

He turns slowly. Perhaps he had mistaken her for a sofa with a black dust-protection cloth thrown over it. He cannot be blamed; even as he stares at her inert, reclined tonnage, he cannot see *what* she is reclining on. That piece of furniture, whatever it is, is a part of her. Something sturdy, no doubt, with iron cross-beams to hold it up, the suspension of an eighteen-wheel truck perhaps.

This the first time he is observing her this close, within touching, feeling, smelling distance.

He lifts his hand to doff his hat, except the hat is already in his hand. The damp Monti Cristo merely goes up and comes down again. 'Don Pedro Cleto Colaco at your service, Ma'am,' he booms.

In the late-evening light that filters through the skylight, her skin has a radiance that he wants to capture on canvas that very minute. He mixes colours furiously, colours he has no names for, but can see clearly in his mind's eye.

She holds out her hand at him, wagging short, stout fingers that look like baby carrots. He transfers his hat to his left hand and taking three bold strides, grabs her podgy fist manfully in his own. He plumps out his lips in an unabashed pucker and presses them down onto her moist, oily skin.

Real men are not afraid to leave a little saliva behind. He lets his lips linger there, aware of a sour, acrid smell wafting into his flared nostrils.

He straightens up, lets his tongue taste the essence that he has hoovered up from that fleeting touch. He tastes sea salt, mingled with curdled milk. Perspiration, that erotic excreta of the human body.

He places her hand gently down by her side, except her fingers are still holding on to his, her eyes boring into him in startled bewilderment.

'Help me up, please! W'at do you t'ink you are doing?' she bleats in a voice that almost shivers with its own frost.

Don Pedro recovers quickly; he retightens his grip. He tugs gently, which has the effect of pulling her arm a little forward in the shoulder socket. He tugs harder; this time her right shoulder comes unglued from the back of the easy chair. She is watching him now with owl-like eyes. His smile tightens, aware that he is breathing a little heavily now. Her sweat-sheened hand begins to slip out of his. He jams his hat on to his head and desperately reaches out with his left, sinking his fingers two inches deep into the dough-like flesh just above her elbow. His back flares up, and his spine feels like an overloaded crane-boom, groaning and creaking under heavy load. She begins to move, slowly but surely; he prays his back will hold. His gut flaps and hot sweat breaks out on his brow.

'Aieee,' she squeaks. 'Your fingers are hurting me! Why you don' use bot' hands?'

Thick veins emerge from under his fine linen shirt and crawl up his neck like baby snakes. 'I am. Using. Both hands,' he wheezes, sounding like a truck climbing a distant hill in low gear.

'Not *your* hands. *My* hands,' she shrieks as she comes up in a lopsided fashion, her torso twisted to the right.

Angie is there the next instant, grabbing the other arm and pulling her up with practised ease. Rosie sits up now, no longer needing help, safe from the hungry clutch of gravity.

Don Pedro straightens up slowly and carefully. There will be lots of Sloan's Liniment tonight if he wants to get out of bed tomorrow. 'Thank you for your help, my dear, um, Alvia,' he puffs at the girl who has intervened in the nick of time. 'But it was not necessary.' He throws his shoulders back.

'Angie. Of course not. You are indeed man enough, but I thought I'd help anyhow.' She gives a little smile and disappears into the kitchen.

'Please sit.' Rosalina points to a chair opposite her. Between them is a little oval table that has an inlay of elephants marching through a sylvan forest at twilight. 'And forgive me for not getting to my feet. Dey hurt from my two walks to church and back. If I don' give dem rest, dey will be useless tomorrow.'

Much like his back, he thinks.

'Would you like some tea?' Rosalina offers. 'Angie! Some tea please, my child! And some biscuits! Dose foreign ones!'

'Beautiful girl. Takes after you, I can see that. In your capable hands, she will grow up to be as charming and elegant as you.'

'I am grooming her for de right moment. Grooming her in my image.'

Rosalina screeches her name from the living room.

'Coming,' Angie trills musically.

Angie places the tray over the marching elephants and steps back demurely. Don Pedro has one leg dangling over the other knee, the saucy, jaunty air of a big-game hunter sitting around the carcasses of a hundred big cats.

'Now look at her,' Rosalina says. 'All dat work I do for udders, God must be saying I am neglecting my own flesh-and-blood.'

'What are you talking about, Mai?'

'About you, my child. Jes' today I made dat Lobo boy meet Florinha, you know, dat Vincent's daughter? God must be t'inking, I am helping udder girls and boys into holy matrimony, what am I doing for Angie?'

'You don't have to do anything for me, Mai. This is the way it is—'

'What do you mean?' Rosie snaps. 'I treat you like my own daughter, no? You have a house, a family, dat is enough, no?' She sniffs. 'I hope God understands, but.'

'I'm sure he does, Mai.'

'De same day Angie became a widow, I lost a son. Do you t'ink God will understand, Don Pedro?'

'His mercy is – er – limitless.' He nods gravely.

Rosie wipes her right eye. 'Today, I am all she has. I go out and help de world, dey are *all* my chilrin out dere. But I am all *she* has.'

'Your mother-in-law was just telling me about how she has united more than a hundred young boys and girls.'

'Not only dat, I make sure dey *stay* good chilrin, go to church, rispeck de elders. My work is *never* done.'

'And I was just telling her how it is a shame that Pocolim does nothing to honour her name.'

'Waiting for me till I die, I t'ink. *Den* dey will do some'tin. We must *never* work for reward, Don Pedro. Dat is de devil's way.'

'They should name the church after you, at the very least.'

'Or at least dis road. All dese roads in Pocolim have no name.'

'Avenue de Rosalina Eucharistica.'

'Yes. Before some bleddy Hindu politician comes and calls it dere bleddy names, like Naik, or Sawant, or Ghedekar or sometin', no?'

'That would be a tragedy,' Pedro thunders.

'All of Goa is going dat way,' yells Rosalina.

'But first!' He grandly gets to his feet and holds out his hands in front of him. 'There has to be a portrait of you. To hang in this beautiful house. I am astonished there is no portrait of you in this house.'

Rosie puffs her chest enormously. She sweeps a hand over the coffee table. 'Please have some tea, Don Pedro.' Her eyes fall on the plate of biscuits at that moment, and they turn to Angie in angry slits.

He picks up three biscuits all at once and pops them in his mouth. The sugary jam and the chocolate interior are absolutely delightful. He reaches out and picks up three more. Rosie's eyes bulge like a fat lizard's that is just about to despatch a grasshopper. Don Pedro holds two in his left hand and proceeds to lovingly dip the third in his tea.

'I was actually thinking of a series,' he says with his mouth full of doughy sweetness. 'Two in the house, one in the church.'

The biscuit goes in and out, and Rosie's eyeballs go up and down in sync.

'And! My dear lady…' The soggy biscuit is whisked away to its death. With both hands he etches out a large canvas in the air as he chews. 'A whole private collection dedicated to *you*! It will be shown in Milan and New York and in London.'

Rosie's eyes follow the fate of the two cookies trapped in his left hand.

'This will be my honour and privilege,' he says. 'Forget the church, forget the residents of Pocolim, forget the municipal corporation. *Don Pedro* will immortalize you on canvas forever! That is the least your humble servant can do.' The humble servant does a humble bow and transfers the two remaining biscuits to his mouth.

Angie gasps. 'That is a wonderful idea, Mai!'

'Umm, I thaw so,' he says, wading through a marsh of sticky chocolate and jam.

'Yes.' Angie's eyes gleam. 'When they name this road after you, Mai, people must know what you look like.'

'And, it wi' be my solemn duty to ensure tha' thi' i' my bes' work ever.' He belches softly. 'That burden is *mine*.'

'Who better to paint you than the world-famous Don Pedro Cleto Colaco,' exclaims Angie in wonder.

The artist looks up at her gravely. 'Yes, child. But that can only be done with the good lady's blessings. People who toil selflessly for the good of others, they are often very shy of recognition. A sad irony of our times. Crooked politicians and thugs get *their* portraits painted.'

Rosalina reaches out a fat paw and snaps up the last two biscuits on the plate.

'Mai must understand that this is not for her gratification, for she needs none,' says Angie firmly. 'This is for all the people she has helped directly and indirectly.'

'A tribute!' he yells. 'A tribute to her largesse!'

Rosie's eyes widen. 'My – my wat?'

The artist crosses his hands and bows his head like a penitent. 'I await your permission, madame.'

'Would you like some more biscuits, Don Pedro?' Angie asks brightly, reaching for the empty plate.

'No need!' Rosie shrieks in terror. She looks up at Angie, her lips trembling. 'You are feeding a wedding party, or wat?'

Angie rushes to the kitchen with the empty plate, nobody noticing the gleam in her eyes. She comes back, wiping her hands on her house-dress.

'When do you want to start, Don Pedro?' Angie asks solicitously. 'Mai will need some time to think it over. She is not a vain person, and you have suggested something that only vain people do.'

'An irony,' mumbles Don Pedro.

'Don Pedro,' Rosie finally squeaks. 'I-I don't know nuttin' about portraits. Or too much about art.'

The artist looks at her in shock. 'You don't?'

The paintings all around them, all over her walls, they are execrable horrors. The sculptures, even more ghastly: a plaster-of-Paris bust of a woman seductively disrobing, pulling a medieval garment over her head. Baring her ample breasts, except the breasts have no nipples, as if some malignant infant has bitten them off. A gargoyle-like cherub prancing around a tree and feeding a couple of stupid-looking, beady-eyed birds.

He wishes he could go around and piss on every one of them.

'*Au contraire*,' he says. 'I can see you have a fine eye for art, Madame Rosalina.'

She blushes and squirms. 'Dis was a different time. My husband used to work on de ship. I would tell him, Albert, you travel to all dese beautiful places, go out drinking and making merry, you *must* bring back sometin' nice for de house. Every trip he would bring two or t'ree pieces.'

'Yes, hmmm, fine choices.'

He wonders what kind of soulless dog Albert must have been, and thankful that he is dead.

They'd had a son and he had bought it early too, mercifully terminating this disastrous chain of tasteless human beings.

Chicken bone, and on his wedding night, isn't that what Father Francis had said? All that choking and kicking with eyes bugging out.

He sees Rosie eyeing him with a mixture of thrill and suspicion. His gift of objectivity, his prescience: he looks into her brain and sees two frolicsome imps leapfrogging over each other. Excitement and Doubt.

Her bosom heaves and dips like an oily sea.

What she is doing is seeing her portrait from several angles, with various backdrops, in different attires.

Her portrait displaying myriad moods: kindly indulgent, righteously fearsome, imperiously grand.

She sees a plaque bearing her name at the head of the dusty road.

First the road, then the Church of the Tireless Lady. Then murmurs and grave heated discussions amongst padres and bishops about the possibility of sainthood.

'You will have to give me some time to t'ink about dis, Don Pedro,' she squeaks. 'It is all too sudden. I have too many t'ings on my mind just now.'

Somewhere in all of this, that other imp, the one of doubt and distrust, sneaks in and has his turn in the air.

The artist speaks to her curves. 'I understand, madame. But remember, the world needs heroes and heroines that they can look up to.'

They need role models.

You are only helping *them*, you are only doing this for *them*.

He sees her struggle to factor in new dimensions: altruism, moral philanthropy.

She squeals in sudden agony. 'My child, get me a glass of water, please!'

'At once, Mai,' Angie says.

'All day I have been t'inking about dis, dat and de udder. Too much, too much!'

The slave girl turns to him and smiles sweetly. 'Perhaps I can show you out as well, Don Pedro, if there is nothing else? I think Mai needs to rest.'

It dawns on him then: he has gone from being in control of the situation to being imminently hustled out.

He is bewildered. All the while he has been staring ahead and surging forward, suddenly he has been side-smacked. Has he made an impression at all? Has he gotten through?

His mojo and libido, galloping like two proud stallions side-by-side just moments ago, are now reduced to two listless street-corner bums picking their noses.

He turns to the slave girl for a clue, and all he gets is a dazzling, empty smile. He slowly gets to his feet.

'Pardon me if I don't show you to de door, Don Pedro,' Rosie says sleepily. 'I t'ink it's time for my nap.' Two plump eyelids promptly snap down like window shutters.

His last bit of prescience: through closed eyes Rosalina sees fame and posterity much better, far beyond anything she can see with her eyes open. She utters a squeaky sigh and lapses into a lazy daydream.

In something of a dream-like state himself, but a bad, restless one, he follows Angie to the door. He looks at her buttocks move tightly under her house-dress, but feels nothing. His libido is slouching, inert and useless.

'So what do you think?' he asks the left cheek, almost mumbling the words. 'Do you think she will…'

Angie reaches the door, opens it and turns around. 'You must not mind Mai,' she says sweetly. 'She gets like this sometime, at the end of a long day.'

'Yes? And?' Don Pedro bleats hopefully.

'And nothing.' Angie shrugs, still smiling that sweet, dazzling smile. 'I think you offered her a wonderful idea. I think I can make her see sense. What are you doing, say a fortnight from now, if I may ask?'

'Uh, nothing. I don't know,' he replies, his first sincere and truthful statement since he has walked in.

'We have to go on a road trip. Will you come? You have a car?'

Don Pedro stares at her, hypnotized by her smile, entranced by her words.

'I will convince her in the meantime.'

You can spend time with her, understand her, observe her up close, she says.

Bring your sketch pad, she says.

He shuffles towards the open doorway like a tired old donkey that has been walking for days and days and has suddenly got a whiff of a second wind at seeing a bright, red, juicy carrot before its nose.

19
SAVIO

Morbid curiosity carries him there, nothing else.

People pass him going the same way, men and women, old and young, clad for mourning and remembering.

Some attempt conversation, but he has worn his come-close-and-I'll-bite-your-nose-off face before leaving the house.

Want to ask me something stupid, his face demands. Kai re, Savio, walking?

He has borrowed a suit from Oscar the laundry-man. Oscar told him it is Kenny's, but Kenny will not be back for a couple of months, so it is okay. Who is Kenny, he asked, did he know him? Oscar had looked surprised and said, '*Our* Kenny, re, dat fellow who lives side-door to Mrs Braganza.'

Oscar had wanted a hundred rupees for an hour, give or take. 'Italian suit, you bugger,' he had said proudly, as if he only laundered the best. They had haggled back and forth, until he had agreed to give him two of Loyola's finest shirts for free in exchange.

Morbid curiosity or not, there was no way he was showing up looking like a bum.

By the time he reaches the Church Hall, he is soaked through and through. The day is no hotter than usual, but when you wade through a marsh of reluctance and impotent rage, why then you may as well have concrete boots on. He needs a drink.

Inside, he sees the snack table. He sees the flowers, orchid bouquets, five in all. The big punch bowl. The snacks themselves: cakes, samosas, popcorn? Is that popcorn? Biscuits, a heap of potato wafers. A hundred chairs, give or take.

He walks over to one side under a noisy ceiling fan. Sticky warm air blows down on him like swamp-breath, sending the perspiration on his face scurrying for cover, but doing nothing to cool him down.

All eyes in the room have swivelled towards him like automated gun-scopes sniffing out a perp. A fourth of the chairs are taken, and there is not one face, man or woman, that he can put a name to, or ever remember seeing in the company of his father, stopping by for a drink or bringing over a Christmas cake, slapping backs and swapping stories.

Or dropping in for some traditional Pointless Conversation.

He scans each face with hot, hooded eyes; one by one the gun-scopes are lowered or turned away.

An old lady totters up to the table and fills a paper-plate with sandwiches and biscuits. She stops at the bowl of popcorn (which must be soggy as a whore's knickers in this heat, he thinks), shoves in one crone-like hand and puts a few into her mouth. Her toothless gums work on them for a minute, and then she shuffles on to the plate of oily samosas that look like they are glowing with a sweat of their own. Strike one for the popcorn, rejected by old Mrs Whothefuck for inadequate freshness and crunch.

He gets a paper cup and walks over to the punch bowl. It is three feet across and a foot deep, full of something that looks like a stagnant pool of yellow radioactive run-off on whose surface cubes of ice float desultorily like glass crocodiles. He pours himself a cupful and sips it; a sugar wallop with a hint of what might be pineapple. Refreshing. He takes another sip and scans his taste-buds for that tell-tale nip of alcohol. None, or very little.

He turns his back to the crowd. He pulls out a half of cashew feni from his inner pocket and empties it into the bowl. He stirs the mixture well, scattering the ice-cubes with soft, pleasant clinks and clunks.

Something shiny and bilious green suddenly looms to his left. He turns to look at the first familiar face of the day.

'Joao, how are you my friend?' he says, dropping his Rottweiler look momentarily, allowing the other man into his space.

'Savio D'Gama, little Savio, eh? Fully grown boy now. Sorry for your daddy, baba. Very sorry. Boro munis, best munis!'

He wonders if Green Disco Ball is the correct dress-code for a memorial, and nods in approval. That shirt may look like battery-powered puke, but it beats greys and blacks any day.

'*Amkam soddam borem kortalo*,' continues Joao, his hand on his heart and genuineness in his eyes. 'Never complain about my bread, *never*.'

The blackened, waxed moustache bobs in time with the lips.

'Man of character. Not crying about dis and dat all de time. Like dese udder fellows.' He shoots a sideways look at the occupied chairs and those still trickling in.

'Have some punch?'

'You try de samosas?' Joao turns his bulbous eyes on the farthest plate. 'My wife made. For Loyola, anyt'ing, anytime, she said!'

'I will. You have some punch first.' He thrusts a paper-cup in his hand. 'Cool you off a little bit.'

'You know, your daddy always said … you know what he said? He said, Joao, your bread is de best in de world. Better dan all de bag-ettes in France.'

'That's a great compliment, considering he never stepped out of Goa all his life.'

'You try de samosas, re, later. Jacinta made dem.'

'You should give the eulogy,' he says, filling Joao's glass and his own. 'I think you are the only one in this room who actually knew him. *Who* are all these other people?'

'All de usual, re. Every time same faces,' Joao says dismissively. He takes a sip from his glass and his eyes light up instantly.

'I made that punch.' He grins. 'What do you think?'

A thick purple tongue sweeps over his boot-polished moustache and eyeballs roll approvingly. 'Little bit strong, no?'

'Nonsense. Should be like this only.'

'Is it okay to drink before de ceremony?'

'You're standing with *me*, no? *I* am the son. Who's going to tell you anything?'

Joao takes another long swig, and emits a belch that is exactly as long as the swig. 'Dese budhas and budhis are going to get fucked if dey drink dis.'

'They have come to remember my father. Let them remember this as well, no?'

'Your fadder...' Joao raises his glass, solemnly. 'Best man, ever. Boro munis. Really. Loved my bread, always told me, best bread ever. Wat you doing in Goa, he would say. You should be making bread in Europe.' His eyes mist over in sadness. 'How to leave, re? Wat, drop everyting and jes' go? I aks him.'

'This punch. It's like your bread, Joao. Better than all the wine in France. Cheers.'

'Put some more.' Joao holds out his cup. 'So, where you came from just now? Didn't see you for your daddy's funeral also.'

'I was travelling. Old man went suddenly, re. No warning.'

'Wat warning you want when you're pushing eighty? One foot in grave, de other on de banana peel. Har, har, har, har.' He points with his glass. 'Nice suit. You buy in Bombay?'

'You like it? Italian.'

Envy dances in the baker's eyes, Europe still on his mind, baking foccaccia and baguettes for discerning gentry. He leans forward and sniffs. 'But funny smell I am getting. Your aftershave or somet'ing?'

He fingers his stubbled face that has not come in contact with any aftershave for almost three years now, it being way, way down on his shopping list, right after must-have essentials like a nostril-trimmer or a butt-waxing kit. He looks down and sniffs.

Yes, there is something, a far-off smell, like something being cooked up in somebody's kitchen a mile away that comes and goes depending on the wind. It is a sweet smell, and not in a nice way. It reminds him of…

From the corner of his eye, he sees Rosalina. She just stands in the doorway, a little sunlight squeezing through the little crack on both sides. Like the moon, she can cause a solar eclipse.

Joao holds out his cup. He fills it, and pours himself his fourth. A kind of a numb, happy feeling is washing over him. Everything feels a little distant, his pennilessness, this ludicrous memorial, his dead father, Rosie's tyranny. Even his hands and feet and body seem to belong to somebody else; everything is somebody else's problem.

Then Rosalina moves forward, and sunlight tumbles through again.

Joao nudges him in the ribs. 'Let's go to the side, re. Udderwise de bleddy cow will have something to say about dis.'

'Fuck her,' he says evenly. 'This is my pop's memorial. I'll stand where I want and do what I want.'

Rosie waddles down the aisle, looking from side to side like some head of state inspecting troops. People look up as she passes, some bow and some greet her. She merely nods.

She stops at the third row. The rippling flesh around her hips jiggles for five seconds before coming to a dead halt. 'Mrs Ferrao,' she squeaks in a tired, resigned voice. 'How many time I tol' you, food is for after?'

Mrs Ferrao, the ancient lady who had been helping herself earlier, almost swallows a stringy piece of chicken that she has been hammering away at with her gums. 'Eh?' she says. Her face keeps folding up in half, the toothless mouth disappearing from sight as she gamely keeps up the fight with the chicken.

'If you eat all de food now, how will people eat later? Dere'll be no food left, no?'

Rosie faking a kind demeanour, but *she's just a fucking bullying bitch*, he thinks disgustedly.

Mrs Ferrao swallows the chicken and clears her throat. 'I'm hungry,' she snaps. She looks two hundred, but if she had teeth, she would sink them into Rosie's hip.

'Who isn't,' Rosie snaps back, fully aware that everyone was watching. 'Every time same story. It's bad manners, eating before de eulogy, you know dat, no?'

Mrs Ferrao pops a whole biscuit into her mouth in defiance. Her battle-hardened gums go for them instantly. Her bony claws tighten around the paper-plate, ready to fight to the bitter end if it comes to that.

Good on you, old girl, he chortles.

Rosie shakes her head wearily and slowly continues her forward roll. 'Dese old people, wat to tell dem, again and again.'

'Go away, fatty,' mumbles Mrs Ferrao, blowing crumbs all over the receding derriere.

Rosie's eyes meet his and instantly her mouth curls downward. 'And look who is setting an example,' she says, loud enough for everyone to hear. 'How am I supposed to teach udder people wat to do, if de family members don't respect de rules?'

'Who says you have to teach anybody anything?' he says calmly. 'We're all old enough.' He lifts the cup to his lips and takes a big gulp.

Go easy on the big gulps, bugger, he tells himself. *Fuck it*, he replies, and fills another glass.

'Yes, your poor dead fadder is watching! *Remember* dat! And he is *very* proud of your behaviour.'

He ignores her and walks back to his original position under the fan. He beckons Joao to follow him, but the baker is trying to hide his cup from Rosie, his nose twitching like a rabbit.

'And you, you have come dressed for de circus, or wat?'

Joao stutters and falters incoherently, but Rosie imperiously rolls on. He is a tradesperson, beneath her.

Angie almost runs in, holding something large, flat and square, wrapped in newspaper. Her hair is tied back in a ponytail and perspiration glows on her skin. She comes straight down the aisle and heads for a little table, which is bare apart from a gaudy red cloth thrown over it on the far side of the snack counter.

'Finally, it's ready,' she pants to Rosie as she passes her.

'Did you run all de way here? Dere is no need to run, I tol' you dat, no?'

Only women of loose character run, harlots and strumpets that are being chased by drunks, irresponsible women escaping the duties of wifehood, fallen women fleeing an angry mob. Ladies walk, no matter the urgency.

Angie tears the newspaper and pulls out a large-sized portrait. She props it up on the bare table, and turns it to face the gathered crowd. He manoeuvres himself to get a better look. He remembers that photo, his father with his face angled slightly downward, but that had been a black-and-white photograph; and even at that distance, from a bad angle, half cockeyed with booze, he can see bright vivid colour.

Angie has brought over two of the five orchid bouquets, and Rosie is ordering her on how to place them. He stops within two feet of the portrait and stares at it.

The background is the original black and white, the dirty grey curtain at Alfonso's Photo Shop that the proprietor (now Alfonso's son) has never bothered to launder, but the rest of it...

Loyola's hair is a shiny black, like he has just shampooed it with fuel oil, the forehead and chin are the colour of white bread gone a little mouldy, the nose is orange, one eye is a sickly yellow, the other bright green and the lips are so seductively red that he is actually embarrassed to see them on his father's face. And the cheeks … the cheeks are pink, a horrible, stomach-turning pink, the colour of cheap candy-floss sold at village fairs, which is somehow even more disturbingly sexual than the blood-red lips. He blanches in horror, and purely out of reflex, tosses the entire glass down his throat. His eyes water as the feni squirrels through his tubes like an industrial drain-cleaner.

'Jesus Christ,' he gasps. 'What is *this*?'

Angie turns to look at him, even as she moves bouquets and portrait back and forth.

'You let him be, my child, and keep doing your work. Now he is pretending he doesn't recognize his fadder. It's all part of his impertinence!'

'This was a black-and-white photograph,' he sputters.

'You t'ink I don't know dat? It was old and fully faded. None of you chilrin took any good pikchers of him, dat is also my fault?'

'But – but why not use the original?'

'I said, it was *old and fully faded*. So Eddie said he will restore it; make it colour, even better.' She sniffs. 'Now at least he looks in de pink of helt'. Dis is how we remember Loyola, dose of us who remember him.'

'He looks *healthy*? You want to make him look healthy? This man is *dead*!'

'One more time you be impertinent, I will give you one smack!'

'Whose idea was this? My father's also? He told you, colour my face, Madame Rosalina. I want to look like a clown?'

'Eddie suggested it,' Angie jumps in hastily, as Rosie takes a big step forward with a dangerous rustle of her skirt.

'Who is *Eddie?*' he yells.

'Alfonso's son!' yells Rosie right back. 'His fadder took de original!'

'So is Eddie retarded? Is he *blind?*'

'It is just a little digital retouching,' Angie offers nervously.

'By whom? A *monkey*? Is Eddie a chimpanzee?'

'You are jes' counting money again now, aren't you?' Rosie says, her mouth curling downward in disgust.

'Jesus Christ, I need a drink.' And he staggers over once again to the punch bowl.

'Yes, just remember Loyola is watching you,' Rosie spits out, her mouth still twisted in derision, eyes still triumphant.

He shakes his head like he's been hit by a brick. 'That is not Loyola. That is not my father.' He fills the cup to the brim with unsteady hands, causing yellow liquid to spill over and stain the tablecloth.

He takes his glass and walks over to Joao, who now eyes him apprehensively.

'Did you see that?' he snarls, tottering into him, spraying feni and pineapple juice into his eyes.

'Eh, what?' says Joao, unable to see anything momentarily.

'My father. He looks like a tart. She has made my father look like a ffff-uckin' ... like a fuckin' set of Barbie Doll panties.'

That is a little beyond Joao's pop-culture knowledge, but he knows what panties are. 'What you're saying, man?' he asks, shocked.

'Pink. And red. And fuckin' yellow and God knows what.' He pokes Joao in one cheek, narrowly missing the eye. '*Your* colour skin he had, dark brown. Now he is multi-coloured. Like a fuckin' rainbow.'

'Shhh, keep your voice down, re, bugger. The ceremony is going to start now. Fadder is here.'

'That's how people are going to remember Loyola. As a multi-coloured clown. What's the point of all this? May as well drop my pants and bend over.'

He demonstrates bending over, wagging his butt at the crowd. Joao has this faint sense of being imminent collateral damage: Savio, the son, will be spared, and he, the innocent bystander, will catch the hail of bullets. 'Stand up, man,' he hisses. 'What are you doing?'

'Yes, what *are* you doing?'

He straightens up and whirls around; Angie is standing there, looking at him curiously.

'Jesus!' He grins and giggles. 'You scared the shit out of me.'

'Are you alright? Did you drop something?'

The world is swaying a little, but he manages to lock her stare. She has rimmed her eyes with that black-something that women use to make them look more mysterious. Her irises shine like gemstones in a dark cave.

'I've got nothing left to drop. Except my dignity, which I will hold onto for a while, thank you.'

Rim your eyes all you want now, he thinks, there'll come a day when it will make you look like a fuckin' raccoon, or like you've painted spectacles on, and he is unbearably saddened by that thought.

'Would you like to take a seat? Father Francis is about to start, I think.'

'I'll find a chair.'

'I've reserved one for you next to us.'

'Sit next to *her*? I'd rather be hung upside down.'

'How is the punch?'

'Best I've ever had.'

A worried frown creases her forehead. 'I might have added too much vodka. You cannot tell because of the sweetness. Is it too much?'

He looks at his glass. 'No, it is perfect.'

'There was an old bottle of Bacardi as well at home. Nobody had drunk it for years. I put that in as well, in memory of your daddy. He used to love rum, you remember?'

He screws up his eyes and pretends to remember, but he is actually wondering how many different kinds of alcohols his brain cells are drowning in.

'But that won't be potent anymore, after all these years,' she says brightly. 'Only for taste.' She reaches out and touches his jacket self-consciously. 'This looks very nice on you.'

'You look nice yourself.'

She blushes. 'Thank you. You don't *have* to return a compliment, you know.'

'I hope you stay that way, but. All this slogging and slaving will destroy your beauty very fast.'

He thinks he sees her blanch a little, but no, that might be his imagination. They go back a long way, don't they?

'Lucky bugger that Gabo was. Caught you in your prime.' He laughs. 'Everyone loved you, Angie, back in the day. Men *and* women. The women wanted to be with you, and the men wanted to be you.' He hiccups. 'Old saying.'

She has taken a step back now and he sees that familiar look in her eyes. The look that says…

'Sorry, sorry,' he twirls his finger vaguely, 'the other way round. Men want to be *with* you, and women…' he trails off.

…the look that says, *Caution, waggy tail or not, he will bite.*

He spies Father Francis over her shoulder, walking their way.

'Here comes the Pope now,' he says gravely, then bursts into more giggles.

'Are you going to ruin this memorial?'

He looks hurt. 'What are you talking about? It's just picking up.'

'Would everyone take their places please?' says Father Francis in his deep pulpit voice, directing the question more at Joao and Angie.

Joao uses the ecclesiastical order to bolt like a rabbit for an empty chair in the second row.

'I'll stand and watch,' he says pleasantly.

'For how long will you stand?' Angie asks him.

'For as long as this circus goes on.'

'No, I mean for how long will you be *able* to stand?'

'Huh?'

'Would you like to refill your cup?'

He looks at her suspiciously. 'Easy. I'm going easy for the moment.'

'And what is that *smell*?' She sniffs the air like bloodhound, then abruptly jabs in, as if trying to head-butt him in the stomach. 'It's coming from *you*. Do you smell it, Father?'

The priest prefers to stick to his routine. 'It's time to start. Please take your seats.'

'Smells like…' She looks up at him, her eyes growing wide. 'Whose suit is this?'

'Mine, of course. Eh, *what*?'

She is looking at him piercingly, slicing through his lie and making him squirm. He is reminded of the day – he must have been six or seven – his mother had sternly asked him if he had pooped his pants, and he had denied it strenuously. He remembers the hiding he had received, he, the runt of the litter, too stupid to run to the toilet in time, and then lying on top of it.

Angie pats his lapel. 'Yes, it's better you don't come over there. Mai has a much more powerful nose.' She turns to leave, then looks back, excitement dancing in her eyes. 'Listen, listen. That letter that Ferdie found? We're going to need that car. I have spoken to Don Pedro and he's as good as agreed. All that remains is for you to fix it. Isn't that wonderful?' She touches his arm fleetingly, giving him a sly, knowing smile and walks back.

He sniffs himself in various places, in both armpits, on the sleeves, and Jesus Christ, there *is* that smell, something sharp, something sweet. Father Francis smiles weakly and hurries away to the table from which a gaudy Loyola D'Gama stares out disappointedly at the gathering.

He looks around wildly for Joao, and his eyes catch a flash of green in the second row; it is sitting like a little boy whose mother has left him all alone with instructions to behave or else.

'Ey, Joao!' he hisses. No less than ten faces turn to him, but the baker may have been deaf, or in another room, or on another planet.

'Joao!' Louder now. More heads turn, but the baker doesn't twitch.

'Come here and stand like a man, re, you bugger. Running away like that.'

'Shhh!' That comes from Rosalina, accompanied by a stare that could bend iron nails.

'Joao! Come here or *I'll* come there!'

That gets through, and Joao, looking a bit like the Ancient Mariner, turns around gloomily to stare at his albatross. Loyola may have been the best munis around, but his youngest is definitely the biggest pain in the ass. Bending over to look inconspicuous, he tiptoes back. Where, instead of being greeted with chumminess, he is lashed with disapproval. 'What, you're scared of her, or what?'

'No, re, I'm jus' giving rispeck to de occasion.'

'Who is Kenny?'

'Who is *who*?'

'Kenny. Some bugger who lives here. Gives his clothes to Oscar's laundry.'

Father Francis clears his throat importantly. 'Good afternoon to all who are gathered here,' he begins, testing his voice, flexing his oratory muscles, practising pitch and throw. 'I hope everyone is in their seats. Thank you for being punctual. We will begin shortly.' He gives a little bow and disappears into an adjoining room where he tops himself up with two fingers.

'Kenny. Kenny. Who Kenny?' chants Joao ruminatively.

'Some Kenny. Must be a young chap, my height, my size somewhat.'

'Kenny. Kenny,' Joao goes off on his chant again. 'Mmmm, which Kenny, re?'

'Jesus, you deliver bread in your sleep or what? After twenty years you don't know the names of your customers? Where's your cup?'

'Left it dere. Let it be, not a good idea, re.'

'Bullshit. It's my pop's party. Wait here.'

Ignoring Rosie's laser stare, he swaggers up to the table and fills two more glasses. His legs feel rubbery, and he isn't sure he can feel his toes. His hands and arms seem to be moving of their own accord, controlled by some remote auto pilot. As is his mouth. He turns to the assembled guests and says cheerily, 'While we wait for Father Francis, please feel free to have a drink. Because I think that is what he is doing back there as well.' He winks at them. Nobody moves. He shrugs. 'If you are feeling shy, just look at Mrs Ferrao and learn from her.'

'Give me a glass,' croaks Mrs Ferrao from the third row.

'Give me a glass, *please,*' he admonishes jokingly, and chortles. 'Of course, my dear.' He almost skips to where she is and deposits the paper cup in one trembling claw. 'You see?' he tells the rest of the crowd. He dances back, fills another one for Joao and returns to his place under the fan.

'You got big balls, man,' the baker says, fearfully. 'She's a devil. You don't know her.'

'What's the worst she can do?'

Joao merely shudders, his overactive imagination helped along by three glasses of naked alcohol in pineapple clothing.

'As long as she doesn't sit on me, I'm safe.' He bursts into a giggle-fit.

Father Francis appears again in that moment, smoothing out his cassock and looking at Rosie importantly. 'Shall we start?'

'Unless you want to wait for Christmas,' she snaps.

'Is everyone here?' he asks stiffly, of no one in particular. He looks at his watch. 'We still have five minutes.'

'Start,' says Rosie. 'It seems people cannot wait.'

'Look at her,' he sighs. 'Day by day getting more and more fucked up.'

'She came out of her mudder's stomach like dis only, I t'ink, to make life miserable for everyone.'

'I'm talking of Angie.'

'Oh yes, she is a bleddy sweetheart. How she sleeps in dat house, God knows. When dis fat bitch snores, keeps me awake next door.'

'It's all downhill for her. Fatty got a two-in-one, a servant who is also family. Convenient.'

'You knew her before, no?'

'She was older. She married my friend, who was also older than me.'

'Tragedy that was. Tragedy.'

'What to do now?'

'Nutting you can do. God's will.'

'Back then she was really beautiful.'

'You also had a little scene wit' her, or what?'

'Mad or what? Friend's fiancée, re. Not possible.'

'I wonder if she will find someone now. If dat bleddy cow lets her. What's wrong wit' your eyes, man? Dey gone all red.'

A big man in a dapper linen suit walks in the door. He has a fancy hat on that you only see in movies. The artist on the hill. The rightful owner of that heap of nuts and bolts that is rotting in his yard.

Don Pedro walks right to the front. 'Sorry if I'm late,' he booms without the slightest trace of apology. He goes straight to Madame Rosalina and kisses the hand she offers. He straightens up, looks around and waves at Father Francis dismissively. 'Start, start. Don't wait for me.' He leans over and whispers something in Angie's ear.

'She doesn't know what she wants to be, that's her problem,' he tells Joao. 'She's at that stage, you know. Asking herself, should I be a slave, or should I say fuck off? And then do her own thing, right?'

'True. Poor t'ing.'

'Even her looks don't know which way to go, forwards or backwards. Will she grow up all beautiful and elegant? Or will she grow all old and ugly?'

'All in God's hands, re.'

'Bullshit, man. All in her hands. I told her the other day, what were you once and what have you become. Fell on deaf ears.'

Don Pedro is now walking towards them even as Father Francis is clearing his throat. There is forcefulness in that walk that is a little intimidating.

'What the fuck does *he* want now?' he hisses at Joao.

'Anudder mad bugger. Go to his place, phaughh, what a stink. I t'ink he does his pissing and cacca in de garden.'

Don Pedro comes as close as one foot away and stops, arms akimbo. He looks both of them over carefully, like a dog-catcher wondering which collarless stray to put to sleep first.

'I know who you are,' Don Pedro tells Joao with a crocodile smile. 'Nice shirt. What, somebody by mistake told you you look like Elvis?' He turns to Savio. 'And you are Loyola D'Gama's son. Sorry for your loss. Your father and I did business together.'

'Uh-huh?'

Don Pedro wrinkles his nose. 'Is that aftershave? If it is, buy another bottle. It's gone bad. Anyway,' he says, 'he died, your father, God rest his soul, leaving you to conclude the business. When will the car be ready?'

'*What?*'

'I understand you might be grieving, but there is no need to overdo it. You people grieve too much. One month is over. Now get on with it.'

'Get on with *what*?'

'Fulfilling your father's obligations. Fix that damn car. I need it, and people are depending on me.'

'Have you seen the *state* of that car – sorry, that piece of rusting, broken-down shit?'

Don Pedro uses his height to good advantage to lean down on him. 'I paid money for a *car*. So come and tell me when it's one. *Soon*.'

'You obviously know *nothing* about these things.'

'Is there a law that says I should?'

'Well, we're going to have to talk about it.'

'Not interested,' Don Pedro sniffs haughtily. 'Talking is a waste of time. Next thing you'll be dead too, and then where will I go?' He slaps him on the shoulder. 'It's either the car, or return the fifty thousand that I gave your father. Stay in touch. *God*, that *aftershave*!' He turns around and walks over to an empty chair in the back row.

'Who the *fuck*…' he splutters, rubbing his arm where the big paw landed, though the four syllables had been like a much harder kick in the gut. *Fif-ty thou … what* the fuck?

'He's like dat only. T'inks he is some conkwistador.'

'Well, fuck him and the horse he rode in on.'

Fifty thousand. Seventy thousand. *Where* are all these magical sums of money? Loyola the high-roller, the big spender. This is a sinister aspect to his father he never dreamed existed. That lugubrious clown-face staring out of Eddie the chimpanzee's photo-frame isn't saying anything, but does he imagine it, or is there some kind of spectral wink and silent nod, some unholy covenant between the photo and that fat, smug toad in the front seat with her chins cascading down her bosom and her bosom cascading down her stomach and her stomach cascading down the chair, like some enormous muddy mountain that is in a hurry to roll down its own sides and merge with the plains?

'I remember who Kenny is,' Joao says, his moustache twitching.

Father Francis begins his sing-song chant, 'Good afternoon, ladies and gentlemen. We are gathered here today, not to mourn, nay, but to celebrate…'

'You should piss in his bread,' he rages. 'Tell me, *I'll* come and piss in his bread. Bake him a separate batch.'

Joao is looking at him. 'Why you aks who Kenny is?'

'No reason. Who is he?'

'Kenny is on de ship. Like his fadder, Julius. You remember Julius? Always well-dressed he was. Always wore suit, like dis one.' He points, from an arm's length away.

'So?'

'Julius died six mont's ago. Old he was. Kenny was on de ship at dat time so dey waited for him to come back. T'ree days dey kept Julius. After Kenny came dey cremated him.'

'So why the fuck are you sharing that information with me?'

'…Loyola was a man who was very much a part of this wonderful family that is our village, our community. He ate off our table and on occasion put food there also. We broke bread with him and drank from his cup. Generous and always giving, that was Loyola…'

'Giving *what*? And to *whom*?' he yells in rage.

He thrusts his hands in his pant pockets and turns them out. The lining hangs down from his hips, limp as a Beagle's ears. He is well and truly plastered now, he realizes. His eyeballs feel like errant yo-yos. And now he is hot. The fan seems to be doing nothing, and that distant kitchen-smell coming off of him is more pronounced. Time to leave, he thinks. Time to get drunk and pass out completely.

'He was a good husband, an exemplary father…'

'Ha!' he snorts.

'…and a brother to all,' finishes Father Francis with a quick nervous look to the side.

'Except now he looks like a sister,' he cackles.

'Shut up, man,' hisses Joao.

'Erm … ahem. In life he gave generously and … and we must likewise be generous to his memory, which is why we are gathered here today.'

'And cheers and good appetite,' he guffaws, rotating dangerously on his axis.

'Cheers,' returns Mrs Ferrao toothlessly from the third row, hiccupping thrice in quick succession.

'Somebody fill her glass,' he slurs. 'All in the spirit of giving. Let us keep giving. And giving. Give it all away!'

'Let us observe a two-minute silence,' says a flustered Father Francis, who is unused to heckling of any kind, 'and, ummm, reflect upon Loyola's, ummm—'

'Pretty face!' he hoots.

Joao, ever mindful of catching that stray bullet, scurries away to his chair, determined never to return.

'Follow me into a two-minute silence, please,' says the priest solemnly, clasping his hands and uttering a quick silent prayer, not for Loyola, but for the earth to swallow up his youngest son.

'First somebody fill her glass! My father would have wanted that, Mr Generous that he was. I would, my dear, but I cannot move.'

His feet feel as though they are nailed to the floor, even as his upper body keeps swaying above. 'Who was that idiot who said chariddy begins at home? Bloody idiot he was. D'int know anything. Should've consulted my father.' He hiccups violently, almost regurgitating the punch. It is that smell. It is all around him now. It is coming off strong, that ghastly sweet aroma, like molasses being cooked over a slow flame. What does it remind him of? What? What?

He grabs his turned-out pockets and holds them up playfully, twirling them around. 'All that out *there*,' he gestures with his nose at the table full of food, 'should have been in *here*, rightfully. But charidddy dush – does not begin at home. Not in Loyola's home anyhow.' He hoots with laughter.

'Shut up!' screams Rosalina. 'Somebody t'row him out!'

'*You* shut up!' he roars back. 'Who invited *you*? Enjoy, enjoy! Eat every crumb and drink every drop. Because remember, anything you waste is *not* going back in *here*.' He thrusts his hips out at the crowd, holding up his pocket-linings like a magician's handkerchief.

The smell hits him again, like an uppercut to the nose, making his eyes water. The sheer force of it … Biology lab class. Eviscerating a plump and very dead frog. Been dead a long time, and pulling out intestines and stomach and heart that should have rotted away, but looked in the pink of health, ready to rock and roll. Preserved by that sweet smell…

Julius. Who was Julius again? Kenny's dead father, kept in the pink of health for three days until Kenny returned…

'You should be taught manners, talking to a lady like that,' says a wall of white that has suddenly appeared before him. He dimly makes out the outline, large, overbearing, brutish, too close, way too close, invading private space.

'You bugger off,' he slurs petulantly. 'Ish not your pocket she's putting her hand in.'

'You ungrateful wretch,' hisses the wall of white.

'Bugger off, bugger off. None of your business.'

And then they cremated him, that old fart Julius, who liked to dress in sharp suits. So, would they have removed the suit before they fried him?

He can feel the alcohol coming up his food-pipe like a backed-up drain, rising, rising. He chokes it back.

'I woulda kept it. Why waste a good fucking suit, eh?' he tells Don Pedro with tear-filled eyes. Jesus, he feels sick. He feels yucky. *He* is the source of the smell, not the suit. He is dead and they have filled him up with sickly sweet embalming fluid. Oscar, you dirty, dingy, sonofawhore.

He feels a hand on his arm, a strong hand that does not intend to go away soon. He yanks it off brutally. 'Piss on you,' he says savagely. ''Scuse me.' He pushes past the artist and locates the doorway that seems blurred and impossibly far away. Like the light at the end of the tunnel. Go into the fucking light, Savio.

He staggers, stumbles, half-runs down the aisle, ricocheting off chairs on both sides, his hand on someone's skinny shoulder now, in someone's hair, brushing an ample boob, kicking somebody's shin. The light grows stronger even as the edges are still blurred. He can make out nothing inside the light.

He shoots out of the door head-first, completely blind, the sun searing his eyeballs. He stops and bends over, gasping for breath, but the world keeps moving past him.

Like an express train exiting a tunnel, vodka, rum and feni roar up his oesophagus and shoot out of his mouth. It is a long train, and it keeps coming. When it stops abruptly, he turns his face heavenward and gasps. 'Sweet Jesus.'

Then he pitches face first into his own puke.

20

POCOLIM

It took him three days to get the smell of puke out of his nose. Until then he smelt it everywhere, in his food, in his bed, in his dreams, in his tool box, in his clothes cupboard. These moments of puke-smelling gave him clarity. Wake up and smell the puke was his new mantra.

He touched the car with real interest after that, sat behind the wheel, inhaled its decaying interior, the mouldy seats, the hot toxic air that it trapped daily. He popped the hood and traced a finger through the cobwebs and dirt, communed with the engine block, with its pipes and tubes and valves, and remembered the days when these things used to grunt and roar and take him away at great speeds from this house and village. And he knew what he had to do.

He decided to stay sober, keep his head clear. It helped that the sight of a feni bottle – or any alcohol, for that matter – filled him with dread and loathing. He knew it was temporary, just a lover's spat; one nose-dive into puke and humiliation from the entire village could not come between years of friendship. For now, though, he would ride sobriety as far as it would take him.

After three days of mulling with a clear head, he finally got down to it on the nineteenth of March, the resurrection of the Dodge. He worked and worked long hours. He crawled under and into. He stripped, cleaned and put back. He made lists and made calls.

Ferdie came around every day, a dog that likes to be around its master, watch him work with love and gratitude dripping from his face; if he had a tail he would have wagged that too as he circled the car lovingly. Sometimes he sat in the driver's seat and pretended for fleeting moments that he was a man of action, part race-car driver, part fighter pilot, with smatterings of rogue, playboy and spy, wrenching the wheel from side to side and feeling the front tyres gouge the earth under him, until Savio was tempted to yank him out and smack his head.

Occasionally Savio would take a break, and the two of them would sit in the front seat and stare at the red ribbon of road ahead of them, and Savio would blow smoke rings past Ferdie's nose and sip lime and water and comment on how, for once in the life of this sleepy village, something vaguely interesting was happening. Even when the Indian army came and the Portuguese left, what was Pocolim doing?

Nothing. Eating, sleeping, fucking and farting. History going on just outside, whole fucking war and peace sagas going on all over the world. But over here, a younger Madame Rosalina was hooking up the accountant's son with the grocer's daughter, and old Bob, my father, was scratching his balls and serving arrack, and housewives were getting porked for the fifth and sixth time in the holy name of procreation and kids were being born and others dropping dead, and everyone either wailing and crying or gossiping and talking shit and falling down dead drunk night after night.

Then, someone has a dream, and he falls out of bed and kicks up a holy ruckus because some mysterious letter comes in the middle of the night, and all of a sudden there is some grand love story that everyone is trying to rewrite and everyone's thumbs come popping out of their arse, and suddenly it's do this, do that and bang – road trip! Out of nowhere, to nowhere. Ferdie would never miss an opportunity to thank Savio, and Savio would grunt and say no, thank *you*, did you ever think that you, Ferdinand, meek and mild and slipping into and out of your little hole like a mouse all your life, would one day make this happen? Be the cause and effect of the biggest event in Pocolim since forever, because nothing has ever happened in this shitsplat village?

And sometimes Savio would get that gleam in his eye when he would talk of the three of them, Angie and he sitting in the front seat, while Ferdinand sat at the back, and never mind that this trip is the dumbest thing he has ever heard, but everyone is making it sound like the best idea since sliced bread, and they're really using Ferdie as an excuse for doing what they all really want to do: get the fuck out of here, even if it's only for a day.

And then the occasional rant against Rosalina, that soul-sucking bitch who is like Russia: an authoritarian regime that kills the human spark. It's a wonder that she is letting Angie go on this trip, Angie who has never strayed further than this village, like she's on a dog-leash that is twenty years long, sweet Jesus, what a life!

And Ferdinand would sit silently and stare at the road ahead, a generic road lined with generic trees and wild shrubs, merely a scribbly line between two points, hooking up with other scribbly lines, forming a vast network that knitted Goa, possibly the whole world into one heaving organism. But all of that has little meaning for him. All he knows and cares about is, down some generic road like this one, some immeasurable distance away, is Millie, perhaps staring out of her window at some similar stretch of mud or gravel or asphalt, waiting and watching without even knowing what she is watching and waiting for.

And thus the days passed.

And Ferdie had no more dreams for all those nights, only because he popped a Restil each night that slammed him slack-jawed into the soft embrace of his pillow until morning. Except on the last night before the journey: even as the Restil began to worm its insidious way though his mind, shutting doors and putting out lights, Millie came.

And the dream was slower than before, sometimes replaying parts of itself unnecessarily just for the heck of it, and Millie was somehow more real, and this time she even touched him. The Ferdinand in the dream was aroused (even as the real Ferdie lay limp). This time, she watched as he rowed away, smiling and not stopping him, and this time he did not fall over the side and drown but just kept bobbing in the surf a little distance away, not getting pulled out but not rowing back to her either, until an early morning haze spread softly over the beach and Millie merged with it, leaving Ferdinand unsure whether the haze descended onto Millie or she ascended into it.

BOOK TWO

THE JOURNEY

I

ANGIE

Dear Mai,

All this has happened so fast. I'm sorry for writing this letter instead of talking to you about it. I did not want to wake you up, because you don't like to discuss all these things late at night. You work so hard in the day with all those important church matters, you need to rest so you can be strong again in the morning.

Anyway, I am travelling to Secaulim tomorrow morning. It concerns a human heart: not mine; I gave and lost mine long ago. Our postmaster Ferdinand fell madly in love with a young, beautiful girl called Millie thirty years ago. He never got a chance to tell her, silly Ferdinand, because you know how shy he can be. And even though sometimes you think that he might not be normal in 'that' way, he still loves Millie very deeply, and that is why, I think, he never took another woman again.

She lives in Secaulim, and it's only two hours away. Ferdinand needs moral support right now, and like a good Christian should do, I have offered to be a pillar that he can lean upon. I have left food in the fridge for breakfast and lunch. You remember the xacuti from yesterday? I'm sorry it's not cooked fresh, but you slept so well in the afternoon after you ate it, I thought you might like it again.

Don Pedro has offered us his car for the journey, so generous of him. By the way, after he met with you, he could not stop talking about how he wants to paint a portrait of you. Several portraits, maybe. He said something like he wants to freeze your grace, elegance and beauty on canvas before the ravages of time take it all away. His words, not mine – they sound so lovely, I'm not even sure what they all mean. So flattering, no? He is coming with us, and you know what, I think he secretly hopes you'll be coming too. But I said no on your behalf, knowing that Pocolim needs your constant attention.You should spend more time with him, Mai. He has such good manners and is such a gentleman.

Also Savio D'Gama will be driving us, as Don Pedro cannot drive. I know how childish this Savio can be. He can cause your blood pressure to rise and your blood sugar to fall. These young boys, they sometimes have no respect for old people.

He is trying to get friendly with me too; maybe it's because he thinks I am single. I have tried to tell him that my life is dedicated to looking after you, Rosalina Eucharistica, who is like a mother to me. He laughs when I say that, and even though I get angry, I think I find him quite charming. Day by day, I am not so angry with him any more. I just hope four hours alone with him tomorrow does not make me do something you would not approve of. But you will be there in spirit, Mai, looking over me, like my guardian angel, helping me to fight temptation.

So, it's Ferdinand and me, this charming artist Don Pedro (who I think is secretly in awe of you) and this bloody rascal Savio, who is quite interesting sometimes, but needs a good lesson in keeping his hands to himself. I wish, I wish Pocolim could do without you for four hours, so I could look to you for guidance every time that charming voice tries to entice me into those rough hands. And also because I'm sure you would love the company of Don Pedro so much. He is so funny and he has so much passion for his art, and I think, for you.

I will return in the evening, and I will tell you everything.

Your loving daughter,
Angie

2
SAVIO

Some days it is just better to stay in bed. But how do you know when that is? You end up sleeping in and missing out, or blundering out and get kicked in the balls.

First, there is the self-loathing that non-morning people suffer when forced to wake up at 7 a.m., which is five hours too early. Especially if you went to bed at four, after celebrating the resurrection of the Dodge with a bottle of Johnny Walker Black which you bought from the extra money Don Pedro gave you to fix the car.

The other eleven bottles are still stashed away, which Savio plans to nurture for as long as he can.

Wake up five hours too early, and you'll find even simple tasks difficult. Like opening your eyes all the way. Finding light switches. Like getting toothpaste on the brush, then locating a mouth somewhere on your face.

The extra money had not come easy. He had, as sullenly as possible, told Don Pedro the truth – that he had no clue where the advance of 50,000 was, that there was no money *anywhere* and he was going to need more. And throughout the conversation, he had felt as humiliated as a beggar at a traffic light, and a dishonest one at that, in the toxic wash of Don Pedro's drooping-lipped disbelief. But the truth is the truth, and if you want that car to run, this is what it is, he had snarled.

Blame Loyola, blame Rosie, but blaming won't make your car run.

He had been surprised at the force of Don Pedro's desire to have that car running at all costs, the speed at which he had signed the cheque, even as he chose not to believe Savio with his eyes and mouth.

Had Angie slept with this man, was his first thought, blooming like the first triumphant cancer cell. He had ground it to a halt but could not crush it, and now it will always be there, in pretend-freeze mode, ready to run rampant if he allows it.

He finds a jar of coffee, briefly contemplates putting a kettle on boil, then merely pours a fistful of powder into his mouth and chews on it bitterly. He washes it down somehow with some cold water, and shambles around, still looking for the light switches.

The early glow of a new day is now creeping around the house; there is something sweet and innocent about that first light settling into the gloomy interior of Casa D'Gama without the slightest hint of disapproval at the decrepitude all around.

He dresses in the amplifying light. Meanwhile, the upstart caffeine tries to wrest control from the totalitarian alcohol. This battle will be positively Homeric, he knows, leaving the battleground scarred and bloodied. He puts a hand in front of his mouth and exhales. Then he goes and brushes his teeth again, giving his tongue an extra working-over this time.

When he steps out onto the porch, his father's old Ray-Ban perched on his nose, he is startled.

The road is untrammelled and pliant, the sky is a soft duvet of violet, keeping the snugness of the night in.

At his usual rising hour of noon or thereabouts, everything looks hostile. If it isn't hostile, it is depressing – either way, unapproachable.

Now, the trees aren't fretful and restless, the sun and sky not despotic dictators uncaring about the harsh conditions of their subjects. And there is not one shambling, bumbling idiot on the road with a head full of Pointless Conversation. He thinks he will give mornings a shot after this trip is done.

The Dodge is resting quietly on its wheels, brimming with power and raring to go. Built at a time when size mattered, built for women to pose full-length on its hood in bikinis, built to carry the family and three dogs for weekend outings. She had come to life with the sweetest purr of gratitude, happy to be alive again.

He looks into the front seat; no ghost there. He will be in that driver's seat instead, flesh and blood, and Angie will be sitting next to him, real Angie, not a memory of her, just like in the old days, and they will put a few miles between them and Pocolim, and he will have all day to tumble into her eyes, back into that Big Bang.

In the back seat, no Gabo, no best friend who will snatch his girl away from him with affluence, just a battered old sod with crazy dreams who will probably sleep through the entire journey.

For the first time in many, many years, Savio feels like he is in charge of things again.

When he drives up to the church courtyard, the engine thrumming quietly, begging to be unleashed, he can hear the choir belting it out, lovely trills overlaying the elegant lower registers. It sounds like a pleasant and fitting soundtrack to the war being waged in his bloodstream. The coffee is winning, and despite the savagery of the opposition, the outcome is inevitable. Mornings, he says to himself again in amused wonder, yes, I should look into them more.

Angie and Ferdie are not there yet; that is fine, he is content to soak in the sounds and sights and wait. He does see Don Pedro standing under a huge banyan tree, lost in thought and looking around. The anal old fuck just there to give him last-minute instructions on driving safe and looking after the car, or else, blah blah blah.

But there are the two bags at his feet, one little and one large. Even as his whisky-soaked mind tries to figure it out, Don Pedro turns, almost in slow motion, and the penny begins its unhurried twirly journey downward. That faraway look he had seen in the artist's eyes turns out to be one of ill-concealed irritation. Down, down comes the penny, sinking through several fathoms of Johnny Walker Black, and it lands softly at exactly the same time as Pedro's upper lip curls south.

He sits motionless behind the wheel. The good mood blows out like an old bulb, lighting up his head with darkness. Slowly, with deliberate movements, he pushes the shades on top of his head, opens the door and steps out. Don Pedro is not looking at him, only at the car.

'Good job,' says the artist. 'Cost an arm and a leg, but I suppose it was worth it in the end, right?'

Everything about the morning is now stale and rank.

'Some problem with your speech?' Pedro grins mirthlessly.

'Are *you* coming along on the trip?' he hears himself ask.

'Well, I am the owner, am I not? If I don't make the maiden trip, who will?'

What good are rhetorical questions, except to bang home dirty and unpleasant truths you have to swallow?

Don Pedro walks around the car slowly, his hands on his hips. 'I must learn how to drive this, one of these days. Can you believe, I cannot drive. Ha, ha, ha.' A finger reaches out and traces a little line on the hood. 'So. Is this one-day-old dirt, or have you never bothered to clean this car since your father passed away? Ha, ha, ha. I know Pocolim is dusty, but this is a bit much, don't you think?' He holds the finger aloft, presumably for all of Pocolim to see. The same finger points to the two bags propped up against the banyan tree. 'These go in the trunk. After that, make yourself a little busy with a cloth, please.'

'A week ago, this car was *dead*. *I* brought it back to life for you. You are talking about it being a little *dirty*?'

Don Pedro knows how to sniff: loud and ponderous sniffs that hang in the air, fat and swollen with scorn.

'That is another problem with you people. Just because you repair the car, you think you can give it to me dirty? What, are you doing me a big favour? When will you people learn to respect your duties?'

'*You people*?'

'There is a lady coming along on this trip. She is my guest, and I certainly do not want her to get into a dirty car.'

His brain yells *clean it yourself*, even as his body moves of its own volition to the driver's seat, and fishes out a cloth from under the dashboard. Retorts and abuses that will never breathe fresh air bounce around in his head uselessly.

'Put my bags in first, please. I don't want red mud getting into my things. Hold on, on second thoughts, I'll take that. Just the other one.'

He pops the boot and flings the bigger piece of luggage into the cavernous interior. He slams the boot shut with such violence that the car sags on its axle.

'Banging things, throwing things. I suppose you young people think that is the way to be.'

He mutters something inaudible, an incoherent mixture of *yeah so what* and *fuck you*, which came out as *fyhecksoyouhat*. He slaps the car desultorily with the dusting cloth. The sun is climbing over the trees now, and the choir singing has stopped.

The church-goers, some of them stop to have a little stare. They are watching him as though he were a train-wreck about to happen. He did not disappoint them the last time, did he?

'I trust the inside is clean, at least? No grease stains on the seats? You washed and aired them out, I hope?'

'They're clean,' he growls.

'Hmm. Leather and sweat don't go too well, smells like pig's piss after a while. Ah, here they come. You. You continue dusting.'

His molars gnash and grind into each other like gladiators. Ferdie, he observes, is all dressed up. A pin-striped shirt that is crisply ironed, and well-creased pants that are tightly belted up just a couple of inches shy of his nipples, leaving a clear view of socks that have some spotted print. His straggly hair is slicked back and he has taken something sharp to the foliage that erupts out of his ears. All efforts to look grown up and groomed and responsible, yet somehow looking like a child that had been dressed up for an occasion it has no clue about.

Angie looks a little wan. He sees her roundness in a form-fitting russet-coloured dress with frilled cap sleeves, her cinnamon complexion top-lit by the morning sun.

If the black rage of betrayal blowing through his head wasn't taking up all the blood, some of it might have been diverted down to his crotch.

'The beautiful Angelina,' Don Pedro says, 'the glow on your cheek and the light in your eyes put the sun to shame.'

Who the fuck talks like that? That malignant cell again, just waiting to proliferate: did she shag him to get the car? Jealousy flares and perches on top of the anger pile like a buzzard on a shit-heap.

'And the intrepid Romeo, the Don Juan of Pocolim, the Casanova of the entire Konkan coast, you are an inspiration to lovers everywhere. If only I had known why you wanted my car! I salute you, sir.'

'And where is the *other* lovely lady? She will be with us soon, I hope? Not that we are late, or anything. This young man is just putting the finishing touches on the car.'

The church bells start tolling, but they cannot match the tinnitus in his ears through which he hears Angie say, 'Mama will be along any minute. Please excuse me.'

Angie walks around hesitantly to the side of the car where he, for want of something to do, is wiping down the door, face a mask, mind in turmoil, heart in a rage.

'Before you hate me for the rest of your life, let me tell you that it was completely out of my hands.'

'Lies,' throttling the word as it comes out, wiping the door vigorously.

'Could I refuse them even if I wanted to? Could I tell them, no, don't come?'

'Fuck them. And you too. And that noodle-fuck Ferdinand.'

'Oh, now that's very mature.'

'I don't lie. I don't trick people.'

'He owns the car. How can—'

'You tricked me into driving this car.'

'He owns the car, Savio.'

'And that fat cow owns you. Live your life that way.'

'She doesn't own me. She is my family.'

'You are her servant.'

'If you had said no to driving, what would happen to Ferdie?'

'I wanted to get away from this village. I wanted us—'

'I had to do it for Ferdie. I had to.'

'Balls to him. And don't talk to me. Go tend to her.'

'Very mature.'

'At least I'm free.'

'No, you're not. You are trapped by having no money, by your behaviour towards others and by your self-pity.'

'At least I live by my own terms.'

'You call that living? Are you denying all the extra income you made just by repairing the car and finally selling it?'

He straightens up. His back is hurting and his jaw is aching from speaking through clenched teeth. The car door shines brightly in stark contrast to the rest of the dusty chassis.

'Here she comes, her royal fatness. Fucking ugly as ever. Go, roll out the carpet.'

'You have to stop feeling sorry for yourself. You behave like the whole world is out to get you.'

She puts her hand on his chest, softly, warmly, then whirls around and walks towards Rosie. He gets in behind the wheel, throws the cloth under the dashboard and looks into the rear-view mirror. Even from the back of that big bullet head, he can tell there is a big grin plastered in front. 'Madame Rosalina. The First Lady of Pocolim village. What a privilege it is to be in your company on our journey. My humble car awaits.'

Now Ferdie is bowing to her, offering to help. She hands him her big, furry handbag and he almost drops it. 'Careful!' she screams. 'Why do you have to drop everyt'ing? Have you got holes in your hand or wat?'

'It – it moved.'

'Of course it moved! It's a cat! Ah, Don Pedro.'

'What a beautiful animal. Is it coming along with us, or has it come to wish you farewell?'

'Ma, are we taking Nereus along with us?'

'Dere is no one to look after him. He will be fine; he will stay wit' me. Look after him!' she snaps at Ferdie, as she allows herself to be led to the car by Pedro.

Savio pops a gum in his mouth. The sight of Rosalina does not agree with his stomach, and the hangover seems to have sprung a sudden coup on the caffeine.

Father Francis suddenly appears, full of bon vivant and brandy. 'Aaah, our travellers are gathered. As soon as you are on your way, we'll say a little prayer for you. Why do you have tears in your eyes, Ferdinand? Are those tears of joy?'

'De-de cat,' he says, his eyes red, his nose twitching.

Father Francis wags a finger at him. 'Get it out of your head, now. We are all God's creatures. We must not be allergic to each other.'

It's only two hours, Savio tells himself, wringing the juice out of the gum.

'You made it work,' says Angie, her hand on the window-sill. 'From *that* to *this*. I believe in miracles now.'

'Miracle?' He pauses, looking at her, trying to ease his eyebrows out of their scowl. 'The miracle of sticking my head under the hood for fifteen-hour days. The miracle of getting the spares. Yes, you could say that.'

He doesn't want to be angry at her, but anger is always slow to leave.

'Our prayers were answered, either way.' She smiles brightly.

Anger, the unwanted squatter, has to be ejected face first.

'Yes of course. God came to me in my dreams a week ago and said, "Don't worry Savio, sleep on; the car will be fixed in time for the journey. You have nothing to worry about."'

'See, I can never tell if you're teasing or being serious.'

'"Give me your spanners and your spares. And stay in bed, son."'

Anger, it seems to be unpacking its bags, settling in.

Rosie is being helped into the back seat by Pedro. The car squeaks as it sinks almost a foot into its suspensions on one side. She has that awful perfume on again. An evil, unseen hand stirs up his stomach.

'I will sit next to you,' Pedro says magnanimously. 'Your lovely daughter-in-law can sit on your other side. 'You, you get in front,' he says to Ferdie.

Ferdie: by now the main target for every microscopic allergen that Nereus's fur harbours.

'Padraon,' Savio nods to him, a little alarmed at the puffed-up eyes and the nose that has swelled up to twice its size. 'Allergic to cats, Padraon?'

Ferdie gives a violent sneeze of assent.

'Good, you deserve it. You knew too, didn't you? Well, chuck it out first opportunity you get.'

He sees Rosie casting him a suspicious look in the rear-view mirror. Pedro and Angie pile in from the other side.

'What a lovely car, Don Pedro.' Rosie smiles.

'Yes, I thought so too, when I first saw it rusting in Loyola's yard. Needed a little work, nothing much. Foreign engineering.'

'Yes, when will we ever learn to make cars like dese? Lifelong dey last, so little maintenance required, no?'

'*Very* little maintenance,' agrees Pedro.

Savio looks down at his calloused hands, the cuts, the burns and the bruises. The traces of grease still under his fingernails. The tiredness in his body.

'Can you drive a fine car like dis?' Rosie's voice booms from the back seat.

He looks at her in the mirror.

'Yes, you,' says Rosie. 'And good morning. It's okay if I have to teach you manners. Your mudder must have forgotten.'

'You are asking me if *I* can drive this car?' His jaw might have dropped at the sheer audacity of her question, but it is too busy grinding gum and teeth.

'Yes, are you qualified? Dis is a foreign car and I hear t'ings can be very different. Like ... like de gears on the udder side and .... t'ings.'

His stomach clenches and unclenches. He wants to cry tears of rage while he stomps her to death. When he is confident of speech, he looks back into the mirror. 'Can anybody *else* in this car drive this car?' he asks. 'You?' He shoots a look of pure savagery at Angie.

She shakes her head, a little frightened.

'You,' he snarls at Pedro. 'Can you drive?'

Without waiting for an answer, he looks at Rosie. 'You, madam? Since you know so much about foreign cars and their gears. Can you drive?'

There is no answer. 'I guess that leaves me then, doesn't it?'

Rosie sniffs. 'I'm not sure I trust dis hooligan to take us safely. Don Pedro, are you sure dis is safe?'

He slams both hands down on the steering wheel. The column takes it bravely and impassively. The horn starts up and does not stop. The Dodge, it blats out a rude and loud raspberry. He pops the hood and gets out.

They all watch him, the occupants of the car, Father Francis, a few straggler onlookers satisfied that they are about to get their money's worth at last. They see him disappear under the hood, grunt around like a savage foraging for food, and then the horn abruptly stops, leaving an even louder silence in its wake. The hood comes down with a crash and a couple of voices speak at once.

'Now, now, Savio, there is no need for ...' That is Father Francis, sidling up to the car so he can lean on it.

'You see? *You see?* Bleddy hooligan!' That comes keening out of the back seat.

He kicks the driver's door viciously, feeling the shock radiate up to his hip. The door swings shut and bounces right back; the *boiiing* is layered by a scream as Father Francis learns the all-important lesson of not leaving his fingers lying around.

He boots it again, and this time it slams shut, leaving the occupants with the sensation that they have been broadsided by a blunt projectile.

He stalks off, leaving in his wake a sobbing priest wondering if he will ever be able to hold a glass of brandy again, four shell-shocked passengers, and three delighted rubber-necks.

He comes back a whole five minutes later – as violently as he had left. Elbowing Father Francis out of the way, he gets in and slams the door.

There he sits, motionless, breathing heavily. His peripheral vision picks up a dirty fur-ball lazing and stretching in Ferdie's lap.

'This is—' Rosie begins, in a strident voice.

Savio jams a finger at her in the rear-view mirror. 'Shut it!' he snarls. 'One more word out of you and I'll drive us all off the edge of a cliff! *One more word out of any of you! Understood?'* He turns to Ferdie. 'Touch anything and you'll be sorry. If that filthy animal comes close to me, I'll make you eat it, you understand?'

He starts the car and aggressively throws it into gear. It shoots forward like a slingshot, throwing everybody back in their seat.

3

THE DODGE

They are used to shuffling into the future, not tearing into it.

There is little conversation. Everyone is lost in thought in these early moments of being in a vast, fast foreign machine that is hurtling away from the village they have rarely been out of.

Ferdie, his nose jammed up from the tip of his nostrils to the deepest recess of his sinuses, is now inhaling Nereus's mites through his open mouth. His allergy escalates to a steady stream of tears pouring out of two slits where the eyes used to be, and a violent snot-projectiled sneeze sprays the windscreen every fifteen seconds.

Angie, all she thinks is, they're back, back in the car where it all began. It sounds the same, that engine, that grunt of gearbox. Inside, it smells the same, the leather, the cured hide of some ancient cow giving off its reliable odour for eternity. All she wants to do is throw a bridge across the empty air and communicate with him.

Ferdie crushes his face into a fistful of tissues, hoping to smother the monster itch that is eating him alive. Flecks hang off the tip his dead nose and all over his cheeks.

'Padraon, you look like shit,' snarls Savio from the periphery of the snot-and-saliva storm.

Savio, still the petulant child throwing a raging tantrum in his head.

Rosie, next to Angie, thinking of her journey from humble foot-soldier to general, all her life in service of the Church, fighting the hordes of Indecency and Heresy. Generals got their portraits painted, of course.

The tissue box empty, Ferdie reaches for the cloth which had shined the car door a few minutes before. Shredded tissue is replaced by broad streaks of dirt, all across his face which now looks like a badly leavened bun.

Savio asks the three animal lovers in the back seat why the goddamn cat is in front.

Rosie tells him to mind his own business.

Don Pedro suggests that Ferdie stick his head out, it will do him good.

Savio says, throw the cat out, the fresh air will do it good.

There is indignant squeaking and puffing in the back seat as Rosie struggles to lean forward and smack his head.

Savio, he thinks of how, from one moment to the next, things change. Instead of Angie sitting next to him and the two of them sharing sweetly silent thoughts, no conversation necessary, there is this sniffling, mush-brained loser who is feebly stroking a dander-infested animal as corpulent and repulsive as his mistress who is spread out like a dissolving blob in his back seat, right next to some arrogant toff who thinks everyone is some measure of the servant class or the other.

Reality: the opposite of perfect, with a few toxic add-ons. A leaky nose being wiped on a sleeve every now and then is proof that forces far beyond his control are stacked up against him.

Rosie lapses into a nap, in which she dreams of filling up the sky with her presence, while a billion humans fall to their knees and bow their heads below.

Don Pedro fidgets next to her, baser thoughts on his mind. This would be a good time to start with a pencil version. He reaches between his feet for his bag.

Ferdie takes Don Pedro's advice and pokes his head out. A passing car almost takes it off. He jerks it back in, hair erect, eyes large as dinner plates and swollen red, wheezing laboriously through his mouth.

Without warning he jerks forward and sneezes violently. Then he sneezes five more times in quick succession, spraying the dashboard and the windscreen. 'Jesus Christ,' yells Savio. 'Use the bloody tissues!'

Ferdie turns to him, mouth wide open. 'I – I shoo-shoo' carry a ha-ha-haaaaaaachooooo,' hurling a bucketful of snot and saliva into Savio's face.

Three minutes later, Savio grabs the cat, gets out, opens the rear door and, conscious of his elbow brushing past Angie's breast, drops the animal onto Rosie's lap.

He is not driving on with that mucus-machine in front, he snarls. Or that cat.

Rosie protests that her daughter-in-law will never sit in front with a hooligan like him.

Then drive the fucking car yourself, he says. Walk, I don't care.

When the Dodge hits the road again with Angie in front, her frilly sleeves blow up with the wind, exposing her shoulder, the same shoulder he had pressed his lips to in a leeching desperation the night of her wedding ten years ago. Her shoulders had been even more exposed back then in that wedding gown, and he had buried his face, his nose, his mouth into the springy muscle, smelling her, kissing her, determined not to let her see his eyes. She had let him, both her hands rubbing up and down his back in that asexual manner of patting down a dog that has strayed too close. And then he had pushed her away and left without a word, using the shadows of the room to hide his eyes through which you could have seen right down to the hacked remains of his heart.

'Twice my agent has told me, twice, that it is important for an artist to stay hungry. Hunger will produce the artist's best work,' says Don Pedro from the back seat.

'What a ridiculous t'ing to say,' says his muse, stroking the cat's fur.

'I told her to go to hell; my ancestors did not believe in starving.'

In the front seat, Angie is preparing Rosie's medicine. Her type 2 diabetes pill, her pressure pill, her gout pill, her cholesterol pill.

Without twisting his neck, Savio sees her breasts jut into his vision right there next to him, a short arm's reach away. He focuses on keeping an erection in check as her breasts jiggle, despite being trussed up in a tight bra, as the ageing suspensions answer each and every tiny bump on the road.

Then there is a pill for her triglycerides, her deep vein thrombosis, her obstructive sleep apnoea, her non-alcoholic fatty liver condition, her osteoarthritis, her lower back pain.

Earlier, while fishing for a cigarette, Savio had found a tiny tablet in his pocket, one he kept for occasions when thinking got too heavy before bedtime.

Don Pedro says, I produce my best work when I'm sated and happy. My agent, he says, she's English. Before they found tea in India, they were drinking hot water. No, she will never understand the Latin blood that flows through our veins.

How this works is, Angie puts all the pills in a paper cup and Rosie tosses the entire lot down her enormous gullet. Savio peels off the foil on his own tablet and palms it.

Angie carefully places the paper cup full of Rosie's goodies on the seat between them. Then she leans down to fill another paper cup from a water bottle that is in her bag at her feet.

Hungry, Pedro snorts. Ha! He doesn't believe in that nonsense about tortured artists, grovelling for that spark of inspiration.

Angie turns around and hands Rosie the two paper cups.

If Don Pedro feels a smidgeon of guilt at that bald lie, he hides it well: the last three months of torment and hate and self-abuse and pounding walls in rage and eating scraps out of a refrigerator and staring at his shrivelled-up cock lying inert on his hairy balls night after night, it all seems a distant past on this magical morning with its scent of dewy earth rushing through the open window, his enormous muse pressing her flesh against his and his fingers clutching a phantom pencil that is flying across a blank page in his mind.

The various pharmaceutical aids begin their marathon swim in Rosie's bloodstream, one of which slips away unnoticed to unplug her central nervous system.

'The role of a muse is often misinterpreted,' Don Pedro says. 'Underrated, even.'

A muse is not a paid model, oh, no, no. A muse … a muse is the pure feminine part of the male artist. She is the yin to his yang. And of course there is intercourse between an artist and his muse. Who is inside of him, you see.

Agents, gallery owners, critics, all the people an artist must surround himself with, they fail to understand the true role of a muse.

'I am referring to spiritual intercourse, of course,' he adds, slamming his sketch-pad down on his crotch that has reacted like a sleepy snake coming out of the charmer's basket.

'A muse brings forth life, from the womb of my mind! It is the classic gender-reversal, the man flat on his back, his legs spread in surrender, as the woman-on-top slowly tugs his life-force upward and outward!'

Of the whole lot, agents, gallery owners, the critics are the worst. Scum of the earth, that's what they are.

'Who are all dese terrible people?' Rosie asks, yawning.

'Philistines,' he roars. 'They are all Philistines!'

'Oh, dose mad fellows,' she squeaks weakly. 'Always shooting guns and t'rowing rocks in de Holy Land.' She rolls her eyeballs that feel as heavy as cannonballs, and a little dribble of saliva leaks out of one side of her mouth.

'To a Bohemian like me, if I may dare to call myself one, a Philistine is like – like – anti-matter. He sucks the life-force out of my soul.'

'He sounds awful – dis Antimatto,' says Rosie, her 'O' stretching away into a yawn that threatens to unhinge her jaw.

Don Pedro leans back in his seat, eyes gleaming. Are they listening to him, these peasants? He needs a break from speaking. His muse is falling asleep again. He whips out his special 2D pencil.

Rosie's head, finishing a slow turn on its axis, droops onto her bosom and lies there.

With carnality hanging right there like two twin clouds, fat and bloated over both front and back seats, the car hurtles on with the unvarying sameness of the Goan countryside whizzing by, a side-screen movie of trees, paddy fields and human civilization in one blurry continuous loop.

In the back seat, Nereus is stirring in Rosie's lap. He wants to lick his fur, but he is lazy. He looks around, a little disgruntled at being ignored, and goes for a walk on the continent of Rosalina's thighs. As cats go, Nereus can be classed as obese, but still possesses that softness of foot, which is why a sleeping Ferdinand does not feel a thing as the cat deftly switches laps and snuggles into his.

The only sounds in the back seat are of a pencil scuffling paper with graphite shoes, a deep rumbling snore, a sniffle and a contented purr.

The highway turns around a clump of trees ahead, a blind corner, which is why Savio does not see the herd of buffaloes ambling across the blacktop in the not-so-far distance. A nanosecond thought flashes through his head as he jams the brakes, were the pads originals or knock-offs? And then they lock, and a lot of things happen in that instant.

Don Pedro almost impales himself on his own pencil.

Rosalina, protected by mass and inertia, barely oscillates a couple of inches.

Ferdinand, the antithesis of mass and inertia, slides off the seat and comes to a halt when his knobby knees hit the seat in front.

Nereus, lazily contemplating the merits of a dilettante's life with a cat's grin, instinctively flicks out his claws and digs them deep into the flesh of his host's skinny thighs.

Ferdinand comes out of his sleep with a start and reacts with his own human instinct, which is to grab the source of the pain and fling it out of the open window.

The tyres squeal, the car slows and comes to a stop.

There is an eerie silence, the only sound that of buffalo hooves scraping the asphalt, their mouths chewing phantom cud as their noses sniff out sweet grass on the other side of the highway.

'Sorry,' says Savio through a mouthful of chewing gum that he has almost swallowed, a little jelly-ish in the bladder area, a little proud and relieved that the brakes (knock-offs, he remembers) have passed their acid test, although he would have preferred less drama.

'Jesus Christ,' snaps Don Pedro angrily.

'I – I – I di' no' mea' to. No, no, no.' There is a rasp and urgency in the voice, like the words are being dragged over a cheese grater.

Angie turns to look at Ferdie, massaging the wrist of the hand that she had thrown out to brace herself against the dashboard.

'Aaagh, aaaagh, aaaagh, I di' no' mea' to, no, no no.'

'What is he babbling about?' asks Savio, but Angie, who should have been able to translate, looks nonplussed and annoyed.

'Oh Je'us, oh Je'us, oh Go', oh Go'.'

'Will you please get your fingers out of your mouth?' She composes herself. 'I can never understand what you're saying.'

There is a soft sucking click as the frozen jaw unhinges a notch. 'It bit me. It bit me.' He is quaking now. 'Oh God, what have I done?'

He throws open the door, lurches out, runs around and throws up by the side of the road.

Savio gets out of the car, looks past the foetal postmaster and sees something familiar in the middle of the road. A handbag. 'You're *kidding* me,' he says.

'Oh God, Oi Bogos. Oh, what have I done? *What have I done?*'

'If you had something to do with … *that*,' Savio says, 'you've signed your death warrant, Padraon, nothing else.'

'*What* is going on?' asks Angie, stepping out.

Savio shakes his head. 'Not even an hour into the journey … amazing, fascinating …' His mind fumbles for more superlatives. 'Wow,' he finishes weakly.

'*What* are you looking at? Oh *mother in heaven*, please tell me that is not—'

Ferdinand retches again, determined to eject all his organs so he can die as painfully as possible.

'There is a big open field here. We can bury you here after she has torn you from limb to limb. Wait here.' Savio walks reluctantly towards the inert object in the road.

Don Pedro has got out as well, torn by curiosity, despite the thrill of having the entire back seat with a comatose Rosie, who looks almost schoolgirlish in repose.

They all watch Savio looking down at the limp form, then scooping it off the asphalt.

'Shock,' he tells them, in a state of mild shock himself. 'No blood. Even neck seems intact. Dead, I think,' saying the words like they are in a very-tricky-to-pronounce foreign language.

'Are you sure?' Angie, her voice keening high. 'He goes into a deep sleep sometimes.'

'Deep sleep? Here, you check.'

There is an extra dimension to the cat's sleep as it lies stretched out in Savio's arms. Even in the deepest dreamless sleep there is a subtle tension of muscle, a hint of an unfulfilled ambition or unfinished business, a residual coil of energy, and there is none of that; Nereus is well and truly uncoiled and at peace.

'He could never land on his feet,' Angie mutters hollowly.

Short falls are deadly for cats, offers Don Pedro. The higher the fall, the more likely they are to land on their feet. Ironic, eh?

'How did he do it? Did he jump? Mai was in the middle. I have never seen him jump that far,' says Angie, her voice a whisper.

Savio shrugs and points. 'I hate to say it, but I think he had something to do with it, though I don't know what.'

Ferdie isn't telling. His expression is packed with a tale, but he does not look like he possesses the vocabulary or the spirit to narrate it.

A loud snore booms out of the back seat.

'She slept through the whole thing? A bloody miracle,' says Don Pedro, meaning it.

'The sleep of the innocent,' says Savio, thinking of a scenario without a knock-out pill, then pushing it away. 'Not a blemish on her conscience. All right. Everybody, get back in.'

He reaches into the back seat and gently lowers the dead cat onto Rosie's lap.

'Do we really have a choice?' he asks them. 'So *stop* looking at me like that. Does anyone want to wake her and tell her what happened? Why don't you do it, Ferdie padraon? Tell her the truth. We'll start digging.'

It smells the same, he says. 'She won't even notice it. When the flies start to come, we'll all stop and mourn the peaceful passing of Nereus the cat, who died peacefully in the bosom of her mistress.'

'Alright by me,' says Don Pedro. 'Sounds like a good plan.'

Ferdinand unbends upward, vertebra by vertebra.

'It's either the bigger picture, or we all go back home,' Savio tells Angie. '*Don't* look at me like that, I'm offering the practical solution. Driving on or driving back makes no difference to me.'

Ferdinand's face crumples at that exact time. 'Look at him,' says Savio, 'do you want to be responsible for *that*? This wasn't exactly a kitten we are talking about.'

'Nereus has been with us for sixteen years,' Angie says tearfully.

'Poor thing, snatched away in the prime of life. Sixteen years? I think Ferdie here has done him a favour.'

He looks around again. 'I'll leave the decision up to you.' He fishes out a packet as nonchalantly as he can, smelling cat-hair on his fingers as he sticks a cigarette in his mouth and holding back an enormous gag-reflex as he lights it.

4

SAVIO

The seats on these old cars! It feels like he and Angie are sitting on a big sofa. Bucket seats, what are they good for? Safety, yes, but what about when you stop to take in a sunset, or veer off the road into a shaded grove?

From the first time he saw her, he had wanted. I want, I would like – the first words that had ticker-taped through his head. This new, shy entrant into the Eucharistica household, with her unselfconscious beauty, her coltish legs brown and beautiful under short dresses that had rapidly become longer as more time passed under Rosalina's eye. Her mysterious orphan-child genes out on display like rare artefacts from another time and place. Who were her real parents? Who had passed on those fine nuggets – the skin, the cheek-bones, the erect spine, the sinewy muscle and, fuck, those eyes.

He had been thirteen then. First there had been that gentle velvet punch between the eyes, then a warm fist slowly enveloping his heart, and then the sensation of his groin filling up with warm water, all in a span of minutes, and it had definitely been some degree of love at first sight. Yes, love always, in some form, pure and carnal locked in battle, first one on top then the other.

You can want and want someone's heart or vagina, dream of it, covet it, sense that she has similar thoughts about you too, but then in one moment no different from the last, she's just a friend, gone from sexual to platonic, two opposite ends of the fucking universe at warp-speed, leaving you holding your limp heart in one hand and hard dick in the other.

Gabo, she was always meant for him, brought in for him, nurtured and groomed for him, while Gabo just stood around picking his nose with that smug complacency of knowing that without even trying, by some fucking miracle of fate and right-place-right-time, he'd be the casual possessor and provider of this marvel of teeth and bone and curves and body fluids. He'd be her exclusive toucher, taster, smeller and all-round recipient of whatever magic of passion and sensuality she was capable of.

Exclusive, that is a word Savio has had the hardest time shaking off. Why the fuck should anything be exclusive for one man?

In the back, Gabo's mother is babbling about being hungry. She had woken out of the sleep-stupor an hour ago, just like the beast she was, like those sedated crocodiles or hippos those scientists clip tracking devices on before releasing them into the wild again, one moment dead and docile and in the next almost taking off an arm or a head.

Her first words had been 'I'm hungry, where are we?' and her first action had been to run her little carrot fingers through dead fur. Everyone had held their breath, but the fingers had continued to stroke while her face had contorted itself in a dozen different expressions of annoyance at the lack of instant response to her question.

All the way there, Savio had hoped, deep down in that region of the brain where all hopeless hopes reside, that somehow, in his own magical way, en route to Millie's old address, the one on the envelope, Ferdinand would manage to murder Rosalina and Don

Pedro too and make it look like an honest accident. But no, there is only so much an ineffectual little fuck can do.

Millie wasn't home. Nothing that resembled Millie was home. The home in question was spectacular, though. It made Rosalina's Casa Fernandez look like a hovel, and even Ferdinand was shocked, adding fear to the already extant emotion of aghast that had not left his face post cat-death.

The door was opened by a white, elderly Caucasian who had not bothered to put on a shirt, and whose torso had several splotches that turned out to be smudged tattoos. His white hair was tied back into a ponytail and his eyesight was kept alive by a pair of glasses with lenses that looked like twin mini-Hubble telescopes. Of the four people lined up outside (Don Pedro had stayed back in the car to pretend to feed the cat), the reactions had been varied.

Rosie had shivered from head to foot at the sight of something so repulsively heathen emerging from a house that should have rightfully been inhabited by someone ... like her. Ferdinand had added despair to the aghast and fear on his face, concluding that this was Millie's husband, Millie who had once flirted and made gooey eyes at this lanky, gawky sailor, promised him home-cooked meals when he returned and then vanished like a puff of smoke right after.

It was a while before they understood that this was not Millie's husband. The man's brains were as weak as his eyesight. For the first five minutes, he pegged them as Christmas carollers, even offering Ferdinand ten rupees if he would just go away, he and his fat wife, inducing a face-purpling rage from Rosalina.

But sometimes the sun would peek through the fog in his head, and Savio, who had been pumping the questions, recognized those little windows and waited for them. After a few more minutes of nonsense came the second moment of clarity, in which the foreigner even let them in, introducing himself as Vladimir Ilyanova, spitting out consonants through an obstacle course of slippery dentures.

The interiors were gloomy and moist and the air had a pulpy-rotten smell of boiled vegetables. That last was explained when in his third cloud-break moment, he invited everyone to try his borscht, which first excited Rosalina then infuriated her as another thick cloud rolled by and he forgot ever offering it to her. In the meantime, Ferdinand, on Savio's instructions, had wandered around the dimly lit room looking for evidence of Millie, even staring up into the soupy gloom fifteen feet above his head as if he expected her to be perched on the rafters. He had eventually spied a photo-shrine of sorts on a little round table. Thanks to his own dim vision and the poor visibility, Ferdie had difficulty telling men from women in the photos. He saw large hairless brutes with cold impassive eyes and weightlifter forearms who had no business having coiffed hair and dressing like farm-girls. He saw a couple of pretty girls in scanty clothes at the beach and zoomed in, briefly wishing one of them was Millie while being simultaneously shocked that Millie would ever wear clothes like that.

'No photos of Millie,' he reported back to Savio dejectedly. 'Dey are all his bredders and sisters, I t'ink.' He had paused and looked around fearfully. 'Mostly bredders I t'ink. But dey're wearing…'

Meanwhile, Rosie was chafing about the no-show borscht, furiously indignant about not being offered a chair or a glass of water, and hopping mad when a bean-bag was kicked her way, because as the old man put it: 'Sorry, madam, thyere are no chyairs in thyis house thyat wyill take your wyeight.' Then, eventually, after a clatter of meaningless conversation, the fourth window opened and information poured out: Millie Furtado had sold the house to him twenty-five years ago, wonderful lady. She had moved to Stotisgaon, which was a further thirty kilometres from there. The government had made a lot of problems about a local selling to a foreigner, but he had married an Indian, so he got lucky.

Lovely lady, Millie Furtado. Did they know her?

And Savio had leaped up from his bean-bag, pushing Ferdinand forward, saying, 'This man here is going to ask her to be his wife. We are desperately looking for her. Do you have an address in Stotisgaon?'

Then Rosalina, hunger gnawing her alive and reacting like an angry leopard that had had a kill snatched away from her by a mangy hyena, had piped in with another demand for borscht, and by the time that had been cleared up, the man's eyes had glazed over and he had snuggled back into the warm, woolly comfort of another thick cloud.

Nothing else to do but leave, Savio secretly chuffed that the journey was going to continue for another thirty kilometres, more opportunities to lever Angie's mind open, bring her back from Planet fucking Platonia of the past.

5

DON PEDRO

Don Pedro is not feeling too good.

It has to be the prawns, he reflects.

'No time for breakfiss also,' Rosie had grumbled. 'Dat naked hippie offers food, and den he says, I never offered *anyt'ing.* Can you *believe it?*'

If they had not stopped for lunch, she would have been uncontrollable. He needs her calm. Ideally, he needs her asleep. That Savio, that alcohol-sodden wretch whose pasty skin speaks of poor nutrition and inadequate sunlight, he has some good ideas sometimes. He likes her asleep even more than I do.

'How far to Stotisgaon?' Rosie has asked Ferdie, Napoleon asking a lowly corporal the distance to Moscow.

'Two hours give or take,' Savio had replied. 'You stick to directions, Padraon, time not important.'

Ferdie, with the map open on his lap, cringed at Rosie's response, screaming like she was talking to someone across a football field: 'It is when someone is starving! Don Pedro, will you please command your driver to stop? He does not want to lissin to a lady. I cannot wait for two hours.'

The mood had been going sour rapidly. The traffic was now crowding in on them, on that stretch nearing the airport – that cusp of North and South, where the tourist taxis clusterfuck their way to and from hotels and resorts that have slashed prices to outdo the competition, to suck in squealing brats on holiday from school and their squalling parents from over the length and breadth of the country, for whom Goa is a bit like leaving India without actually leaving its shores.

Them and the honeymoon couples, young girls fresh out of parental oppression, gearing up for in-law oppression, with their flashy bangles and tight tee-shirts, the guys strutting like peacocks in their knock-off shades, possessing that gauche swagger of kids who have completed their rite of passage and wondering, now what?

'Even Nereus has eaten,' the muse had snapped, her fingers slithering through the cat's fur-like baby pythons, 't'anks to Don Pedro.'

'*Fuck* this traffic.' Savio banged down on the horn repeatedly.

'Really, Don Pedro, I don't know how much a lady can stand dis always fildy tongue. This trip is not easy for me, I jus' want you to know dat.'

'Mind the language,' Don Pedro had said automatically, not really putting any authority in his voice. 'Just basic decency, in the presence of *two* ladies, not one.'

Clever to insert the slave girl into the equation, forcing Savio to maybe reconsider throwing out the fuck word a bit too much.

'And stop for lunch when you see a suitable place, please.' The final word had come from Don Pedro. Power-play buzzing back and forth over the front and back, who was really calling the shots, overall?

A lot of Savio's rage was coming from the slave girl now sitting in the back seat again, Don Pedro deduced. Switching with that hairy-eared noodle, who is now navigating, right after their first stop. Must look into the rutting habits of the working classes, he had mused, this elaborate mating ritual that is playing itself out. She, making him work too hard.

They had eventually pulled up outside an eatery, situated in full view of a little cove of sea, the bridge across the Zuari visible in the distance, faint radio sounds coming and going on the wind. Quiet. Pretty. Even the mighty Arabian Sea that was gearing up for monsoon assault – already tumbling and battering beaches further on down the coast – was merely trickling up and lapping the shore of the cove with soft sucking sounds. The board had said 'Eutilda's Corner. The Dhaba for All Goan Delicacies.'

It was, coincidentally, right next to a pharmacy.

Even then his muse had not been entirely satisfied.

'Dis is a daba,' she had said. 'Dabas are for drunkards who like t'ree pegs of rum with badly cooked sorpotel. It's for ruffians and people with foul mouts who scratch demselves all de time.' Turning to Savio: 'You would fit right in.' And then, 'Dey don't wash dere hands properly even.'

'Maybe it's not a dhabha,' Savio had replied. 'It says Eutilda's Corner and it's not on a corner. Are you hungry, Don Pedro?'

Yes, he had confessed, he could eat a buffalo.

The prawns. And the peanuts. And the butter chicken, before the mutton chops. It had to be a combination of all that. And the beer. He had been too distracted by Rosie's woman-scent, his first real tactile encounter with her.

He had forgotten to chew, he had simply shovelled.

At the table, with the beer and the peanuts and the papadums, when Savio had come back from the pharmacy, Don Pedro had said, 'I like you, despite your manners. Despite your attitude. You remind me of me.'

He tried to give this fool some advice on women. On their dumb Machiavellian games. The wretch, of course, had taken it all wrong.

'I remind you of—? You mean, except for the silver spoon sticking out of your arse?'

'What's money got to do with anything?' Don Pedro had smiled patiently. Yes, his father had been rich, so what. 'Harness your desperation, control it,' he said. 'Money does not stop people from being hungry. Controlling it and focusing it are the key factors. With all that pent-up anger in you, if you started steering it, wow, who knows where you could go? And second, be nice with the ladies. See the benefits of that.'

He had patted Savio's hand in an avuncular manner. 'Nice touch about the cat, by the way. I approve.'

Rosie was ordering. 'Butter chicken. T'ree helpings. No, make it four. Two plates of mutton chops. Wat you have in fish and prawns?'

They had left the cat on the back seat, covered in a sheet, with the windows cracked down. The sheet was to ostensibly delay the onset of flies, but word had already spread through the insect kingdom, Don Pedro noticed. The kingdom had despatched two emissaries to scope the territory. Just as he had left the car, he had seen them buzz in and alight on the white cloth-tarmac.

'And get one empty plate also. For my cat,' Rosie had ordered the waiter.

Ferdinand, he was babbling. 'At dat house. I-I was very nervous. If I am going to be so nervous, how am I ever going to talk to her?'

'Let your eyes do the talking at first,' that imbecile mechanic had advised him. 'The words will come later, don't worry.'

Advice from a moron to a retard. Letting that servant girl trample all over him with her feminine wiles, giving another idiot advice on women. Jesus.

'Recite your favourite poetry to her,' Pedro had told Ferdie, through a mouthful of peanuts. 'Something from – from Shakespeare. Or from Neruda. Even Frost.' And he had popped another fistful of peanuts into his mouth and drained half his beer glass.

'I haven't read poetry since I was seven,' the retard said.

'Well, then, you must be careful,' he cautioned. 'Baa-Baa Black Sheep might not be the best declaration of love.'

Rosalina, who was arranging the napkin over her bosom, had laughed like it was the funniest thing she had ever heard. Her chest and stomach heaved like mountains in the grip of an earthquake.

'What am I frightened of?' the retard had asked the table.

'Good question,' replied the moron. 'The answer is, of nothing.'

'Nothing?' The word had filled the retard with mortal fear and made his hands shake.

'We'll start with some things, Ferdie,' the servant girl had piped in. Another fucking expert. 'Nothing is a little hard to achieve all at once.'

'I don't know,' Don Pedro had muttered to Rosie, 'if I had to see that face in the mirror every morning, I'd be frightened too.'

And Rosie had giggled.

'Especially with that hair standing up.'

Rosie had giggled even more. He must do a portrait of her giggling. Capture that flesh in motion.

Hunger was getting her all excited, he'd noticed. It was making her frisky, like an elephant in the first throes of sexual heat gearing up for a little rampaging.

What had she been like young, he wondered. Before the glands went nuts, before the gluttony set in, before the self-loathing? Did that thick mass of hair, dyed a monstrous black and trapped in a bun, ever flow free, was it tossed and rumpled, teasing young boys in her day?

The food had come just then, interrupting his thoughts. Large, plastic dishes sliding across the table like flying saucers effecting emergency landing. As the aromas flew past, Rosie's jowls jiggled, her nostrils flared and her knees knocked against the table legs.

'So I tot we'd eat somet'in we don't eat every day,' she'd announced, her words squishy with saliva. 'Proper daba food. Where is de empty plate?'

The waiter, he'd showed displeasure at the thought of a cat's tongue coming in contact with his crockery.

'Wat's de difference?' she'd snapped, cranking out her enormous bosom like a puffer-bird in a reflex of intimidation. 'Cat eating or human eating, you still have to wash, no?'

'No-pet policy,' snapped the waiter right back, ignoring her expanding chest like an exemplary professional.

'He is not pet, he is fam'ly!'

'No pets. My udder customers will not like.'

'Wat udder customers? We're de only ones. You were catching flies before we came.'

This lowly, underpaid help at a highway eatery, he'd just looked down his nose at Rosie with the hauteur of a trained maître d'. 'How you know someone else won't come while your cat is eating?' With that question hanging somewhere over Rosie's frontage, he'd pirouetted elegantly and left.

The retard was looking at the food with wonder and trepidation, his hands in his lap, his shoulders hunched over, his nose still a little red, eyes carrying a hint of moistness. Fear was the retard's thing, like anger was the moron's. Both emotions with their million avatars, endless fuel to burn, bottomless pits of chemicals on tap.

Rosie said they would give grace before eating. Nobody argued. Ferdie shut his eyes ferociously.

'Oh Fadder, t'ank you for dis food at our table …' she'd begun.

Don Pedro had devoured his first mutton chop before Rosalina had finished, wiping his hands and licking meat out of his teeth by the time all their eyes opened, the 'amen' fading away in the quiet air.

'And … and please give me de courage. Please, please, please,' blurted the retard, seizing the moment while God was still on the line.

'Can you believe dis fellow? I am giving a prayer of t'anks and he is aksing and aksing. Always aksing, never t'ank you. Ungrateful wretch.'

Ferdie's lips moving soundlessly, clasped hands bone white, shaking in their own grip on one another.

One fat paw had whistled down and smacked them smartly. 'Stop dat!' His muse, looking like a boiler whose pressure was about to blow. 'Dat is why you will never have anyt'ing! Ungrateful people never have anyt'ing!'

There was no defiance in his look, no rancour or resentment. There was only compassion; he had looked almost saintly as he'd cocked his head and stared at her with moist eyes; like something out of a medieval painting, the Good Angel in a white striped shirt going toe to toe with the Angel of Death in black – allegorical, symbolic, brilliant.

'Dere is a time to be grateful, and dere is a time to aks,' he'd said. 'Dis is my time to aks.'

His head moved a little, changing the way the sun hit it, snuffing out the halo effect. In an instant, he was a quaking mortal again, looking around the table for support. He'd said, 'You have so much, so you have reason to be grateful ...'

Rosie's torso had leaned into the rickety plastic table, spilling gravy from the butter-chicken bowl. 'You wretch!' she'd hissed. 'You of all people saying dis! Do you know wat I have gone troo in dis life? Do you not? First my husband, den my son!' Her voice was a strangled whisper.

Eyes sweeping the table wildly, she grabbed up a plastic fork. 'I ought to stab you in your evil heart for saying somet'ing terrible like dat!'

And that was when he'd got aroused. Forgot to chew.

She'd waved the fork over her head like a demented goddess while her chest bulldozed the table away from her.

He helped himself to another mutton chop, almost swallowing it whole.

Savio had grabbed Ferdinand's empty plate and thrust it in his hand. 'Go feed the cat. Make yourself useful.'

The slave girl had grabbed his shirt sleeve and yanked him upright. 'I will help you.' She'd dumped two slices of fish and a handful of prawns onto the empty plate, dragging the retard away like a rag doll, his head swivelling around, still looking at the fork in her hand.

'You will go to hell for saying terrible t'ings like dat!'

She turned to a disinterested cottony cloud overhead and bellowed, 'Did you hear dis man? Does he know de trials and tribulashins you have put me troo?'

The dispassionate cloud had drifted away, blotting the sun and casting a shadow over the table. For a moment it had looked like she was going to stab herself in the chest, but then the hand had come down heavily onto the table top, causing three mutton legs and a dozen prawns to jump out of their plates.

That was when he had started shovelling.

'There, there, madam,' he had said, kneading her flesh with one oily hand, pulling her close. 'That man has no sensitivity, no feelings. Ignore him, please.'

He'd moved from the shoulder onto the jiggly triceps area, and then boldly down to her waist, allowing her to believe that she was moving towards him on her own. When she'd finally cleaved her body to his, he had smiled inside all the way down to his frisky loins that wanted to come out and play.

'Dat man has no fait', Don Pedro. Widout fait' where are we, wat are we, I aks you?' Making funny snuffling noises, like a pig wading through a trough.

'Nowhere and nothing, madam.'

'You t'ink I would have survived dis far widout fait', Don Pedro? Even as he took away Albert, and den Gabo, he gave me courage. Dat courage only comes wit' fait'.'

'There, there, madam. Hush now.' He was aware those adorable snuffling sounds could ruin his linen shirt if not checked.

'Crying all the time, spoiling everyone's sleep. For nuttin'. God has given him everyt'ing.'

'Everything, except a spine.'

'Me, he gave and took away everyt'ing.' She'd emptied her nostrils onto his shirt while she ground the paper napkins to shreds with wringing fingers. 'Bleddy cruel fellow,' she'd wept.

After he had gently pushed her away, he reached for a fresh batch of napkins and applied them assiduously to his sleeve.

'Come, we must eat, Don Pedro. We need our healt',' she had said, sitting upright and dabbing her eyes and nose.

'Where is dat horrible man, Don Pedro?' Rosie had turned to look.

But by then he was eating. Hand to mouth, food had flown. Tastes had tumbled over each other as prawns, peanuts, mutton skipped his tongue like flat stones on water, cascading down his gullet like debris down a storm-drain. And butter-chicken. And beer.

He had never believed in that shit about hungry artists. He wanted his sketch pad, he wanted his brushes *now*.

'You weren't joking about the buffalo,' Savio had said later, sweeping his hand over the empty dishes all around.

'If you have the stomach of a sparrow,' Rosie had said scornfully, 'you will be small and timid like a sparrow only. Like him.' She jerked a thumb over her shoulder at the car.

But now, the car with all its own aromas crowding his nostrils, odours of dead flesh emanating from the ball of fur that is at Angie's feet, it is the start of things. The car hurtling forward, taking blind turns, the thick trees on either side forming a tunnel, branches entwined at the top like fingers. Claustrophobia begins to smother him.

His stomach is turning away the food, ordering it back up, but Don Pedro is damned if he is going to tell Savio to pull over.

He stares at Rosalina's sleeping form, a sight of slovenly beauty, her breasts piled on top of her stomach like baby seals flopped on top of mama. This woman fights gravity every single moment of her life, but when gravity wins, it is magical. Only an artist can understand that.

6

THE DODGE

'Are we almost there yet, Padraon?' Savio asks Ferdinand. 'No bloody signs on the road.'

Ferdie snaps out of his sleep with a wild-animal snort and looks down myopically at the map on his lap. 'Dere is a big right turn coming up. You haven't passed dat, no?'

'No right turns yet. Road is straight as an arrow. You've been telling me about this right turn for half an hour now.'

Savio raps the fuel gauge with his knuckle. 'Either this car is excellent on fuel-saving, or …'.

'You bin in love also?' Ferdie asks Savio.

All those muggy nights in Bombay, Savio thinks, usually in some two-floor walk-up squirreled away in the ventricle of the red-light district fed by veins and capillaries of lust and decay, his limbs entwined with some sweet, plump, organic woman's, among sheets that smelled strongly of camphor oil and the skin-shavings of other men who had ground their groins there earlier.

After a long pause, Savio replies. 'We all have, haven't we? At some point or the other, I mean.'

'I look at her, and I t'ink sometimes.' He wags a tentative thumb in the direction of the back seat. 'My poor little Angie. I hope she loves again.'

I hope she loves again, now there is an interesting thought. Has she ever loved? Whom?

Ferdie's voice drops to a whisper. 'And every time I t'ink about *her*, my heart bleeds.'

'Where is that goddamn turn?'

'Dat's why I try to be nice to her always. But she just—'

'Who you talking about now?'

'Her, her.'

'Her who? Fat Rosie? Jesus, save your sympathy. She's a bloody crocodile, cold-blooded and vicious.'

'Shh, shhh, shhh.' Ferdie curls himself into a ball of panic. 'No need to shout.'

'Relax. She's out for the count. Gave her two this time,' Savio assures him.

'Two what?' It is as if somebody has taken Don Pedro's voice, full of brio, and slammed it on its head with a sledgehammer.

'They use them when they have to transport large and dangerous animals. Keeps them sweet and docile. You okay, Padraon?'

'I'm fine,' Don Pedro says in a voice normally heard uttering last words. 'And don't call me Padraon.'

'Okay, Padraon.' He nudges Ferdie. 'No need to whisper, is what I'm saying.'

'Poor lady. I've always wanted to hold her hand and give her comfort—'

'Except she'll take your hand off. Balls to her. You focus on Millie.'

'First husband, den son. What I said back dere was all wrong.'

'So you and Millie … When you were together, how was it? Did you … you know?' He pumps an imaginary horn with the heel of his palm.

'Wat is dat?'

'Okay, that's a dumb question. Did you, like, hold hands?'

'Yes, we did.'

'Did you kiss?'

'A – a little.'

'What else, a blow-job? A hand-job, maybe?'

'Wat is dat?'

Savio tells him, in straight simple English. 'No big deal,' he says. 'It's devotion, Ferdie, whether it's her mouth or her hands, or both.'

'Tell you a secret?'

'Where the fuck is that turn, Ferdie?'

'It's coming. Tell you a secret? Promise not to tell?'

'This is not the time to confess that Millie doesn't exist.'

'You know Albert and I used to be shippies? Albert, her husband?'

'I heard.'

'We sailed togedder, de last time, before he never came back.'

'Yes, I've seen photos. Looked like a nice chap, nothing like her. You were on the ship with him when he died?'

'Did not die. Jus' never came back.'

'What?'

'Did not die. Never came back. Wrote her a letter, tol' her he was never coming back. Tol' me to give to her.'

'Jesus Christ, wasn't there a memorial? Rosalina the grieving, pregnant widow, husband buried at sea, some bullshit story like that. Why?'

Ferdie's fingers wrestle each other in his lap. 'I don' know. I t'ink he found a girl. In Madagascar. Jumped ship and disappeared.'

'No, I mean, why fake a funeral and memorial? Why not just tell the world the truth?'

But he knows the answer to that, and Ferdie knows he knows.

'Dat's why she hates me. Because I am de only person who knows, apart from her and Albert. Not even Gabo, she never told him. Not even Angie. Now you know.'

'Damn, that explains all the bitterness.'

'Promise not to tell?'

'Jesus, that is a big one. But I promise.'

'Or at least wait till I am dead. Den you can tell.'

'You stick around. There is no need for you to leave. Now where is that fucking turn?'

'It's coming.'

The prawns are winning, concedes Don Pedro.

Those two halfwits are jabbering in front. One of the halfwits has slipped something to his muse, something strong, judging by the quantity of drool that is wetting his right shoulder and the slave girl is dozing. Timing-wise, it cannot be more perfect.

A spasm that starts in his stomach and ends at his throat jerks him upright like a hooked minnow. He pushes his big, bullet head out of the window. Relief floods his entire being as he throws open the gates, and the eviscerated crustaceans charge it like hardened death-row convicts seeking freedom.

A passing tree-branch smacks him violently in the face. He jerks his head in. His mouth fills up with a roar, nothing can stop the powerful pulsation of the freedom-seeking effluence now.

One nanosecond of panic at the thought of soiling himself, and then in a pure reflex of self-preservation, he leans over the other way.

They come out in a tumble, the front-liners, the ones with the battering ram, with barely a sound. In the front seat Savio hears something that sounds like a wet hiccup through the roar of the rushing wind.

The masticated crustaceans spill silently down the hillside leading from Rosie's chest onto her lap, where they pool in a valley of polyester. Then there is a respite, giving Don Pedro enough time to stick his head out of the window and unload the rest. Nobody hears that either, but Savio sees the artist pull his head in, face ashen, lips vomit-flecked, eyes all loopy with weak relief. And then comes the smell.

'Oi, oi, what is going on back there?'

'Nothing. Just keep driving.'

'Are you sick? Should I pull over?'

'Just keep driving.'

'What is that hanging off your lower lip?' Savio, an expert in regurgitation, asks belligerently.

'Keep driving, damn you.' Don Pedro reaches for a toilet roll from his bag and unravels a yard or more of it. Very carefully, like a collector taking a dust-cloth to a priceless objet d'art, he gently dabs at Rosie's chest. Savio adjusts the mirror and whistles.

'Look at that. Did you do that on purpose?'

'Keep your eyes on the road and mind your own business.'

'Except you've stunk up the whole car now.'

'It's not your car.'

'But the air I breathe is mine. And the air right now is shit.'

Don Pedro, he is beginning to wonder if the mutton chops will not soon join the prawns in a burst for freedom. He takes the absorbent paper to Rosie's contours; his hand roams all over her breasts, the largest and the most copious he has ever touched, and instead of this being a thing of pleasure, he is revolted by it.

'There go your plans of painting her,' says Savio. 'Phew, what a stink.'

Ferdie, a little slow on the uptake, dreamily sniffs the air like a retriever. 'Yes, wat's dat smell?'

'Don't ask. Even I can't believe it.'

'It's coming from …' His nose oscillates from side to side for a bit, and then slowly begins its backward turn.

'Look in front, you!' snarls Don Pedro, baring his big teeth at him. To Ferdie's dim eyesight, it looks like there are bits of bloody flesh hanging from them. He snaps his head in front. Is the beast chewing on raw meat? What raw meat?

Rosie's sleep thus far has been deep, dark and silent as outer space – 60 mg of Restil has hurled her into a soft, enveloping cosmos where there is no sensation. Her jaw is slack, her brow smooth and untrammelled as a mill pond.

But now she twitches. A furrow suddenly appears in the middle of her forehead. A pulpy tongue snakes out and licks her dry lips. The edges of her mouth tremble in uncertainty, unsure of which way to go, outward in a smile or downward in disapproval.

There is the tactile sense of being caressed or fondled, she doesn't know which. Caressed is good, fondled is bad; her mouth and forehead deliberate on which it is. She hears sounds but no words, just pleasant basso rumbles and tenor overlays.

'So how are you planning on getting out of this one?' Pleasant tenor.

'You'll see. When the time comes.' Basso rumble.

'I can't wait.'

'One wrong word out of you—'

'And what?' Pleasant tenor with chuckle that gurgles like running water.

'And I'll tell her all about the cat.'

'Why would she believe you?'

'You think she'll believe you? You? Ha!' Pleasant basso rumble with contrapuntal loud thump. Rosie jumps a little.

'The cat doesn't have a scar on it. Your puke, however, is all over her.'

'Who said it's my puke?'

'You're gonna pull that one?' A whistling teapot over the tenor.

And then that sensation again, the one that makes her mouth and forehead flip a coin: caress or fondle?

'Should've just told me to pull over, no?'

'What for?'

'Unless you were too macho to do so.'

'What are you yakking about?'

'I remember how you looked at me after I threw up. Outside my dad's memorial. Like I was some low-life.'

'You are a low-life.'

'Like puking is something only weak people do.'

'Yes, weak, drunken sods who can't control their intake.'

'Appetite of a lion, my ass. Insides of a girl.'

'Shut up and drive.'

'Insides of a sissy girl. Eating like a glutton.'

'Shut up and drive!'

'And not even man enough to admit it.'

In lieu of getting in the last word, Don Pedro's fingers clamp and squeeze.

'Wat is dis … wat is dis … wat is going on?' she asks, her voice building up slowly as the thick Restil fog begins to clear.

He regroups. He leans close and stares sadly into her eyes.

'Just a minor accident, dear lady,' he says. 'The food must not have agreed with you.' He dabs. 'Nobody knows. This will be our secret, you have my word.'

Rosie slowly looks down. Her eyes bulge out of her head and, in a gesture of utter futility, she tries to shrink away from her dress.

'It's almost all cleaned up, madam,' Don Pedro pushes confidently. 'As soon as we stop, we'll get a little water on it and you'll be as good as new.'

'Gimme dat!' she squeals breathlessly.

A little civil war rages inside her brain. It cannot be. But here it is.

'D'aba food,' she squeaks in a whisper. 'I tol' you.'

'Happens to the best of us, dear lady.'

She grunts with effort and disgust. 'Give me some more paper, please. Shh, tear it quietly. T'ank you.' She rubs and scrapes and continues to squeak and grunt like a pig being poked in the ribs.

'Dere is a water bottle in my bag. Please get it out for me.' Her big, round eyes keep darting fearfully from Savio to Ferdie in the front seat. She sees one of Savio's eyes in the rear-view mirror.

'Please tell dat hooligan to adjust dat mirror,' Rosie squeaks in stage whisper.

'You! Please adjust your mirror. Madame is making some adjustments to her dress.'

'Can't. It's a safety issue. My eyes are on the road. Madame can do whatever she wants.'

'Just a little adjustment won't hurt. Do it. Please.'

Savio gives the mirror a token fiddle, not changing anything. 'Where is that goddamn turn?'

'It's coming,' says Ferdie.

Rosie drenches the front of her dress and wipes vigorously. 'Please hand me dat perfume bottle,' she whispers.

Don Pedro holds his breath as Rosalina splashes herself.

'Phuaagh,' gags Savio. 'That smell again. Is someone having a bath in the back seat? Jesus.'

'You shut up and drive.'

'Dere it is, dere it is. Look!' Ferdie starts jumping around in the front seat.

'That's a turn? You sure?'

'Yes, yes. Look. Jus' after dat big tree.'

'I see it. You're right. About bloody time.' He shoots a worried look at the happy gauge that still announces a full tank.

Ferdie leans forward in his seat, his chin almost resting on the dashboard. His knees knock together and his scrawny butt grinds the upholstery.

'Sit back, Padraon. You want to stop for a piss?'

Ferdie shakes his head violently, making his earlobes slap against his cheeks.

'Be man enough to tell me. There are enough smells in the car.'

Ferdie pushes himself back and whirls around.

'Why are you jumping around like a jack-in-de-box, I aks you?' Rosie screams, dropping the perfume bottle out of sight.

Angie's eyes snap open, and she instantly wrinkles her nose. 'What is that *smell*? Have we reached?'

'My fellow passengers,' Ferdie says, his Adam's apple bobbing like a trapped alien life-form. 'I-I-I-I could not have done dis without you.'

'What're you up to, Padraon? Giving a speech now, or what?'

'I been quiet all dis while, but my heart has a few words to say.' He puts a hand on Savio's shoulder. 'It is bursting with gratitude. Please – please understand, I may have sailed de seven seas…'

'One sea. You just sailed one sea,' squawks Rosie.

'… but my heart has never been on an adventure like dis one. *You* all made dat possible. Without you, you and you, and especially *you*,' he turns around at an impossible angle to point to Angie, 'my – my heart was like a bird with a broken wing. It could not fly.'

'That's so sweet, Ferdinand.' Angie smiles sleepily.

'Are you delirious? Like, with fear or something?' Savio asks.

Pedro nods. 'Not a bad speech. You better have one just like that for Millie when you see her.'

'My eyes will tell her everyt'ing she needs to know,' he gibbers. 'I may never need to open my mout'.'

'Might be a blessing,' says Pedro.

'Do de same for us, den. Jus' talk wit' your eyes,' says Rosie.

'He's lost it,' murmurs Savio.

Ferdie is licking his lips. 'Today I have realized, dis body of mine is just an empty shell. Widout love, it is nutting – we are nutting. All dis is nutting.'

His hand waves clockwise as his Adam's apple goes the other way. 'Love. Love is de engine, and love is de fuel. Love makes life unpredictable! Er – I'm just going to turn around; I'm getting a crick.'

He snatches at the rear-view mirror and adjusts it. 'T'ree hours ago, I had nutting, just bad dreams. Now, I have everyt'ing. Millie is dere, around de corner.' He points ahead vaguely. 'Whatever happens, *whatever happens*, my friends and well-wishers are behind me. I am surrounded by love. Dere is only love.'

'Friends and well-wishers? Love?' Savio asks.

'Madame Rosalina, you were right! Everyone in the world should be as lucky as me!' He sobs and laughs at the same time. With a grand flourish, he roars, 'And take a right here!'

They take the right.

Ahead of them, as far as the eyes can see, possibly as far as the world's biggest telescope can see, is an endless row of paddy fields. In the distance, at the edge of the world, the sun is setting in a shimmery fashion, like in a jerky film. You can still hear Ferdie laughing that triumphant laugh as the fuel-pump gasps out its last bubble of gas to the engine.

BOOK THREE

ENDTIME

1

SAVIO

It's odd, he reflects; no, not odd, unfortunate, that amidst such beauty, he feels murder in his heart. He looks down at his feet, at the patch of drenched earth which is still frothing with his piss, and communicates with it. I don't suffer fools, why should I? I don't get spared when I am one, the world is just waiting to get a kick in. My fucking turn.

He is sorry his bladder is empty. It means he will have to pack up his tackle and turn around soon. The sun is blowing holes of soft, fading light through the rain trees in front of him. Birds and other day-job fauna are heading home; the night-shift is getting ready to take over. Some overzealous crickets have already started up. This is far better than any scenery back in Pocolim, even the trees look bored there.

Unfortunately, once he zips up and turns round, the worst of Pocolim is waiting right there, behind him. It has followed him all the way here to this beautiful paddy field.

'Will someone tell me why we have stopped in dis jungle?'

'Hush, Mai, I think the car has stalled.'

'Why has it stalled? Where is dat no-good fellow? How dare he jus' walk away!'

'I think we are out of petrol, Mai.'

'Why are we out of petrol? Why was de tank not full?'

'I gave him money for a full tank, I assure you, dear lady.'

'He must have filled half and put de udder half in his pocket, dat rascal! Where is he? I will box his ears!'

'I'm sure the tank was full, Mai. We have travelled longer than we thought.'

'Gone to find some alcohol, I'm sure, wit' all dat extra money. Let him come back, I will break dat bottle on his head!'

'I think he's just as upset as you are, Mai.'

'And where is Stotisgaon? Why are we in dis jungle?'

'Er, I think we read the map wrong. We are … somewhere else.'

Of course we read the map wrong, he reflects, not moving, holding his limp penis in his hand wistfully. The map is a square piece of paper, which means there is one right way and three wrong. Why expect Ferdinand to pick the right option, when there are three more tempting ones for the shit-wit to choose from?

He looks around and tries to guess where they are. At what point did they leave the highway? Porvorim. And then? Perhaps he should not have snatched that map from Ferdie's quivering hands, slapped him across the face with it five times, then flung it into a paddy field on the side of the road; might have come in handy just to get a location.

Darkness falls all around him like a diaphanous curtain. 'Night is coming!' comes one plaintive wail. 'Why are we in dis jungle? Don Pedro, do sumtin!' But nobody answers her question, and if Don Pedro is doing sumtin', he is doing it silently. Peace at last.

He looks around him, in no hurry to put his cock back in his pants. Branches and leaves rustle around him as if speaking a beautiful, sibilant whispery language. Stolid tree-trunks commiserate with him like ancient, silent yogis. Loamy earth, hot air greeting the cool of night and spawning dew; nature stretching and putting its feet up, quiet and restful, unminding of all the uglies in human form with their petty beefs and rancid neuroses.

Humans are cunts, really, the lot of them.

Look at him, prime example.

Goa, the land of amazing biodiversity, compared by some to the Congo and the Amazon; how much does he know of it? Cannot name more than five trees, not a single one in sight right now, oh wait, except for that banyan. All those nature hikes taken with Dad and his brothers, who were really all more like his dad's friends, older people he had no connection with.

Loved only one girl, did he ever tell her, let alone bang her or marry her? Waste, all a fucking waste. Birds are calling out to one another, birds he cannot identify even though they have lived around him all his life, calling out in precise bird-language to come on home, succinct and musical. No pointless conversation among birds, ever.

Humans are such cunts.

He hears a twig snap, followed by the sound of tall grass brushing against legs. It is a light tread and by process of elimination he knows who it is. He hurriedly zips up.

'Savio?'

He does not reply, partly because his temper has not fully abated, and he is likely to snap if aroused. But mostly it is because he wants her to come closer.

'Savio, are you there?'

He sucks her in closer with his silence. The footsteps advance, the grass yields.

'What *are* you doing there?'

'Just got him out of my system, that tall, useless stream of piss.'

'Are you talking about Ferdie?'

'Trusting him to read a map. Like asking a chimpanzee to read Shakespeare.'

A cricket party starts up close by. Savio stamps the ground lightly. They stop.

'Well, he seems to have disappeared too. That was hardly any way to treat an old man.'

'Too bad. It's been a rough day. More for me than anyone else.'

'He is very sensitive.'

'So am I.'

'He's disappeared in the dark. And he might just never come back. You humiliated him.'

Savio turns around. He stares at her silhouette. He cannot see her face at all, which is just as well.

'Listen. I don't give a rat's ass about him, is that clear? All the time it's somebody else. She is old so she's grumpy, he is eccentric so he behaves weird, he is stupid so everyone must excuse him. Well, fuck all of them. They're all assholes, you hear?'

Silhouette stares at silhouette. Not visibly, but both tremble a little.

'You think it's okay to speak like that all the time?'

'You think it's okay to treat me like I'm an idiot child all the time?'

'Did you spend every day of your life in Bombay fighting with people? Because that's what you seem to be doing here.'

'Better than being a doormat for the whole world.'

'Old people need patience and understanding.'

'Old people use their age to be tyrants. Or to be stupid. Ferdie's gone old so he gets away with being stupid. People have actually forgotten that he was born stupid.'

'He is your friend. He considers you his friend. Not like … those two over there.'

'Ah, and what are they up to right now?'

'I-I don't know. I came away. Don Pedro is comforting her. She is afraid of the dark.'

'Is he feeling her up? Undressing her with his eyes?'

'Stop that!'

'Painting her with his penis?'

'Savio!'

'That pencil is only symbolic, Angie. It's actually his penis.'

Shadowy hands go up and cup shadowy ears. 'I'm going back to them. I thought your company would be better, but I was wrong.'

'You didn't know about this when Don Pedro came to your house, tripping over his tongue? You didn't make this happen?'

He thinks he sees two pinpoints of light flash momentarily in the dark. 'I did it for Ferdinand.'

'Good, so now let them be. They're on this trip to fulfil their roles, which includes breaking my balls whenever they can. Maybe they'll hook up, get married.'

'That is a shocking thought,' she says, a hint of a frown in the voice.

'Look at the bright side. Once they get married, she'll forget about smothering you and let you live your own life.'

The frown in the voice deepens. 'He seems the demanding type. I don't want to look after him also.'

She sees a row of teeth appear in the black blob of his head. 'That's the first thought that comes to your head? Looking after him? What about looking after yourself?'

'I look after myself.' Automatic response, no conviction.

He stares at her. There are no details, but he observes the outline of her hair, now tied carelessly behind her head, strands out of place and fanned by a gentle night breeze. He observes the way her neck slopes out into her shoulders, the shoulders swooping into a waist, the waist blooming out into hips, and then the final taper down to her ankles. Flesh flowing elegantly, no sharp edges, just roundness. He wonders what underwear lurks beneath: functional and prosaic, hard wires pinching, scrunching up, trapping meat? Or lacy and yielding, caressing and soothing, going along for the walk?

He wonders what she will smell like after a day on the road. He tries to remember her smell that one night, ten years ago, that night he had . . . what was that musk?

'You think I'm being mean to you, right?' Grass sighs as he moves towards her. 'Going on and on about how you should be free?'

'I'm sure you speak from experience. Never having to look after anyone, only living for yourself.'

'See, now you're making me sound selfish. I used to send money home from Bombay, nobody talks about that.' That is a complete lie.

Her head tilts up as he advances. There is enough starlight to make out her skin, creamy with a light dusting of cocoa in it. The sheen on it, of old sweat and country air.

Animal, that was her musk, mingled with fresh soap, and that subtle perfume dotting her throat. That musk that had pulled him right in and made his lips seek her neck. And that beautiful wedding gown she had on, that beautiful wedding face she had on, happy yet bewildered, achingly sad and hopeful at the same time. He had cried that night and she had held him, her grip oscillating between warm affectionate and horribly platonic.

Tonight, her lines are softened by the heavy hand of darkness. This is Angie from ten years ago. He stops at arm's length; any closer, this soon, and he will be invading.

'We are a lot like each other, Angie,' he says in a husky voice, feeling like the ground has mysteriously tilted away but he is still miraculously on his feet. 'Just ten years back, not a care in the world. We used to smile and laugh a lot.'

Alluring lines appear on her forehead. By day they would have piled years onto her face.

'These days, the only time *you* smile or laugh is when you are making fun of something. That is not laughter. That is the braying of a donkey,' she says.

He needs a little time to recover from that. 'You're telling me you're happy.'

'As happy as anyone my age, in my situation. I don't go skipping through the fields, laughing gaily. But happy? Yes, I am.'

'Happy cooking and cleaning and being somebody's maid twenty-four hours a day?'

'So what are *you* unhappy about? Not a care in the world? Nobody to look after, no cooking, no cleaning?'

Her accuracy is deadly, he reflects. She is winning on accuracy. And reach, she seems to have a longer reach.

'First of all, I don't drink all day, damn it. I haven't had a drink in three weeks.' Not counting the buddy-bonding with Johnny Black last night, this is true. Considering there are still eleven of his brothers waiting back home, this will not be true in the future, but for now this is as fucking *veritas* as it is going to get.

'And I was busting my ass trying to get that car working the last three weeks. That is what made this whole fantasy trip possible. I work when I have to work.' He is getting a few in now, he realizes. Little jabs are good. Avoid the big hits. 'And that big mansion? It needs big money to look after it. It's falling apart all around me. Big dump is what it is.'

'Spend time on it,' she says. 'Restore it to its original glory. Be *proud* of it. It's your heritage.'

'Restore it with *what*? I've got twenty dentures, ten shirts, five pants, three socks and two underwear. That's all dear daddy left me. Do you know what it costs to restore and maintain a house like that?'

'Oh,' she says, 'it's different when you come from an orphanage. I have no cause to moan and complain because I never had a house of my own.'

Her voice is right, it belongs to the night, blending perfectly with the rustle of leaves and the mating calls of insects. But her words are all wrong.

'So,' she says softly and matter-of-factly, 'coming back to that, where is all the money you made in Bombay? You must have *something*; you were away for ten years.'

He has asked himself that same question a dozen times over without a satisfactory answer. No answer comes now either.

'Maybe your investments are all wrong,' she says. 'If we plan wisely, we can do up the house little by little. But until then,' she gently places her hand on his shoulder, 'I'll come and help you clean the place up, what do you say?'

Even through his shirt he can feel the potential strength of the fingers, the calluses on her hand. But the touch is tender, it is from ten years ago. His tongue scours his dry mouth, as if looking for words lying around that he can scoop up.

'There is no money,' he speaks through a mouthful of cotton-wool.

He sees her smile. 'I'll *still* clean your house.'

His fingers claw their way upward, finding purchase in empty air, heading towards her shoulders in the dark.

'For free,' she says solemnly.

Up, up go the fingers, like stealthy mountaineers.

'And then I want to see some of that old Savio back.'

Old Savio? Her voice seems muffled as if she is speaking from under a pile of clothes.

His fingers reach her elbows and rest lightly there. Base camp. Just a breather, and they will be on their way again.

'Angie, I missed you these ten years. I swear. I thought of you a lot.'

'Yes, I thought of you a lot too.'

'Bombay is not easy. I had to hold on to memories to stay sane. And the memory was of you, all the time.'

Saviya, while I was fucking her, I thought of you the whole time. Maybe even cried out your name but Saviya never noticed. Or just let it slide, happy to be pity-fucked.

She rubs one of his shoulders tenderly. A blood fist rockets into his brain. From there, it bounces and plummets back into his loins. He feels like those machines at amusement parks, where strong men swing hammers to make the bell go ding at the top.

'So is it a deal?'

'Ug, what deal?' A centrifuge machine seems to have started up in the pit of his stomach, hurling sensation outward.

'The old Savio comes back. The same—'

Fingers scurry up her firm biceps like fleet-footed spiders. They reach the spur of her shoulders, then ski uphill the rest of the way to the slope of her neck.

'Baby, I never went away,' he says, gasping like he is starved of oxygen. He pulls her into him, head first, making her totter, and smothers her lips with his own.

Dry, is his first impression. Dry, not as in temporarily dehydrated. Dry, as in a topographical phenomenon, as in no rain clouds come this way, ever. Her lips part a little. His tongue snakes in, thirstily seeking the moisture that the surface is denied. Perhaps an old water-table, left over from when this patch of earth was young…

Something loud explodes in his right ear. Even as the tinnitus starts up, he becomes aware of a smarting sensation on his face. By the time strong hands push him back, his mind has gone into full-blown shock.

The silhouettes square off, but there is a change in the language and vocabulary of each. One is now tiger-ish, and the other distinctly sheepish.

'*What* are you doing? Are you *drunk*?'

That hurts, that really hurts. Hurt takes the path of least resistance, and nestles in comfortably with the anger that has already been there earlier.

'Jesus Christ! Was that necessary?' he asks with feeling, rubbing the side of his face.

An edifice is crumbling in his head, an edifice of commonality, of an alliance against the rest of the fucked-up world, of shared childhood memories, of spiritual bonding. Everything falls with a crash and he stares at the wreckage in mute, dismal disbelief.

'Have you gone *mad*, Savio?'

He wishes then that she could see his eyes. They are asking the hundred questions he has no voice for, his mouth the mortar and pestle that smashes and crushes words before they can tumble out.

She doesn't stalk off, leaving him there, humiliated and wrecked. She stays and burns the dark space between them with her eyes, tearing little strips out of him.

He dredges up a voice from somewhere, something that sounds like it comes from the mouth of a corpse with a bad throat. 'So, you are thinking that I'm good enough for a little charity, good enough for a house-clean, but one peck on the lips and suddenly I'm the devil? Is that it?'

'What *I* am thinking? What are *you* thinking?'

'So, who am I to you, Angie? Just some stranger, some guy from the past? Who means nothing?' His lips tremble and his body shakes. 'Just some … some … did I never mean anything to you?'

'Don't you *dare* start feeling sorry for yourself again. That's all you ever do.'

'So what was all that "we" stuff about? We'll clean up the house, we'll do this, we'll do that? What the fuck was all that about?'

Eyes glitter in her black face and her mouth hisses, 'We. You and I. I help you and you take my help. That's what friends do.'

'*Friends? Friends?!* Jesus Christ, *friends*!' He sobs, thinking he can go on and on echoing that word like a madman. 'Haven't you had enough of that *friends* bullshit? Back then we were friends, *now* we are friends. *When* is this *friends* bullshit going to stop?' He wants to cry now.

She does not reply, just stares at him.

'And when *friends* kiss? What happens then?' He wishes she would say something, so he can concentrate on her words and not on her heaving breasts that now seem as distant and unreachable as another galaxy. 'You are not in school anymore,' he rasps. 'You're not sixteen anymore, hanging out in playgrounds, watching your … your … body grow, trying to hide your tits. *You're thirty-five years old, for God's sake!* Grow up!'

The crickets go silent as if holding their breaths, waiting for her comeback. The two silhouettes heave and pant in the dark.

'I'm going back there,' she says. 'I suggest you stay where you are and *think*.'

'Yes, go back there. Crawl back into that sexless, servile life of yours.'

Her body goes into a little shivery spasm as she contemplates an answer. Then the grass sighs and parts as her skirt swishes away into the black night.

The crickets start up again in her wake.

2

FERDIE

He wishes he had not walked so far away. When he had started walking, he had resolved to never stop, to keep going till his body dropped.

His initial intention had been to circumnavigate the globe, twice if necessary. He had not counted on the dark being a solid obstacle in his path, like a spongy wall that he could poke with his finger. It had slowed him down. Then it stopped him as surely as if he had smacked his nose on it.

Now he just stands there, a forlorn human being, on a landscape as dark and alien to him as his own cloudy personality. His thoughts, which have been floating behind his head as he walked, now catch up and blow a lonely wind through his head, one that churns up dust and detritus of the past, near and distant.

Barely twenty minutes ago, when the last sting of the map-slap had worn away, when the map had been flung into the field, he had stood there motionless, like a car at a filling station, topping up on humiliation and death. After he had crammed in all he could, he had willingly let it spill over, feeling the cold prickle of self-hate as it cascaded down, his skin cringing from its touch. Then he had set out, with a full tank, determined never to stop. If he encountered the ocean, as he knew he would, he'd merely walk around it.

Fifteen minutes and two hundred yards later, after squelching through wet mud and tripping five times on hidden roots, he has stopped. Now he is torn: the engine of self-loathing and expiation urges him on, but his fear of dark slams the brakes.

He turns on his axis slowly, and is astonished to find that at all points of the compass, he only encounters black, an impenetrable black. Vertigo washes over him, his legs crumble and he sits down heavily on a wet patch of earth. As moisture spreads all over his hind quarters, an unnecessarily mischievous thought surfaces: snakes love paddy fields, particularly wet, squelchy ones. And they like the night.

He springs to his feet like a rocket trying to flee the atmosphere. His legs tremble for a couple of scary moments, but they hold. He teeters in the dark, trying not to cry. At no cost is he going to cry. Crying like a baby is not part of the expiation process.

Even as a boy, he has never been attacked so viciously, and with so much anger and disgust writ on the face of the attacker. Physically, there was very little pain as the paper whipped his face, but psychologically, spiked boots have stomped all over him. As he stands there, swaying and bumping into only blackness with every oscillation, trying not to whimper, he aches all over. He feels bruised and battered.

How far away he is from anything good, so far he cannot even measure it, other than know that it can never be reached again. There is only one memory left. All the other trillions of cells packed with information about his childhood and teens and later adult years have died, blacked out forever, data irretrievably lost. Recollection and recall are distilled down to a handful of remaining cells that contain only Millie.

Millie in her ballgown that one time they went up to Panjim and danced to Johnny and his Jolly Lads … her smile more dazzling than her pearl necklace, the hint of her breasts chocolatey warm and luminescent as they disappeared into that silvery gown, her hand fan in tremulous motion, urging him to dance with her, while Johnny and the lads belted out a medley of cha-chas and twists.

The other time, in her strappy sundress perched side-saddle atop the bar of his bicycle, his nose too shy to snuggle her neck but enjoying the girl-scents that billowed out of her hair and thinking, this surely was the heaven that priests and parents spoke about.

Millie, his soft peach. How can he explain to people that he could never eat *any* pulpy fruit after that?

Three months of his life. She was in Pocolim to stay with some ailing relative before she went back to resume her – what was it she did, something secretarial up in Madgaon – and he was gearing up to become a deckhand on a steamer. He should never have left, *never have left*.

Millie, the reason he woke up every morning. Otherwise what is there to wake up for? Millie, the last thing he thought of before he went to sleep at night. And later, Millie, the cause of his insomnia.

Millie on the quay, waving him goodbye. That dirty water of Vasco Port, every second taking him exactly five feet away from her. When he looked up again, only sea, no land, no Millie.

The letter he wrote. The first of many they would write each other. She would say, come back, Ferdie, come back, or something like that.

He shuts his eyes. He can hear Rosalina's treble squeaks demanding to know what is going on, and the confused angry replies provided by the others. They all hate him.

He balls his fingers into fists and opens his eyes. Outside, there is still only black. He looks up and sees stars, thousands of stars. They wink coldly and remotely. Everyone has fled planet Earth, gone away to those distant lights, and left him all alone – a lost, abandoned, blind, bruised and battered, useless piece of shit.

He still does not cry.

3
ANGIE

She sees the silhouette of the car ahead and stops. There is one solitary road-lamp ten feet from it that flickers on and off. When it chooses to cast its weak glow, the car is briefly illuminated, as is the broken road, and the dead light-poles and dusty trees that line it. Then the image disappears, leaving behind a faint hologram of its existence.

This is far enough, she reckons.

Far away from Savio, and not near enough to her mother-in-law, who has decided to follow Don Pedro's counsel and not stray too far from the car. She hears their voices, and is satisfied that there does not seem to be a tone of distress in them.

Don Pedro, if he thinks he is going to woo his way into Rosie's life and home, he is welcome, as long as he picks up after himself, shares cleaning chores and brings some of his own money in.

There is someone for everyone, she thinks, and if they like each other, let them have each other.

She sits down upon the dewy grass, perfectly equidistant from a spurned and furious Savio and a wooed and pampered mother-in-law, and wonders who there is for her.

Pocolim. Her mind goes from door to door like a secret service squad delivering midnight knocks, starting from the east end and moving in. There are lots of young men her age, she reflects, and she mentally pulls them out of their homes and lines them up. She snaps off a blade of grass and sucks on it, tasting its leafy, muddy, dewy essence, and moves through the only village, the only community she has ever known, house by house.

She has no idea what the time is, but she knows she has plenty of time. She is determined to come to some kind of conclusion tonight; the issue of her life is off the shelf.

Savio is not in the line-up. He is the Outsider, the guy who left, who started out with piss and vinegar, but instead of walking a straight line, kept veering to the left like a gimp-footed drunk, until he landed back in the same place he tried to get away from. He carried out, in his personality, a tiny amount of Pocolim, and come back in with a truckload of Bombay on his shoulders, an unwieldy weight that he isn't used to, that keeps toppling him face first in mud.

She examines the line desultorily. They are a nose-picking bunch, an arse-scratching bunch, they are all drunks in some measure, they are all church-going, God-fearing and Rosie-terrified. They have a feeble glow about them, like their life-force has never really lit up, and if she wants to get more depressed, she only has to look at each and every face and project it twenty years into the future. They are all interchangeable, their faces with their names, Gregory, Edward, Kenny, Benny, Lenny, Alfred, Robert; throw away their names and call them all Pocolim. They look like Pocolim, talk, think and act like it. They have not had one original idea amongst the lot of them, ever. There are other villages, but why will anything be different?

She lies down on the grass and looks up at the stars. She can hear Rosie and Pedro's voices. She hears Rosie giggle and Don Pedro chuckle. Somewhere in the field around her is Ferdie, cowering from them, probably weeping. Everyone playing their role, nothing ever changing. She feels tired, disgusted and helpless.

Why did she never leave? How come her feet never picked themselves and just walked out of that door? Go somewhere, get some vocational training, throw herself at the world and take what came? Never knew how. Her feet, her brain, never read the instruction manual on how to work themselves. She just took out the batteries and stayed.

She sits up.

The Bombay that Savio carries around on his back, like a sack full of stones that he keeps throwing at the world, she wants to take a closer look at that. He had sobbed on her wedding night, he had sobbed *on* her on her wedding night, his tears soaking her neck and her dress, told her he was going away and she was the reason. She had let him, she had not pushed him away, not even when Gabo had blundered in, already three drinks down, staring at them all clasped together like that. Her sad eyes had met Gabo's drunk ones over Savio's shoulder, and then Gabo had grinned his weak *oh-shucks-I'm-sorry* grin and slunk out, and probably got hammered some more. And an hour later he was dead.

Angie sighs, a long sigh that parts the night air.

She gets to her feet and starts walking. She traces back the soft plop of stones to a shadowy figure sitting on a little mound throwing them in a dejected manner. She comes in from the side to avoid being hit by one, choosing sound over stealth, walking as though she is fifty pounds heavier and a whole lot clumsier. His arm goes up with its latest missile, and pauses at the top. She hears a carefully constructed sigh that says *there goes my peace* and sees him get to his feet.

'Please don't get up.'

Dusting his pants now, his movements vibrating with an unspecifiable frequency.

'I just want to sit here,' she says softly, non-threateningly.

'There are fifty other paddy fields. Maybe five hundred. Go find your own.'

'I want to sit *here*.'

'So sit. I'm off.' And he moves away, his shoulders hunched over.

'Will you *please* sit down?'

He stops and turns around. His outline shivers like a plucked string.

'Listen, Angie, why don't you fuck off? What have you come here for? To hold my hand and feel sorry for me?'

'No.'

'Well, then bugger off, because I have nothing to say to you.'

She has never experienced this before, but has read about it a lot, in the girlie magazines at Dr Britto's clinic. The ego, the rejection, the hurt. How often has she wistfully wished to actually see all of that first hand, normal stuff that happens in normal relationships to normal people, either to be its cause or to feel the effect.

She is careful to keep the thrill out of her body language, and is glad that the dark hides the excitement on her face.

'Being mature again, Savio?'

'Don't use words you don't know the meaning of, okay?' Even the trees seem to wince as bitterness scorches the air. 'You're on some other planet. Planet Angie. Stay there.'

Even as the words lash her, she shivers in a breathless glee. Gathering herself, she hisses. 'So tough you are.'

'What?'

'To use any language you choose to use. Especially to a girl?'

'Girl!' he spits out.

'I *will* come and smack your face. I am not frightened of you, Savio. Of your language or your stupid attitude.'

The hostile vibrations in his outline stutter momentarily.

'I have nothing to say to you,' he says feebly. 'Please go.'

No 'bugger off', no 'fuck off' this time.

He is learning something here: if you are going to be angry all the time, make sure you are *angrier* than the other person. Otherwise there's no point; you will just get beaten.

'But you had a lot to say earlier. Half an hour ago. Don't you remember?'

'That was a mistake. It should never have happened. I don't know what I was thinking.'

'You were thinking? Actually thinking?'

'I was thinking that there was something there. But I was wrong. You're as frigid as a polar bear's tit.'

She takes two sudden steps towards him and he shuffles back hastily.

'Have you ever thought of anybody but yourself? Ever?'

'Oh, please. Don't start with that now.'

His body language has recovered some of its snarling, wounded vocabulary, and she lets it, knowing she can crush it anytime she chooses to.

'No, Mr Mature, tell me. You know me, you thought there was something there. What did you think was there?'

'You … and I. You and I, we were … you and I were close, remember?'

'Yes, we were eighteen. No, you were eighteen, and I was twenty-five.'

'Age has nothing to do with it! Do you remember how we were?'

'Yes, I was your best friend's fiancée.'

That clocks him one, which he blinks and recovers from. 'You only remember what you want to remember. That's why there is no point in talking to you.'

'I was *not* your best friend's fiancée?'

'That is not relevant!' he roars. 'All I'm saying is I'm not some bloody stranger who is hitting on you. We have something … *had* something.'

'Go on.'

'If Gabo hadn't been around, it would've been me. I mean, if I had stuck around and—'

'If you had stuck around . . .' She muses. 'No, I'm glad you went away.'

'Go find another paddy field. Why are you here?'

'No, I mean that in a good way.'

'You're just like her, you know that?'

'Like who?'

'Like who,' he mimics. 'Like that fat sow. Hurt people, kick them around, taunt them.'

'Oh, Savio.' She sighs. 'You are feeling rejected and humiliated because I . . . spurned you?' She has never used the word 'spurned', and it thrills her as it rolls off her tongue.

'Spurned me? You keep spurning life.'

'Come here, I want to make it up to you.'

'No, you bugger off. Hey! Hey!'

But he hasn't moved back fast enough. She is almost standing on his toes, her mouth an inch away from his throat. He almost pisses his pants at the suddenness, the strength and the stealth with which she is on him.

His breath catches in his throat as her breasts touch his body, compress a little and stop. They stand there in that state of dynamic tension, pull and push in perfect equilibrium. He stands his ground, but more like a deer in the headlights.

'The last time I was kissed,' says her mouth to his throat, every syllable and consonant burning his skin with hot feather-bullets, 'was on my wedding day.'

'It was fifteen minutes before my husband choked and died,' she says, 'eating his own figurine on top of the cake. It wasn't a chicken bone, as the story goes. It was the figurine, and it wasn't made of icing, it was made of plastic.'

Her mother-in-law was trying to save money.

Her son was so drunk, he tried to swallow it whole, and by the time he found out, it was stuck halfway down his throat. Nobody was around to save him in time.

There is a respite from the feather-bullets as she pauses to inhale. He shuts his eyes.

'That was my first and last kiss. And it was ten years ago. And you think I did something wrong, slapping you today … Is your ego hurt? Where does it hurt?'

'No,' he tells her forehead; he cannot manage anything more challenging than that. 'No.'

'You think after waiting ten years, a girl would not like it to be done properly?'

'No. I mean, yes.'

'Good. So now finish what you started.'

What has he started? He opens his eyes and blinks to clear his head, but the mechanism seems to be a little bust. He can smell her hairline directly under his nose; the hairline, where two terrains meet, old shampoo mingling with old face wash, both basted in old dried sweat.

'The ground is a bit hard,' he says in another man's voice, wondering why anyone would say anything as stupid as that.

She shrugs and leans into him. 'I don't know any better. I'm a virgin.'

4

ROSIE

When Don Pedro unpacks his bags, it is as if he has actually planned and plotted for the car to come to a dead halt miles from anywhere. The gleam in his eye – which goes unnoticed, because there is no one around to see it except Rosie, who is gleam-illiterate and half-blind – suggests a sinister omniscience.

Rosie, who has been composing sword-sharp paragraphs with which she will tear Ferdinand's head off when that coward emerges, is suddenly mesmerized by Don Pedro's smooth unhurried movements. He is whistling as he works, a tune that is so note-perfect and trilly, it could have come from a genius nightingale that has somehow absorbed an entire oeuvre of some lovelorn Fado lyricist. His composure in the teeth of a potentially horrible night that does not involve a comfortable nightgown, oils and unguents, a mattress that buffers and absorbs is so impressive that it rattles her.

She has never met a human who is more in charge of a situation than she is. It excites her but also makes her resentful.

But when a crisp, dry, double-layered, emperor-size sheet is pulled out and unfurled upon that cold and insect-teeming grass, she utters a sigh that drips with erotic innuendo. 'Oh, Don Pedro.'

There is barely a fluctuation in the smooth notes emerging from his lips as Don Pedro smiles diabolically in the dark. In a voice that could only have rumbled down from a benign heaven, he says, 'I would have offered you a chair, but in the circumstances, allow me.'

His silhouette reaches out and two warm, strong hands envelope her own. Her legs move of their own will, scuffing grass and scattering insects as she moves towards the magic carpet that this efficient wizard had laid out. 'Gently now,' the God-like words rumble as his grip grows firm.

She does not notice the stiffening of the body and the tightness in his jaws. She lowers herself onto the sheet, which is to say her muscles bear the weight a third of the way down. Don Pedro, veins bulging in his neck and eyeballs threatening to burst, takes up the slack on the rest. The last six inches are actually free fall, but Earth, used to massive asteroids and angry meteors bashing it all its life, bears it manfully.

Rosie racks her memory for proper sitting etiquette. Her skirt is way too tight for cross-legged and her joints way too stiff for the Japanese tea-ceremony pose. She settles for reclining on her side, propped up on one elbow, imagining she looks a bit like Cleopatra, which is not very lady-like, more like slutty-royal, but it will have to serve.

She sees Don Pedro reaching into his bag and out comes something that clinks pleasantly, making her flesh quiver. The streetlamp in the background brings her environment into brief flashes of focus, and she does not like anything she sees, apart from the mesmerizing movements of the artist. He looms over her, solid as a rock and twice as dependable, holding something in each hand. Then he is by her side, on the soft, warm blanket. A candle is lit and placed in the grass six inches away; the flame reveals a bottle and two glasses on the sheet between them, something thick, golden and lava-like glowing inside the bottle.

'One of the finest brandies known to man,' he says in a voice like velvet-coated thunder. 'Azteca de Oro, which I am sure you have had many a time in your life, madam.'

How can she say no, she has never heard of the damn thing? She merely smiles and puts on an expression of possessing deep knowledge, which is completely wasted even had there been sufficient light, because Don Pedro is looking at her body and not her face, like a man in the throes of a dream trying to hide his delight that this is all real.

'My husband and I,' she says, temporarily forgetting what he is called, 'we used to have evenings like dis all de time. I tol' you, no? He was a shippie and—'

'Tonight is to us, madam.' The sound of a cork popping, liquid sloshing elegantly into one glass.

'He was a shippie and—'

'Is he here?'

'W'at?'

'Your husband. Is he here?' While her jowls jiggle wordlessly, he fills the other glass. He hands one to her and waves the other in a circle, indicating the cosmos in general. 'Perhaps he is somewhere up above, floating on the clouds, looking down at you and smiling in approval. But tonight, it's just us. To us, madam.' He clinks her glass. 'May you continue to inspire, and may this humble servant of yours continue to be inspired.'

Well, when he puts it like that … His words speak of being humbled by her, so why is it she who feels weak and helpless? As if allergic to dilemmas, she hurls the brandy down her throat like medicine.

Azteca de Oro may have been a top-shelf brandy, one of the finest known to man, but there is none of that in the bottle. Rosalina's gullet burns as Doctor's Brandy, brewed in Goa, rakes its talons down her throat. By the time it reaches her stomach, it has curled itself into a fireball with the feel and texture of a chain-mail fist.

The ground shakes as Rosie goes into an involuntary spasm, and a few fruit flies are incinerated on the spot as she belches out angry fumes. She spasms for a bit, losing a large chunk of her Cleopatra composure in the process, grinding out a crater of pulped grass and crushed bugs underneath, and when it all goes quiet finally, she looks at Don Pedro's shadowy outline with smoggy eyes, her bosom heaving, her mouth drooling, her muscles all over her body slack.

'Whoooooeee,' she says in smoky, school-girly voice. 'Dis is good stuff, Don Pedro. Dis is wat dey call de bee's knees. Haaaaaaagh.'

'Indeed, madam,' says Don Pedro, sipping from his glass, aware that he will also have to help her to her feet at some point in the evening. The thought fills him with an unnameable fear, and like a sensible warrior, he decides to cross that bridge when he comes to it. He refills her glass. 'I see you have the fine palette of a sailor on shore-leave, madam. No doubt you get it from your husband.'

'My husband,' she repeats in the throat-charred manner of a noir-vamp with a carton-a-day habit. 'Whoooeeee, wat was his name? Albert, yes, yes, Albert. You t'ink he is watching?'

'Let him. Why should he have all the fun in heaven?'

'Lots of fun he had always, non-stop. Dese sailors. Dirty people, no rispeck for dere wives at home. Not my Albert. He was fait'ful.' She grows morose for a moment, then hiccups and has another swig, a more measured one. 'Whoooeeee.'

'And why would he be unfaithful? A magnificent woman like you waiting for him at home?'

'Yes, yes.' Another swig, more gurgles of pain and pleasure, the air around them now thick with her belch-gas. 'Bleddy rascal he was. I tol' him. Albert, you come back smelling of udder wimmin, if I see lipstick on your collar, dere will be no person in de world more angry dan me.'

'Must have been hard on him.'

'He was sweet. Always fait'ful. A wife knows dese t'ings.'

Is that moistness he sees in her eyes? A little quiver on her lips?

'If I had been your husband, madame, I would never have gone to sea.'

'All lies. All you men, all lies. And if you don't go to sea, den who will pay for everyt'ing, your fadder?'

Don Pedro goes into caution mode. He has been blindsided by her before. He squints and moves in close. Yes, her eyes are a little moist, and behind the wet curtain dances the twin fires of the candlelight. But as he looks closer, he realizes it is her eyeballs themselves that are bouncing all over the place like free-spirited ravers. Does she have some gastric bypass line that makes alcohol flow to her brain directly?

'How is the brandy, dear lady?'

'Call me Rosie. Nobody else does.'

'Rosie is a wonderful name. Somehow it suits you.'

'Even Albert called me udder names, never Rosie.'

Don Pedro sips and observes. She is having a little difficulty staying propped up on her elbow, he can tell. He excuses himself and gets to his feet.

She is saying to his ankles, 'Pussycat was his fav'rit. Is dat supposed to make me feel good, calling me pussycat? In public? In front of friends? Wat if he said it in church by mistake? One time he called me Estella. Anudder time it was sunmtin else, sumtin foreign. Crazy fellow. Dat is why I got a pussycat in his memory. Oooooh, Don Pedro, dis is … t'ank you.'

'You looked uncomfortable,' he says, stuffing two big pillows under her torso. She sinks into them with a sigh and a belch. It will be impossible now, he reflects, to hoist her to her feet. This is a job for a tow-truck.

'Now the picture is perfect,' he says, almost to himself, but loud enough. She stares at him in a cock-eyed manner, addressing his left ear. 'Please sit down. I cannot look up and talk to you.'

'I wish I had my easel out now. And I wish there was light.'

'You want to paint me sleeping like dis? People will t'ink I am lazy.'

'There are a few details that need changing, but you are perfect.'

'You can't put de glass in. People will t'ink I have drunk and passed out.'

'You are a very sensual woman, aren't you, Rosie?'

'Perhaps de bottle. So dey know I'm not drinking jus anytin'.'

'Lucien Freud would eat his heart out right now. He would kill himself if he saw this. Madame, you are perfect.'

'An' stop moving. Why are you moving so much?'

'Let me refill your glass.'

'Whoooeee,' she says in anticipation. 'Please pour small. Ladies don't drink as much as you men. No, little more, jus a little more. O-kay, t'anks.'

'They held back, you know? Botticelli, Rubens. Pah, the whole concept of Rubenesque. Flesh, flesh, they all wanted flesh, but when they had it, they held back. Freud went further, he broke the boundary, painted outside of it.'

Rosie yawns like a hippo being offered a loaf of bread. 'And den?'

'But he had never seen this. Never dreamed that this existed.'

'Which Floyd? Not dat useless fellow in the pork shop?'

'I cannot wait, Rosie. I cannot wait.' He kneels by her side and slowly strips off her dress with his talon-like eyes. His hands cut through the sweet-scented night air, tracing circles as he drapes an imaginary blanket around her – the same blanket she is resting on – drapes it in various ways, first with one and then both breasts exposed, he plays with show of thigh and stomach, plays with light and shadow in the space between, getting progressively dry-mouthed and flushed with red-hot blood all over. His body feels weightless, as though floating on a cloud.

'Wat are you doing, Don Pedro?' she snaps. 'Magic tricks wit' your hands? I cannot see anyt'ing in dis light.'

'It's all magic, dear lady. Will you call me Pedro?'

'Dat will be too familiar. I'm sorry, no.'

'These titles are stifling. They form barriers.'

'I hardly know you,' she says primly, her mouth pinching up disapprovingly.

'That, my dear lady, is all going to change tomorrow.'

'Oh Pedro, the words you use make … dey give me a funny feeling in my stomach. Haaaaaagh.'

'Drink slowly, my dear. There is plenty more where that came from.'

'We should eat, no? All dis drinking … eeeeeeeeek, who is dat?'

Don Pedro, shocked out of his waking wet-dream, whirls around, except he is on his haunches and ends up with his head in the grass, brandy down his shirt and convinced he has twisted an ankle. Glancing up, he thinks one of the lamp-posts, following a very badly written horror plot, has come to life and crept up on them, but then it speaks.

'I have come to tell you my decision,' it says, in a familiar voice.

'Jesus friggin Christ,' Don Pedro snarls at a blade of grass that is probing one nostril. 'Who do you think you are? Some goddamn commando? Creeping up like that?'

The lamp-post twitches, considering the question. 'I wanted to knock,' it says, 'but dere was no door.'

'Clear your goddamn throat next time.'

'My t'roat is not blocked. I have come to tell you my decision.'

'Who gives a goddamn for your goddamn decision?'

'Tomorrow I will get petrol. Den I want all of you to go back and I will carry on to look for Millie.'

'Who asked you anything?' roars Don Pedro, resentful of everything.

The lamp-post takes a step forward, revealing violent trysts with Mother Earth who seems to have slapped and punched him. But there is a glint in the eye that suggests he has borne it all like a man.

Don Pedro hears a giggle behind him.

'Is dat grass in your ears? Or is dat your hair?'

Ferdie reaches up and gives a tug. 'It's hair,' he says morosely. 'De scissor does not reach everywhere. I don't want to bodder anybody anymore. Tomorrow at de crack of dawn I'm off.'

'Well, why don't you bugger off now?'

Again that careful consideration. 'It is dark. I am afraid of de dark.' A little hand-wringing follows, the kind that precedes difficult words. 'Dat is anudder fear I have to overcome.'

'Listen to him,' sneers Don Pedro. 'Overcomes his fear of dark by walking in the day.'

Rosie is attempting to sit up; in her vision Ferdie is canted at an impossible sixty-degree angle and it is giving her vertigo. Eventually she gives up the struggle and tries to align just her head with the vertical but does not possess the neck to do it with. 'Come here and sit down,' she squeaks, letting her mass settle into the ground again, tired and out of breath.

Ferdinand does not move. He has been visited by wisdom during the last couple of hours all by himself in the paddy field, and one of the points in that insight is that he must keep a safe distance from dubious objects. 'I have said what I came to say. Now I will find a tree to go to sleep under,' a shudder racks his voice and body, 'somewhere around here.' A long, lingering look at the candle follows.

'Shut up, bleedy eeeediot,' Rosie gurgles pleasantly. 'Come and sit. Have brandy.'

'There's a nice big tree over there,' Don Pedro offers, pointing.

''sgood brandy. Haaaagh.'

'But only two glasses, I'm afraid,' Don Pedro, still pointing.

'Hic. Urrrrp. So wat. You can drink from mine.'

'T'ank you, but no,' says Ferdinand, drawing upon another nugget of the visited wisdom, of never polluting stoicism with weakness of the flesh.

Rosie struggles to get upright again, makes it about three inches this time, then collapses, giggling. 'Don't – don't make me get up, udderwise I will come and smack your head. Sit down, you bleddy fool. All dose nights you used to come over, drinking wit' Albert. Forgot?'

Ferdinand has not so much forgotten as he is not quite sure it had ever happened. Figment of his imagination, perhaps. Wishful thinking, most likely.

'Used to come to our house, Don Pedro, he and Albert, bot' shippies and he used to drink all Albert's fine whisky. Now look at him, all high and mighty. After Albert disapp— passed, what happened to him, God knows. Sit!'

Wisdom prevails again and prevents Ferdinand from counter-asking, 'What happened to you?' Instead he concentrates on not getting yanked forward like an unwilling puppy at the word 'sit', and the tone of *or-else* it comes wrapped in.

'As diff'rint as a pea and a potato, he and Albert. He was the pea and Albert the potato, round like me.'

'Boring vegetable, the pea,' says Don Pedro.

'Welcome change from de potato, sometimes. Gives me gout, all dat starch.'

Ferdinand looks at her sympathetically and, though the others miss it, with a touch of envy as well.

'Let him go where he wants to, Rosie,' Don Pedro says, seizing the moment, nipping a nostalgia trip in the bud. 'A little quiet reflection might make a man out of him after all.'

'Nonsense. I cannot drink all dis by myself. Whooeee.' She goes off into a peal of giggles normally heard only behind walls of Happy Homes for the Unhinged. 'It is very bad for my legs.'

Ferdie's feet break free, taking a step closer to the blanket. 'G-g-gout, madam?' he asks.

'No, no, it makes dem spread, whooeee.' She thumps the mattress and earth winces. 'Sit, I order you!'

Like a hooked trout, Ferdie's feet almost do not touch the ground en route to the blanket.

5
SAVIO

It's karma, he thinks. Well, what do you expect? he asks Orion, who is spread-eagled above him like some voyeur peering down through a glass ceiling. All that crap they tell you about fucking a virgin. He is exhausted, finished. His postcoital cigarette feels as heavy as a pool cue in his fingers.

Is that sex they have just had? Or a Hong Kong kung-fu movie choreographed fight?

Thrust, parry, feint, block, yield, strike. Angie has muscles. And they have been conditioned to counter every amorous manoeuvre, grope and feel like a trained ninja.

There had been desire and there had been fright. There had been breathless yearning and there had been iron-muscled resistance. There had been collapsing surrender and then a sudden second-wind of vicious below-the-belt techniques. Press the gas pedal and the brake at the same time, and you get the idea.

Well, serves you right for fucking your best friend's widow, Orion tells him.

He turns around to look at Angie. They are a mess, both of them, aren't they? His tee-shirt is torn, his elbows bruised, his head concussed. His lower lip is swollen and his balls hurt like the dickens. There is mud and grass in his hair and eyes and down his shirt. When he finally pulled his pants up, they came with clods of dew-soaked earth that is now making his butt itch like crazy.

She, on the other hand, bathed in starlight from a trillion miles away, looks like she is growing out of the ground, a fertile, sensuous, goddess-symbol of Mother Earth. She seems to be checking her body parts as she lies on her back, like him, staring up at the night sky, skirt rucked up high, panties ripped off and thrown away, her dress lying around her shoulders, her bra askew. One hand is now on an exposed breast, then scampers down to her bush, back to the stomach, her fingers stroking and searching.

He reaches out and puts a hand on her stomach, flinching involuntarily when she makes contact, her hand over his, remembering that just twenty minutes ago she might have tried to break his fingers, either in self-defence or ecstasy, he will never know.

'You okay, baby?' he asks, the words feeling strange and alien, but somehow necessary and imperative.

She nods, not at him, but at the sky.

Was it good for you? he asks her voicelessly, telepathically, searching the airwaves for her answer and picking up nothing. Was it good for you, almost biting my lip off, knocking my nose askew, gouging canals down my back, nearly fracturing my cock?

'Would you like a cigarette?' he asks loudly instead. 'Like, just a tradition you know? Afterwards?'

She is quiet, reflective, unnerving, like she has a million things to say, but not to him. He reaches for the packet and yelps as pain flares out from his third finger, on which she had bitten down like a dog trying to crunch a bone when he had tried to muffle her banshee yells and moans.

He lights a cigarette and tries to relax, tries to hush the pockets of pain that scream on silently, tries to remember just the pleasure moments, like when she had first gripped his penis at the base, all hard and smooth as warm marble, that ivory-tusk texture which had taken him a while to build up, so startled and frightened had he been at first. Like a guy just been told he has won the lottery.

Made it worth the bloody arcs she left behind when the fingernails dug in. Those will now need some antiseptic cream urgently. He smokes on, shooting sideward glances occasionally.

'You okay, baby? Really, you okay?'

'Yes, I'm okay. Lying and watching the stars,' she says, in a voice that is barely above a whisper.

'Come here and show me that you're okay. I want to see. Come here.'

'No. No need.' Again, whispered, as if it hurt to speak normally.

'Talking is good, baby. It's nice to talk, despite all the stuff they tell you about how men just like to turn around and fall asleep.'

Especially since this is not really a bed we are lying on, this hard fucking ground not exactly the best place to turn around and go to sleep. And not when pain is rising out of every square inch like heat haze on a blazing desert road.

'Talk. What is that, also a tradition?'

'Well, not if you don't want to,' he says, a little stung. 'But my God, this ... this thing ... what just happened, I thought you would like to talk about it, y'know.'

'No, not really.'

He smokes on, blowing rings at the centre of Orion's belt. He will have to teach her, gently and patiently, not to jump so violently on his cock when she is on top, pounding his scrotum with her springy, taut ass, and definitely not jump so high that she is almost airborne but not quite, his tip still inside her, and then free-fall clumsily like a sack of laundry. Penises get ruptured that way.

He is going to have to get stronger, he realizes, pump weights maybe, in order to control that muscular bounce.

Oh and yes, get her to trim her fingernails, until she learns how to use them.

'Back there, for a moment, I swear I thought she was going to come running to check. I'm surprised the nearest village did not come running to check.'

'Who? Who are you talking about?'

'You were making a bit of sound, you know.'

'Who would come to check?'

Maybe her brains are a little scrambled, he has fucked her so much?

'Never mind,' he sighs, wanting to shut up but his mouth motors on. 'Though, speaking of which, it's gonna be fun when she finds out.'

Smugly satisfied is how he feels. Sweet revenge delivered. I am fucking your adopted daughter now, your daughter-in-law, widow of your only son. Sure, go ahead and hate me now.

'Savio, who are you talking about? You're mumbling and babbling, you know that?'

And when he tells her:

'Again you are talking about Mai? You are always talking about Mai. Why do we always have to talk about Mai?'

'Angie baby, don't be naive. What are you going to tell her about us?'

That seems to get her attention. She actually turns over, props herself up on one elbow and peers at him. Her earth-breasts flop down to one side, gleaming with perspiration. 'Why should I tell her anything about us? Have you gone mad?'

'What do you mean?' He does not mean to sound alarmed, but that is how it comes out.

She doesn't reply. There is a dangerously confident aspect to her. He lights another cigarette.

'What do you mean you're not going to tell her? Is this a one-time thing, that is all this is to you?'

Why do we ask questions we don't want to hear answers to? Stupid brain, why can't you shut up?

'No, I didn't say that. I am hoping there will be more times,' she whispers. 'And I am hoping it will get better also.'

'What do you mean, better?'

'What do you mean? This was the best it ever gets?'

'Er, no . . . but—'

'So, better.' She falls back onto her back.

'You didn't make it any easier for me,' he chokes in protest. He continues to stare at her. She is a vault, whose main door he has managed to crack open, barely, only to see a dozen more inside, each with their own insidious locks and tumblers and cryptic combinations. The burglar in him is flummoxed. Break and entry is supposed to be an easy thing, like 1-2-3; this is more the cube root of pi to the tenth decimal place.

All those frigid years, neuroses locked away. This isn't a job of finesse and watch-maker fingers; he has to burn this house down once and for all. Fuck the burglar approach, try arsonist instead.

He gets up and straddles her, registering the look of mild surprise and – is that annoyance? Probably.

'My sky,' she says.

'What?'

'You're in the way of my sky.'

He laughs, almost scornfully. 'I've got better stuff for you.'

She puts her hands behind her head. 'Really? What?' Genuine curiosity in her voice.

'Tonight's our night, Angie. And there's lots left of it.'

'What are we going to do that is so different, this time?'

He leans into her face. She still has that flush, he only has to pick up from where they stopped. And his cock, like a wounded soldier, seems to be shakily getting ready for another round. 'Try not to fight me so much this time,' he hisses, kissing the valley between her breasts. How well Mother Earth has chosen her representative, he thinks, his mouth going dry.

One hand gently nudges him away. 'Wait, Savio, listen.'

'What?' he asks savagely, aware that the arsonist's torch can go out if it goes on like this.

'Can we talk? Can you get off me so we can talk?'

'Talk,' he repeats disbelievingly, but she mistakes that for go-ahead.

'For you this is just another … right? For me it is a huge leap, like I've just jumped over a huge … what do you call those?'

'Chasm?'

'Yes, that thing. For me, I have jumped all the way from there to here. I don't know, I'm just … confused.'

'Confused about what?'

'Maybe confused is not the right word. There is just too much thought, too much feeling. I don't know if you really understand me, Savio. I mean, is this me you are … you know, or could it be anybody else?'

'Fucking. It's called fucking. Start using the word.'

'So answer the question then. Honestly, truthfully. Is this me or could it be anybody?'

It could be anybody of course, except they aren't as *wholesome*, nobody is. And they do not have all the colours of an innocent cosmos in their eyes. Mostly they are skanks, and the skanks do not fight back, they go along and cheer in sex-speak, meaning nothing and everything, you never know.

'I'm not even sure if I understood what happened the first time. I'm dealing with it. I'm dealing with a *lot* right now. Can you understand that?'

Despite the urgent call-to-arms from his testicles, he listens.

'After all these years, it's just a figure in the dark on top of me, on this hard ground. I know it's you, but do you know it's me?'

'Yes, goddamn it, Angie. I know it's you. Who the hell else could it be?'

Getting fucked for the first time, all that writhing and bucking and screaming, like ten years of Christmas presents denied her suddenly being heaped on her all at once, you'd think she'd be grateful, slavish, weepy with joy.

She sighs. 'It's all a bit too much. Let's talk about it later. But not now, now I just want to … be.'

He looks down at her, feeling a cramp snake up his right calf. 'All those magazines you read. Telling you it has to be special. Telling you how men think, how men are bastards.'

'I don't need a magazine to tell me that. Do you know how long I've waited? I *know* it has to be special. There *is* simply no other way.' Her eyes are shut now, her head resting peacefully on her hands again.

'What do you mean by special? Do you even know what that means?'

'Stop talking. Get off me.'

He rolls away and sits up looking at her, massaging his cramped calf.

She makes no effort to put her clothes back in order. She just lies there, a perfect snapshot of seduction, indeterminate in time and mood. A viewer might wonder, is this pre? Or did she just have some? Is it pain? Pleasure? Anticipation? He can look at her all night long, the alluring tranquillity of her body, the chaos of her clothes.

'Aren't you going to … put your things back together?' His voice sounds like it is being strangled by his own testicles.

'Maybe, maybe not. Why don't you try and sleep? Let me be?'

'What kind of shitty attitude is that?' he asks angrily.

'Listen. If I had not come to you, you'd still be sitting there sulking and sucking your thumb. So I'll do what I want. Let me be.'

'Fine,' he hurls out his retort, injured and stung. He smokes on in silence, telling his brain, his mouth to shut up, or he will bite his own tongue off.

6

THE PADDY FIELD

Nobody really sleeps that night.

In varying degrees they are all aware of the passage of time, walking through the night with the shuffling gait of an arthritic octogenarian. The seconds seem heavy-footed, the minutes feel tired and drained of energy, and the hours are the worst; the hours feel like they would throw in the towel any minute and collapse like dying mules with glazed eyes and heaving breaths.

Angie:

She is on her back the whole time, at least she thinks so because that is the position she wakes up in.

Her entire body has been alive and twitching with electrical impulses all night, like the remains of a circuit board that is still sparking after a huge electrical fire.

At first it was creepy, the sensation of rough male hands sand-papering her skin, lips and teeth sucking and biting, her first reaction being to swat it all off. There was only one man on top of her but it felt like multiple limbs, an attack on all fronts, too much tactility, too many flavours and smells, all new, all different, and her brain struggling to differentiate between pain and pleasure, friend or foe.

But in the middle of all that, in the thick of battle, there had been that moment when she had gasped.

And each subsequent gasp removed a smidgeon of mortar, and then the gasps grew longer and the defence wall began to fall off in chunks of brick and cement, and eventually nothing remained.

For a long time, she lay on her back and surveyed the wreckage with closed eyes and forensic fingers, retracing every gasp, allowing memory to steer, stopping at areas that still glowed, embers still fertile, ready to burst into flame if a passing moth so much as beat its wings over them.

She had underestimated her body.

She had touched herself in the past, but she has no name for this pleasure she has just felt, and if this is pain she would not mind some more.

Her panties had been torn and thrown away and her vagina was behaving like a kidnap victim that has just had its gag removed.

Mysterious juices pooled and stung the soreness that she felt, abrasions left in the wake of his finger, and then his penis. Cock? Should she start using that word now? Penis sounds fuddy-duddy, like something spoken in a lab.

Cock feels crude to her ears, but it also feels urgent, earthy, sexy.

Has she done the right thing, she asked herself. Has she been a little foolhardy, a little hasty? Could she not have waited till they got back? Waiting, waiting, waiting, so tired of waiting.

Then she had slept.

She has woken up all alone, Savio nowhere in sight, her first sight of a violet sky with birds wheeling around in it. She has a million bites over her body but she feels nothing.

Savio:

For him, the sensations are not as memorable and prolific. His balls hurt, his cock feels like it had been fondled by a cheese-grater, his ego is a little contused and his mind is swimming sulky laps inside his brain. He had toyed with the idea of sleeping in the car, but he remembered the smell, the smell of Don Pedro's insides covered by

Rosie's perfume and the thought of it made him gag. And who knew where the dead cat was?

He had scratched and swatted all night instead, on his own little patch of ground a little distance away from Angie, far enough from her so he was not compelled to stare at her and wonder what was going on in that head.

Rosie:

Much further away, she had passed out with her mouth open, her body a benign, unhaughty, unguarded Cleopatra. As the alcohol in her grew bored of mischief and passed out through her pores in a sticky sweat, her flesh wriggled and squirmed of its own accord, yearning for a familiar mattress.

Ferdie:

He had curled up into a little worm-ball at her feet, his head using one fat ankle as a pillow, dreaming restless, tortured dreams where he seemed to have lost his pants and was running around butt-naked – sometimes on his bicycle, his balls flopping on either side of the seat and swinging in the wind; at other times singing in the choir, the parish's attention focused not on his warbles and trills but on his hairy, unglamorous ding-dong, as though the voice and the words were coming from there.

Millie, mercifully, did not appear.

Don Pedro:

He slept in the car. Smells did not bother him. His seduction had not worked out as planned. How could he have known the results of mixing cheap brandy with Rosalina's brain? Practical as ever, his blanket usurped by the spineless retard, he had knocked back three stiff shots and spread himself on the back seat of the car, his head resting on a woolly garment that someone had left behind, probably Rosie's or Angie's. It could be said that he slept the best.

Early mornings in the countryside have a twinkle in the eye about them – a promise, however naïve, of only good to follow.

There is not one twinkle in the five sets of eyes that open, only caked crud. Then there are dew-soaked clothes, frozen necks, stiff shoulders, bursting bladders, spasming colons and mysterious bites and welts to contend with.

Savio has disappeared into the bushes at the crack of dawn to have a cigarette and drop his pants, hoping the leaves he uses are not the itchy kind. He is itchy enough from the night.

Angie, her dress zipped up, her creases smoothed out, goes to look for Rosalina, wondering how they will do their toilet. Savio comes to their rescue on that one, finding a couple of empty wooden crates a little distance from the car.

'Tell her to park one cheek on each, make sure no one's looking, and check that we are all upwind. If one of these breaks, there's a spare. If two break, well, then she shat herself out of luck. Same goes for you.'

He walks away with the cigarette stuck to his lower lip without even looking into her eyes or saying good morning or giving her a smile.

'Where is he going?' Rosie asks him, a little later, gathering up all the aspects of lady-like manner that she had somehow misplaced the night before.

They are staring at Ferdie, who has walked to the edge of the road and is standing with a jerry can between his legs. They have not seen or heard a car or truck or motorbike since they have stopped.

'Against my better wishes, I have agreed to let him go and get back petrol,' says Savio, inhaling on his third cigarette. 'He insisted.'

A total lie. It is Savio who encouraged him, knowing it will buy him more time, good precious time, delay their eventual return. Isn't that what *everyone* wants, he thinks.

'Dis is sometin' you should be doing. He won't know w'at to get.'

'What do you think he's going to bring back in that jerry can? Apple juice?'

Another drag, a long, lingering one, savouring the throat-grating, lung-burning light-headedness. He blows smoke which the wind carries past Rosie's head. He waits for some shrill comment on his manners and attitude, but she looks a little subdued. One night out in the open, shitting perched over two poxy wood crates has taken the piss out of her.

'Besides,' he says, 'it's his journey, not mine. Time he stood up and took responsibility.'

'He will get lost and never come back,' she says morosely, 'jus' you wait.'

'So you go look for him then. You and Michelangelo over there, while you look for him, he can look at more of you.'

Something of that old dangerous spark flashes in her eyes, but it lacks wattage. 'Are you t'inking wit dat dirty mind again?'

'What other mind do I have? Speaking of dirty minds, wait till he pulls out his, uhm,' snapping his fingers, 'what's the word, uhh, paintbrush?' His chapped lips crack into a leer.

He will not tell her anything about last night, Angie does not want that, but he can still gloat.

A sound precludes Rosie's comeback. They see Ferdie jumping up and down like a battery-operated pogo-stick. As the unmistakeable sound of a motorcycle dopplers louder and louder, they see him run into the centre of the road, flagging down the source of the sound that they cannot yet see. As announced, a motorcycle appears, one with the characteristic kick-drum beat of the Royal Enfield, no mystery there, but the rider, even at that distance begs attention.

A female, no doubt, face triangled perfectly, like a guitar pick, eyes set wide apart, oriental, with blonde dreadlocks. Thighs emerging from denim cut-offs that look like mahogany baseball bats at that distance, perfectly rounded and tapered. Halter top strapped tightly over a chest blessed with breasts the size of, say, Japanese tea cups. Spurred boots festooned with large feathers, as if she has just been in a kicking fight with a gang of eagles. At least we're still in Goa, thinks Savio, soaking in the vision.

The woman stops reluctantly, her machine slowing down to a patient idle. They see Ferdie limp over to her and deliver a pantomime performance, and he seems to be giving her Acts 1 to 7, starting with his life as a postmaster back in Pocolim, a letter received, a backstory of Millie whom he last saw standing on a dock, the hunt for a car, a detailed description of his fellow travellers evinced by a lot of pointing in their general direction, some anguished semaphoric gesticulations that are meant to convey the dastardly unreliability of maps, finishing up with a heart-wrenching finale of sorrow, pain, abandonment and redemption.

He holds up the jerry can just as the curtain falls on his performance.

'T'inks he is some opera fellow, always. See wat we have to deal wit' in church every day?' Rosie impressed, nevertheless.

'I was gripped,' says Savio. 'Pity he didn't start at birth.'

Either the oriental is a patron of the arts or has tons of time on her hands or both, she never hustles or hurries him; her machine too beats on impassively.

Then Ferdinand is throwing one long leg over her back seat, settling in, waving to them with both hands, almost toppling off backwards as she pops the clutch and roars off down the road.

'Bring back some apple juice,' yells Savio through cupped hands.

They wait till hush reigns over the countryside, and Don Pedro is the first to speak. 'You think he'll be back?' A touch of derision in his voice. His mood has not been great after discovering what that woolly pillow had been.

'Of course he will,' squeaks Rosie, louder than necessary.

'Unless she kidnaps him and makes him her entertainer slave,' reflects Savio.

'Chhe. A buffoon like Ferdie, who would want him?' But Savio detects a little reluctant admiration in her voice.

Don Pedro laughs obsequiously, perhaps noticing that inflection too. 'The wit of a lady,' he bows, 'never falters in a crisis.'

'I think I'll go for a second round of shitting,' Savio growls, his lip curled in disgust.

'I'm going to de car. Angie, help me please.'

'Allow me, dear lady. The time is at hand.' Waving away Angie, Don Pedro looks up at the sky, clocking the exact position of the sun, giving the impression that this is the hour of magic for artists everywhere. He comes forward, takes her hand and elegantly leads her away.

'I'll feed Nereus, Mai,' says Angie, temporarily taking her mind off Savio who is standing not three feet away.

He throws a sideward glance at her. 'Get him back here. Let's get some shade.' He's feeling fourteen and gawky all of a sudden.

'I'm not coming with you while you … do your toilet again.'

'That was a figure of speech. That guy could give anyone loose motions. Let's go and watch them from there, those trees, and you'll see what I meant.'

'Why, what do you think is going to happen?' she says, looking at him, curling a lock of hair with her fingers.

'Watch. See how the wolves really work. This is it. The whole cause and effect of your clever manipulations.'

'I wish you wouldn't use that word. Is … is she safe?'

'Of course. Nothing is going to hurt *that* rhino. She may be blind and stupid, but she's not to be messed with. Now get the cat before she gets to the car.'

'First, I am going to freshen you up with a glass of orange juice, my dear Rosie.' Don Pedro's words like a distant drum-roll announcing a full-moon sacrifice in the deepest Congo. 'It is not chilled, I'm afraid, but vitamin C first thing in the morning will make your skin glow.'

Rosie frowns briefly, wondering if she finds the use of her Christian name appropriate, faintly dredging up some memory to that effect, and then dismisses it, mesmerized by the timbre of his voice. He sits her down comfortably in the back seat, goes around to the trunk and unpacks. While she sips on her juice, he pulls out his canvas, a folded easel, a pouch of brushes and a bag of little colourful bottles.

He walks back to her, and clinks his glass of OJ with hers and holds up his favourite paintbrush like it is the key to the Kingdom, wondering why a look of alarm suddenly glazes over her face like a noon shadow.

'Wat ... wat are you going to do wit' dis ... paintbrush, Don Pedro?'

'Call me Pedro, dear Rosie. Remember we made a pact. There cannot be walls anymore.'

'Yes ... umm ... ummmm.' She slurps the juice noisily, her piggy eyes staring at the well-worn bristles. They look gritty and mature, a bit like his voice and personality, but somehow holding a promise or threat of more.

'What am I going to do with this, you ask?' His face eclipses the sun as it draws close, she can feel his breath, and each word that emerges comes coated in the richest velvet. 'You feel the need to ask an artist that question?' Rosie's thigh muscles quiver and a hot wind blows around her enormous panties.

'Aah, I understand. The usual simple answer will not suffice. I forgot you can be a lady of rare sensibility, so allow me to be a little poetic.' A gentle hand on her shoulders, a surgeon's touch, a safe-breaker's caress. 'With this brush, I will gently lift up the soul that exists within this magnificent body ...' Dramatic pause. '... and I will put colours on it, colours the world does not have names for yet.'

He lets his hand drop, and her bladder almost lets go as contact is lost.

'With each daub of paint, I will give this beautiful soul a new skin, a skin that will make God wish that he had left the creation of woman up to me.' He extends one leg-of-lamb hand, fingers moving as if in a dream of their own. 'Be my muse, Rosie.'

Deep within her flesh, in a mythical Atlantis a countless fathoms below, a dam bursts and warm liquid spreads almost biblically.

'Oh Don Pedro,' she squeaks inaudibly. 'I-I-I cannot feel my gout pain anymore.'

7
YUKO OHTSUKA

She has ridden bikes since she was eleven.

Her father's garage-hands had nicknamed her Yuko 'Honda' Ohtsuka. She grew up in the central district of Kyoto, a little rental and repair shop in the heartland of ancient Shogun country. The district seemed to be in a perpetual ceasefire between the old and the new, the garage nestled equidistant between the glorious Nijo Castle and the ultra-modern glass-and-steel Kyoto Station.

That is where she had learned the noisy art of shredding tyres before popping wheels (she could pop them front and back, and turn on a needle-point); by thirteen she was side-sliding under sixteen wheelers and ramp-jumping over decrepit Nissans and Subarus.

She could probably have cooked Soba noodles and eaten them leisurely while screaming down Teramachi Street at 120, though she had never actually tried that. She has, however, successfully rolled several joints while whistling down from Anjuna to Vagator on the back of her trusty Enfield, without even coming close to any kind of bodily harm.

Yet, she is having difficulty keeping the handle straight on this well-tarred smooth country road.

'You sit stirl, goddamn it! You move too much!'

Ferdie cannot help it. His butt itches. Sitting down in that paddy field was a mistake, and he had picked the wettest patch to do it in. Mud, squelchy and loamy, has hitched a ride on his pants along with, of course, the usual residents of the area, mostly microscopic but with surprisingly sharp teeth, which seem to be nipping chunks out of his leathery hide all at once in some kind of communal feeding frenzy.

'I take baboon on the back, baboon sit better,' yells the irate veteran of the two-wheeler.

They are making good time, thinks Ferdinand, looking at the bright side of things.

'You hor' me. You must hor' me,' she shouts, the wind carrying her words back in fragments of pitch and volume.

Ferdinand does not know what she means, until a lean muscled arm snakes around, grabs his free hand and brings it around the waist. The hair on his neck climbs a tree as his fingers encircle her smooth, rippling belly. He retracts his arm in shock.

'You hor' me,' she screams. 'Otherwise you for. You mus' hor'. You or' man. Why you worry?'

He opens his mouth to say something, but his brain has not formed the words yet, and only saliva dribbles out, whipping wetness past his head.

'Why you no hor'? You have dirty mind?' Now she seems amused, and he is shocked to hear a sudden teenage giggle.

'I – do – not – have – a – dirty – mind,' he gasps, and as if to prove that, he flings his free arm around her waist and clutches it with authority.

She is right. He feels better anchored now. This is better than bicycling, he thinks, as he sticks his head this way and that on either side of her slender neck, on which he notes with some trepidation the tattoo of a gargoyle that seems to be following his movements with predatory eyes.

The girl navigates the bike expertly down the narrow Goa roads. Ferdinand places the jerry can between his legs in case his penis decides to go for a walk. Dust and random insects keep going into his eyes, but he does not want to miss a thing. He reluctantly blinks, but only when he has to.

Another violent swerve. 'You no move lef' right!' She lifts one hand from the handle and points. 'This side Goa.' She points the other way. 'This side orso Goa! It or same. You sit straight!' She elbows him sharply in the ribs to show she means it. 'Or you walk!'

He moves his head in line with hers, and through a red, moist mist, looks at the back of her neck. The gargoyle glares back hatefully.

'I t'ink I will buy a motorbike,' he proclaims loudly, 'as soon as I find my Millie. We'll go around Goa, she'll like dat.'

'First you rearn ride bicycer. You very dangerous on motorcycer.'

He gasps, stares hard and long at the malevolent eyes of the inked beast. 'I am already an expert cyclist!'

'You sit straight now. Or we crash and die and you never see your gir'friend.'

'She's not my girlfriend.'

'Your wife, then.'

'She's not my wife,' Ferdie says sadly.

'Then why you forrow her?' her voice rises a notch. 'You stalk her?' She looks at him in her rear-view mirror.

'No! I am trying to find her.'

'Why she run away? You beat her?'

'No,' he sobs exasperatedly. 'I love her!'

'If man beat me, I no run away. I beat him back. He run away.'

Ferdie leans into a wall of wind and bellows in her ear. 'It's a long story! You din't you hear a word I said back dere?'

Her slender shoulders shrug. 'You speak funny. You talk lot, but say nothing.'

He throws up both hands in theatrical frustration, one of them carrying the jerry can, which is a mistake because a powerful side draft of a passing bus catches the can and yanks it out of his hand.

Ferdie manages to grab the string of the halter top just in time, the part that goes around her neck. She gags as her head snaps back, the bike swerving uncontrollably. The jerry can tumbles away down the dusty road behind them. A passing truck roars over it, crushing it, making it completely useless.

She pulls over by the side of the road. Ferdie, wild eyed with shock and fear, is still holding onto the string of her halter. She wrenches his fingers free and pulls him off the bike. He totters away to sit under a tree, shaking much like the leaves that offer him their canopy.

She dismounts and stands over him. 'Why you come?'

'W-wot you mean?'

'There are five peeper in car. Why they send you?'

'Because – because we – we ran out of petrol.'

He stares at her face and wonders if the gargoyle is modelled on her in some abstract way.

'Because – because we got lost,' he stammers.

She keeps glaring.

'Because – because I read de map wrong. We got lost and we ran out of petrol,' he says in a rush.

'So it your faurt,' she hisses at him.

'But I chose to – to be responsible, and – and take petrol back, so we could continue.'

He looks forlornly at the remnants of the jerry can, which has scuttled off, wind-assisted, to the side of the road.

'You ter me … this gir'friend of yours. Is she rear?' the two-wheeler terror of Kyoto demands, her eyes blazing.

'What do you mean?'

'Is she rear? Does she reary exist? Or you litter crazy and you maker her up?'

'Of course she's real,' he gasps. 'And she lives in Stotisgaon, where I will find her.'

'No, I think maybe you one of those crazy peeper who make up story. You ord, no wife, no nothing, so you make up this imaginary gir'friend you want to see after forty years.'

'You are mad. She is real and I will find her.'

'And then?'

'And then I'll ask her to marry me.'

'You rike a chile.' She sucks her thumb lewdly for emphasis. 'I see your eyes. You just a chile.' She shakes her head. 'Woman need a man, not a chile. Look at you, you are crying. Why are you crying?'

'I'm not crying,' he says, wiping his wet eyes. 'It's the dust.'

She shakes her head at him sadly. 'You no ready for any marriage, any wife. You just a crazy or' man. Useress.' She barks, 'Stop crying!'

'I'm not crying! My eyes are burning.'

She fishes out a little bottle from her jeans pocket. 'Here. Put drops. Crazy man, no sungrass also.'

He raises his red eyes to the sky and tentatively squeezes off a couple of drops in both.

'Even the jerry can is destroyed,' he mumbles.

'Can not important,' she shouts angrily. 'You important. We find can at petror-pump, we buy one in market orso. But where we buy you … this, what you cor this?' She turns around and runs one finger down her back, from gargoyle chin to the top edge of her thong that peeks over the waistband of her cut-offs.

He blinks, a little distracted. 'Sp-spine?'

'Yes, where we find you spine? And where we find you these?' She cups her crotch, giving it a little longshoreman-like heave.

Ferdie only gapes. 'Dose – dose I have,' he says finally, after going through several possible answers.

'You have, you no use. I think you never use. You useress. Now come on, we go.'

He gets to his feet very reluctantly. She is checking the bike, brushing down the seat, opening the fuel cock. She turns around to face him. 'I no understand one thing. You go rook for gir'friend, why other four peeper in car?'

'Dey – dey came to help me look for her.'

'Why? Why you no go arone?'

'Because I cannot drive a car!' he shouts, now genuine tears welling in his eyes.

'Why you no go by bus? Why you no walk?' She looks at him witheringly. 'One love of your rife, you need four peeper to help you.' She shakes her head disgustedly. 'You rearly useress.'

He drops his head, the tears coming on strong now. 'What do you want me to do?'

She says, 'You are or' man. This is your rast chance. Remember that. Your gir'friend see you like this …' She shakes her head. '… your rast chance gone.'

He looks up at her, his eyes red, the tears swelling and falling. She fishes out the bottle again. 'Put more drop!'

8
ANGIE & SAVIO

It is creepy, thinks Savio, that she is walking with a stiff, dead animal in her arms.

'Has she even seen the cat? Asked for it? Played with it?'

Angie looks down at the still form of Nereus. 'She trusts me to look after him.'

They walk on in silence, which is awkward because they both know this morning is not meant for trivia. Still, trivia just keeps intruding, steering them on parallel paths that are safe. But neither of them want safe, both are waiting for the other to flick the wheel over and converge, collide, cause a pile-up from which they will emerge a little banged-up but clear-headed.

'You think about Gabo a lot?' he asks, tweaking the wheel a little to the right.

'I try not to.' She unconsciously strokes the cat's fur, which is now freaking Savio out. 'But I'm living with his mother, and there are photos all over the place. In a way that's better than trying to forget – facing it, I mean.'

He licks his dry lips. 'Look, don't think I'm not aware of ... things. You are my once-upon-a-time best friend's wife. Sorry, *were* his wife. Bugger is six feet down now, God rest his soul. Someday we will be, too. But right now, right now, I see you, I hear you, I can smell you, I can … touch you.' Another lick, but even his tongue seems dry. 'What I'm saying is, I want to cut out the bullshit between us. I thought about what you said. You were right, I don't know you, but I would like to. And you've got to trust me too.'

Her body language says, uh-huh?

'I mean, don't fight me. Last night was a fight. That … kind of defeats the purpose.'

'I wasn't fighting you. I just did not know what to expect. Besides, isn't that how the cavemen did it?' she asks, a little smirk suddenly appearing out of nowhere.

Is that supposed to be funny? 'We're not … cave-people.'

'No, but it's still nothing to complain about, is it?'

'I'm not complaining,' he snarls, even though he is.

'So, how many girlfriends did you have in Bombay?'

'Will you please put that cat down? It's creepy the way you keep petting it.'

She sighs. 'I keep forgetting he is no more with us.'

She sits down on the spare yellowed grass, placing the limp form beside her. He stands, butt aching from all that hard ground, and noting that the cat is now definitely giving out a foul odour.

'Answer my question. And don't think I'm jealous or anything. I've heard that you might think that, y'know, if I ask you about your girlfriends?'

'Heard that. Who tells you all this rubbish?'

'Read it, actually. It's not important. Tell me.'

Savio pauses. Do whoremongers have girlfriends? He thinks honestly, had they ever really talked to him? Did they know his name? Would they remember it, pick him out of a crowd?

Was Saviya a girlfriend? No, but she would have been an enormous pain in the ass if he had not left at the opportune time.

Dear daddy, I ought to thank you for your timing.

'A few,' he says. 'A couple,' he corrects. 'But nothing that lasted.'

'No money, no girlfriends.'

'You don't have to put it ... are you rubbing my face in it?'

'Are you getting defensive again?'

'I didn't go to Bombay to look for women. I was busting my ass earning money. People have this impression,' he says, 'that you go to Bombay, pick up a stone and you'll find money underneath, just waiting there for you. Bullshit. All you get is a bad back. And dirty fingers.'

She shrugs. 'Well, you tried.'

It sounds terrible, the part she doesn't say ... *but you failed*.

'I left Goa because of you. I loved you then, Angie. I fell in love with you. Couldn't you tell? Could you *not tell*? Ten years have passed. And I still—' His fists bunched, trying to fill the blanks with gestures. 'What do *you* feel, Angie? It's time *you* said something, no?'

'Didn't I say whatever needed to be said last night?'

'No, we haven't spoken. You didn't want to speak, remember?'

'I did speak, but you were not listening. You get to know me, I get to know you. We take it a day at a time and nobody has to know about it.'

'In Pocolim, you're going to keep something like that a secret?'

'I'm also genuinely going to help you clean up your house.'

'You're not afraid of that Gestapo fatty finding out? Poking her nose everywhere.'

'You sound like *you're* frightened of her.'

He'll have to do some quick, rudimentary cleaning as soon as he goes back, he thinks. Put his clothes away. De-mould the cupboards. Slap dust off the furniture. Change the sheets. Buy some air-freshener for the toilets. Run the brush under the rim of the commode, scrape off the hardened crust of his splattered shit. Buy some hand-soap, fresh towels...

As if reading his mind, she suddenly says, 'You know the times I have been tempted to come up the stairs and knock? But it always looks so gloomy, it's scary. I just pass by and see the door open and there is just darkness inside, and I somehow imagine you scrabbling around like a blind man looking for this and that. It's *awful*.' She gives a little shudder.

'It's just a couple of bulbs that have blown,' he deflects. 'You know that house was always dark, it never really admitted much natural light.'

'Never this scary dark. You need to get more powerful bulbs.'

'I know, I just keep putting it off.'

'One quick trip to the general store, that's all it takes. In half an hour, you're done.'

And then what will I do tomorrow? he asks silently. *If I do everything today, what the fuck will I do tomorrow?* The classic procrastinator's quandary, how will she understand that?

'All that junk left in the house,' he says instead. 'Everyone left something behind, and dad never threw anything away. Clothes of seven kids, all lying there neatly folded up in cupboards, all smelling old and looking like shit.'

'The orphanage will take them. Which reminds me, if you see a pair of panties, will you pick them up please? They're here somewhere.' She pats her crotch the way people pat pockets looking for misplaced wallets.

She crosses her legs and her skirt accordions up her thighs like a curtain going up on an installation. It stops just short of the zone of shadows where everything becomes illusion, suggestion, promise. Sunlight does not reach her pussy, but Savio, dry-throated and suddenly stiff-cocked, sees it clearly, mushy as a ripe apricot and deep as Alice's rabbit-hole.

'Jesus Christ, Angie,' he gasps through a mouthful of sticky molasses.

'Funny you should mention that. There was a time, not so long ago, I thought of becoming a nun. I thought that was the only way out for me. I'd wear a ring, I'd be married to Jesus, and he would give me everything I ever wanted.' She looks at him. 'Now I'm glad I didn't.'

'N-nun?' He superimposes a habit on her, with all those silly little buttons that would wear a man's thumb down to a nub getting them open. 'You're joking. Why?'

'I don't know, I was running out of options, I thought. I was neither here nor there. Neither fully devoted to any one man, or to God. I always knew there was a middle road, but I didn't know how to find it.' She looks at her fingernails, which probably still have slivers of Savio's skin underneath them. 'My idea of men was all based on the ones I saw in Pocolim. Jesus was definitely more attractive.'

Emotions circle Savio's head like a herd of horses in an enclosure. Gabo had gotten lucky, years ago. He, Savio, had only watched, *could* only watch.

And now ... and now it had been neck and neck with Jesus Christ, Saviour of Man, the Ultimate Cool. And he has won, he has pipped the Son of God to the post by a nose, by a nostril hair.

The Second Coming has been delayed a little, kind of, sort of.

That revelation seems to weigh a couple of tons, and he sits down abruptly next to her.

9

DON PEDRO

In the field, Madame Rosalina Eucharistica is being prepped for posterity. Nature is cooperating, providing the props, the lighting and the soundtrack. He has chosen a spot for his muse under the shade of a large banyan tree. Its secondary roots hang down like beaded curtains in some dingy den of sin in the psychedelic sixties. The banyan also comes with a natural stool, one thick, gnarled root that sticks its knee out, on which she will perch.

The only problem with the entire production has been the styling department, the stylist being Don Pedro himself, or more accurately, Don Pedro's loins that are dancing to commands issued by Generals Testosterone and Dopamine, both recently promoted to five-star and gone power-crazy.

Once, long ago, while swanning in the art circles in the University of Florence where he had been invited as a guest speaker, he had been offered a line of cocaine at some after-party. It made him feel like he could've bungee-jumped off the moon. He feels pretty much the same way now. He has always believed in signs, but signs have never lined up so well, so perfectly before, ever; everything around him on this beautiful morning in rural Goa seems to be a smiley-faced signpost, everything seems to have both thumbs up in approval.

Everything but the styling department.

The black dress that covers her flesh, that black dress will never do. It has grown heavy and sticky with overuse and sweat and soaked-up crocodile tears. Not to mention a little patch of puke. Even detergent and a good spin-cycle will not get the drabness, the unsexiness out of it. May as well give her a burqa to wear.

Getting her out of it, however, proves almost as challenging as skinning an elephant.

But he does it, finally, with honeyed words and effusive flattery. He has a pounding headache just coming up with adjectives that will make the tumblers of the lock-that-is-her-mind drop. He composes odes to her skin, delivers soliloquies to her flesh, rattles off verses about her volume, and blathers teary-eyed on her roundness like a mathematician who has just discovered pi.

She is eventually mesmerized by the words and the train they rumble in on, looking like a very fat Mowgli under the spell of a hissing Kaa, colourful concentric circles radiating outwards from her pupils.

In a trance, she disappears behind the banyan, the only tree around for miles that can conceal her girth, and emerges fifteen minutes later with an enormous bedsheet draped around her shoulders, the same sheet that had doubled as a bed the previous night.

After that, it is par for the course for the despot and his generals.

10

FERDIE

Yuko stops the bike, and points to a row of shops on the road. Ferdie, exhausted, travel-dazed and viewing the world from behind a thick soup of his own tears garnished with road-dust and bug-wings, looks but does not dismount.

'Jerry can,' she rasps, the syllables knocking on the front-door of his consciousness and skulking on the stoop, waiting for someone to answer.

'Ooo-ow,' he yells, his throat tired and dusty, as she turns around and pinches him in the sensitive area of his left nipple.

'You awake or sreep? You no sreep on motorbike.'

'I no sleep,' he moans, the shooting pain making his grammar sloppy. 'Why we stop?'

'Jerry can.'

Ferdie blinks and shops shimmy into view. He looks grumpy, but she can pinch, this mad woman, so he reluctantly gets off and shuffles towards one shop that, as far as he can make out, is just a blur of colour but no shape.

'No that one. You buy jerry can in dress shop, you crazy man?'

He veers to the left, his eyes itching madly, barely making out something that looks like some domestic hardware store in a row of the usual trades on display. He walks towards it, then abruptly walks back to her.

Scratching his stomach and shuffling his feet, he looks down at her navel, which has a ring running through it, the flesh around it pinched and red; he takes in the porcelain quality of the skin that stretches over her stomach, her muscles rippling like a beach at ebb tide.

'Can you – er – loan me some money?'

'You come to get petror, you no get money?' Her voice is coming from somewhere high above that modern-art belly.

'I – I changed my pants dis morning.' He decides to lie, but sees in his mind's eye the wallet that he had placed carefully on the grass next to the blanket before lapsing into slumber on Rosalina's meaty-soft calf.

'So what you want now? *I* give you money?' There seem to be a dozen breathless question marks appended to that query.

'I will give you as soon as we go back. Honest mistake it was, I swear.' Then, going out on a limb, he throws in, 'It could happen to anybody.'

'No.' Her head moves dangerously from side to side. 'It could no' happen to anybody.'

In deadly slow motion, she nudges out the side-stand which grinds its toes into the soft mud as the heavy bike sighs into it. 'Now,' she says, her words gliding off her tongue like hot lava, 'you stay here and don' move. You only move to breathe.' She pokes a finger into his bony chest. 'No move otherwise.'

'But listen, dere is no need to trouble yourself. I can—'

'You no can nothing. I give *you* money, between here and there you roose it, I guarantee. And then? We both no have money. No move.' The last request is accompanied by steel fingers that dig into his shoulder like a bear trap. Then she swishes away, her pound-cake bottom in denim fish-tailing elegantly from side to side.

Ferdie surrenders to the moment, wondering in all honest despair when this is going to end.

Everything has a shelf-life, even great ideas and risky plans, even love and luck and hard work. He thinks it significant that he did not dream of Millie last night. Perhaps it was his rather unusual pillow, or maybe it is just that Millie's telepathic signal is growing weak.

She is losing hope perhaps, sending out her dream communiqués in vain, and instead of getting closer, he is only moving further and further away. Perhaps she is watching him, in some clairvoyant manner he cannot understand, and getting despondent at his bumbling ways. The mad girl with the gargoyle on her neck is right, his uselessness is now getting to be legendary.

'Oi Padraon,' says a rude voice in Konkani. 'Move the bike, re.'

The words hang in the air for a bit, while Ferdie, not the best of multitaskers, concentrates his energies on doing what he does best: feeling sorry for himself. Mark Antony might have launched into a famous speech about borrowing ears three feet from him, but Ferdie would have only heard one voice, his own, in these deeply introspective moments.

'Oi, you're deaf or what?'

I'm coming, Millie, his mind sobs. Just a little detour, a little deviation. One more day you can wait, Millie. One more day I will be dere. No more cock-ups, I promise. You will see a new man before you.

Ferdie practises a few shoulder pull-backs, though it is hard to keep them there. Muscle memory is elastic; they keep drooping forward.

A strong stench of stubble-sweat mounted on a drunken steed of halitosis rides all the way up his nostrils and cuts through his telepathic yearnings.

'Two times I'm telling you. T'ink I am talking to myself or what?' It is impossible to ignore the face that seems to be blotting out the sun; short though the stubble may be, it gives Ferdie's aura a good scratching up. He recoils, almost toppling backward.

A brute stands before him. The red drunken eyes lend the man a certain mad pit-bull demeanour even though there is a sadness to the mouth, the kind that comes from regret at not having bitten off Ferdie's ear when he had the chance.

'You t'ink I like being on de highway? No business all morning, chhe, from eight o'clock I open, and then you park the bike right in front of my store?'

These are technically questions, but Ferdie takes one look at the arms, which are thicker than his own thighs, and decides that they aren't the kind you offer answers to, just listen quietly and later do as they command.

But he does have a point to make. 'It is not my bike,' he says.

'I know. Your bleddy girlfriend bike, no? Walking around like she is on de beach in dose hot pants. Move de bike!'

He reminds Ferdie of Joao, the way the moustache bristles and rotates around the mouth as the man forms words, except Joao lacks the pure malevolence that this man possesses.

'Front of my store,' growls the brute. 'You t'ink customer wants to walk around de bike? You t'ink customer likes de hard work? Dey go to somebody *else's* shop, because of your bleddy bike. Psychological!' he roars, thumping his own temple with two Goa-sausage fingers. 'Move now, bleddy inconsiderate!'

Ferdinand looks around wildly for the biker girl, but there are about sixteen shops and she has disappeared into one of them. Ferdie totters to the bike and looks at it doubtfully. It is heavier than his bicycle, that much he knows, and it has a kind of intimidating quality, as if it is daring him to touch if he is man enough.

Aware that there is something grunting and growling about how it is the middle of the day and the cash drawer is still empty as an aged hooker's pussy blah blah, Ferdie reaches out and touches the bike. The bike touches him right back, with its solidity and its weight and its sheer immovability.

The threat of death, or even worse – extreme pain – forces him to think. This fat bug with its bulging neck and pudgy abdomen has wheels, and wheels turn. He grips the handle, edges it off the side-stand and pushes, and for a while it seems the bike is pushing back and his breath locks in his throat and all his internal organs feel like they are mushing into one big porridgey mess and his backbone is cracking in three different places, and then the damn thing actually moves.

It moves forward, reluctantly, petulantly, annoyed at being disturbed from its repose and trying its hardest to lie down again, on either side, it isn't fussy.

'Not in the mud, push it on de road, re,' Ferdie hears over the noise of blood rushing through his ears like an express train choo-chooing through a tunnel. It is a kindly voice and Ferdinand can dimly make out the outline of another shopkeeper as the source. 'Not in front of my store. Keep moving,' the kindly voice says. 'Push on de road, not in de mud.'

'Please … help,' Ferdie gasps, and the kindly voice comes out of his shop and helps Ferdie get the bike off the mud and onto the hard blacktop, where to his delight it starts moving without too much effort, with an almost head-hung docility, like an intractable horse that has been broken in.

He pushes on, feeling stronger by the minute, elation rising within him and spreading like a balm, numbing the agony of his twitching muscles and wobbly joints. When he is well clear of the shop-line, he pulls in the reins, and gently, deftly, like a man in control, he eases the lazy beast back onto its crutch. Without a word or a neigh of thank you, it appears to go back to its deep power nap.

Ferdie staggers back, wishing the fire in his lungs would go out and those winking fireflies in his vision would stop hovering and flitting about.

Leaving the bike a clear three feet well into the blacktop line, he finds a milestone that says 'Panjim 40' and sits down upon it. Rightly or wrongly, he feels a little proud of himself.

The beast fought and he showed it who was boss, with plenty a sob, granted, but without a tear.

He sends out one more mental telegram to Millie, stating – I am on my way stop nothing can stop me now stop don't be disheartened stop I am coming to take charge darling Millie stop you'll see stop all my love Ferdie.

And then a truck barrels around the corner doing at least a hundred and using up all the road to make the turn successfully and head-butting the snoozing Enfield a clear twenty feet through the air, causing it to whizz through Ferdinand's star-spangled vision like an asteroid narrowly missing Earth, embedding itself nose-first in a field of wild-grass, mangled beyond use, giving a new dimension to the old saying 'Its ass and neck are now one'.

11

ROSIE

Epiphanies are usually grand phenomena, awakenings one is likely never to recover from.

They are rare, these climactic ones. But several are had by ordinary people every other week – minor ones, tiny ones that will barely produce enough brain spark to light up a flea's fart, and it's these mental pipsqueaks that add up to our overall understanding of what we are all about.

For instance, it comes up on Rosalina in a flash what a bowl of fruit must feel like, or a sunset or a landscape or some plump lady called Mona Lisa in the sixteenth century. This revelation hits her long after delirium has already set in, sitting bare-rumped on a tree root that has more bark than a rabid chihuahua, her skin raw and sore, her flesh gradually radiating numbness upward into her hips and downward into her toes, her back breaking from no support, and worst of all, her modesty being slowly torched to death like a witch on a stake.

The delirium itself, it comes long after various other stages of consciousness, the first hour or so passing in visions of grandeur, of the far-reaching importance of giving her best three-quarter profile to the canvas, all her wisdom and virtue stacked up in her eyes like knick-knacks arranged neatly on a shelf. When the first of the cramps hits her, the historical importance of looking wise quickly slips into the current necessity of looking uncomfortable. She squirms and makes minor adjustments to her limbs, which draw stern but gentle reprimands from Don Pedro reminding her of posterity and using phrases like the Final Sacrifice, making her feel fleetingly like Jesus in Gethsemane. Then the next flare of pain tears through her calves, causing her to squeak and sweat.

And when she requests the artist for a toilet break, she does not know which hurts more, the humiliation of perching on two creaky mango crates behind a bush again, or the disgust in his eyes and scorn on his lips when he grudgingly lets her, muttering dark, foreign words under his breath and kicking unseen stones.

Next in her parade of thoughts, somewhere between hour two and three, comes the Float of Troubling Questions: Is she being treated the way a lady should?

Is he heartless to not offer her a drink of water at least?

Is he a bumbling amateur who needs four tries to get a stroke or daub right?

Does it make sense for a paragon of human virtue, a lighthouse for future generations to sail safely into the Harbour of Good Christianity, to be dressed like some faux-Grecian courtesan draped titillatingly in a crusty, insect-infested blanket that smells faintly of Surf Excel and mostly of cupboard-mould?

'Madame Eucharistica,' he booms, all sweaty-browed and flushed, barely looking at her, 'could you please drop the cloth a little off your left shoulder?'

Rosie? Whatever happened to can-I-call-you-Rosie? She straightens her spine and looks at him, hurt and haughty. 'You know, I don't t'ink dat is really—'

'Drop it, I said!' he roars, causing a flutter of wings overhead and one panicky bird to drop a load of shit on the root right next to her. His eyes lock with hers and she feels herself go weak again, her pupils floating away into the back of her head. 'This is art, my dear lady. No compromises,' he says, sounding like a wolf growling in a graveyard, in a voice as cold as the Ice Age.

Her overheated brain is aware of the wet spot of steaming guano right next to her hip, but she is too terrified to move even a couple of inches away. Her lips tremble. 'I – I – I – I'm not comfortable.' Her mouth is too dry to say any more.

Don Pedro walks up to her, stands over her, smelling of power and brute force, eyes shining like bright, hot stones in a demon's forehead, fingers coming up to grip her shoulders, one hand moving up to her face, caressing it, tilting her chin upward. 'When this is over, madame, your other journey begins. There is—'

'R – R – Rosie?'

'When this is over, Rosie, your other journey begins. A soul like yours can never rest. You are now entering history. May you always walk through its pages, my proud and dearest muse. Bear with me a little longer.'

Her defence sags like the axle of an overloaded truck, and she smiles beatifically through dry and chapped lips, making one more enraptured appeal to the milk of human kindness that oozes from this magnificent man. 'I – it's just dis robe … dis, dis blanket you know? Is it – is it…?'

'Is it necessary?' he volunteers, tilting her chin further up. 'It is merely a garnish, just a detail. The sheet will hardly be there in my painting, I assure you.'

'Okay,' she squeaks, 'okay,' wanting this man never to release her from his delicious touch, and this is precisely when the delirium sets in, later followed by epiphanies of fruit bowls and Mona Lisas.

Don Pedro swaggers back to his easel, leaving his muse feeling light as a feather, though the tree root might have disagreed with that.

12

ANGIE & SAVIO

They, oblivious to Rosalina's entry into history books, are looking for Angie's underwear. Savio, spying it in the green, scoops it up when her back is turned and stuffs it into his pocket. It is only temporary, of course, before she gets home and slips on another pair, but for now her snatch is a political prisoner out on bail.

All this hunting around gives them something to pass the time. This reunion of sorts, it has to be approached carefully. Time is one thing they will have a lot of when they are back in Pocolim. He is acutely aware of this: he does not possess a deep enough personality for her to plumb endlessly.

His load is light, and he does not want to shoot it all at once. Scratch that built-up mystery, and she might find him as bland as the other ball-scratchers she has eschewed in his favour. And then?

And then there will be others. She can now walk through the world and fuck anyone she chooses; he has provided her with the taste and the memory.

Every time she bends over to chase a false lead and her skirt sighs up over bare skin, no line or bump of waistband polluting the untrammelled roundness of her cheeks, he stares at her unblinkingly, like a cat eyeing a mousehole, keeping his wriggling fingers in check and thinking:

Now I've got to *keep* this.

He has tucked his penis into the waistband of his briefs, up in noon position, otherwise it wags uncomfortably at ten o'clock all the time, solid and perpetually turgid in her presence, the skin around it raw and red from all that friction with her bristly pubic hair that crowds her pussy like a possessive grove of spiny trees. Chicks who don't get fucked never trim their pubic hair, why is that? he wonders. Even Saviya, the bush rich and huge while the body gaunt and sallow. Weird.

He touches her a lot, and she touches him back, and they smile when they do, and they keep the air around them charged with eroticism. But, for now, he does not venture beyond that, not just because he is in a lot of pain, but because there is something preciously delicious about this particular delaying of gratification, a coming to fruition of something he has waited fifteen years for.

13
FERDIE

Far away from these lurid tableaus, a few miles to the south west, Ferdinand walks hunched over, holding a newly purchased jerry can.

Yuko 'Honda' Ohtsuka, feeling the absence of a throbbing steed between her legs like a phantom itch, clumps behind him in her feathered boots.

Once or twice, a scuffed boot-tip nudges Ferdinand's withered flanks when he slows down or breaks pace.

When Ferdie tries to flag a car or truck down, she twists his thumb savagely. 'You walk!' she barks, her knee prodding his buttock. 'No car, no wheels for you. You walk!'

'How far?' he wails.

'Very far.' Her words are like Uzi bullets that wing him, her voice could make sheet-metal curl.

'I can't,' he blubbers. 'Dis heat.'

'You can. And you wir.'

An invisible leash hangs between them, lengthening and shortening as she sees fit. She keeps talking, mostly in Japanese, her consonants hissing and spitting like a nest of cobras, her vowels nicking and cutting him like a rusty katana blade. Is she talking to herself, this mad woman? No, she is talking to him, and even as her words buzz incomprehensibly like hornets about his ears, he has a creepy feeling that at some deep instinctual level, he understands everything she is saying. Or maybe it is just the heat-induced delirium.

She gives him water every once in a while, just a couple of sips. This was after she had stood over the wreckage of her motorcycle, communing with its soul like a Shogun princess mourning her warhorse with royal restraint and dignity. She had not said a word to Ferdie after that, merely walked back to buy the waterbottle, returned, grabbed his collar with one slender arm that seemed to possess the strength of ten dead warrior ancestors, and they had started walking.

'Please. Please.' He sobs now, staring at the shimmery road that winds before him, like the backbone of some subterranean monster-worm that has partially emerged for a little tan. 'I am an ol' man,' he whines.

She pauses in the middle of what sounds like a particularly vitriolic Haiku to say words that Ferdie has heard countless times before, though never with so much bite and gouge. 'No, you are a stupid man. Stup-pid-do,' breaking up the word in three rabbit-punch syllables.

'It was the truck's fault! What?' he yells, as a boot-tip goes a clear inch up the crack of his buttocks.

'Stop putting brame. Shut up and walk.'

'How much farther?'

'Very much farther. Today you rearn.'

'Today I learn what?' He looks up at the burnt-out sky, stares at the scorching road. Heat is a ping-pong ball that is being batted back and forth between these two giant paddles. What is being taught here?

She breaks into Japanese again, words that have the sound and feel of fat, colourful bumblebees. 'Today you rearn to finish what you start,' translating the bumblebees for him.

'What you mean? Ow!' Another boot practises proctology on his bum.

'No srow down. Finish what you start. You make mess, you fix. At the end of this, you rearn,' she says. 'Now you shut up and rissin.'

Which bewilders him, because she has switched her Uzi to Japanese mode again.

For the next hour he does not utter a word. Sounds come and go: her low, foreign mutterings, vehicles whizzing past that he does not dare raise a throbbing thumb for, sing-song conversations that sound like bad radio transmissions when they pass a village or small town. Above all that, the land speaks with its multilingual vocabulary, the birds wheeling and squawking, the wind slithering through the tall grass like a platoon of clumsy guerrillas, trees creaking and stretching their limbs. Pain scurries up his legs and back down, harrowed couriers ferrying distress messages, his stomach growls in a rich tenor reminding him that he has not eaten a thing since … since forever.

Slowly, one by one, sounds seem to fade, as if someone has silently shut a door on them. At the kernel of that distant, subdued noise, a little mantra throbs and glows: today you learn to finish what you start.

His thoughts merely circle the mantra the way birds circle a neon sign at dusk, intrigued by its weak incandescence. In the deepening silence that follows these tight sorties around the mantra, he feels he can almost hear the sound of a distant ocean, although that is impossible. Maybe it is the sound of the sun's rays singeing the air. He sips water when it is offered and walks.

An hour later, he feels an arm encircle his rounded shoulders, the touch of her bare skin cool against his sweat-soaked shirt is simultaneously warm and comforting. A whimper breaks through his chapped lips, but no tears (no tears, ever) and his entire body sags against her shoulder. She does not flinch at his weight, but they both slow down.

Bumblebee wings tickle his right ear as she whispers, 'No' rong now. Be brave, and you wir finish. Okay?'

Another sip of water, and the arm comes off the shoulder, leaving a void where there had been a gluey, sticky intimacy. Her hand comes down and takes his, her palms cool and dry, his overheated, and to him it feels like being hooked up to an IV bottle that is slowly releasing a measured dose of strength and comfort, drop by drop.

They walk for an hour more.

He only remembers the part when they stop. Some rented villa somewhere; somewhere that is another time, another place from wherever it was he had started. He has walked four hours across a baking landscape he has no name for other than Goa. In which direction lies Pocolim, the Dodge, Millie, he has no idea.

It is the middle of the day. She has assured him they will be back to the Dodge by two, on her partner's motorcycle. Rest for an hour, she says. He would have liked to rest for a week.

His entire body is singing a chorus of pain, his lower body a little louder on the higher registers and his torso taking up the backing basso. Night is still a long way off, but inside his body it is already creeping in, in the form of stiffness and soreness.

The villa doubles up as an exclusive two-room spa and massage centre on the outskirts of Anjuna, run by Yuko and her partner Kanako. They are famous, and they are busy, and their rooms are booked every day until May, except weekends. In addition, they also do house-calls for reiki and feng shui, which is what Yuko had been out for today; she was on her way back from Pernem, all the way up near the Maharashtra border.

Yuko tells him all this as she and Kanako watch him sip his green tea. They have tenderly removed his shoes, unpeeled his threadbare socks and put his feet up on a little ottoman.

They must be very, very close friends too, Ferdie thinks deliriously, watching them touch each other in fond and strange ways, even kiss passionately once. Perhaps these are Japanese customs between business partners, he thinks, deciding he has learned something of cultural value today.

Yuko is tired and she announces she is going to have a deep, meditation-induced power nap from which she will awake fresh and rejuvenated. They point to a couch and suggest Ferdie do the same.

When he tries to get his feet off the ottoman onto the floor, he cannot. When they help him do that, he cannot get out off the chair. His muscles have bid nighty-night and buggered off to bed. Kanako looks at Yuko, a nod is exchanged, and that is how Ferdie finds himself lying on the massage table, getting the rub-down of his life from the magical, oil-lathered hands of Kanako Kobayashi.

If sleeping has crossed his mind, the minute he lays his forehead on the cushion, it is run over by a heavy traffic of pain that erupts as steely strong fingers goose his exhausted muscles awake. They are deep sleepers, his muscles, much deeper than their skittish host. They rage like tantrumy infants at being woken up, and Ferdie hears every waking shriek, every howl of rage. But it feels … heavenly, much better than that awful feeling of everything shutting down.

Kanako does not speak at all. He only knows she is there because he figures she is somehow attached to those hands that are kneading and digging and caressing, hands as soft as flower petals but with the weight of a hydraulic press behind them. He feels better. He feels stronger. He feels loved. He feels privileged. He feels empowered.

'Finish what I started,' he gasps. 'Yes, I must. Finish what I started. I always start, and then I get scared,' he pants. 'From now on, finish what I start, yes.'

The mantra, it's a mouse trying to escape the clutches of a playful lynx.

She taps him on his shoulder, and with a silver-toothed grin that causes her eyes to disappear altogether, she motions him to flip onto his back. Then she starts on the front.

Ferdie, shutting his eyes, begins to daydream now, seeing Millie on the screen of his closed eyelids, Millie in his house, in his kitchen, cooking and cleaning and sewing and smiling and beaming, Millie walking the streets of Pocolim with flowers in her hair and Millie being addressed as Mrs Fernando D'Cruz. In the foreground, he keeps mumbling *I will finish what I started*, like some tuneless soundtrack for his movie. His mind floats away from his body, which in response to pure stimuli, begins to act on its own.

Her giggle cuts through his daydream. He opens his eyes and immediately becomes aware of three things: her hands have stopped, she has stripped him expertly to his dirty underwear, and she is looking down at the biggest hard-on he has ever seen on himself.

Her hands are over her mouth, little girlish trills of laughter escaping from between her fingers like butterflies. She reaches down and strokes his penis through the fabric of his underwear, causing his aching limbs to go into involuntary spasms.

She deftly lifts his rump and pulls his underwear off. Ferdinand's head falls back in horror, finding himself incapable of staring his naked erection in the eye. He hears her speak for the first time:

'You no worry,' she says. 'This is normar.'

She rakes her fingernails gently over the shaft. She strokes it two more times like it is her favourite pet, then she looks at him with crinkly eyes that seem to be having a quiet chuckle on their own. 'You want wank?' Her words caressing his ears just like her fingers have caressed his cock.

It's devotion, Ferdie, Savio had said. Wrong girl, but still.

It has been thirty hours since they have left Pocolim; the most tiring, trying thirty straight hours of his life.

He started off his journey wearing a chastely buttoned-up shirt, sharply creased trousers and combed-back hair, the perfect suitor setting off on a two-hour journey to find his lost love.

A day and some change later, he is lying starkers in a massage parlour with the most magnificent erection he has never dreamed himself capable of. And there is this woman staring down at it, a complete stranger, who is fondling it like they've known each other all their lives, his penis and her.

'Yes,' his mouth says. 'Oh Jesus, yes,' succumbing to the moment, letting go, his brain taking its first coffee-break in fifty years, give or take.

'I come back, okay?' she says, giving her new, oldest friend one final tight-fisted hug. One finger trails an erotic line on his face that gives him goosebumps where no goosebumps ought to be. Then she leaves the room.

Ferdinand passes the time getting to know his penis. There is a lot to catch up on. They communicate silently. He wonders how she will return. Will she have no clothes on? Or will she disrobe in front of him, slowly and seductively? Will she come back with Yuko? Yuko of the machine-gun jibes, and also Yuko of the warm, soft touch.

He shuts his eyes in a thrill of terror. He shuts the door on Millie as well. Or he will not be able to face her when the time comes.

He communicates with his penis, and tells it, *dere is some devotion coming your way*.

Then they communicate some more, and he wonders if the time is nigh, when right on cue he hears soft footsteps outside the door, two sets of footsteps. Two sets of butterfly giggles, the door sighing open, the rustle of flesh on silk, he hears them enter, and he turns his head to them, his eyes glazed over and pleading, holding down his turgid cock like it is a rocket about to blast off into space, and then Yuko's face over his, asking him, 'Okay, you finish? We go now.'

14

THE PADDY FIELD

'You have good heart. Weak mind, but good heart' – Yuko's parting words to him a few metres away from the Dodge, straddling Kanako's bike, Ferdie standing on the shoulder with a jerry can at his feet. 'When you find gir'friend, you must make mind strong,' she says. 'Mind like steel. But continue dreaming with your heart. You keep heart soft.'

'Wait,' he says. 'I go and give them petrol. And then I find my wallet? And then you drop me to bus stand?'

She looks doubtful. She thinks she has done her bit, and she wants to get back and get a massage of her own, complete with the bliss-ending. Leave this calamity-magnet to his own devices not a moment too soon. But she looks into his eyes, and asks him instead, 'How much time I wait?'

'Five. Maybe ten minutes. I must say goodbye to Angie. De udders … I don't care.'

'I rook at watch,' which she does, 'and in ten minutes I go. Okay?'

He picks up the can without a word and turns around. There is not a soul near the Dodge. In it, however, is a decomposing cat, flies partaking of a late lunch, and a smell you would need a chainsaw to cut.

He places the jerry can in the little shade offered by the car, straightens up and calls out to Angie.

Rosalina hears him and jerks out of her stupor. The little jerk sends tremors of pain rippling through her stiff and sore body and she almost topples off the tree-root. 'Ferdie,' she squeaks. 'Ferdie is back.' She attempts to get to her feet but her legs are not up to it. Don Pedro looms again and grins a skull-like grin. 'A few minutes more, madame, is all I ask of you. Don't move!' And she cowers back into the hard, poky hole of her aching body like a frightened rabbit.

Angie and Savio are too far away for the wind to carry Savio's feeble call. They have found a shady spot whose temperature is at least five degrees cooler than ambient, the gargantuan foliage of two old banyans soaking up the heat and spitting it back into the atmosphere.

They lie side by side on the cool grass, turning each other over the way a child turns over a brand-new toy. Their fingers and lips are super-tuned probes, plucking out knowledge and the essence of the other. Their stomachs are belting out a duet of acute hunger, Savio's rock-star rasp answered by Angie's hell-chick growl, and they both giggle.

Ferdinand calls again (drawing mountain-lion snarls from Don Pedro which still Rosie), and then he sticks his head into the concrete marsh of dead-meat stench, bangs open the glove compartment and fishes out a piece of paper (a laundry receipt for Loyola's clothes) and a pen.

On the back of the receipt, eyes watering from Nereus's death-musk, he begins to scribble.

Yuko watches him, her peripheral vision alert for potential misadventures that might fall out of the blue sky or barrel out of the woods as long as she is within the force field of this human. But nothing happens and Ferdie, tongue sticking out and brow scrunched up, finishes his note.

Dear Angie, Madam Rosalina, Don Pedro & Savio,

I think it's time to leave you. I had an experience today that made me learn many things about myself. My love for Millie is strange. I don't understand it; how I can expect you? I am just like you, you know? I also hope for good things but never did anything to get them. From today I will finish everything I start.

Madam Rosalina, I have dreams of you often but always in a good way. It is not your fault that you look at me like a simple fellow; perhaps in our next lives we will be friends.

Savio, you have given me the strength to think for myself. I know, I know, a sailor cannot read a map, but what to do? I am a postman, and I was never good at delivering mail also. Now that will change, you'll see. I hope you consider me your friend after this.

Angie, you are the daughter I never had; and you are the wife I hope Millie will be. And I wish my mother had been more like you. Now what more to tell you, whoever you touch is the luckiest bugger in the world, even if they don't know it then.

Don Pedro, I hope you immortalize the lovely Madam Rosalina in your painting.

I hope each of you fulfils something in your lives. Will I see you again? Maybe, maybe not, I don't know what plans Millie has for me.

I respectfully remain,

Yours truly,
Fernando D'Cruz

He places the note under the jerry can and walks with heavy feet and a heavier heart back to the bike.

15

DON PEDRO

When the final stroke is applied, he dips his brush tenderly into the gloop on the palette that looks like the remains of a fully dressed clown gone splat after a twenty-storey high-dive.

He swirls the brush dreamily in the clown's colourful entrails, and touches the canvas with it: a final daub of paint signifying the end, a splotchy *quod erat demonstrandum* that appears on Rosalina's left thigh just below the blanket line. A birthmark, a bruise, a lover's hickey? It is ritual, always to end with a full stop, why should writers only have that privilege?

What is it like for Don Pedro to complete a work of art? Is it like cresting a peak, or going over the finish line after a trans-ocean swim?

He steps back, looks at it, and savours that familiar feeling of extreme relief. His own very private one, of having just had the best, longest, sweetest, smelliest dump of his life, a sentiment never shared with journalists when they ask him, *So, Don Pedro, how does it feel blah blah blah?*

He is exhausted but elated. It is the middle of the afternoon. While Rosalina has been in the shade, he has been out in the hot sun. His bald pate feels ready to receive an egg, sunny side up. He is starving and he feels weak, but what does that matter? His loins are crackling and sparking, and he is ready for a quick round of sweaty love-making, another ritual from back in the day when men were men and artists were insatiable.

He looks at her, still sitting on that tree-root, looking miserable, looking like her dog has just died. Or cat, ha ha ha, wait till *that* one comes out of the bag ha ha ha.

'It is done,' he says.

'Oooh, oooh, is it finished?' Her brain lazily comes out of its coma, sputtering like an engine that had not been started all winter. 'Help me up, please,' she grunts, trying to wiggle her toes and will some life into her muscles.

He walks away to the car and returns with an aerosol can, the contents of which he sprays liberally over his canvas. 'Don Pedro,' she pants, giving up on her struggle and holding up one plump, limp wrist in his direction.

He looks at her and smiles. 'Not that, oh no, not that any more. My back cannot take it, dear lady.' He goes back to his spraying, a look of sheer love softening his expression as he stares at the canvas.

'Don Pedro.' A little force in her squeak now, a little asperity, a little alarm.

'You'll have to lose a lot of weight, madam, before I give you my hand one more time, oh ho, I'll tell you that. Not one good chiropractor in all of Goa, let alone Pocolim.' He steps back. 'There, as good as dry. Five minutes in the sun and we are, as they say, ready to boogie.' He begins to gather up his brushes.

She stamps her foot. 'Don Pedro, please, I want to see. You t'ink Fadder Francis will like it? For de church, I mean?'

He looks at her, his muse. Looking at her the way Casanova might have looked at a latex rubber doll.

'Father Francis?' he says. 'Is that how far the reach of your lowly mind goes?'

The limited elasticity of his facial muscles prevent his lips from curling all the way down to his toes, but that is clearly his intention.

'To some drunken sod, little more than a bureaucratic clerk in the employ of a dusty, fossilised institution, for whom art is the label on a bottle of cheap brandy?' he enquires.

His eyes skewer her and turn her around slowly on a flaming spit.

'Do you think I have painted this so I may get a whistle of approval from some insignificant church-mouse? I may as well line up all the cockroaches in Goa and teach them how to clap.'

She stops struggling and tries to pay attention, her breath stalling in her throat. Something of great importance is being said here, some great change taking place in this universe of hers, though she has no idea what it is. She has no idea why each of his words feels like a drop of molten lava raining down on her skin. She shivers and flinches. Her brain has a little more luck struggling to its feet than her body does.

'Wat wat … Fadder Francis … wat wat,' says the sputtering engine.

'It is done. This is just the first, and there will be others.' He stares at his finished work, and then swivels his head to look at the object that has inspired it. 'Seldom have I been so wrong,' he says softly, in an axe-murderer's voice. 'How could someone so magnificent to look at be completely empty from the inside? How has all this marvellous flesh accrued upon your bones with no wealth of experience? Where has your mind been while your body was working its magic, filling itself out, becoming an innocent and deadly lure for artists?'

He peers into her thoroughly frightened face. 'Do you know the hardest part of finishing this painting, madame? Your eyes. Where and what is your soul? I do not see it. I had to make it up. It is like making love to you and thinking of another,' he says. 'You mentioned last night your husband used to call you other names.

Now I understand. He may not have appreciated art, but he knew soul. And you have none.'

A grave shake of his head. She feels like screaming in terror but all her faculties have frozen up, shut down.

'How could I have been so wrong?'

Dragging his curled-down lip behind him, he turns around and stalks away. After ten steps, he says over his shoulder, 'You are free to go. I am done with you.'

16
ROSIE

She watches his sweaty, receding back.

Pins run up her legs and pass batons to needles who run down. She finally takes a deep breath, purely an involuntary need to get oxygen to the brain. The air feels hot and her lungs feel like they are doused in paraffin.

Vision swimming and jaws clamped tight, she places her hands on her knees and jerks herself upright, throwing one arm out against the stolid banyan for support. Her blanket falls off her shoulders and pools at her feet. She sees Nature ogling her stark naked body, the trees, the clouds, the wheeling birds, the unseen insects in the grass, everything pinching its lips in disapproval.

Humiliation is the true death. Life flashes before your eyes until there is no life left, and at the end of it you are still alive, burning in shame's acid juices.

Her mind roams the past, looking for comfort. All that comes is a patchwork of hazy events, places and people, and not one of them offers her a landing spot or a little hole she can snuggle into and forget the present.

And worst of all, the single event in her life that she has sat upon and smothered all these years, as effectively as she might smother a squirming mouse under her enormous bottom, the death of Gabriel

Albert Fernandez, her son; it rises. A mother's defence mechanism: tricking memory cells into blurring the ghastly picture of that final, dreadful moment, taming memory's wild-dog tendencies to bite and claw at her dreams all these years; it crumbles.

The images rush back, etched out and clearer than they have ever been: of her getting there first, kneeling next to his body rigid and ridiculous in that 800-rupee wedding suit, and peering into his mouth and seeing ... seeing that little replica of himself that he had drunkenly tried to eat, and which ate him instead, and reaching in and pulling it out, but it is too late, the gates have been shut forever.

For the first time in ten years, she weeps. Copious wetness trickles down her neck and body, some of it nestling in the folds of flesh, the rest soaking the blanket at her feet. And all the time, Nature just hisses and claps and boos. And she weeps and weeps.

After a while, a long, long while, the tears lessen. Long fingers reach into the deepest recesses of her brain and shut off the tap of grief, cracking open the one of anger instead.

Anger, it is a trickle, but it unglues her body, gives it enough strength to bend over carefully and gather up the blanket around her body again. She glares at the voyeuristic trees and bares her teeth at the nosy sun. Giving that grief-tap one last tweak, she finds her clothes where she had left them and puts them on one by one. They make her feel secure and protected, but inside she feels filthy, pawed all over by harsh words, cruel eyes and scornful lips. She is not sure a hundred baths will ever clean all this.

Her lips compressed so tight her mouth almost disappears, she steps out into the clearing and looks around for her sweet Angie; sweet Angie whose memory has not offered her succour just moments ago. She spies the easel and the canvas lounging on it, drying off like a beach bum. She walks over to it, even as she sees Don Pedro walking towards her with the stride of a hungry lion, a roll of plastic sheet in his hand. She reaches the canvas first and looks at it.

A hundred hands paw her all over again, lecherous and dipped in faecal matter. She checks to confirm that she is indeed fully clothed. She feels faint. She feels stabbed and hacked. She shuts her eyes, but phantom fingers pry them open again.

The cloth around her body in the painting is exactly as she had wrapped it. Except this one is gossamer-thin, diaphanous and flimsy. It is the hint of a shadow thrown by a wispy cloud on the burning desert floor. She is, for all intents and purposes, as naked as the day she was born. And had she not sat with her legs together?

He comes and stands beside her, breathing heavily. 'Good, my dear lady, it is not too late to learn to appreciate art. You have your rightful place in history now, as the latest and most prolific muse to Don Pedro Cleto Colaco.' He sighs and touches the painting, testing it for dryness. 'It's a pity your husband, whom I feel a sudden kinship with, by the way, is not alive to see this moment. Might have taught him a thing or two as well, God rest his soul.'

She shuts her eyes and opens them again. Everything is still there.

'Mind you, a bigger canvas would've been more appropriate,' he says, unwrapping the plastic sheet. 'Anyway, what was I going to tell you?' He snaps his fingers. 'Yes, that the petrol is here, along with a badly scribbled note by that halfwit which looks like a drunken centipede with inky feet has meandered all over the page. He's gone, so we can pack up and go back. If we can only find that good-for-nothing and that servant girl, we can be off. Know where they are?'

At that precise moment, they saunter into sight, at a distance. They may have been holding hands, but that could have been a trick of light.

'Right. Wouldn't you know it,' he says. 'Like attracts like. Turn around for a minute and they are rutting like animals.' The artist flashes his widest grin and waves, motioning them to the car. Then he proceeds to wrap his latest masterpiece.

17

SAVIO

He gets to the car and picks up the letter from under the full can of petrol. While he reads it out loud, he keeps glancing at Rosalina. There is something definitely off here, something way beyond fatigue, something radically amiss.

Her lips look glued together, like they will never move to form words ever again. Or smile or open to eat food. Her shield, her invisible electrified fence, seems dormant. He could tweak her nose and she would not react. The current is switched off. She looks like she has unplugged herself from life.

'Don Pedro, I hope you immortalize the lovely Madam Rosalina in your painting,' he reads. Did those lips quiver just then?

'I hope each of you fulfils something in your lives,' he continues. 'Will I see you again? Maybe, maybe not, I don't know what plans Millie has for me.'

This time he is sure he hears a sob. He folds the letter, looks around and catches Angie's eye. She holds up the cat and nods imperceptibly, a terrified look on her face. He responds with an imperceptible shrug.

'So wat we do now?' Rosie speaks, making Savio jump. Those lips have moved, and yes, they are definitely quivering.

'We go home, no? You heard what he wrote in his letter. He's gone on his own.'

'So we leave him jus' like *dat?*' she hisses, her bosom heaving in and out like a giant beating heart.

'You want me to read this letter to you again?' He wonders, why the fuck did we not run away in the opposite direction when we had the chance?

'I understan' English perfeckly, t'ank you.'

Another opinion is called for. Has he been mistaken? She has not unplugged from anything. There is a viciousness he has never seen before. Her squeaks are legend, but he has never heard her hiss and she is definitely hissing. And spitting.

He takes a step back, ready to run for his life if necessary.

'Selfish, dat's wat all you men are!' A nest of snakes speaks from somewhere in her throat. 'Selfish, t'inkin' only of *yourself*.' Spittle rains all around and he takes one more step back. Her eyes are unfocused now, looking past him, through him.

'So,' Don Pedro booms, 'what are we waiting for?'

He has come up on them, the canvas rolled and packed neatly in one hand. She shoots him a sideways look and shudders literally from head to toe. In it, Savio instantly reads everything he needs to know. Pissed of at *him* for whatever reason, taking it out on me.

Fucking typical. Just having a hissy fit, that's all.

'We were about to leave, but madame has other plans,' Savio tells the artist.

'Do you care for *anybody* but yourself?' she screams, parting his hair, spraying his face with saliva, knocking sleeping birds off branches, making grass quake. 'It should have been *you,* not Gabo, that night,' she hisses. '*You*, you selfish no-good fellow, it should have been *you* that died, but God takes away the good and leaves behind the trash.'

Somewhere low down inside Savio's stomach a trapdoor opens up and hot rage flows upward. He cannot really see her through a red-black mist. He is now a self-loading shotgun with the trigger jammed in shoot.

'This is not Pocolim,' he roars. 'This is not your fucking house, or your fucking pop's village, or your fucking pop's car, do you hear?'

He leans into her. She leans back, jowls jiggling like blancmange.

'And I am selfish? You stupid, self-absorbed fat beast, walking around the whole time with your head up your arse, I am selfish? I'll show you who's fucking selfish!'

He storms around the car, grabs Nereus from Angie's hand, even as her eyes plead, *no, no*. But he can barely see the red-black outlines of things. He storms back to Rosie and throws the cat at her bosom. It bounces off, and she fields it before it hits the ground, cradling stiff, dead meat in her fat forearms.

'Your precious cat, your precious light-of-my-life cat has been dead for a *day*! As dead as *your fucking son*! Have you fed it *once*? Looked after it *once*? What are we, your fucking pop's servants, to look after it while you pose like a tart, thinking you are some high-society madam? A tart, a fucking tart is what you are!'

Even shotguns need a break, even those gone mental.

'And now suddenly, it's Ferdie, Ferdie, Ferdie?' He gives her a full view of the inside of his raw and ravaged throat. 'You treat him like shit, all your fucking selfish life you have treated him like *shit*, like the mud on your fucking shoe, and now suddenly it's Ferdie, Ferdie? Well, Ferdie my ass, I'm getting into this fucking car and driving off, and if you don't, well, then walk!'

Mercifully, the shells run out. Rosie looks like she's had a concussion. The unplugged look is back. She looks down at the lifeless cat in her arms, looks up, looks all around her. Her eyeballs go up into her head to look in there as well, and then her body begins to move.

It oscillates about its own axis, slowly at first, overcoming that formidable inertia, and then picks up a little velocity, expanding its diameter as it goes.

Savio sees it happening and reflexively throws out his arms, his mouth forming an O, but now she is now toppling away from him, straight into Don Pedro's arms.

He nimbly skips away, and all 300 pounds of her crash to the earth, causing birds' nests to rattle for a mile around.

18
THE DODGE

There is savagery in the silence.

Dehydration and hunger do not help.

The fifth passenger, sitting where Ferdie might have been sitting, is the smelly ghost of the cat. The physical body had been interred just fifteen minutes back with minimum fanfare, its main mourner out cold.

They had tried to revive her, but it was almost as if she had preferred to stay unconscious, a state much better than her recent waking reality. Nereus went under the ground only marginally more stiff and immobile than he had lived above it.

Don Pedro has a spring to his body language that is completely absent in the others. He did not assist them in the revival of his muse, did not lend a hand to help her to the car.

Savio is brooding. Rosie is diagonally behind him, her presence hovering on the outskirts of his vision like a stalker animal. He feels as if his heart is being used as a trampoline by impish leprechauns. He feels terrible, he feels low.

There is an ugly taste of no-victory in his mouth. He disgusts himself. Angie, what will she think of him now? Her eyes are vacantly staring at the road ahead, her fingers twirling her hair, her head propped up in her hand that in turn is propped up on the window-sill.

Another soft sob from the blind sector behind his right ear, and hobnailed boots go boing-boing on his heart.

In the midst of the melee, there is one sudden nanosecond of clarity, a lone firefly flaring briefly in a pitch-black night, glimpsed through a fleeting window of silence. His hands and feet, moving of their own accord, are already slowing down the car and pulling it over to the side of the road.

A set of lips curl expertly downward in the back seat. 'What is it now?' they ask.

The engine purrs and sweet sounds of late afternoon waft in. 'We're doing this all wrong,' Savio says. 'We should be going that way.' He jerks a thumb over his shoulder.

'Which way is home?' the down-angled lips enquire.

'This way,' pointing ahead, 'but Stotisgaon is that way,' pointing back, 'literally round the corner.'

'And what is in Stotisgaon that is of importance to us? We all read the letter, didn't we?'

'Food. For your legendary lion's appetite.'

'I won't die if I don't have food for another couple of hours. And neither will you.'

'No, but if I pass out while I'm driving, we all will.'

Don Pedro's lips purse, pout, sneer, do back-bends and handstands, and then finally speak. 'All right. So maybe you're being cute, and you think I'm stupid. Maybe your heart is bleeding and you actually want to pick up that walking-talking whining-crying good-for-nothing insult to men. All right, I'll give you the benefit of doubt. Do one thing: when we get to Stotisgaon, drop me off at the bus stand so I can get home. You bring the car back to me, cleaned, serviced and polished. Polished, you hear?' He yawns. 'Yes, really. The longer I spend in this august company, the further I can feel my IQ falling, tumbling down the hill like Jack and Jill, and the sooner I rescue it the better. Ha ha.'

There is a crash of gears and the occupants feel some considerable centrifugal force as Savio swings the car around and barrels down the road in the opposite direction.

Wind makes conversation obsolete. It disperses the ghostly smell of cat in the car. With dried-up words and rumbling stomachs, they hurtle towards Stotisgaon.

They spot him at a distance, on the side of the road, as they crest a steep incline just where a milestone says '3 kms'. The road angles down as steeply as it has climbed, and then curves away to the right, out of sight, the turn marked by a thick grove of oaks that look massive even at that distance.

On a good day, Ferdie might pip the six-foot mark, with his hair standing on end. On this worst day of his life, he looks about three feet tall. He is slouched over and his feet make little arcs in the mud, scraping and dredging earth as he staggers on. He does not look like he has 30 metres left in him, let alone 3 kilometres. On and on he goes, shuffle following shuffle, looking like his essence has evaporated, leaving behind some indestructible core which keeps on keeping on.

'Lo and behold, Romeo crawling towards his Juliet,' sneers Don Pedro. 'I knew it. This is why you turned.'

The car accelerates as it hits the steep down-gradient. Angie reaches across and jabs the horn thrice: loud, jubilant blasts that stretch out long fingers, carrying a message of succour.

'Oh, grow up,' snarls Don Pedro.

Ferdie turns around, still bent over, still in the twilight zone of exhaustion, too tired to even straighten up.

Yuko had dropped him to a nearest bus stand and whizzed off. There had been no bus to Stotisgaon. They had cancelled it on that day, not enough passengers. The old Ferdie would have ... He didn't know what the old Ferdie would have done, but the new Ferdie had started walking. And he had walked and walked, wondering how many miles a pair of feet was good for in one day? Would they just stop on their own?

At the sound of the horn, he turns and looks. Slow as a summer dawn, a smile spreads across his face.

Even Savio gets a lump in his throat. He eases his foot off the gas pedal and pushes the brake in gently. The car does not slow at all.

He punches down hard, twice, feels the piston sigh through air instead of the reassuring resistance of oil. The car accelerates, gravity hungrily sucking down all two tons of it.

'Jesus Christ,' he hisses.

Bewilderment on Angie's face, Ferdie's wide, tired smile suddenly going slack, Don Pedro coming alive and alert in the back seat.

'What's going on?' he demands harshly.

The speedo needle climbs as the American monster, with its evil chromium-grille grin, ducks its head and charges the oak-grove at the end of the road. Rosie, who has been clawing empty space on her lap where dirty fur should've been, suddenly snaps out of her daze.

The knock-offs, thinks Savio, *the fucking knock-offs!*

A wild keening scream erupts in the back seat. 'Help me,' it yells.

Except the vowels are a yard long, in a volume that might have woken up a dead cat. The car rockets past Ferdie, almost knocking him over with its side-draft.

'Help me,' screams Rosie again, adding another foot or two to her vowels, and even as her life flashes before her eyes for the second time that day, she forgives Don Pedro and leaps into his arms.

He swats away her plump hands, places two size-ten palms on her shoulders and heaves her back. He grabs his rolled-up canvas and his bag of sketches and throws them out of the window. Lips muttering something about sacrifice and posterity, he pushes open the door, stares fleetingly at the whizzing foliage, takes a deep breath, and hurls himself out like a sack of potatoes.

The car hurtles at a hundred miles an hour towards the clump of fat, gnarled, impassive oaks, carrying its remaining three shell-shocked occupants to a certain death.

19
SAVIO

But nobody dies. They age rapidly towards another death, at another time, but not on that day.

And the car isn't even scratched.

Savio, dialling in desperately to a God he has not spoken to in years, downshifts and grinds his jaw. A howl of rage erupts from the gearbox, and the speedo needle jerks back briefly as though someone has lassoed it, but the Dodge is heavy and gravity is a bitch.

They come upon the turn, a blind hook to the right. In front of them, the oaks grow in size, in width, girth and solidity. He downshifts once more, and wrenches the wheel to the right, putting his entire weight behind it.

Two tyres lift as the car takes the turn, the other two bite and hold, and Savio mutters thanks that Rosie is on the other side, her tonnage keeping her end down. The sturdy Dodge contorts horribly, stretching its tendons and ligaments to the maximum, nuts and bolts holding on with teeth and fingernails, burning rubber screeching and polluting the air and then—

And then, nothing. The road ahead angles up again, looking as new as a freshly unfurled ribbon, and the Dodge cruises on its new heading, the gearbox clearing its ravaged throat but otherwise no worse for wear. Up, up it goes, until it runs out of steam, and just as it sighs to a stop Savio cuts the engine, leaving the car in gear.

Vertigo washes over him as the tide of adrenaline recedes, leaving behind a weak and gibbering thought: he is alive.

'Exhale, exhale,' he tells Angie in a small-boy voice, causing all her trapped air to whoosh out and the purple edges on her face to recede.

His ears pick up sounds that are similar to, but not quite the sounds of nature. A suggestion of a freshly whelped litter of piglets in the vicinity. He peeps over the seat, observes Madame Rosalina staring up at him from the floor of the car. Like a meticulous hand has tucked her in there neatly.

Is Don Pedro *under* her, being squashed to death? He sees the passenger door swing lazily on its hinges. Not exactly as clear as two and two, but he gets the gist.

'We need help,' he tells Angie, that little-boy voice slowly growing a little hair on its chest.

As Angie manoeuvres her mother-in-law out, kilo by kilo, he walks back, down the slope, past the clump of jilted oaks that had welcomed them with open arms and armour bodies, and takes the turn back to where they had come from.

He sees Ferdie immediately, still standing where the car had almost knocked him over. In the foreground, a sack that has been carelessly thrown to the side of the road. The sack moves, it grows a head and limbs. It groans. Savio trudges up the incline and looks down at it.

Don Pedro, he is scratched and bleeding and covered from head to toe in the browns and greens of the great outdoors. One ankle is twisted badly, looking like someone has stuck a hamburger down his sock. His neck is seriously whiplashed and his wrist and fingers hurt when he tries to move them. The way he looks up at Savio groggily suggests the possibility of concussion. Savio looks around, spies the rolled-up canvas that has snagged onto a passing bush.

It is well wrapped and sealed; he digs in his thumbs and tears through the plastic. He opens it out and holds it up. He stares, fascinated.

He is repulsed. And he is transfixed. And he is terrified that he can be aroused by something so abrasively disgusting. And he is shocked when his lips go into whistle-mode on their own and icy feet tap dance up and down his spine.

'Jesus Christ,' he whispers, voice all phlegmy and thick, hands shaking. 'This is – fucking – *brilliant*.'

He can stare at it all evening, and into the night, and the next day, but he forces his fingers to roll it up once again. He walks back to Don Pedro and stands over him. This man, genius or not, is still an obnoxious cunt, but the observation now streaked with a grudging awe.

The artist has made it up to his elbows and is panting with effort, head drooped down, bald pate glistening, snot and spit dangling like pearly bracelets from his face.

Savio grins. 'Nice jump. That bus you wanted to catch? Whenever you are ready.'

20

FERDIE

They make it into Stotisgaon just as the hour creeps up on five, the engine red-hot as Savio crawls in first or second gear, a warning light winking on the dashboard. Savio thinks, there goes the bloody radiator as well. But they make it, five humans and a car, in various states of decay and disrepair.

Stotisgaon is a small village, smaller than Pocolim, and it announces its existence with a stone marker bearing its name jammed into the earth at a jaunty angle between two hefty banyan trunks. Then you drive on for an agonizing ten minutes wondering if the stone marker was a practical joke, or if the entire village has relocated taking with it every brick and stone. Suddenly, thick forest gives way to the first of the houses. And humans become visible, early-evening loiterers that make the narrow roads even narrower, and the Dodge has to elbow them aside politely as it winds its way towards the village square, with the obligatory church and taverna, the Information Centre as far as villages like that go.

The car attracts attention, as do the travellers. They look like they have driven in from Inner Africa, or Outer Mongolia maybe, passed through exotic lands, faced grave dangers and much hardship.

The big, bald man with the torn shirt and concussed face looks like he has seen the inside of a croc's mouth before fleeing to tell the tale.

A scrawny, sunken, hollowed-out human in the back seat might have crossed the Gobi on his hands and knees. The humongously fat lady with the dour expression, the jungle queen that has been kidnapped from the Congo, and that sweat-sheened beautiful girl next to her, her handmaiden perhaps. The driver; well, the driver is the least remarkable of them all, but his eyes look like they contain a library of tales that could regale men all night if plied with continuous grog.

Savio enquires the way to the church. He is guided by bored individuals who dart questioning looks around the car.

'Millie Furtado, Millie Furtado,' Ferdie croaks through cracked lips at every neatly combed head that peers in, only to be met with a hardboiled voyeur's stare and no other response.

They see the church long before the narrow road opens out into the large square, its grey steeple and weathered cross poking above the trees and cottages. It is much prettier than the Pocolim church, the façade recently whitewashed and gleaming, and Rosie, despite everything, makes mental notes.

There is a procession leaving the churchyard just as Savio kills the engine. 'I'm going to look for some brake oil,' he says. 'And I'll ask around.'

As they all step out to stretch their legs, the quiet evening is pierced by a sound, a very familiar sound. Technically it is a tune, but that only becomes apparent a few bars later, as if the musicians have, after scrabbling around a bit, finally found the note they were looking for.

'Oh damn,' says Savio.

As the scratchy notes of '*Lord, I'm Coming Home*' waft over the low wall of the churchyard, the musicians heave into view. Two trumpets wag their noses in the air – neither of which have come in contact with brass polish in years. Two atonal violins and a drum – its skin may have been cut from the withered flanks of an ageing donkey – attempt tricky syncopation.

The musicians, who no doubt hold day jobs where they exercise their true talents, march with a sober expression, tinged with irritation at being pulled away from their sundowners. The suits are as wrinkled, their shoes as scuffed, as their inclination to scratch, toot and thump music.

The coffin emerges, a large one, carried by six, burly youths who are wishing that there were six more helping them. The deceased is a big person and undoubtedly well loved, judging by the mourners, mostly men, honking into handkerchiefs with swollen noses and red eyes. Perhaps an outstanding member of society, a good drinking buddy, a gentleman who has lived well, gorged well and fed well.

Then Ferdie straightens up to full height, his neck craning forward and a jitter in his body frame. One shaking hand comes up, one bony finger extends outward like a probe, and they all hear him say above the cacophony of the music: 'Millie.'

Their eyes follow the line of his finger and alight upon, yes, a lady walking in a group of other ladies, but this one somehow different, not because Ferdie is pointing at her, but because of her carriage, her body language, her beautiful skin and a face that is lovely, obvious even from behind her veil.

Ferdie, except for a finger that shakes uncontrollably, looks like he has turned to stone. Savio forgets about the brake oil, Don Pedro stops caressing his sprained ankle, Rosie forgets about her notes to Father Francis, and Angie clenches and unclenches her fists.

'Go for it, Padraon,' says Savio. 'If you are sure, that is.'

Ferdie, his bulging eyes ask, *if* I am sure? *If*?

'Alright. But stop pointing, for fuck's sake. It's rude.'

Angie has moved up beside Savio. 'Is this … do you think … are you thinking what I am thinking?' she asks. 'This … Millie? And this?' She points to the coffin.

Then Rosie steps forward. She puts one hand on Ferdie's shoulder and squeezes it gently. 'Go an' talk to her, Ferdinand. We have travelled far. You are not a sissy boy anymore. Dere is nuttin' to fear.'

Ferdie, whispering words to himself that no one can quite hear (though Savio thinks he catches something that sounds like 'finish what you start'), takes one step forward. And then another.

The beautiful lady walks past, her head down, sobbing silent tears behind the veil. Ferdie falls into step behind her.

'Millie,' he calls out.

There is a noticeable stiffening of her body, which is only picked up by him and his co-travellers.

He tries again. Her head snaps back.

'It's me, *Ferdie*!' he hisses.

And then he reaches out and gently takes her hand.

21

BRAZ'S TAVERNA

When I come back from the restroom, the boy and girl, they are talking to the old guy at the next table.

The old coot, he is dressed like he stepped out of a Mario Miranda cartoon. Coat, trousers, thin black tie, jaunty hat, smoking a cigarette, sucking on his glass.

It is night out. Inside, the air is thick with smoke. Almost every table is full by now.

The boy, he is leaning forward and nodding. The girl, she has a little camera out, looking around her, her gun-finger poised to not miss a thing.

In a cartoon, the old coot would have been called Manuel Batista de Baltazar e Barbosa. Or Bartolomeo de Costa. Or Patrocinio Pimenta. Something egregiously Goan, a caricature of himself.

The girl, she looks for subjects to photograph. The Wedgwood chairs, the marble-top tables, the labels on the feni bottles, the rakish glints in the eyes of the drunks, their slack jaws, their toothless grins, all of this will be super exotic to folks back home. Her eyes keep going back to the wall, to the photos and paintings hung up there. The still life up there drags her eyes away from the moving life around her.

'Can you believe it,' the old coot is slurring. 'Found her after forty years.'

'Thirty-seven,' says the boy, who has been paying attention, 'But still—'

'That *is* romantic,' says the girl. 'The timing, almost a miracle—'

'She was beautiful,' the old coot is saying, eyeing me as I sit down. 'More beautiful dan he remembered her. When her veil came off ...'

The girl stares up at the wall, her eyes scanning left to right, taking her time on each wall hanging. Her pupils zooming in and out.

'You don't mind if I take pictures, do you?' she asks me politely.

I say, go right ahead.

'When her veil came off,' the old coot is saying, 'de whole procession came to a standstill. What a beauty! Like she had not aged only.'

'What a shock it must have been for her,' the boy says, nodding and shaking his head at the same time.

They are from Minnesota. They are engaged. They are both in between jobs. They've both been forced, mid-career, to figure out what else they're good for. Recession and downsizing have made them look for new tricks to turn. This is their sabbatical.

'Folks said she cried and cried. Wet her whole funeral gown wit' her tears.' The old coot cackles.

The boy raises his glass. One of my father's specials. 'Beautiful. Tears of grief, followed by tears of joy. Death, and a brand-new beginning.' He throws out his hand. 'I'm Phil. And this is Tracy.'

'Pleased to meet you,' says Tracy, tearing her eyes off the wall, transferring the camera to her left.

The old coot, his hands shake so much, it takes him a while to grip theirs.

'Oscar,' he says. 'Laundry. Every single shirt, pant, dress, gown, bed sheet, tablecloth in Pocolim, las' fifty years.'

'Oh! You are—'

'Wow, just like in the—'

'Rubbish!' roars a man from two tables down.

The boy and girl, Phil and Tracy, they turn, startled.

Two tables down, a man glowers at them. He has turned his chair out to face them, his belly hanging down, straining the buttons of his gaudy shirt at its widest, bits of white stomach hair visible through the gaps.

'W'at you t'ink dis is? A fairy tale or what?' he asks, mildly annoyed, his black moustache bristling like a caterpillar. A strand of jet-black hair has escaped his pompadour, and he pats it back in place.

'W'at you t'ink, she did yoga all dese years or w'at, dat she did not age?' he growls pleasantly.

He drains his glass and licks his lips with a thick purple tongue, eyes bulging enormously. Tufts of white chest hair spill out over his top button. His jet-back rockabilly hair, swooped in a ducktail style, glows under the overhead lamp.

'When de veil came off, dere was a pin-drop silence,' he says.

22
FERDIE

She reacts as if she has been nipped by a dog.

She snatches her arm away, turns around full frontal, lifts her veil and socks Ferdie on his shoulder. 'What do you think you're doing?' she yells in Konkani, displaying a fine talent for temper.

The band, not really needing an excuse to goof off, takes an impromptu break. The pallbearers thump the coffin down, wiping their brows, checking that their shoulders are still in their sockets.

When the veil comes up, there is a sharp intake of breath from four people simultaneously.

'Oh crap,' says Savio.

'Oh dear,' says Angie.

'Oh my God,' squeaks Rosie.

'Ha ha ha ha,' laughs Don Pedro.

'What do you want?' the girl demands, her cheeks pink with fury.

The funeral entourage stretch rubbery necks, yearning for something juicy to happen. All they get is a pathetic bleat.

'Millie? Isn't it you?'

The girl gasps. The audience is divided, some look sanctimoniously aghast, others titter behind coughs. The violinist lights a cigarette and the drummer sneaks a quart of feni out.

'Millie,' he mumbles again, his cheeks burning red like he has been slapped.

'Get away from me, you pishya!' she roars, scaring the violinist into stubbing out his cigarette. 'Millie is my mother!'

'Your mudder,' he gasps. 'Your mudder. Your …' Hope floods his face, and then slowly the bottom falls out of him. Angie rushes in to support him.

'Jesus Christ,' mutters Savio, looking up at the sky as if to say, *now, really, was this necessary?*

Rosie's plump little mouth falls open and a few inquisitive fruit flies come to check it out. Don Pedro, a frown on his contused forehead, hobbles onto his good foot and edges closer.

The girl, looking at Ferdie's shocked face, his legless aspect, wipes her eyes and squints at him commiseratingly. The light is soft, fading.

'Who are you?' she asks gently.

Ferdie finds his feet, taking some of the weight off Angie.

'Ferdinand,' he says, speaking to himself, as if the world and everything in it, animate and inanimate, has shrunk to the size of a shoe box and there will never be any need to raise his voice from here on.

'She used to call me Fernando. She was Millie Furtado then. We met in Pocolim.' No tears come, even though he has obligingly opened the floodgates.

'She never mentioned anyone by that name,' she says.

Ferdie tests his balance briefly, before gently removing Angie's arms. He walks on newly born gelding legs to the coffin and pleads to the young girl with his eyes. She nods to the pallbearers, one of whom pulls aside the lid.

His lips move around looking for words to form and his bushy eyebrows contort into wriggling worms of doubt.

'Dis is …?' he stammers.

Nobody notices Don Pedro who has limped over as well, and nobody notices the hungry look in his eyes as he takes in the weight and width of the coffin.

When he peeps in, nobody notices the hundred-volt shiver that wracks his entire body either.

Nobody hears him say, 'Fuck me sideways,' in Portuguese. Or limp back to his bag and remove his sketch-pad.

Ferdie turns to the girl and whispers, 'Today? She passed away today?'

'Early morning. She has been ill for about a month,' she tells him. 'Living in her own world, recognizing no one, talking to herself only. Last night, she went into a coma.' Her face crumples.

About a month? His body feels numb. Empty, like he has no organs left that can feel anything. He wonders how he can feel so much grief and still not cry. It isn't empty space in his body after all, it is all grief, wall to wall, floor to ceiling, like dark matter in the universe.

In her own world, talking to herself? Sending out little puffs of memory into the ether, this woman who has occupied his thoughts for near-on four decades but whom he cannot recognize right now.

Last night, slipping into a coma, switching off her transmissions for good…

Like dark matter coalescing to form a star, his grief balls up and rises, from his stomach, up, up into his throat. It comes floating up on something sweet, something kind.

'She came to me in my dreams,' he whispers, dry-eyed. 'You t'ink I'm mad, but she came to me in my dreams. Are you her only daughter?'

'From her second marriage, yes.'

'W'at do you mean, how many marriages has she had?'

'Four,' chuckles a pallbearer. 'Altogedder she took out one cricket team, from four marriages. Can't you make out?' He grins, flashing crooked teeth.

The girl's eyes flash. 'Pick it up and let's go!'

The pallbearers give their tired shoulders one more rub and mutter private words of antipathy. The drummer hurriedly stuffs the quart into his coat pocket. The trumpeter, seeing his solo moment, toots a tuneless reveille.

The girl gently touches Ferdie's shoulder and lowers her veil.

In the gathering twilight, Ferdie's stare can be measured both in distance and time. His eyes alight on nothing in the square or anything in the village. Standing there, between the blank walls of his past and future, he feels, for the first time his life, a strange contentment.

He thinks of his little room back in Pocolim as he stares his light-year stare. He yearns wistfully for his bed, for his kitchenette, his solitude. The bed looks benign and harmless, not a vessel of bad dreams and tortured thrashing.

Just a bleddy bed.

His feet ache, his calves scream, his thighs judder, but he reckons he can easily walk back to Pocolim if he chooses to.

The funeral procession disappears out of sight, nothing personal, they are just doing what they need to do. Just planets carrying on in their preordained orbits. It could be said that Ferdie once bravely flew out of his orbit for a bit, for a cause.

Planet Ferdie, surrounded by his motley satellites, contemplates a return. He reckons he can hate the sound of trumpets forevermore, just like he hates the sea because it came between him and Millie once.

Yuko would scorn him for that petty thought.

He turns to Savio. 'She remembered,' he says.

'I'm sure she did, Padraon.'

'She was ill and not herself, but she remembered.'

They wait. He runs fingers through his hair. He barely possesses the strength to chew his lip. They barely hear, 'I am hungry. Shall we eat sometin'?'

The equivalent of a hypnotist snapping his fingers.

'We were all thinking the same thing. Yes, we must,' says Angie.

'Not eaten properly for a whole day. Did not have lunch also yesterday, no?' says Rosie.

'I wasn't hungry den, but I'm hungry now,' in that the-world-has-shrunk-to-a-shoe-box voice.

'Or should we just drive back? After I've fixed the brakes?' offers Savio.

'I'll buy us some fruit and snacks. Let us drive back,' says Angie wearily.

'Yes, I t'ink you should get de brake oil,' Ferdie's lips concur.

Rosie puts her hand on her stomach. 'We have food at home?' she asks.

'There is xacuti in the fridge.'

'Chicken?'

'No, mutton.'

'Come eat wit' us tonight,' Rosie says.

'I think I'll go and look for the brake oil.'

'Anyway Angie is always bringing food for you. Better you eat wit' us from now,' says Rosie, with gentle firmness.

'Albert,' she says, 'he would have wanted it dat way.'

As Savio walks away, Ferdie turns to him.

'Er, jus' one t'ing. You came back for me. T'anks for dat. T'anks to all of you.'

'Savio's idea,' says Angie.

Savio stops, turns around. The expression on Ferdie's face…

'May as well tell you now, no?' Savio says, the expression on his face deflecting the gratitude.

'Tell me w'at?'

He licks his lips, thrusts his hands in his pockets. 'That letter that came under your door. My father used to be a postmaster years and years ago. One of the many jobs he did in Pocolim.'

He waits for pennies to drop but not one *ka-chink* is heard in all the faces that look back at him.

'It must be tradition, in Pocolim, to never deliver letters,' he says. 'Misplace them, take them home to dispatch later, forget about them.'

It must be the general tiredness, he thinks. Their faces are blank.

He shrugs. 'He was shit at his job, maybe even worse than you.' And for Rosie's benefit, he adds, 'Loyola, the outstanding, hard-working member of his community.'

Then Ferdie begins to tremble. And Angie looks at Savio like she is meeting him for the first time. And Rosie looks away.

'I need to see a doctor,' growls Don Pedro but nobody pays him any attention.

'Yours was the only one that belonged to somebody still living, still in Pocolim. Tore up the rest.' He turns around and disappears to look for brake oil.

Ferdinand walks over to a row of pigeon-shat benches outside the church wall and sits down. He stares at his knees and plays with his fingers. Angie walks over after a while, followed by Rosie and they flank him like mismatched bookends. Don Pedro sits in the Dodge and sketches. Dusk gathers.

'I need a drink,' says Ferdie, just as the sun gives one last wink from over the rooftops and ducks its head.

'Dere is some ol' brandy of Albert's also at home.'

'I need a lot of drink.'

'There is plenty, Ferdie,' says Angie.

'I want to drink till I am fully drunk. Till my eyes close.'

'You must stay awake for de xacuti.'

'First the xacuti. Den the drink,' whispers Ferdie, not to them, but to the dusk gathering before his nose.

'I will drink wit' you.'

'Me too,' says Angie.

'Bleddy hot day it's bin, no?'

'Uff. Wait till May, den you'll see.'

'I t'ink I walked for fifty miles today. Xacuti mutton from Gregory's shop?'

'Now run by Maria. And her son.'

'Useless fellow, dat Warren. Fat he's become. Which girl will want him? Always smelling of meat.'

'Good meat, though.'

'Can keep for five days in freezer and still will be fresh.'

Twilight goes on for a bit in these long days of summer, the sun inching its way up the elliptical ladder, night coming in slower and slower each day like a shy guest. Back in Pocolim, he reflects, he'd be scurrying back to his abode like a frightened animal trying to outrun the dark.

Down the road somewhere, there is a burial taking place, another human exiting, taking her body and personality with her forever, never another one like her.

Taking away the unique reasons why she was loved, hated, missed, coveted, leaving nothing behind, not a trace.

Wrap up the memory of her in a paper bag and chuck it down into the hole with her.

'Good times,' Ferdie murmurs to a spot of darkening air in the middle distance. 'Good times.' And then so quietly, even he doesn't hear himself although he can swear he shouted it, 'T'ank you.'

23

BRAZ'S TAVERNA

'Thank you? He said thank you?' the boy, Phil, he asks, looking a little blindsided. But, after two of my daddy's specials, they usually do.

'Ferdie, he was a gentleman,' says the guy with the hair-do. 'A gentleman knows how to take it on de chin.'

'But that is so tragic,' says Tracy, the sweet Midwestern girl.

'Credit where credit is due,' says the old dude with the jet-black rock 'n' roll hair. 'Fucked up my sleep in the morning wit' his bleddy singing. Sounded like a cat being tortured. But only a gentleman displays grace when his world falls apart.'

Mind your language, I warn him.

'You call it tragic because you believe in fairy tales, dat's why,' says this pompadoured fool. 'W'at tragic, why tragic? Dat's how real life happens,' he says, running a comb through his Elvis hair.

'Poor Ferdie,' says sweet Tracy, empathy pouring out of her eyes. Eyes that keep going back to my wall. My wall, with its own storyline, its own characters. 'What happened to him then?'

He tucks his comb in his breast pocket and starts playing with the white hairs that protrude between buttons.

'He got married to Rosie. Double wedding it was. Angie, Savio. Ferdie and Rosie.'

'Really? That's amazing,' slurs the boy.

'I remember reading about Pedro Colaco,' says the girl. 'In our final year in school.'

'Rosie changed,' says Joao. 'That trip took all the piss out of her. She was nice to everybody after that.'

'You went to art school?' I ask her.

'After Ferdie moved in with her, there was peace in Pocolim. Fool stopped crying, she stopped shouting. And I started sleeping.'

'University of St. Paul,' she says. 'Contemporary Asian Art.'

'Yes, different kind of happy ever after,' says Joao, 'but what de hell. Cheers to Ferdinand.' We raise our glasses solemnly.

'I studied Pedro Colaco,' she says. 'I can't believe it all happened right here,' sweeping her hand, covering the whole of my little shitsplat village. 'What a coincidence,' she says, rolling her eyes.

Then he, Phil, turns to me. 'That was some story.'

I pour him another. Told you, didn't I, I say.

'Except I don't know why you heard the end from these idiots.' I point to Joao. 'He has Alzheimer's. Can't remember whether he wants to piss or shit. Goes to do one, ends up doing the other.'

They look at me shocked. Joao grins and continues to play with his belly hair.

'Wears diapers now, full time.'

The girl, her eyes roaming over my walls, says, 'Pedro Colaco's last showing was a success. The best ever.' She pulls out an iPhone and starts scrolling. 'I have it here somewhere.'

'And this fellow,' I point out Oscar to Phil. 'Been inhaling bleach all his life. You listen to them tell you the world's greatest love story?'

'Sorry,' he says, 'they just jumped in.'

'Continuing the tradition of "Women on Canvas",' Tracy reads, squinting in the dim light, 'no doubt inspired by prolific predecessors such as John Singer Sargent and Lord Frederick Leighton, but perhaps borrowing heavily from the legendary starkness of Lucian

Freud during his Fifties heydays, Don Pedro Cleto Colaco unveiled his newest collection of staggeringly vivid portraiture in the Chiostro Del Bramante today.'

'They came in one by one, after that mad road-trip,' I tell them. 'To drink and talk. My job is to listen. Yes, it is true Millie died that day.'

'Appearing after being out of the public eye for near on five years, his latest offering to the art world drew divided comments from the critics. Experimenting with a distinct departure from his past associations with surrealism blah blah, Don Pedro seems to have finally found a home in the Realism style of the eighteenth century.'

'Savio came in the most,' I tell them. 'Once a drunk, always a drunk. I told him, so Savio, now you have a girl, when you gonna smile, be happy? Still looking like he's misplaced that tube of balm for that imaginary boil up his arse, you know? Just like his father.'

I turn to Tracy. 'Pardon my French.'

She is half-listening, reading on.

'Almost exclusively nudes, the style ranges from thin paint, a nostalgia for his earlier works perhaps, to a thick impasto technique blah blah blah. Critics who commented on the homogeneity of his collection, calling it "almost an obsession", they nevertheless admitted to being mesmerized by the kitchen-sink realism of his treatment, where the ugly and sordid are merely guises for a deeper beauty, perhaps seen only by the artist himself.'

'Ferdie came in three or four times. First time in sixty-five years, he came to drink and talk.' Phil is half-crosseyed by now, but listening to every word I say. 'Never used to come in before. My clients, not classy, you know. Ferdie, he always thought, he'd be a lightning rod for their dark energy, y'know.'

'When asked about the identity of his muse, Don Pedro, smoking his customary Partagás cigar and tweaking his signature worn-and-weathered Monte Cristi hat, looking more like a Patagonian rancher than famous artist, merely smiled mysteriously and proclaimed his muse to be a figment of his imagination, stating with his usual baritone laughter that he "needed to break away from the suffocating barrier of muses in portraiture, preferring instead to paint outside the boundaries of what could be possible in living, breathing live models". Besides, he said, where on earth do beautiful women like these actually exist?'

'Marry that mad bitch Rosie?' I look at Joao accusingly. 'What you think this is, a fairy tale?'

'On being asked for the reason behind his retirement, Don Pedro looked away sadly and dreamily, and after a long pause, he merely said: It is finished. I have nothing more.' Tracy puts away her iPhone.

'Ferdie, when he came in, he sat over there, at the bar,' I tell them. 'Looked me in the eye and talked. Like a man. Never asked for credit, never wanted my shoulder to cry on. Didn't even pretend we were friends.'

'Did you know?' Tracy said, pushing her glasses up her petite nose. 'Pedro's showing. It made him so much money, he bought a villa just outside Lisbon. Nobody has seen or heard from him since. He lives like a recluse, just like he did here.'

'Yes, I know,' I speak to her directly. 'Sold me his car before he left. I'm going to write him a postcard one of these days, tell him the brakes are still shit. Thrice a week, I take lessons up in Panjim.'

'I hope you have a receipt for it,' says Tracy. 'It will be worth a lot one day, way more than just a car. After he's dead.'

I shrug. 'Ferdie, he had grown a leathery skin around his old self. Every evening for ten days, this sack of new leathery skin would sit on his favourite stool,' I point to that stool, 'and his eyes would hold mine with manful candour in them, throwing out a challenge, telling me, go ahead and laugh, scoff, taunt if you want.'

I put my hand on Phil's arm and lean into him. 'I'm probably the best poker player in all of south Goa. I just listened, deadpan, rinsing and wiping and filling them up as he spoke and hurled alcohol down his throat, never once blinking as it blazed on the way down.'

'But you know the funny thing,' Tracy says, her eyes dancing, her bum shifting around in the chair. 'That collection that he showed, sixteen works of genius, that wasn't all.'

'When he played that last card, even I did not see it coming, so much for my poker skills.' They are both listening now. 'Played it like a pro,' I say, 'not a hint of a tell, his eyes as bland as my wife's cabbage soup. He finished his story, timing the last of his narrative perfectly with the fifth glass of my specials, his sips and sentences pacing each other nose-to-nose towards the finish line, the empty glass coming down at the precise moment that he said, "You know what I said? T'ank you, I said t'ank you."'

Phil is looking at me, at what he thinks is me, but he is seeing double. He is looking past my left ear, at my double image. His fiancée, she is playing with her camera, still working her ass round and round on the chair, like she wants to pee or something.

'He placed a hundred on the table and asked for one last one for the road. Then he turned his back to me and drank in silence, his shoulders slightly hunched, one leg lazily swinging in the air. When he was done, he politely placed the glass on the bar-top like a gentleman and left.

'And the next day,' I say, 'he was dead. Died peacefully in his sleep, discovered by the coconut boy. What a card player, that man! What an elegant move that was! Doc Rodriguez, who wrote out the death certificate, said he might have stopped taking his medicine, and I think about it and wonder, would it have helped if he had kept popping the nitros?

'Had he popped a single tablet on that marathon walk across Goa with that crazy Jap?' I ask them. 'Or yearned for one as he sat on that bench, hearing the toots and thumps of Millie's final journey down the road?

'An inconsolable Angie said it might have been sleeping tablets,' I say scornfully, 'but no, his medicine cabinet was full, there was no empty strip found in his waste-basket. Even his jug of water was untouched. He went out like a man, no note, no maudlin messages, just a peaceful smile on his face.'

'Oh man,' the boy leans back in his chair, my daddy's specials smacking him around good and proper from the inside.

'I suspect,' I say, 'if old Tomaso De Souza's wife went before him, he would follow in a day or two, naturally, happily, no more buses to Mapusa Hospital to see her off on to. These are rare, special cases. Me? I love my missus, but if she goes before me? Fuck that, I'll carry on.

'Pardon the French,' I tell Tracy.

Rosie took care of everything, I tell them, made sure everyone came for the funeral. I think she went around to every house and yanked them out. She looks a bit hollow these days, like that enormous volume of flesh is slowly evaporating inside her, her skin is flopping around the empty space. She cried the most. Her eyes were hot springs that continuously gushed, her mouth forming a miserable little O, and when she looked up to the heavens, as though checking out Ferdie's next stop, she looked like a fat seal about to twirl a ball on her nose.

'Forgive me,' I say, 'but it's hard to feel sorry for that bitch.'

Savio and Angie, they are still around. Still fucking. Rosie doesn't know. Or doesn't care. Someday they'll marry, have kids, grow old, die, no big deal.

I'm thinking of inventing a cocktail, I tell them, and naming it after Ferdie, call it Ferdinand's Fling. Kind of sounds like Singapore Sling, no? It's not going to be anything classy, just some coconut feni with 7Up and mint and lemongrass and lime. Keep it simple yet strong, a bit like Ferdie was in his last days.

'In the middle of all the nudes,' Tracy says, 'there was one portrait. Of a man. A thin, long face. That one, it fetched the most.'

'Really?' I say, giving them a hint, story's over, you can now fuck off, pardon the Français, go back to your guest house, hotel, wherever.

'Critics say it was the most expressive, intense portrait seen this entire century,' she says, 'or the last. No two views were ever the same. Some saw the most elegiac despair, bleakness. Others saw madness. Some likened it to a war-victim photo, a man who had watched his entire family massacred. Others said it was a mass-murderer looking slyly repentant.'

It fetched 468,000 pounds, she says.

The fat nudes, they were the side-show, said some critics. As if he was saving up his mojo for this masterpiece, she says.

Rumour has it, he did a whole series of them, maybe five or six, but no one knows where they are.

If they are found, they will be priceless. After he dies, even more.

The man in the portrait, she says, looks like that man up there, she points to my wall. Looks like that painting.

They leave. I clean up. Who would've thought, I muse, Ferdie and his daft love story. New leathery skin and fresh mojo notwithstanding, still Ferdinand. Invisible in a crowd of one. Insignificant as an appendix. Useless as a wet wick. Boring as a nun's dream.

Irony, I tell myself. I will probably never sell that painting.

But I may sell the others, if I can get them back.

I gave two to Angie, one to Rosie. The two Angie has, one of them is of a man shuffling down a road, bent over with defeat, yet going on. The other, a thin, tall man staring into the coffin of an enormous lady. They give me gooseflesh every time I look at them, the look and expression on that man's face.

Experts will join the dots. Say it is the same guy. The one that went for – how much?

Alive, worth 468,000 pounds. Dead, three times that. Bloody hell, I should have such choices for everything in my life.

Rosie has made hers into a shrine. Candles and incense and fresh flowers every day. The most expensive shrine in the world, soot from the candle giving it that old, gritty feel over the years. Of an old man singing in a choir, his face etched with lines of devotion and bliss, staring up into some golden-halo light in the high recesses of the church.

All I told Don Pedro was, no nudes. So he gave me the others.

I didn't know he saved one for the showing, in the Chiostro.

I can easily wait for the fucker to die, if I'm greedy. He won't last long in retirement. Guys like him, they're like Great Whites. Need to keep moving, otherwise they die. Water stops moving past their gills, they die.

But waiting might be a folly, now. I must try and get the other paintings back. Somehow. Before the girl, what's her name – Tracy – before she goes back and shows her art teachers the photo. The photo of the portrait on the wall. Before the collectors and gallery owners and art thieves from all over the world descend upon my little village, sniffing around houses, pulling stuff off walls, tearing down shrines.

When you ignore the bigger picture of your own dreams and aspirations, and focus on the minutiae of others' lives, it is better than television.

My half-assed way of saying, like everyone else in Pocolim, I wasn't really good for anything else.